Meant to Be His

ELENA MARKEM

Books by Elena Markem

Fable Notch Series

Once More With You
Meant To Be His
This Time For Us

Dedication

For my Aunt Florence Kamphausen
who discovered romance novels later in life,
but who has always understood the power of love.

Chapter One

♥

Staring out the kitchen window of his home, Nick Hanson didn't know what to do next, a situation he hadn't been in since he was fourteen. How had everything gone so wrong in such a short amount of time? Fortunately, he hadn't liquidated his real estate assets when he gambled his financial future on some risky investments. If he had, he might be homeless as well as nearly broke. Instead, he was back in Fable Notch, New Hampshire, the town where he grew up, staring out the window and wondering how his life had become such a shit show.

At least the house was gorgeous. He'd been imagining the Craftsman style home since he was a kid, sketching it and dreaming of the day when he'd have it built. When last year's bonuses were more than double what he'd expected, he'd used the money to make this house a reality years before he'd planned. What he didn't imagine was that his first visit would be because he needed to put as much distance as he could between himself and Wall Street.

Six weeks into a three-month suspension from his mergers and acquisitions job, he was finding the boredom and monotony beyond frustrating. The days had gone by in a blur of avoidance as he slept in, roamed the city from midtown north avoiding the Financial District, and went to his twice weekly mandated therapy appointments. Which weren't doing any good. He didn't need to sit on a couch and talk about what had led to the epic panic attack that sent him to the hospital. He needed to get back to the plans that would make him successful. This time, he'd keep his focus and not get distracted by the possibility of fast returns. No more cryptocurrency investments, no more venture capital. He knew how to make money for himself and his clients.

How he was going to get the partners at the firm to believe this was something he hadn't figured out, but he would. Ever since he'd written his first five-year plan back in high school, he'd been able to meet—even beat—his original timeline. He could get that edge back.

He had to. He would not accept any other possibility.

Twenty-four hours ago, he'd still been in New York. He'd woken up and decided it was Day One of the next five-year plan. He sat down with a pad of paper and... nothing came to him. He'd paced around his home office for hours without a clue of how to get his career and life back on track. A walk outside in the late July heat did nothing but make him sweaty and mad. He didn't know how much time had passed until he found himself on Broad Street, standing in front of his office, three miles from his apartment. From a distance, he watched people come and go as his heart raced, and he hoped no one would recognize him. Picturing the bottle of Xanax pills sitting by the bathroom sink, he thought, *I've got to get out of here.*

Splurging on a cab back to his apartment—a few months before he'd taken them daily without a thought to the cost—he spent elena rest of the day preparing to leave. The next morning, he waited for rush hour to clear before heading north. It had taken him less than six hours to get from the city to New Hampshire. It felt—as it always did—like a world away, which was exactly what he wanted. He had no idea how he was going to fill the time here anymore than he knew what to do in New

York, but at least he didn't have to see people getting on with their lives the way he was supposed to be.

He decided not to tell anyone he was back yet. Tomorrow would be soon enough to reach out to his foster parents, Millie and Martin Sinclair, and his brother, Theo, who'd moved back in May. Once he spoke to them, he'd have to explain why he was here, and he wasn't ready to say the words out loud: I failed.

He walked mindlessly around the house, stopping to look at the beautiful view of mountains and trees from the wall of glass doors that led to the back deck. The sight should have calmed him, but instead panic bubbled up. After all the work he'd done, all the plans he'd made, he was the worthless screw up his father always said he was. He closed his eyes and rested his head on the cool glass, trying to practice the breathing technique his therapist had taught him. In for four counts, hold for four counts. Out for four counts, hold for four counts.

It wasn't working. He was hearing howling.

At first, Nick thought it was the noise in his head, another part of the endless cacophony of judgment he'd been hearing since his suspension. Xanax helped with anxiety, not self-criticism.

The next howl was longer and louder. He wasn't hearing things. From the way it made the hairs on the back of his neck stand on end, he was certain an animal was in trouble. Normally, he would have ignored it and assumed someone else could take care of it, but since his house was fairly isolated and he was happy to have anything distract him from his thoughts, he opened the back door and headed out.

He stepped off the back deck and into the soft ground. Two steps later, mud nearly sucked the shoe off his foot. Only years of skiing allowed him to correct his balance fast enough so he didn't wind up on his ass. He pulled his foot out of the muck to see his leather shoes covered, probably ruined. He considered going back to change, then realized it didn't matter. They were shoes, for fuck's sake, and he had shelves full of them.

He continued walking, this time more carefully, until another howl told him he was going in the wrong direction. *Figures*, he thought. More wrong turns. Before the animal could call out again, he found a beautiful chocolate brown dog leaning against a tree. As Nick approached, it took a step toward him, hobbled, cried out, and fell. That answered the "what was wrong" question. The dog's right front leg was injured. Nick looked but didn't see any blood, which he took as a good sign.

Nick approached the dog slowly, doing his best to maintain eye contact, speak in a calm tone, and keep his palms up and out. A former girlfriend had planned to become a veterinarian, and when they were dating, he remembered seeing her do this with a hurt animal. He hadn't thought of her, or the way she'd broken his heart, in years.

It seemed to take forever before he was near enough to pet the dog gently and allow the animal to give him a sniff. "You're hurt, boy. You have to let me take you to someone who can help. There's a doctor in town, and I'll drive you there. He'll fix you up."

Nick kept up a steady stream of conversation as he put his hands under the dog's belly. For a moment, their eyes met, and Nick sensed the animal sizing him up, deciding if he could trust the human who held him. Whatever the test, Nick must have passed it, because he allowed Nick to lift him. Once in his arms, the dog rested his head on Nick's shoulder and gave out a small, chuff-like sigh.

They headed back, and it wasn't long before Nick was feeling the strain of walking through soft ground carrying at least an extra fifty pounds. His lower back strained with every step. He wanted to adjust the dog and make it easier on himself, but he was afraid any jostling would cause the dog to jump, which would increase the injury. "So much for my expensive trainer and gym membership, huh, boy? Now when I need those muscles I supposedly built up, where are they?"

The dog didn't answer. That seemed typical for Nick these days. Lots of questions. No answers.

When he got to the car, Nick leaned back to take the weight of the dog more against his chest so he could free up a hand to open the back door of his Lexus. He gave a brief thought to the leather seats, then let that go as he got the dog settled. "I need to get my keys, pooch. Stay here. I'll be right back."

He shut the door gently, so he wouldn't alarm the dog, ran inside, grabbed what he needed, and got in. "This shouldn't take long. I know where Doc Wheeler has his practice, and assuming it hasn't moved—and let me tell you, nothing moves in this town—we'll be there in no time." He received a short "woof," which was good enough.

Nick drove out of the driveway and down his sloping street. He hoped someone would be available. Small town offices kept small town hours. For all he knew, the office closed early on Tuesdays, or they weren't open at all. Once on the main road, it took him less than fifteen minutes and three turns to arrive at the veterinarian's office. There were two other cars in the lot. He took it as a good sign. He parked as close to the main entrance as he could, went to the back and lifted the dog out, then pushed the door closed with his foot.

Next came the challenge of getting into the building. Like most older businesses in Fable Notch, Dr. Wheeler's office was in a modified colonial house and while it was handicap accessible, it didn't come with an automatic door. Once again doing the chest balancing act, he managed to get inside, gratefully acknowledging this was the last time he was going to have to open a door with his arms full of dog. Soon the animal would be someone else's problem.

A bell over the door jingled as he entered. He stood there looking around the waiting area, noticing the bulletin board covered with pictures of happy animals and their owners. Flyers for the upcoming Dog Days of Summer Festival were tacked up between posters about flea and tick prevention. The last time he'd been here was the summer before college, and he'd been in love with… no, that was an old mistake. He had plenty of new ones to keep his thoughts occupied.

Before he could call out, a young woman with a name tag which read "Beth" came in. "Hello, can I help—" She stopped as she took in his situation, grabbed a clipboard, and stepped out front. "Okay, let's go straight to asking what the problem is. Follow me to an exam room. What's your dog's name?"

"This isn't my dog. I found him in the woods behind my house. He's hurt his front leg. I didn't know what to do for him, so I brought him here. Is Doc Wheeler around?"

"No, today's his day off, but you can see Dr. Dani."

Nick's mouth went dry. Had he left one screwed up situation to walk into another? So much for not seeing anyone he knew. Wouldn't that be perfectly in line with all the other shit going on in his life. "Dr. Dani," he repeated.

Beth laughed as she opened the door to a small room. As she helped him get the dog situated on the table, she said, "Her name is Danielle Vaughn, but she goes by Dani, and that's what she's asked everyone to call her. I think it makes her more approachable and puts people at ease, don't you?"

No, at ease was not how Nick was feeling at all.

Chapter Two

♥

Dani Vaughn checked the IV on one of her sweet, furry, but very sick patients. She gave the dog a gentle rub under the chin and had her gloved hand licked in response. Animals gave love easily and unconditionally. It was one of the reasons she enjoyed working with them. Show them kindness and attention, and you had a friend for life. So much easier than people.

Seeing an improvement in Snuffles eased her heart, but Dani intended to stay in the clinic bedroom overnight so she could monitor them. When Snuffles and her brother, Pepper—their owner wasn't going to win any naming awards—arrived that morning, both schnauzers were listless and unresponsive. As soon as Dani saw their eyes, she diagnosed distemper. Dani didn't know why they hadn't been vaccinated against such a contagious disease, but some people didn't understand the risks until it was too late.

She made a note in the animal's chart and went to check on Pepper. When the other dog showed similar signs of improvement, Dani breathed a sigh of relief. She lived in fear of the day when she had to give the first person end-of-life news. It would happen, and she'd done it before, but hopefully it wouldn't be necessary until she'd been here longer.

Dani ran through what she still needed to do, including walking and feeding her dog, Otis. She also needed the Yankee pot roast with mashed potatoes and buttered carrots from her Aunt Rosie's diner. Her mouth watered. She looked at her watch and tried to calculate if she had time to go to the Kinsman Diner if she called in her order in advance. She was reaching for her cell phone when Beth poked her head into the room.

"A really cute guy showed up carrying a dog with an injured leg. Says he found her in the woods. Looks like a hound. Female. I scanned for a chip, but there's nothing. I've put them in room three."

Dani attempted a smile and said, "Great." She didn't mean it. The current Hollywood heartthrob could be waiting with a dozen roses and a box of Godiva, and she'd be in no hurry to see him. Well, she'd take the chocolates. And a lost dog meant no vaccination history. Dani rolled her shoulders and refocused. Whoever was here, it didn't matter what kind of day she'd had. An animal needed her help. "I'll be right out."

It had been a long day, but even the toughest day in Fable Notch was better than any of her time at the pet hospital in Texas she'd left five months ago. She didn't miss the large, more impersonal practice or the people. Especially the people.

She removed her gloves and the disposable medical gown covering her clothes, and washed her hands. She'd let Otis stay in the office. He was an enormous dog and sometimes overwhelmed strangers. Slipping the copy of *People* magazine from the stack of paperwork on her desk, she dropped it on the pile of magazines in the waiting area before heading to the exam room. Taking the clipboard from the holder outside the room, she gave a quick knock before stepping in. She was still looking at the paperwork when she said, "Hi there. I'm Dr. Dani." As she held out her hand, she looked into the familiar blue eyes of the man who'd broken her heart.

Eight years disappeared in a heartbeat, and any emotional distance she'd gained from that time evaporated. *Oh, this cannot be happening. I'm not that unlucky, am I?*

Apparently, she was.

How could he be standing there? A thousand memories of Nick ran through her head, starting with the day she met him at Martin and Millie Sinclair's house her first summer staying with Aunt Rosie, and ending with the last time they made love. Her body betrayed her by flushing when that image hit. Thoughts of being in bed with him, laughing with him, even arguing with him brought back old hungers and longings she would rather have kept in the past. Along with the pain of leaving him.

Finally, she managed to say, "Hello, Nick." Good, her voice sounded calm. "This is a surprise."

"For me too, Dr. Dani," he said, emphasizing her name and title. It sounded strange on his lips. She hadn't been a doctor when she'd last seen him.

She couldn't stop staring at him, noticing what was the same, and what had changed. His dark brown hair was a little longer than might be considered professional, which only made it sexier, and it was clear he hadn't shaved that morning. And his eyes, as heartbreakingly blue as ever, had circles underneath. His black polo shirt hugged a strong and muscular torso. Everything he wore looked expensive and fit him perfectly.

It wasn't fair. He had a desk job. He was supposed to get heavy and flabby. Maybe even have the beginnings of a receding hairline, although, she thought with more than a touch of bitterness, he could always pay for whatever cosmetic surgery would fix the issue. But no, he was as gorgeous as ever, and she hated that for a moment, her hands ached to reach out and brush his hair away from his forehead.

Unfortunately, she knew she didn't look as good. He was seeing her at the end of a long day. By this time, she'd be wearing none of the minimal makeup she'd put on this morning, and her ponytail was probably off center. *This is why it's always important to look your best.* Dani heard her mother's critical voice. Not what she needed. Small talk. Dani had to come up with small talk, not think about her appearance. "I hadn't heard you were in town."

"I got here a few hours ago. It was a...." Nick paused, and Dani thought she saw frustration in his expression. "Spur of the moment decision."

That was a surprise. Nick didn't do things on a whim, especially not leave New York. There was something going on, but she couldn't let herself worry or care. "And where did this dog come from?"

"I heard him howling. When I found him, he was limping." Nick put his hands in his pockets and rocked on his heels. "I expected to see Doc Wheeler."

Dani stiffened. That's what most of their clients said when they saw her. They wanted the veterinarian who had been in charge for over forty years and were disappointed to have the "new doctor." Every time it happened, she worked harder to make a good impression. No place had ever felt more like home to Dani than Fable Notch, and she was determined to be accepted. "Doc recently celebrated his seventieth birthday. I'll be taking over his practice when he retires in the next year."

"Seventy? That's not possible." She watched as he mentally did the math. She'd had a similar reaction. He made a soft whistle. "I take that back. It's possible."

There was silence. Neither of them were good at small talk. A small yip from the exam table brought her back to the present. Right, there was a dog who needed her attention, and it didn't matter who brought her in. She would focus on the dog, not Nick. Not now, not ever. "Okay, sweet girl, let's see where you're hurt, shall we?" She turned to call Beth for help, but the young woman walked in as Dani reached for the door. Good. She hated to admit it, but she wasn't comfortable being alone with Nick.

Beth put a hand under the dog's head then stroked her flanks to keep the animal quiet as Dani examined the leg. They didn't want the dog to become agitated and kick out, possibly injuring herself and others more. She spoke to the dog in a soft voice, explaining what she was doing. Dani believed talking helped them understand she was there to help. Continuing her exam, she asked Nick, "Was there a road near where you found her?"

"No, he was in the woods behind my house, up Prescott Hill Road. There's only one other house even remotely close." Nick always did function better alone. Better to execute his plans. "It was muddy and slippery along the slope where I found him. I almost lost a shoe a few times." He lifted a foot, and she saw he was muddy to his ankles.

Aww, poor dear, did you ruin your $300 shoes, she thought bitterly. He'd be able to replace them in no time, she was certain. "We've had a lot of rain the last few days which means more soft spots in the ground. People and animals end up turning an ankle or worse. From my palpitations and her relative calm, there isn't anything to suggest a break, but her leg is a little swollen and warm. I'd say it's somewhere between a Grade I and a Grade II ligament sprain, which is a good thing, isn't it, honey?"

"In non-doctor terms for the rest of us," Nick said as Beth wrote the diagnosis in the file.

Dani took a treat from her pocket. The dog didn't look malnourished, but from the way she snatched the food, Dani guessed it had been at least a day since she'd been fed. "It means she needs a leg brace and has a several week recovery period she's not going to enjoy, but she doesn't need surgery or a cast." She brushed a hand across the top of the dog's head between her ears, then asked Beth to get a large front leg brace. Dani kept her focus on the dog when she and Nick were alone again. "Nope, no surgery for you, only some anti-inflammatory medicine that we'll put in a treat." The dog's ears twitched at the word "treat." She may not be tagged or collared, but someone cared for her and was probably missing her.

When Beth returned, Dani worked quickly to fit the brace to the dog's leg, making certain it was tight enough to give support without causing more strain. "Let's see how you do walking on this, girl." Sliding her arms under the dog with Beth there for back up, Dani lifted her and placed her on the floor. The animal hesitated which, Dani thought, was likely a combination of worrying about the pain, and uncertainty about the brace. Pain and uncertainty. Dani understood both. She watched as the dog took a few steps, then a few more. Dani gave her another treat and some encouraging scratches. "Good job, sweetie. You'll be better in no time."

"Glad to see he's in good hands." Nick reached into his back pocket and took out a leather wallet. She recognized the Gucci logo. "Whatever the cost, you can charge it to me."

Dani stopped petting the dog as her jaw tightened. She should have known he'd say that. Money—the universal problem solver. As soon as he had it, Nick used it whenever possible. She'd been running through a mental list of volunteers who could take an injured dog for a day or two, but when Nick assumed all he had to do was throw some cash at the problem, Dani changed her mind. "You think a ridiculously high credit limit is going to handle this situation?"

"Don't go there, Dani." He sounded as annoyed as she did as he took out a plastic card. "I'd think you'd appreciate my help. This mutt is nothing to me. He's a stray who needs care, and I'm willing to pay for it. There's nothing wrong with that."

"The dog—who's a mixed breed with a strong presentation of hound—is a she who needs care and a place to stay while she heals."

"Then let her stay here. I know there's space for animals who can't go home."

"Except today. I have two dogs with distemper. It's highly contagious. Since I have no idea if she's vaccinated, this beauty is going home with you."

The hand holding the card dropped to his side. "That's not possible."

She was not going to let him win this. "Why? Is your place unsuitable?"

He stiffened. It was a low blow, and she didn't feel good about having said it. She knew the struggles he came from and how run down the house he'd grown up in was, but she was annoyed. Apparently, he was, too. She heard irritation in his voice when he replied, "No, it's new and spacious, but I'm not a pet owner. I have no way to take care of a dog, especially an injured one."

"Are you leaving tomorrow? The next day?"

He didn't answer, and Dani didn't understand the look that crossed his face before he said, "No, I'll be here."

"Then you and your credit card are in luck. I can sell you everything you need, from food, to bowls, to a toy to keep her happy while she's with you." As she waited for Nick to protest more, Dani pushed at the cuticle on her thumb, concerned she was making a mistake. He'd have to watch the dog for no more than two days, but as much as she wanted to show Nick money wasn't the easy answer he wanted it to be, it was more important for the animal to get the right care, not for Dani to have some petty revenge. Then the dog in question lifted her head and nuzzled Nick's hand. Dani chuckled. Guilt removed. "She likes you."

"There must be another way."

She continued as if he hadn't said anything. "The brace will take her some time to get used to, but at least you won't have to worry about changing or re-wrapping any bandages. Keep it dry. If it turns out you can't handle her, call me, and we'll see if it's safe for you to bring her back."

Nick rubbed his hands across his forehead as his eyebrows drew together. The gesture was so familiar, it made Dani's stomach clench. "Guess I don't have much of a choice."

"I'll help in any way I can. I'll even come to check on her tomorrow." Damn, that was stupid. She wanted to avoid him, not offer opportunities to see him. But the dog's care came first.

"Fine," he said, although it was clear from his tone it was anything but. For a moment Dani thought he was going to say something, but then it passed. "Tell me what to do."

"She needs food, water, and rest. Pretty standard stuff. She'll have trouble jumping onto beds and couches, so you may need to help her. Beth, could you get Mr. Hanson a starter kit, collar, and leash? And carprofen." At Nick's confused look, she said, "It's for pain and inflammation."

Beth made notes in the file and asked, "Three days' worth?"

"Better make it five." She saw Nick's jaw drop a little. It was fun to play with him. She could get the dog from him Thursday, Friday at the latest, but she didn't need to tell him. Instead, she took the credit card that was still in his hand, gave it to Beth, and said to Nick, "You can return whatever you haven't used when you bring her back." Before leaving the room, Beth took a picture of the dog that they would send to other clinics to see if anyone reported a dog missing. When they were alone again, Dani found herself too aware of Nick. The exam rooms weren't large, but his presence made it seem smaller. After years apart—and too much time spent thinking about him—he was close enough to touch.

Not that she would.

Even though she wanted to.

Instead, she kept her hands busy petting the dog and encouraging her to take small steps. After too much silence, she looked at Nick to find him staring at her. She wondered if she had something on her face and wished she knew what he was thinking. Trying to stay focused on her patient, she asked, "Do you want to give her a name?"

"Me?" He looked surprised and sounded almost panicked.

"Who better? She's going to be with you for a while. You should choose."

He thought for a moment and then said, "She's a hound?" Dani nodded. "Well, since she's a girl, Elvis won't do, so I guess it will have to be Presley."

"What do you think?" she said, looking to the dog and rubbing under her chin. "Do you like Presley?" The dog stepped happily in response, or so it seemed. "She approves. Try to use it frequently so she knows you're talking to her. The one thing new owners—even temporary owners—need to remember is not to overfeed. Start with a cup of food, then wait at least three to four hours before giving her more. Even if she asks."

"Asks?"

Nick would learn soon enough that animals communicated. "Barks, pushes her bowl around. Howls. Hounds like to howl."

"I heard that. It's how we met."

His words had her thinking of how she and Nick met. She looked at him and nearly got lost in his eyes. This was not good. She needed to finish this appointment. He needed to leave. "We'll give you something to put her medication in so she takes it. Keep her water dish filled. She doesn't look badly dehydrated, but she's likely gone a while without drinking. I think that's everything. Do you have any other questions?"

"Just one," he said. Dani had no idea what the question was, but a moment later Nick closed what little distance there was between them, put one hand on the back of her head, and pulled her in for a kiss. She was better off not knowing what he was thinking.

Chapter Three

♥

As soon as Dani walked into the room, all Nick could think of was kissing her. She wore no lipstick, nothing to make her mouth stand out, but it took willpower not to grab her as soon as she looked at him. Everything from the last six weeks—hell, the last six months—disappeared as he drank her in.

She was as beautiful as she was the last time he'd seen her. Maybe more, if that was possible. She was at her "happy weight," the extra pounds she carried on her frame when things were going well in her life. She got skinny when she was upset. Today she looked lush and irresistible.

As they kissed, he breathed her in. He noticed the clean scent of the antiseptic soap she used for work, but under that was the smell he remembered. Something soft and welcoming, like honey.

All Dani.

She fit perfectly in his arms as she always had, just the right amount shorter than his six feet so that when he held her, she was pressed against all of him. As her body shifted and she responded to his touch, he deepened the kiss, moving his tongue into her mouth, tasting her, and letting his mind fill with the memories of other kisses. Their first happened not far from where they were standing, the summer they were fifteen. After that, he couldn't stop kissing her. There had been a time when he thought she'd be the last woman he'd kiss.

Presley chose that moment to give a bark, startling them both. They broke apart, but Nick wasn't ready to end the moment. He kept a hand at her back as she placed on one his chest. He couldn't read the look on her face when she asked, "What kind of question was that?"

"I wanted to know if kissing you would still drive me crazy. It does."

She gave a glance down to his crotch, then jumped as Beth came in with the supplies for Presley. He watched, aching, as she and Beth went through the box, making certain they hadn't forgotten anything. It was so mundane he could have screamed.

He wanted to kiss her again, make her moan and sigh against him. Her gorgeous auburn hair—he was always a sucker for that color because of her—was up in a high ponytail and his fingers itched to grab whatever was holding it back, pull it out, and run his hands through the long strands. He stood there remembering what it looked like spread out over his pillow when he kissed her in the mornings.

"I think that's everything you need," she said, interrupting his thoughts. *Ha,* laughed the voice in his head. Everything he needed? Not by a long shot.

Presley, who had been seated at her feet, stood carefully as Dani attached the collar and leash and handed the end to Nick. "Beth will help you to the car. Remember, you have our number if you run into trouble or if she doesn't seem to be doing well. Call if you have any other... questions. Have fun, Nick, and take care." She stared at him a little longer than polite, as if she were about to say something else, then walked out of the exam room.

He almost called her back, but he didn't know what he'd say. Okay, there was still one more question to ask, but it would wait. Beth asked, "Are you ready?" and it took him a second to realize she was talking about the dog.

"As I'll ever be," he said. She held the door open as he adjusted to walking with Presley by his side.

Beth followed him to his car, carrying the supplies and keeping up a stream of chatter. "You've got enough food to get you through several days, but in case you go to the store, there's a list of brands we recommend. We have a great pet store in town, Significant Paws, and they specialize in things for dogs. She may have a little trouble settling down after the trauma of the day, but there's also a chance she'll be exhausted. I gave you Dr. Dani's cell phone number in case you need to reach her directly."

Her cell phone number. That piqued Nick's interest. He wasn't sure when he was going to use it, but there were things to talk about. As long as he was going to be in town, they may as well get things out in the open.

With a little help, Presley got into the front passenger seat, and moments later, Nick and his new roommate were on their way. He couldn't believe the dog was still with him. After he helped her from the car, they walked in. Presley hesitated at the door, then entered the foyer, seemingly unsure about what to do next. He didn't know if it was that the place was new to her or walking with the brace was weird. "Make yourself at home, girl. There's more than enough room."

He took off the leash, and she gave him a woof, then walked and explored, sniffing and rubbing. He could only hope she wouldn't feel the need to mark anything. He probably should have asked. He'd had enough surprises. As Presley wandered, Nick went to the bedroom, opened his luggage, and changed out of the muddy shoes and socks. Looking at what he'd brought, he realized it wasn't going to be enough for the time he'd be here. His credit card was going to get a workout after all. He sat on the bed and, needing things to arrive quickly, opened up the Amazon app on his phone. Not the best clothes, but they'd be quick to arrive and budget friendly. Shirts, jeans, socks. A pair of basic sneakers. He was annoyed he hadn't taken the time to pack better. He didn't have money to toss around anymore. Yet when Presley came in and gave him a nudge, he chose a few things for her, figuring he could donate them to the clinic later. Trying not to hear Dani's voice about throwing money at a situation, he placed the order.

He stood and walked to the kitchen. Presley followed. "Hungry, girl?" She did a little dance in place as an answer.

He took out the things Dani had given him, put a place mat on the floor at the end of the island, filled the dog's food and water dishes, and put them on top. Tail wagging the whole time, she ate almost everything in her bowl in moments. She left a little at the bottom, which Nick found amusing.

As she drank her water, Nick went to the living room and stared at the boxes piled against the wall. The remnants of his life before leaving Fable Notch; the few things he'd wanted to keep. They'd been stored at the Sinclairs', and Martin had brought them over when the house was done. Nick had planned to come up in the fall to unpack, see everyone, and maybe have a housewarming party. Another plan shot.

He wasn't up for unpacking anything more tonight.

Deciding to follow Presley's lead, he went back to the kitchen to find something to heat for dinner. He stood there staring at the food he'd bought, unable to decide.

"If anything moves, let me know," said a voice in his memory, and he smiled thinking of Millie, the woman who was more of a mother to him than his own. He didn't know how many times he'd open her refrigerator to look for something to eat, but, overwhelmed by the options, stood there staring. His mother had spent most of his childhood drinking. Cole, his oldest brother, managed the household money and bought the bare necessities to make sure they'd have enough for bills. At the Sinclairs' there was always plenty of food. Nick had a long list of things he was grateful to Martin and Millie for, and while keeping him and his brothers out of the system was at the top of the list, what he remembered most about when they came into his life was finally not feeling hungry.

He'd see the Sinclairs in the morning. He didn't want them to hear about his arrival from anyone other than him. Damn, they were going to be disappointed when he told them what happened.

"The only one who's disappointed in you is you." This time he heard Martin in his head. It was his junior year in high school, and he'd choked on a chemistry exam. He'd worked hard, but for some reason, when he got to the test, he'd blanked out on everything he'd studied. That night at dinner, he barely ate. Martin took him aside, and Nick told him everything. "I'm disappointed *for* you. For me to be disappointed in you, you'd have to do something that went against who I know you to be."

"What does that mean?" The question had come out snarky. Nick hadn't wanted wisdom. He'd wanted a good grade so he could get the scholarships he needed for college. He'd already planned to ask the teacher what kind of extra work he could do to improve his grade.

"Well, if you'd cheated on the test, that would say something about the person you are. Instead, it's a shitty situation, but it happens. Disappointment in the results is different from disappointment in a person. Do you understand?"

Nick did then. But now? He wasn't sure.

A bump to his leg told him Presley was curious about what he was doing. "I'm trying to decide on dinner, girl." He opened the freezer section, found a small chicken pot pie, and popped it in the microwave. It wouldn't be as good as Millie's, or Rosie's over at the Kinsman Diner, but it would do for tonight.

A few minutes later he was sitting on the couch, dinner on his lap while he channel surfed. Presley came over to give his meal a sniff and licked her lips. He promised to give her the leftovers. He ate without tasting the food, and barely noticing the television. Normally he'd be reviewing the day's financial markets, even the ones he didn't deal with directly, hoping to discover something he could bring to his bosses. Tonight though, his thoughts were a jumbled mess of memories combined with the awareness of how he'd fucked up his life.

"Work can't keep you warm. What good are your goals or your paycheck if there's no one to share them with? You can be addicted to things besides drugs and alcohol."

Damn, this time the voice was Dani's. The empty house was getting crowded. She'd said it to him a few days before she'd left. He told her he wasn't addicted to work. He loved what he did, and it was getting him what he wanted.

That summer was supposed to be a chance for them to spend time together before she started veterinary school at UPenn in the fall. He'd graduated college in three years and had been in New York for the last year. The first weeks had been great, but he'd been working long hours. She'd been alone a lot and hated it. Soon he'd tense before walking into the apartment, wondering if he'd find her sulking, annoyed, or asleep. Nothing like that had ever been part of their relationship. He'd tried to make it up to her. When he received a bonus and a promotion, he'd bought her a simple but beautiful necklace from Tiffany's. It was the most money he'd ever spent on someone. The next day he found a note: *Good luck with your plans,* the necklace next to it.

He'd tried to reach her, but his calls went straight to voice mail. He checked with her Aunt Rosie, who'd said Dani wasn't there. Even if Dani were in New Hampshire, he couldn't take time to go to Fable Notch to find out. He'd texted Dani several times a day and called every night when he got home. After two weeks, he'd stopped texting. After a month, her phone number was disconnected. Message received. Plan revised. He'd put his focus and his time into what he could control.

So much for that.

And now he was here, and so was she. He wondered what she was doing. No, he couldn't allow himself any distractions, even one as appealing as Dani. He was here to get focused, figure out how to get his career back on track, and return to New York, not start something with the first woman to steal his heart. The only woman.

Nick wished he could call his closest friend, Henry. Talk to him about this setback. Whenever one of them had a problem, the other could always come up with an idea of how to fix it, get through it, and, usually, come out better than before. Henry had tried to warn him about the investments he was making. By the time Nick had lost almost everything, Henry was gone. Nick would give anything to hear his friend say, "I told you so."

A howl from Presley had Nick jumping. "What is it, girl? Are you okay? Did you hurt yourself again?" Presley went to the back door and got nose prints on the glass. Then she howled again. "You know what? That sounds like a great idea, but we're not going back into the mud. Deal?" He got a woof for his answer.

He put the leash on the dog and stepped out into the warm night. They did a lap around the driveway so she could do her business, then walked onto the back deck. Presley sniffed around, barked at a squirrel darting past, then looked into the night sky, threw back her head, and howled. Nick watched and then did the same. For a moment the dog looked at him, and he swore she smiled before starting again. As Presley got louder so did he, and the release of the sound and stress brought him a moment of relief he hadn't expected, but desperately needed.

Chapter Four

♥

D ani did not need Nick as a distraction, not when she had to stay focused on her work as well as do a good job co-leading the silent auction for the upcoming Dog Days of Summer Festival. She wouldn't let Nick being around for a few days throw her off.

She'd gone home soon after Nick left to grab dinner along with the things she needed for her night at the clinic. After Beth went home, promising to come in early so Dani could have some time in the morning, she checked on the dogs, then went to her desk to do paperwork and inventory checks. Anything to keep busy and keep her mind off of Nick.

It wasn't working.

Two hours after he'd left, Dani's lips still tingled from his kiss. The worst part was, she wasn't entirely upset about it. She couldn't stop brushing her fingers over them, reliving the feel of his mouth, the taste of him. It was as though a part of her that had been asleep since she'd seen him last had woken up and was starving.

As she tried to read through a file, her thoughts wandered. She still found him ridiculously sexy. When he kissed her, her brain turned to liquid. Feeling the hard muscles of his chest under his shirt had her aching to touch his skin. All she'd wanted after Presley interrupted them was more, as if she didn't know the world of hurt she was in for if she followed that desire. She'd made the right—if difficult—decision eight years ago to leave him to his plans for financial domination. She wouldn't live in her mother's world where the material was valued over the emotional.

And still, if Beth hadn't walked into the room, she might have grabbed him. Wouldn't have that done wonders for his ego. Why did she have almost no control when it came to him, even after all this time?

Maybe because it had been so long since her last relationship. There was no one she'd been serious about since Nick, and she hadn't made it past a third date in years. Could it be because there was still something unfinished between them? She didn't like that thought.

Questions about Nick were still swirling through her head when she grabbed her tablet and crawled into the twin-size bed of the on-call room. One advantage of having a business in a renovated house was the space upstairs. Some was storage, one former bedroom was the office she and Doc Wheeler shared for doing paperwork and managing the business, and the smallest had a bed and nightstand for when someone needed to stay overnight. It was cozy; nothing like the sterile room of the city animal hospital in Houston where she used to work.

She opened a streaming app to continue the series she was watching, but she couldn't concentrate on that, either. All she noticed was how the leading man wasn't as cute as Nick.

At least Nick wouldn't be staying long. He'd be going back to New York and his plans. Nick was all about following a schedule and making money, and he did both very well.

He kissed very well too, damn him.

Frustrated and realizing she couldn't remember what she'd been watching, she switched to reading and tried to get comfortable. At least Otis was with her, snoring in his dog bed, the twin too small for him to join her like he did at home. She wondered if Nick would let Presley sleep on the bed with him.

Nick. Bed.

No.

She would not let her thoughts go there.

Too late. If only that kiss hadn't been so incredible. If only leaving him hadn't been one of the hardest things she'd ever done. If only she could keep her distance from him when he visited. As she drifted to sleep, her thoughts betrayed her one more time.

If only he'd kiss her again.

Dani woke early and not well rested, which wasn't entirely because she had to check the dogs in the middle of the night. She poured herself a mug of coffee from the pot she'd set to start automatically and added plenty of the sweetened creamer she liked. She looked in on the puppies and was pleased when they perked up the moment she walked in. They might be ready to go home as early as tomorrow, which meant she could take Presley back from Nick. Good, one less reason to think about him.

Beth came in at eight thirty, giving Dani ninety minutes to grab breakfast with her aunt at the diner. She needed Rosie's comfort and understanding. As she parked at the diner, her phone buzzed. The number wasn't familiar, but the text told her all she needed.

Made it through the night. Presley says hi.

She was glad the dog was doing well, but she didn't like Nick having her number. She assumed Beth gave it to him since Dani often offered her direct number to concerned owners. It would have been fine if it hadn't been Nick. As soon as she got Presley back, she'd delete the texts and move on as if he'd never walked into the clinic.

She went into the diner and took a deep breath of the familiar smells—bacon, warm toast, coffee—combined with the sounds of things sizzling on the griddle and pans moving on stove tops. The diner was about a third full, typical for a Wednesday morning. Dani saw a few to-go bags ready for pick up.

She made her way to the back corner booth with the U-shaped bench. Unless the diner was full, this was Rosie's table. It was where she sat on breaks to balance the books for the day, or spend time with her three closest friends: Millie Sinclair, Valerie Stewart, and Leslie Franks, who came in for lunch every Thursday. Dani spent hours at this table every summer, even on the days when she worked waiting tables.

"You need coffee," Rosie said, coming over with a mug and a full carafe.

"I do, thank you," Dani said, taking a sip of the hot liquid, then nearly spitting it out again when she discovered she'd forgotten cream and sugar.

As she doctored her coffee, Rosie sat across from her and put a hand over Dani's. "What's wrong, sweetheart?"

The list was long, but Dani only mentioned the dogs with distemper. Rosie sat waiting for Dani to say more. Usually she loved that her aunt knew her so well and cared so much. Not today. "Nick showed up at the clinic yesterday." A last name wasn't necessary. "He's in town and found an injured dog on his property. He brought her in to see Doc Wheeler, except I was on duty."

Rosie's face softened, and she gave Dani's hand a squeeze. "Are you okay? Is this the first time you've seen him since—"

"Since I left him in New York, yes. Am I okay? I don't have an answer yet. Part of me still thinks it's some stress induced hallucination."

"Dani, you have got to stop with the stress. That's one reason you came here, remember? To be where you belong."

Dani took a deep breath and a sip of coffee. To be where she belonged. It was what she wanted more than anything. Fable Notch had felt like home from the day she arrived, but years of her mother's criticism had her regularly doubting herself. All she could see was where she wasn't doing enough or doing this right. "I know, but I can't let Doc Wheeler down. And the Dog Days Festival is less than four weeks away. We still need a lot more donations to reach the goal, or the library isn't going to get its new young adult room."

"You know all of those things aren't entirely on you?" Dani liked the sound of that, but believing it was a different matter. "It's all going to be fine."

Rosie walked away to pour coffee and take orders, leaving Dani to her thoughts. Her aunt was right. She needed to relax, but this mattered so much. As she sat there, she texted her best friend, Laurel Stewart. *Nick's in town. Saw him last night.* She wouldn't get an answer for a few hours because it was before ten in the morning. Laurel ran a brewery and restaurant and got to bed late. Dani would hear from her friend after lunch. By then, maybe she'd have a handle on what she was feeling about Nick and that kiss.

Yeah, like a few hours was going to make a difference.

She took out her notebook on the silent auction created by her co-chair, Nancy Douglas. This was Nancy's third year managing the auction, and Dani was grateful for her experience. As she looked at what needed to be done in the next week, Rosie served her a bacon, tomato, and cheese omelet with home fries on the side. Dani hadn't ordered it, but her aunt had a knack for knowing what someone needed. Diets and cholesterol be damned. Dani filled her mouth with eggs and potatoes and let the home cooking relax her.

"This is so good," Dani said when Rosie warmed her coffee.

"You looked like you needed a little fortification, so I figured it was a morning for your favorite. Busy day ahead?"

"Nothing difficult, but a full schedule. And there's a meeting tonight for the Festival. I think Nancy and I are behind on her timeline." More stress, but at least she had help.

"I'm sure you two will figure it out. Don't leave before I give you some food to take with you for later."

"Thank you, Aunt Rosie," Dani said. She was so lucky to have her aunt. Rosie couldn't be more different from Cynthia, Dani's mom. Cynthia was the younger sister and wanted nothing to do with Fable Notch or the family business. She would rather have someone else cook, clean, and take care of things—including her children. It was hard to believe the two women were related. Rosie got all the warmth.

As she finished her breakfast, Dani decided that nothing about Nick's being in town mattered. Not even her body's reaction to him. She'd keep her focus where it made a difference. She'd managed without him for years. She could do it again. He'd be gone soon enough.

When she made her way to the door, Rosie handed Dani a bag of food and gave her a huge hug. She let herself relax into the strength and comfort of the embrace. One of the best things about moving here was the availability of hugs whenever she needed them. After her rough night, Dani couldn't help but think of the first time Rosie hugged her. She and her brother, Xander, had arrived for their first summer and were confused and uncomfortable with the easy offer of affection. Her father's way of showing love, especially after the divorce, was with large checks. Her mother hardly showed it at all, and never physically.

Dani thanked her aunt for the food and headed out, then turned around and said, "Nick got into town late yesterday. Please, wait before you call Millie. Give him a chance to see the Sinclairs first."

"Danielle Angelica Vaughn." Dani laughed. The outrage was feigned. "What makes you think I'm going to call her?"

These were the moments Dani wished she could raise one eyebrow. Instead, she stared at her aunt until the other woman laughed, then gave Rosie another hug. "I love you."

"Love you too."

Dani wondered if Aunt Rosie waited until she was out of the parking lot before calling Millie.

Chapter Five

For the first time in years, Nick's first thought when he woke up wasn't about work. It was Dani. True, it was due in part to the fact that he'd shared his bed with a dog, but it was also because of that kiss.

Nick would never admit it to anyone, but it was nice to wake up with Presley. Her weight and warmth had gone a long way to helping him have a better night's sleep than he'd had in months. The night before, he couldn't decide if he should let her sleep on the bed. He didn't know what the dog had or hadn't been allowed at her previous home, but she'd clearly learned the art of the woeful stare. When she added a tiny whine, he gave in. He'd had to give her a boost because of the leg brace, but once she was up, she found a spot against his legs where she could receive warm pets and scratches while he read. He'd fallen asleep with a hand on her flank.

As the coffee pot worked its magic, Nick put Presley's pill in a peanut butter treat the way he'd been shown, then gave her breakfast. After pouring himself a mug, he sent Dani a text saying he and Presley had made it through the night. If he remembered correctly, the last text he'd sent to her had said something like, "Fine. Have a nice life." Her leaving had thrown him into a funk, and it wasn't until he almost made a mistake with a client that he realized how much their breakup had affected him.

After that, he never let a woman get in the way of his work.

Well, she couldn't get in the way now. He didn't have any work. He'd managed to get in his own way.

He was going to be here for a while. Could they talk about what had happened when he last saw her? At least resolve what her sudden departure was really about? If he were honest with himself, what he wanted was to get her alone and kiss her until she begged him to carry her to bed, but he was willing to take one step at a time.

His stomach growled, which he took as a good sign. He hadn't had much of an appetite recently. In New York, his breakfasts typically consisted of coffee and a protein shake, but that didn't appeal. The Kinsman Diner was out. He was afraid to face Rosie. He considered finding a place in town, but if anyone saw him and called Millie and Martin, he'd never hear the end of it. He needed to visit there first.

When Presley finished eating, leaving a little in her bowl again, he put her leash on her collar, took her for a quick walk, then headed to his car. He helped her in, but he must have done something a little wrong because Presley gave a yip. *Please don't let me screw this up, too.* Something had to go right in his life.

He drove down the hill and less than ten minutes later arrived at the Sinclairs'. He sat in his car staring at the white Dutch colonial and let himself remember. This place was where he and his two brothers found the family they needed after his father left and his mother made alcohol her priority. After he, Cole, and Theo set fire to the shed behind their house when he was ten, Martin, the town's fire chief, came to put out the small blaze, then surprised the three of them by taking them home for dinner.

Not quite ready to face them, he sent Theo a quick text. *In FN. Having breakfast with M & M. Want to meet up later?*

Knowing he couldn't put off the inevitable, Nick got out of the car, helped Presley, then walked up the front steps. Before he knocked and went in, he froze, embarrassed to realize he was nervous. This was going to be a rough visit.

A quick rap on the frame, a twist of the doorknob—it was never locked—and he walked into a scene so familiar time seemed to rewind. The living room with the worn recliners facing the television. Books on the armrest. A pile of old magazines next to the wood by the fireplace. Photos on the mantle. Still no available pegs on the coat rack by the door, even though only two people lived here.

He heard sounds from the kitchen, so he walked to the back of the house, Presley on his heels, and came face to face with Millie as she was closing the refrigerator. She was a little grayer and had a few more wrinkles, but she was still beautiful. Theo always said she looked like Ellen Burstyn, and Nick agreed. "Hi, Ma, I'm home," he said. He'd been the first of his brothers to call her that. Her smile was as big for him today as it had been then.

"Nick, what a wonderful surprise," she said, wiping her hands on the dish towel she was holding and opening her arms wide. He didn't miss the look of concern that flitted across her face as he leaned in and hugged her, taking in her scent of vanilla and lilacs. Presley pushed between them, clearly wanting a little of this attention. "And who do we have here?"

"This is Presley. She's staying with me for a few days."

"Hello there, lovely girl. Theo has a dog, too. You'll have to introduce Presley to Harlow. Wait, why do you have a dog for a few days?" He explained how he found her. "Poor thing," Millie said, squatting down to offer Presley more attention. The dog gave Millie's face a nuzzle, clearly and quickly in love. Millie had that effect on people, too.

Nick decided to tell her more about what happened. "I took her to the clinic, but she couldn't stay because there were dogs in quarantine."

"Guess the doctor has his hands full."

"Her. Her hands full," Nick said and paused. Millie said nothing. He had a feeling that would be her reaction. "Doc Wheeler wasn't on duty. Dani was."

"You and Theo—running straight into your exes." Millie looked embarrassed. "I probably should have mentioned she moved back, but we haven't heard from or seen you in so long."

Millie didn't mean it to hurt, but he felt the sting. He couldn't remember the last time he called. Another example of how he let work dominate his life. Wouldn't Dani be pleased to know her prediction about work taking over had come true. "I know, Ma. I'm sorry. I've been busy, and this trip was unexpected." That was an understatement.

"Well, sit down and get comfortable. I was boiling water for eggs. I'll add a few more. Have you eaten?"

"Just coffee."

"Well, there's more of that if you want and some mini muffins." As she took out the eggs and a loaf of bread, Martin came in through the back door.

"Everything is looking good out there, and the temperature—hey," he said, interrupting himself. "Did I miss a message, or is this a surprise?"

"It's a surprise," Nick said, going over to give Martin a hug. Martin returned the embrace, clapping Nick on the back with a loud slap. Presley gave a short bark, clearly not wanting to be left out. Nick explained again.

"What's with you Hanson boys and dogs? Your brother has one too, although Harlow is also his partner."

"He saw Dani when he went over to the clinic," Millie said.

Martin went to the coffee pot to pour himself a mug, noticed Nick didn't have one, and poured a second. Nick could see that Martin's heart attack a few years ago had changed the man he considered a father. Martin was thinner, which made the lines in his face appear deeper, especially as he smiled at Nick. And while there was more salt than pepper to his hair, he still projected an aura of strength that probably served him well as the town's fire chief. Handing Nick the mug, he said, "Ah, more surprises."

"You could say that," Nick said, adding sugar to the drink and taking a sip before asking, "Has she been back long?"

"She arrived, when was it, Millie? March?"

"April," Millie said, putting thick slices of bread into the toaster. "Rosie and Helen are so happy she's here. She was living with them, then moved into a little place of her own at the end of last month."

Nick couldn't stop from imaging showing up at her place, getting some answers as to why she left him, then carrying her off to her bedroom to remind her of how good they'd once been. Damn, his mind was a dangerous place to be.

To redirect his thoughts, he focused on Millie making breakfast. It conjured memories so vivid and different from the last few months of stress, it almost brought tears to Nick's eyes. He took a long drink of his coffee, hoping to get himself under control. Martin's small talk about what Millie was growing in the new greenhouse Martin had built for her was a good distraction, but when the food was served, including a small plate of eggs on the floor for Presley, Nick knew it was time for the questions to begin.

He didn't have to wait long before Martin said, "So, what brings you up so unexpectedly?"

"I finished a big project at work." It wasn't exactly a lie. The project did end. It didn't end the way he wanted, but it was definitely over for him.

"So you're going to be here for a few days? A week?" Millie looked at him with a combination of hope and concern.

"It might be longer." Another half-truth. He wasn't used to keeping things from them. Theo and Cole were the ones who got into trouble. Nick was the one who kept his head down and his focus on what needed to be done next.

"It's too bad you won't be around for the Dog Days Festival," Millie said, passing him a plate of what almost looked like bacon. He gave it a skeptical look after smelling it. "It's turkey bacon. Less fat. It's better for you and tastes fine."

Martin snorted. "Since my heart attack, she's made a few changes to our diet."

Millie slapped him on the shoulder. "Is it my fault I want to have you around for another three or four decades?"

Worry was part of love to Millie. Nick took a piece and gave it a taste. "It's not bad," he said honestly.

"You'll live longer, too," Millie said.

That made him think of Henry, and he almost choked on the food in his mouth. This wasn't going to work. He had to tell them more. "I lied."

"About the turkey bacon?" Martin shook a finger at his wife. "See, told you it wasn't good."

"It's not the bacon." He stared at his plate, trying to decide how much to tell them. "A few months ago, I screwed up some personal investments, as well as a big deal at work. I lost a lot of people and myself a lot of money. I won't bore you with the details, but the upshot is they suspended me."

Their silence was awful. Finally, Martin asked, "What does that mean?"

It means my life has fallen apart. It means I'm a failure. It means I don't know what I'm going to do next. It means my dad was right. It means I need help, and I have no idea what kind of help that might be. "It means I've been suspended. It's been six weeks, and there are still six more weeks before the partners have a meeting to see if they think I'm valuable enough to bring back."

"Oh, honey, I'm so sorry," Millie said.

"It also means I won't be able to put anything into our account for a while." God, he hated saying that and could hardly look at Martin as he admitted it. He hoped it wouldn't be too much of a problem. When he was a kid, Martin had been the co-signer on his first bank account since Nick had been too young to open one on his own. Nick had kept the joint account, and for years, he and his brothers had put money into it to make sure Martin and Millie were never in financial straits. When they told the Sinclairs what they were doing, Martin said it wasn't necessary, but it was for Nick. He needed to show Martin his belief in him wasn't misguided. Nick was sure it had helped when Martin had his heart attack and when he was out of work after getting injured at a fire earlier that year. One more place Nick was failing. "I'm sorry."

"Not to worry, son," Martin said. Nick met Martin's eyes but couldn't read his expression.

"Besides, we—" Millie started, but Martin jumped in.

"We want you to focus on yourself. It sounds like it's been a tough few months."

Nick got the sense Millie was going to say something else, but he didn't want to press. "It could have been worse. They could have fired me outright. And I didn't lose any of the real estate I've invested in." The silence returned. Not wanting to worry them, he said, "I needed the break. Didn't see the warning signs. Guess I got into a black diamond area when I thought I was in blue square territory."

Martin gave a chuckle, and Nick knew he was remembering the time when Nick, barely fourteen, had been too confident on the ski slopes one season and didn't pay attention to signs along the downhill trail. He was a strong skier, but not ready for the toughest trails. He'd veered off the intermediate course, marked with blue squares, and ended up in advanced territory. He'd taken a nasty fall, which led to some serious bruises, but the only thing that broke was his ski. He'd been lucky then. He was not quite as lucky now.

"You've always had a 'ready, fire, aim' way of doing things, my boy."

"What do you mean?" Nick wasn't sure it was a compliment.

"From the time you were young, you knew what you wanted, and you were going after it, no matter what it took or if you were ready for it. You would learn during the process or, if necessary, from your mistakes. Like that day on the mountain. How long before you were on the trails again?"

"As soon as I could buy another ski." He'd used some of his precious savings to replace it. "Two weeks, maybe less."

"And how long before you tackled the black diamond trail knowingly?"

"About a week or so after that." He'd been determined not to let that mountain get the better of him. He hadn't done it well, but he had done it.

"Like I said, full speed ahead," Martin said.

Nick thought about that as he accepted more coffee from Millie. She put a hand on his shoulder as she poured, and gave it a squeeze. He knew she was saying, "I'm going to worry no matter what. Don't try to stop me." He'd known she would.

His phone buzzed on the table, startling him. He turned it over and saw a message from Theo. *Out of town until tomorrow. Breakfast at the diner Friday if you're still around?*

He'd still be there. He texted back suggesting they meet at 8:30. Theo replied with a thumbs up.

"I'd say no checking your phone at the table, but I caught a glimpse of a smile, so I'm going to let it go this time," Millie said.

"It's Theo. He's out of town, but I'll see him at the Kinsman on Friday. I hope Rosie doesn't throw me out."

Millie looked shocked. "Why would she throw you out?"

"Because I screwed things up with Dani." Maybe mistakes were more of a pattern than he thought.

"You're adults. Things happen. I'm sure she doesn't hold it against you."

Presley chose that moment to put her head on Nick's lap. He appreciated the comfort and gave her head a rub. He was feeling better with Millie and Martin knowing about his setbacks. It was good to feel their love even he couldn't let go of the shame. He hadn't told them about Henry's death or the panic attack, but if he didn't say anything, he didn't have to think about it. Right?

"Since you're going to here for a while," Martin said, breaking into his thoughts. "What are you going to do?"

The million-dollar question. Too bad he no longer had the million dollars or an answer.

Chapter Six

♥

Dani got to the clinic with time to spare before her first patient arrived. She checked on the quarantined dogs, then called Mrs. Becker to give her an update and was glad to hear the joy in the woman's voice. She loved being a part of people's relationships with their pets. She may not know how to make her own relationships work, but animals were easier and so much more accepting. They didn't judge you for your pop culture addiction or make fun of your competitive streak.

Her last appointment of the morning was with Mrs. Turner and her eight-year-old cocker spaniel, Chandler. She stepped into the room, saw that Mrs. Turner was about her mother's age, and braced for what she knew was coming. "Good morning, Mrs. Turner. I'm Dr. Vaughn." She didn't use Dr. Dani with her older owners. "I'll be taking care of Chandler."

In the moment before Mrs. Turner took her hand, Dani saw the doubt and concern pass across the other woman's face. She braced herself for what was coming. "Dr. Wheeler isn't available?"

There it was. Eventually people would stop asking and eventually her stomach wouldn't fall every time they did. Eventually she would be accepted and trusted. "No, I'm sorry. I'm the doctor working today."

"Oh, I wasn't expecting... I'm just used to... I mean, I'd heard the doctor brought in a younger assistant to help him." Accent on the young, which Dani knew many people equated with inexperienced.

Everyone wanted and expected a familiar face. Doc Wheeler and Aunt Rosie reminded her soon she would be the familiar one, but every time she got a reaction like this, her heart squeezed in worry. "I understand your concerns, Mrs. Turner, but I assure you, Doc Wheeler wouldn't have brought me on if I weren't right for the job." *Please let that be true,* she thought. "Let's take a look at Chandler and see what we can do for him."

Lying on the exam table, the dog was lethargic and looked underweight. A glance at the paperwork told her he'd lost almost four pounds since his check up in May, a significant percentage in a dog this size. "Could you tell me when you first noticed symptoms?"

"I think it was sometime after Father's Day. He'd be low energy for a day or two, then back to his usual self. But then the off days happened more frequently. When he first lost some weight, I thought it was good. Chandler's always been a little heavy. I feed him too much people food," she admitted. "But now... there's something very wrong." Her voice broke as she finished her sentence, and Dani's heart went out to her.

Dani examined Chandler as Mrs. Turner talked, checking his heart rate and blood pressure. The dog was lethargic and had no response to Dani's actions. He also had the cutest birth mark on his nose that made Dani want to give him a boop. Why was it that odd fur patterns and big bellies made pets more lovable and people less attractive? It wasn't fair.

When she finished her examination, she gave the dog a kiss on the top of his head. "We're going to take good care of you, sweet boy, and you'll be playing again in no time." She looked at Mrs. Turner and saw tears in the woman's eyes. *Sometimes I do the right thing.* She gave Mrs. Turner's hand a quick squeeze, then asked Beth to bring her some IV fluids. As she prepared a syringe, she explained, "Chandler is displaying the symptoms of kidney problems. I'm giving him fluids so I can get a urine sample and taking blood so we can run some additional tests. Because you love him, you noticed this quickly. There's a good chance we've caught this early and can treat him with diet and medication." When Beth came back, Dani got the IV hooked up and the fluids flowing. "This will take a few minutes. I'd like you to watch as I do this because you'll need to do this at home for a day or two." Mrs. Turner gasped, and Dani took her hand again. "It's very easy, and Beth and I will make sure you're confident about how to do it. For now, Mrs. Turner, stay close and hold his paw or pet him."

"Beatrice, but everyone calls me Bea." Dani smiled and repeated the name. "I've been so worried, Doctor. I adopted Chandler a few months after my youngest child left for college. I know it's cliché, but the empty nest was overwhelming. I was driving my poor husband crazy."

"I understand. Our pets become family members, and anyone who says differently doesn't have a pet." Which reminded her of Nick. He'd sent the text, but she should probably check in with him, make sure he hadn't left Presley behind somewhere.

Once the IV was going, Dani left Mrs. Turner—Bea—and Chandler to prepare the blood sample to be mailed overnight to a lab in Concord. They could do a basic CBC in house, but Dani wanted to have a serum biochemistry profile run as well. These were the moments she missed being in a city. In Houston, the lab was part of the hospital, and they had results quickly. Things moved slower in Fable Notch.

When the sample was ready, she responded to Nick's text. She started and deleted three messages before sending: *Glad all is well with Presley. Let me know if you need anything.*

She stared at the phone after hitting send, but there were no telltale dots telling her there was activity on his end. It was weird to be texting him after so long, even if it was about a dog. She'd known when she moved here she'd see him since he visited the Sinclairs, and he'd be at Theo and Eden's wedding, whenever that was. Still, it would have been better if she'd been feeling more confident, or at least wearing something other than a lab coat and leggings for their reunion.

Dani needed to get her thoughts off Nick and on work. She opened the bottom drawer of a cabinet, took a small bag of M&Ms from her stash, and poured out and ate a handful. That helped. There was something about chocolate. Before going back, she brushed her teeth and printed a list of recommended foods for Chandler.

When Dani walked into the exam room, Bea was talking to the dog. Dani offered Chandler a high calorie treat—she wasn't the only one who needed them—which he ate quickly before sniffing her hand for another, which she gave him. A good sign. As the IV bag emptied, Dani heard about Bea's children, her husband, and her volunteer work. Dani may not know what was wrong with the dog yet, but she'd won over Bea Turner, and she welcomed the victory.

After Bea and Chandler left, she went to the kitchen and sat the table with the chicken salad sandwich and chips Aunt Rosie had packed and did some Internet research about kidney conditions on her tablet, wanting to make sure she hadn't missed anything. Then she reviewed what needed to be done over the next few days for the Festival's silent auction, which was three weeks from Saturday.

When she came back in April, Dani couldn't wait to take part in all the Fable Notch festivals as a resident, not a visitor, and the August festival was one she'd loved since she was a kid. She went to the first planning meeting expecting to play a small volunteer role, but when Nancy asked her to co-chair the silent auction with her, Dani agreed before she realized what she was getting herself into.

As she was finishing her lunch, her phone buzzed. She hated that part of her hoped it was Nick. Instead, she had a response from Laurel. It started with a poop emoji. *Holy shit. Guess you couldn't avoid him forever.*

But Dani would have liked a little warning or time to prepare. Or to lose weight. *Was at the end of the day. I looked awful.*

Triple dots told her Laurel was responding. *I'm sure that wasn't an issue for him. He always loved how you looked.*

Dani once thought so, but by the end of their last summer, she wasn't sure of anything. *I made him take home a dog.*

Laurel sent a head exploding emoji and wrote, *This I have to hear. Come by 7BB tomorrow night?*

7BB—Seven Brothers Brewery, Laurel's business named for her crazy big family. Dani sent a thumbs up and was glad to have something to look forward to. She was so grateful for her friendship with Laurel and the others she'd met. Maybe someday she'd have as close a group of friends as Aunt Rosie did.

Assuming she didn't screw it up like she did with her last set of "friends." Dani shook her head to get rid of the thought. At least one good thing had come of that disaster. She'd moved back here.

She was putting a file in Beth's pile when her phone buzzed again. This time it was Nick, a picture with him and Presley, both with their tongues hanging out. She couldn't stop the laugh. She'd forgotten his playful side. It hadn't been there those last few months. She stared at the image, then considered deleting it. She didn't need a picture of him. The ones in her head were enough. She didn't need to remember how cute he was or how sweet he could be. She needed to remember what it was like when she saw him looking at a slender blond woman or putting making money ahead of everything. Because despite how much time had passed, he hadn't changed.

She couldn't let herself fall into old patterns, or worse, old feelings.

Chapter Seven

♥

After breakfast, Nick sat in his car with Presley, Martin's question rattling in his head. What was he going to do? As his heart rate climbed, his hand trembled as he put the keys in the ignition. Recognizing the signs, he stopped and reached into his pocket to take out the prescription bottle. He dry-swallowed the pill and glanced at the dog, who was giving him a questioning look. "Yeah, I've got medicine to take too, girl. Maybe I should put mine in peanut butter like we did for you." A quick bark was his reply.

Deciding he need to see something that made him feel good, he drove over to the house he grew up in. Renovating this place was one of the first things he did once he had money and, pulling into the driveway, he was proud of how it looked and the rental money it earned for him and his brothers. They never imagined how successful it would be when he proposed the idea.

"Knock yourself out, kid. If you want to put in the time and effort, have at it," said Cole.

"As long as I never have to see the place again, whatever you do is fine with me," Theo had said. Turned out to be a good thing they'd kept it, since Theo stayed there when he came in May to help Martin find and stop an arsonist.

Nick got out of the car and took it in. The house was completely different from the one in his childhood memories. Nothing sagged, nothing was falling off. He could still picture the dull grayish-blue paint, see the dishes piled in the sink, and the empty gin bottles in the garbage. For years he'd filled sketch books with how he'd redesign this house, and he'd managed to do it well ahead of his original plan.

Yeah, look where those plans got you. Right back where you started.

Damn snarky internal critic. He needed to shut that voice up.

The quick double beep of a horn brought him back to the present and he turned to see a familiar van with the logo for Franks and Sons General Contracting on the side. The driver waved as he passed then parked in a driveway two houses down. After helping Presley out of the car, Nick walked over. He'd spent countless hours in the summer working for Ed Franks, building and repairing homes around town.

Ed greeted him with a warm hug and a slap on the back. "Good to see you, my boy."

Nick couldn't remember the last time he'd been hugged so much in one day. "Same, Mr. Franks."

"Come on. It's Ed now," he said as he went to the back of the van and opened up the double doors. As Nick peered in, everything looked as though it were in the same spot as it was the last time he'd seen it. "No more of that 'Mister' stuff. You're grown with a business of your own."

Sort of, said the voice again.

"Taking some vacation time to see your new house?"

"Something like that." *Nothing like that.* "Things in New York got a bit... complicated, so I'm taking a break, getting my head together. I'll be here for the next four weeks or so." Maybe more if he couldn't convince them to take him back.

Ed stopped pulling things from the van to stare at Nick. "Complicated. You want to be more specific?"

"Not really." *Not at all.*

"Well, there's nothing like a change of scenery to give you perspective. How are you enjoying the new place? I have to tell you, that was one of my favorite projects."

When it came to the contracting for his house and the renovations on the old one, there was no one else Nick would have given the job to. Not only did Nick trust him, but it was a way for him to thank Ed for all he'd taught him. He'd gotten his appreciation for craftsmanship and a job well done working with the Franks, as well as the importance of having a plan you could rely on. "It's terrific. It's everything I'd ever hoped it would be." Even if nothing else in his life was, at least that was true.

"Martin and Millie must be thrilled to see you."

Thrilled and sad, Nick thought. "It's good to see them, too. How are things for you?"

"Busy, I'm happy to report. I'm not saying those fires in the spring were a good thing, but besides this job, we're working on rebuilding the apartment building that burned."

"The place where Eden was living?" Theo told him how Eden had lost her home to the arsonist.

"That's the one. Gene is managing that project," he said, referring to his oldest son.

"Guess there are silver linings to every situation." Too bad there wasn't one for him.

"We're also helping your future sister-in-law convert the old Elks Lodge into her new dance studio." Theo hadn't proposed to Eden yet, but everyone knew where things with them were heading. "And come the fall, we'll be a part of the team building the new addition on the library, assuming all the funds are raised."

And around here it was always a possibility funds wouldn't be available. It wasn't that projects couldn't and didn't fall through in finance. They did, but it didn't cause the kind of income fluctuation even one lost job could cause Ed. No matter how much Nick enjoyed working with Ed, he'd sworn he'd never get into a business that depended on the weather being good and the economy being strong. He didn't know how much Ed struggled over the years, but it couldn't have been easy raising a family on unpredictable income. Without money, there was uncertainty.

As he watched Ed prep things for the day, he had a thought and without analyzing it, he asked, "I know this sounds crazy, but you wouldn't have room for an extra guy on your crew, would you? I've got the time. You don't have to pay me." Ed didn't make much profit with each job, and an extra man could make that disappear.

Ed's smile was wide and sincere. And welcome. "I'd love the help. I've been a little short this season, and I don't want to get behind."

"Then put me to work," Nick said, reaching into the van to grab a sawhorse and a tool belt. As he followed Ed into the house, he had to stop and rebalance his load, not used to carrying more than a briefcase. They dropped the equipment in the open garage and turned to get more. Presley met him halfway down the driveway. Nick gave her some quick scratches. "Is it okay if she stays nearby, or should I bring her home and come back?"

"Shouldn't be a problem. The Uptons won't mind if you use a bowl to give her water," Ed said, giving Presley a pat. She took it as her due. "Never figured you for a pet person."

"I'm not. Presley found me. Well, technically, I found her in the woods."

"Guess she's your silver lining. Why is she wearing a brace?" Nick told him about Presley's injury and running into Dani at the clinic. "She must have been pleased to see you."

Nick gave a shrug. Apparently, not everyone in town knew how they'd split up. "I don't think I'd go right to pleased."

Ignoring the remark, Ed went on. "She bought a cute two-bedroom ranch over on Juniper Drive. I helped her with the home inspection and fixed the chimney and fireplace for her. Close to the clinic and the perfect size for her and Otis."

Nick's stomach clenched at the mention of a man's name, and he tried not to let his surprise show in his face. Dani hadn't said anything about there being a man in her life. Damn, how much of a mess of things had he made by kissing her? "Otis?"

"You didn't meet Otis? He's usually at work with her. Hope he's not sick."

This was getting worse. "He's a doctor, too?"

Ed laughed. "Not exactly. He's a dog. A big one. I swear he weighs more than she does."

Nick's relief was immediate. "Could be because there was a dog in quarantine overnight. That's why Presley couldn't stay there."

"Might be," Ed said. They went back to the van to get more supplies. "Boy, when Dani came into town with that dog, I don't know what people were talking about more. Her return or the size of her sidekick. He's a beauty though, light brown and sweet as a puppy. Hey, you shouldn't be doing that in those clothes."

Nick had picked up some lumber and was shifting it against his body to get the balance right. He didn't know what Ed was talking about until he noticed what he was wearing. Sure, it was his casual clothes, but the polo shirt and chinos were from Ralph Lauren, and the top-of-the-line hiking boots probably cost more than everything Ed was wearing. He made a mental note to wear only what came from Amazon later today. "It's no problem. They're only clothes. Completely replace-able."

"Still, let me get you some coveralls. And gloves. Your hands aren't used to this work anymore."

That was an understatement. Other than fixing a leaky faucet in his apartment, Nick hadn't done manual labor since before graduating from college. He'd hated how working with Ed made his hands rough and calloused. When Ed handed him the coveralls, Nick slipped into the well-worn cotton, smiling that the name on the patch was Ed's middle son who, if memory served from conversations with Millie, followed a girl to Arizona and worked as a teacher.

As Ed told him about the job—they were converting the garage to a family room then adding a garage—two more workers arrived, and introductions were made. Ed gave them directions and let them get to work.

Once the clothes were on, the routine came back, and Nick found himself slipping into the process. He was surprised by how little instruction he needed to do things he hadn't even thought about in over ten years. He'd learned well the first time around. Ed was a good teacher, patient and thorough, and Nick remembered how great it had been at the end of each day to see the progress they'd made and, ultimately, the pride in a job well done.

When was the last time he'd experienced that? How long had it been since a deal had given him anything more than a larger bank account?

After a few hours that passed quickly, Nick went in search of a bottle of water, then checked on Presley, who'd discovered a patch of shade under a tree and was sleeping comfortably. He took her for a quick walk, then snapped a quick silly picture of them and sent it to Dani before getting back to work. When his stomach gave an embarrassing growl, he glanced at his watch and discovered it was after one.

"I heard that," Ed said.

"Guess it's time for lunch."

Ed came over and checked what Nick had done. "Nice job on the drywall. This room is going to hold a lot of love and fun, thanks to us." One reason Ed was so good at construction was because he always saw the benefit of what his work brought to others. "You haven't lost your touch."

Nick couldn't stop the good feeling that came from the easy compliment. So unlike New York. "Thanks, I'm as surprised as you are."

"Oh, I'm not surprised, just pleased. Time to take a break. We both need lunch, and I've got to go with Leslie to her doctor's appointment this afternoon."

His wife was sick? "What's wrong?"

"Oh, nothing. She got hearing aids a few weeks ago and is having them checked today."

First Doc Wheeler was retiring, now Leslie needed hearing aids. The town may not have changed much, but the people had. "But everything is okay?"

"Absolutely, and you should come by for dinner. Leslie would love to see you." Nick was happy to agree. "You'll join us again tomorrow?"

It's not like he had anything else planned. "Tell me when to be here."

"You should also stop by the Community Center tonight."

"Are you renovating that, too?" The center was in one of the town's old Victorian mansions, and Nick could imagine it needed work.

"No, there's a committee meeting for the Dog Days Festival. Since you're around, come and see where they need help. I'm leading the temporary structures team." Figured. Ed didn't even get a break from building when he was volunteering, but Nick didn't think the man wanted one. He loved his work.

Thinking about spending another night in front of the television didn't appeal, so Nick said, "What time?"

"Seven. Leslie's baking cookies."

That alone could make it worth going to the meeting. "See you there." After saying goodbye to the other team members, Nick walked over to Presley, who heard him coming and jumped up from her nap, stumbling for a second as she remembered the brace on her leg.

He put his coveralls in the back of Ed's van, then headed to his car. As he thought about what to do for lunch and how to fill the time before the meeting, he glanced at the house. Time really had sped by as he worked today, and he found himself looking forward to coming back. The thought led him to another question.

When was the last time he'd looked forward to work?

Chapter Eight

♥

Sending samples to the lab was a do-it-yourself process at the clinic, and regular trips to the local package store were needed. Usually Beth handled these, but Dani needed the change of scenery and some time in the fresh air, so when she had a break between appointments in the afternoon, she headed to the center of town.

She hoped being out of the office would help her stop thinking about Nick. It wouldn't be so bad if she were thinking about yelling at him or putting him in his place for the way he treated her during their last summer together. Instead, all her mind could call up was the feeling of yesterday's kiss, which brought up thoughts of other kisses and more. It was almost as bad as her first weeks in Fable Notch when she'd fought the reminders that came up with nearly every place in town.

Overnighting the package didn't take long, so she walked along West Street, the town's central street, enjoying the day and letting the sun warm her skin. Even without Otis with her, she received waves and nods from familiar faces. It reminded her she was building a life here, settling in.

As she headed to her car, a bark had her turning around. Presley. Which meant Nick on the other end of the leash. At least today she didn't feel as though the day had run her ragged. She probably even had some eyeliner on. He, of course, looked wonderful, expensive, and put together, but it was his blue eyes that captured and held her gaze. And her heart fluttered at his smile.

Damn it.

Be professional, Dani. He'll be gone again before you know it. It was a good reminder. "You've saved me a call," she said as he came close. "Thanks for the text and photo. Seems like Presley is adjusting to her brace, and you're adjusting to her."

"She's fine until she forgets she has it on. Then she'll try to jump into my car or onto something and stumbles a bit. Every time she does, I panic." Dani was glad her decision to send him home with the dog wasn't hurting Presley. "And she's training me very well." He held up a bag.

She recognized the logo from Significant Paws, the local pet store, and smiled. "I can't walk in there without buying way too much." Dani bent to check on Presley. "Let me see your paw, girl. I want to make sure nothing has changed." She smoothed a hand over the leg, touching it through the brace, making sure the skin wasn't heated or inflamed, which would suggest an infection, and checking that the brace was dry and tight. "She took her pill this morning?"

"With breakfast."

"Everything looks fine. Keep watching to see the brace doesn't get loose. If it does, tighten the Velcro or call me if you're concerned." She had to stop suggesting he call her. She stood, but Presley wanted more attention and bumped herself against Dani's legs. Unprepared for the shove, Dani stumbled into Nick. His arms came around her, steadying her. She didn't fall, but she didn't feel steady. She could smell his aftershave, his mouth was close enough to kiss, and, heaven help her, there was a part of her that wanted to. Where was the part that wanted to slap him for the pain he caused her?

She put a hand on his chest, intending to push herself away, but he tightened the embrace. As they stood there, she allowed herself to enjoy his warmth and strength, remembering how he once made her feel, how they once couldn't get enough of each other. Talked of a life together. She waited for him to let her go, but when he didn't, she asked, "What are you doing?"

"Holding you. I thought that was obvious. You almost fell."

"I'm fine." She wasn't certain of that. "You can let me go."

"What if I don't want to?"

That gave her the emotional shove she needed. She had wants and needs, too. And since what she wanted in the moment was to kiss him again, what she needed was distance. She stepped out of his arms and took an extra step for good measure. As she tried to think of something to say to ease her discomfort, her phone rang. The Carnival of the Animals tone told her it was the clinic. "Excuse me." She spoke to Beth for a few minutes and assured her she'd be back shortly. "I need to go."

"Duty calls. We'll walk you to your car."

"It's only a block away." She tried to stay ahead of him, but he was next to her in two strides. Damn his long legs.

"Great. You said Presley shouldn't overdo it."

It took willpower not to bolt for her car. She didn't want Nick to know how much being near him rattled her. She gave a loud mental groan when she fumbled getting her keys out. *Keep it together, Dani.* When he opened her door for her, she knew he'd noticed.

"Guess I'll keep seeing you around," he said. She gave a quick wave, closed the door, and drove off, trying desperately not to speed and definitely not looking at him in the rearview mirror.

After stitching the ear of a cat whose play fighting with a kitten had a real consequence and seeing her last scheduled patient, Dani was surprised to discover an unexpected voicemail from Nancy. They were seeing each other at the committee meeting tonight, so the urgency was concerning. She called, and when Nancy answered on the first ring, Dani knew something was wrong. Nancy had two kids, was expecting her third, and managed a busy bookkeeping business. She was efficient but didn't live with the phone by her side.

"Dani, thank goodness you got my message. You aren't going to believe this. I'm on bed rest for the remainder of my pregnancy."

Dani pulled out the nearest chair and dropped into it. "What's wrong?"

"Placenta previa." Dani's stomach clenched as Nancy explained the condition and what it meant. "I'm not going anywhere until it's time to deliver this little girl, which hopefully won't be for another five of six weeks."

Which was weeks after the auction. "I'm so sorry. What do we do next?" She kept her voice calm when she felt anything but.

"You need someone to take my place. This is too big a job for one person. I can make calls, but that's about it." As Nancy outlined what still needed to be done, Dani did her best to take notes and stay focused, but her head was a jumble of concerns. Nancy was the one who knew what she was doing, and this year's auction had the biggest goal ever, almost fifty percent more than they'd ever raised.

As soon as they hung up with plans for Dani to stop by before the meeting and pick up Nancy's files, Dani promptly freaked out. Opening the bottom drawer of her desk, she ripped open a bag of peanut M&Ms and paced. When the bag was almost empty, she called Rosie. After explaining the situation, Rosie told her to put away the M&M's—Dani didn't need to tell her she was eating them—and trust she would get whatever support she needed. She reminded Dani that Nancy hadn't fallen off the face of the earth, things were in motion, and people wanted this to be a success. When they said goodbye, the M&M's were gone, but Dani wasn't as confident as her aunt.

She spent the next few minutes before heading to Nancy's reading through her event binder and covering it with post-it notes of questions and trying not to second guess herself. She should have known better than to take on such a big role. But, still smarting from what had happened with her so-called friends in Houston, she'd been so happy to be included that when Nancy asked Dani to co-chair, she'd said yes.

First Nick, and now this. She wrote a post-it note reminding her to buy more M&M's and stuck it on the front of the binder.

Chapter Nine

♥

For a first day, Nick thought, it hadn't been too terrible. Running into Dani had been a pleasant surprise, and having her unexpectedly in his arms was even better. He was certain he saw a flash of desire. He didn't know what he was going to do with this information, but it made him grin, and that was enough.

When he and Presley got back to the house, he turned down the air conditioning, gave her one of the treats he'd bought at Significant Paws, then tackled the boxes stacked against a wall in the living room. The first box held books. Favorites from childhood—even a few picture books he remembered reading with his mother—and some from high school. While his peers read *Harry Potter*, his English teacher, Mrs. Keller, introduced him to Harry Dresden. He was hooked after the first book, taking one after the other out of the library and scouting used book sales for more. The first dozen of the series were in the box, and he put them on the built-in shelf next to the fireplace.

When he opened the next box, the bubble wrap told him he'd found pictures. As he unwrapped each, memories came flooding back. There was one of him with his brothers and Ryan Sinclair on Christmas morning. Another of Martin and Millie laughing. One of his mother

Susan that all the brothers had because it was the only good one they had of her.

And one of Dani.

He'd taken it the summer before his senior year of college. She had nothing but criticism for how she looked, but he thought she was gorgeous. He'd had it printed, then splurged and bought the picture a good frame. Not knowing if he'd have room for it when they got to college, he didn't take it with him. He had a copy on his phone, and that was enough. After she left him, he deleted the image. Seeing it again, and the joy in her eyes, made him think of how sad she'd looked the last time he saw her in New York. Before he left, they had some more things to talk about.

The next box held old gifts from his brothers and a Nintendo DS that had been a birthday present from Dani for his sixteenth birthday. It was the most expensive thing he owned at the time. He'd considered returning it, but the chance to have what some of the other kids did had been too appealing. The following summer, she brought hers with her, and they'd competed fiercely for high scores.

There were more memories in these boxes than Nick expected. He was about to stop, then decided to open one more. In this one, he found a treasure. His sketch books. Even before he'd worked with Ed and learned what construction required, Nick drew houses. Huge ones with more rooms than anyone ever needed. Apartments overlooking cityscapes. As he pulled out the books, he found a plastic bag of pencils. His heart clenched at the sight. He'd packed them because he couldn't bear to throw out anything that could be useful. A scarcity mindset that ruled his life for years. Maybe he shouldn't have let it go entirely?

He continued to look through his old ideas, stopping at one house he'd drawn with a huge yard and a dog. That was supposed to be for Dani. Back when he'd woven her into his plans and dreams. She was everywhere—all over his past, his memories. And no matter where she was now, she was less than a fifteen-minute drive away.

Fifteen minutes and eight years.

As he flipped through the books, he saw some of his sketches were pretty good, and it was fun to watch his work improve. He found the first drawings he did to modify the house where he grew up and the ideas for the home he was currently sitting in.

He couldn't believe how close he'd come to his original sketches. He discovered Frank Lloyd Wright while watching *Blade Runner,* and after, read everything he could on the architect. From then on, his drawings were filled with clean lines and flat roofs, which had to be changed because they weren't practical in snowy New England. But more than the pictures he drew were the dreams behind them. Looking at his drawings, Nick could remember the intense desire behind every line he made. As he created those houses, he believed with everything in him that he'd make them real one day.

And he had. He willed this place into being with plans, determination, and hard work. It didn't matter that his net worth was nearly as low today as when he'd arrived in New York. It didn't matter that he didn't know how he was going to get his job back. He would find a plan, sketch it out, and will it into being.

He went to his home office and fired up his laptop but ended up spending the time staring at a blank document and mindlessly searching the internet. Presley would be happy. He'd ended up back on Amazon and he ordered her a bunch of toys in addition to a new sketchbook for himself. He needed to stop overworking his credit card. How long would it be before he couldn't make more than minimum payments? He ran some math in his head, but when his heart rate increased, he closed the computer.

He needed something else to focus on. He'd come up with the right idea. He had to. And in the meantime, he'd go to the Festival meeting.

After dinner, he left Presley at home and drove to the Fable Notch Community Center. It was another business in a converted house, a pale-yellow Queen Anne mansion. He knew ridiculous details about the place because he'd been forced to write a paper in the fifth grade about a local building. It would be the center for information and a few events on Festival weekend.

Seeing the full parking lot, Nick had second—third?—thoughts about being here. The room would be filled with familiar faces and questions he didn't know how to answer. He didn't think he was up for stares and whispers.

Growing up, he and his brothers were used to people talking about them. When your father runs off, your mother needs to be regularly brought home from the local bar, and the fire chief and his wife become your legal guardians, you're the family who gives people something to talk about. But this time was different. He was the one who'd made the mistakes, not his folks.

As panic rose, he considered leaving, then saw Ed's truck with a space next to it. Deciding it was a sign, he parked. He was here. He might as well see what was going on. There'd be bad coffee and Leslie's great cookies. And it's not like he had anything else to do.

He'd barely walked into the main room when Ed spotted him and came over. "Glad you made it," he said.

Nick tried for humor. "It was tough to fit you into my busy schedule."

Ed must have heard something in Nick's voice, because instead of bringing him into one of the many groups of people milling about, he put a hand on Nick's shoulder and guided him to the side. "Son, when we met, I was taller than you. I've never known anyone with more drive and determination. I can see the disappointment in your posture, but I'll tell you what else I see. I see a man with a good heart who's helped his family, follow his dreams, and make something of himself despite a tough start." Nick said nothing as his throat closed. He'd love to see himself that way. "Whatever tangle you've gotten into, you'll untangle it. It may take time, but you'll do it. Nothing worth building is built fast. Now, go get one of Leslie's peanut butter cookies and talk to Brenda to find out where you can help."

Nick couldn't stop himself from giving the man a hug. It was the most encouragement and support he'd received in months. Or was it years? Fine, he couldn't remember the last time someone said something that kind to him. Pats on the back weren't given at Wall Street firms. Compliments were paid in cash bonuses.

He did as Ed suggested and made a beeline for the refreshment table. As he enjoyed the still warm cookie, he checked out the easels highlighting this year's fundraising project. There was a festival every season and, starting in the fall, money was raised at each event toward that goal. This year the plan was to build a young adult room onto the library that would feature places for teens to hang out, a larger, more targeted reading selection, and increased computer access, including laptops kids could take home and use during the school year. That part punched him in the gut.

Computers and internet had been a challenge for the Hanson's. The only way to have one on their mother's limited income was through a rent-to-own plan. By the time they owned it, it was out of date. There were many days when Nick stayed after school to use their computers or went to the library hoping to find a free one, hovering until someone left. If his workload was heavy, he got up early on Saturdays to be at the library when it opened. He remembered when the Sinclairs bought a second computer. They claimed it was because Martin wanted to use it and Ryan was always on the one they had, but Nick suspected it was, so he and Theo would have one when they came by. When Nick graduated from high school, Cole gave him a top-of-the-line laptop because his band was doing well. Nick was over the moon.

He did a double take when he saw the list of estimated costs. It was the smallest bottom line he'd seen in years. Did the Festival always have such low financial goals? When he noticed the cost assigned to laptops, he realized that a year ago he could have written a check to cover it.

A familiar voice broke him out of his thoughts. "Is that Nick Hanson?"

He turned to see his sophomore English teacher. "Hello, Mrs. Keller. Or should I say, Mayor Keller?" He offered her his hand to shake, but she hugged him instead. Yup, worlds away from New York.

When she let him go, she said, "You're not in my class anymore. Call me Brenda."

"That may take some getting used to, but I'll try."

"Good. What brings you here tonight?"

Oh, I have nothing to do with my time because I've got the real-world version of detention. "I'm planning to be here for the next several weeks. Ed Franks suggested I see if there was something I could do. Is there a team or committee that could use some help?"

"Is there? This is wonderful. Your timing couldn't be better." Something else he hadn't heard in a long time. "We lost a key volunteer this morning. One of the co-chairs for the silent auction dropped out because of a medical emergency. If you're up for it, I could use you to take over her job."

That was more than he expected. As a kid, he'd been too young to participate in it, but he knew that the auction was a big responsibility. The last thing he wanted was to be in a situation where he might let people down. Before he could think himself out of it, he said, "As long as my partner knows I've never done anything like this before."

"Not a problem at all. Nancy—she's the volunteer who dropped out—worked on this for the last two years, so all you need to follow her plan. It's not rocket science. And here's your partner now. Let me go tell her the good news."

Yesterday a dog, today a role in the Festival. Barely over twenty-four hours in Fable Notch, and Nick was having trouble recognizing his life. He braced himself and turned. When he saw Brenda walking over to Dani, he decided his luck could be turning.

Chapter Ten

♥

Dani arrived at the Community Center frazzled and anxious. Her time with Nancy had been helpful, but she was in a panic about finding someone to help her at this late date. Everyone had their assignments and commitments. She walked into the main room and braced herself for what was sure to be a difficult meeting. Before she could find a familiar face and plead with them to join her, Brenda came over. She expected the other woman to look concerned, but the mayor was beaming. She grabbed Dani's hand and talked as she moved them through the room. "I have such good news for you. We've found someone to take Nancy's place. And even better, it's someone you know."

Dani wondered who it was. It couldn't be Laurel. She was too involved as one of the coordinators for the blueberry competition. Maybe Sheridan or Eden had decided to help her so she wouldn't fall on her face her first-time volunteering. When Brenda stopped in front of Nick, all Dani could think was, *This is not happening to me.*

"Dani, Nick has volunteered to help with the auction. I recall you two being good friends during the summers when you visited." Brenda turned to address Nick. "Did you know she was back? She's working with Doc Wheeler at the vet clinic."

"We've already crossed paths," said Nick.

"Wonderful. I will leave you two to figure things out. Don't talk too much, though. We're going to be starting in a few minutes. Dani, you'll be able to give us an update when we get to that part of the agenda?"

"Absolutely, Brenda." She was glad her voice didn't wobble or come out as the scream she wanted to release. As soon as Brenda was out of earshot, she turned on Nick. "What the hell are you doing?"

"Volunteering for the Festival. Thought that was obvious." He crossed his arms in front of him. Why was he defensive? She was the one having her life invaded.

"And how are you planning to help on a project this big from New York? Do you have any idea how much work needs to be done in the next three weeks?" She was realizing how many details still needed to be taken care of. "How did you convince Brenda this was a good idea? I cannot mess this up. I need someone who's here."

He pulled her aside, which was a good thing since her panic and voice were rising. "I *am* here. I'll explain more another time, but I'm not going back to New York until after the Festival. I'm more than willing to help. But if you don't want to work with me, I'll find something else to do, and you can find another partner."

She *didn't* want to work with him. She didn't even want to see him. And why was he going to be around for weeks? This was almost as stress inducing as Nancy's news. She took a deep breath to clear her head. If he was her only option, she'd make it work. She had to. "Fine, but you'd better pull your weight. This is a serious commitment."

"I'm aware of that. This isn't my first Festival," he said. "I'm a little surprised that of all the available jobs, you chose the auction. Isn't this the kind of thing you said your mother did at the country club?"

Dani squared her shoulders. She was nothing like her mother. Her mother led committees to get noticed. "When Nancy asked for my help, I thought it would be a great way to get to know more people while helping." Unfortunately, by agreeing, Dani had taken on more than she could handle, and now she risked disappointing everyone. "I wanted to make a difference."

"Then I'm sure you will. This is a place where every penny counts." He motioned with his chin to the jars available for people to put out at their businesses to encourage customers to drop extra change. Several filled ones had been returned.

"Those bring in an extra thousand or two dollars every year. I realize that's not much to you, but—"

"It's not like I don't remember when that was a fortune." She heard the anger in his voice and dropped her eyes. She knew how difficult things were for him and his brothers. It was when money became more important than anything else—when he'd rather work than be with her—she had an objection. But that had nothing to do with today. He looked as though he were about to say something, and if it was sarcastic or mean, she'd deserve it, but Brenda called the meeting to order. "Let's find seats," he said.

The chairs were arranged in two circles, one inside the other, allowing people to stand where they were when it was their time to talk and be easily seen. Dani liked the way the arrangement was less formal and made it easier for to feel a part of things. But tonight, with Nick sitting next to her, Dani wasn't looking forward to speaking. As she pushed at her cuticle, she looked across the room and gave a wave to Eden, Janelle, and Sheridan. Normally, she sat with them. She met Sheridan's questioning look and mouthed, "Tell you later."

As they went through the agenda, Dani was distracted by Nick's nearness. She could see the late day stubble on his cheeks, smell the lingering aftershave on his clothes. She hated being so aware of him. Attracted? No, that wasn't an option.

"Dani," Nick said under his breath and nudged her arm with his elbow.

"What?" she said, a little too loudly.

"You're up."

She stood rapidly. "Sorry, everyone. I'm still getting my bearings after today's change. As many of you have heard, Nancy is on doctor's orders to stay in bed for the remainder of her pregnancy. Nick Hanson has stepped up to take her place. We're committed to making sure the auction is a huge success, so don't worry." *Please don't let them be worried*. She was worried enough. She went on to talk about some new donations and asked people to come to her or Nick with other ideas and contributions. "Nancy and I are grateful for all the items we've received so far, but as you know, the goal for this year's auction is significantly higher than last year, so we're going to need more items and bidders than ever."

"Nicely done," Nick said when she sat down. She wasn't sure if he was being glib.

"Thanks," she said. She hoped people believed the auction was safe in her hands, but she couldn't be certain. She wasn't even certain herself.

The meeting lasted a little over an hour and as soon as it ended, people came over to Nick to welcome him and thank him for stepping up to help. Great, he got to be the hero. Dani scooted over to where her friends were standing by the drinks and cookies.

"Spill it," Janelle said. The other woman was good at getting to the point. Dani was still nervous around Janelle Novak and Sheridan Behr, since she didn't know them well. She wished Laurel was here, but nights were the brewery's busiest time, so Laurel was never at these.

Dani rubbed the spot between her brows to release the tension and gave them a quick update on Nick, the dog, and his suddenly becoming her partner.

Sheridan, a college friend of Laurel's who'd moved to town two years ago, handed her a bottle of water. "His getting assigned as your co-chair was an accident?"

"Fate. I think it was a cruel twist of fate. And if we're going to work together, we're going to have to talk about what happened when we broke up."

"That turned out well for me and Theo," Eden said, the woman's dreamy expression giving away how much in love she was with Nick's brother.

What happened to Eden wouldn't and couldn't happen to Dani. "You're a special case. Nick will develop hives if he's away from New York for too long. Helping on the Festival is nothing more than a time filler for him, although I don't know why he's going to be here for so long." Another thing they were going to have to talk about.

"Hey, Dr. Auction, I've been looking for you." A baritone voice had her turning around. She smiled at the familiar face.

"Chris, what can I do for you?" Like her, Chris Farrell was new to town, although he didn't have the familial history she had. Instead, he was someone who came to ski and decided to make it home. He had a Channing Tatum sexiness to him and a better physique than the owner of a marketing and web design business needed. Young, single, and happy to let any interested woman know he was gay, he'd volunteered to manage publicity for this year's event.

"I want to thank you for doing that video with Otis. It's bumping up the hits to the site like crazy. You're practically viral."

"That's great to hear." A few weeks before, Dani had been reluctant to agree to Chris' request that she an Otis appear in a video, but Chris had persuaded her and, for the good of the Festival, she'd said yes. "Otis is a natural in front of the camera."

"You were, too." Dani was relieved. The process had been awkward until Chris told her to focus on Otis. That made things easier. "I'm very grateful. You're making me look good."

"Then I will use that gratitude. Have you come up with a donation for the auction?"

"I have. I'll offer a website review and a round of copy suggestions."

"Really? That's wonderful. Thank you." Every donation counted, and his sounded like one a lot of local businesses might bid on. She was so happy to have some good news, she gave him a hug.

"Sorry to interrupt," Nick said, coming up behind her. She let go of Chris and turned to see Nick scowling. Apparently, he was having doubts about his new assignment. "We have an auction to make happen, and I don't have a clue what I'm doing. When can you bring me up to speed?"

His tone was abrupt and almost rude. It wasn't as though she liked the idea of working with him either. Chris must have noticed, because he put a hand on her shoulder. She appreciated the comfort. "I can see you tomorrow after my last patient, mid to late afternoon. Would that work?"

He nodded in agreement. Personally, she didn't think anything about this was going to work, but she had no other choice. "You can come to my place." He gave her the address, and she handed him Nancy's auction binder.

"See you then," she said. It was another few seconds before he walked away. "That was awkward."

"He's totally hot," Chris said appreciatively.

"No argument, but he's my ex."

"Which explains why he was shooting daggers at me."

Dani didn't understand what Chris was talking about. "He's probably having second thoughts about helping."

"Oh, he's having second thoughts, but they are about you, sweetness, not the auction. Did you see his expression when I touched you? He looked like a man who wanted a fight. If you want to torture him for a little while, let him think there's something between us."

Dani snorted. "I'm sure he didn't notice that at all."

"Want to place a bet on that?"

Bet on Nick hurting and disappointing her? Maybe. Bet on him being jealous of her touching another man? Not likely. Bet on her wanting to kiss him again? Not going to think about that because Dani knew her priorities, and Nick was no longer one of them.

Chapter Eleven

♥

After the meeting, Nick arrived home in a daze. He dropped his keys and the enormous notebook Dani handed him on the hall table and headed to the living room. He'd think about the auction tomorrow.

What he couldn't get out of his mind was the image of the muscled man with his arms around Dani. Not to mention the possessive way he put his hand on her shoulder. Nick shook his head to clear his thoughts, then wondered if that actually worked for anyone. Dani's social life didn't — couldn't—make a difference to him. He had work to do, plans to execute.

At not even 10 o'clock, it was too early for bed, but he was considering it. He didn't know if it was the physical labor he'd done earlier in the day or the emotional labor of seeing everyone. Either way, he was exhausted. He headed to the living room, Presley on his heels, and he helped her onto the couch before dropping beside her. As he flipped through channels hoping something would catch his interest enough to kill time, he realized he hadn't checked his emails all day.

For the first week of his suspension, he'd checked his emails obsessively, hoping there'd be something to tell him there'd been a mistake, either with his job or with the investments he'd made that had evaporated. It didn't take long before he'd turned off the notification setting and only checked in a few times a day.

There weren't many new messages today, but he was curious about a Google alert about Jeffries and Waters. Wondering what happened at his firm, he clicked the message to see a list of articles on the same subject—a new client announcement in the mergers and acquisitions department. His department. He opened the first link and scanned the article, his heart rate rising as he read.

It was a major deal, and he could see the potential in every aspect of the project. He'd heard rumblings about it in his last weeks at the firm and did what he could to drop hints with the senior managers in charge to let them know he was interested in being a part of it. He'd expected to finish the deal he was working and use it as a springboard to the next big thing.

Yeah, that didn't work out as he planned.

His head started swirling with questions. Would any of those men trust him again? Even if he did get his job back, what was it going to take to prove himself? How long would it be before people didn't look at him and wonder when he was going to screw up again or if he was going to collapse?

It wasn't as if he could get a job anywhere else. He'd thought of it when they first suspended him, then realized he'd never get a recommendation. Not that he wanted to leave Jeffries and Waters. It was one of the best firms in the city. Nearly any move would be a step backwards, and Nick didn't believe in those.

He had to prove he was worth it.

And he couldn't let the Sinclairs down. Not after all they'd done for him and his brothers. He'd been so proud when he'd started helping them out. They'd never asked or even suggested it was necessary, but it was something he'd wanted to do since he was a kid. What if they needed that money? Relied on it?

And now there was the auction. Dani was relying on him to be her partner and create a success for the town. He saw the horror on her face when she found out they'd be working together. Heard the surety in her voice that he was going to bail. What if he let all of them down? What if his father was right, and he was a waste of space?

Nick tossed the phone away from him, startling Presley as it landed on the other side of her. He pushed off the couch, earning him a bark and a howl. Great, someone else not happy with his actions. Pacing around the living room, he tried to get hold of his racing thoughts.

Work. The Sinclairs. Dani. Job. Money. Plans. Success.

How had he gotten so off course? His plans were there to make sure he hit his goals. What was he going to do to get back to those?

And why was he sweating?

The air conditioning was going. It was perfectly comfortable a few minutes ago. Had something else gone wrong?

No, he realized as he struggled to pull in air. Not the air conditioning. It was him. His heart was racing, and he was lightheaded. He didn't have much time before his vision got narrow and his chest hurt. He made a beeline for his bedroom and grabbed for the pills by the side of his bed. His hands shook as he fought to open the damn bottle, then he scratched his throat as he dry swallowed a pill. He sat down, put his head in his hands, and waited for the medication to kick in. He needed to breathe. Slowly. In for four counts, hold for four. Out for four counts, hold for four.

It wasn't helping.

He was about to start pacing again when Presley bumped against his leg and gave him a look as though she were worried. He reached under her belly and put her on the bed. When she laid down, he stretched out against her, putting his head on her flanks, and letting his focus drift to the sound of her breathing.

He didn't know how long it was before his heart rate came down, and he thought he could sit up without the room spinning. Shifting on the bed, he piled some pillows on top of each other and leaned against the headboard. Presley, missing his nearness, moved so her head was on his leg. Smart dog. It put her in the perfect position to get attention.

Glancing at the bedside clock, Nick saw less than thirty minutes had passed since he read the email. He wasn't surprised that it felt longer, but it was too soon for the medication to have kicked in effectively.

Presley.

She'd given him something to focus on other than himself, and in the process, he'd calmed quicker than ever before. He reached behind her ear to give her scratches. Something akin to a doggy moan told him he'd done something she liked. At least there was one person in his life who thought he could do the right thing. Okay, she wasn't a person, but it was a start, and he'd take it.

He let his mind drift, this time on driving somewhere tomorrow where Presley could have a fun walk as a reward for helping him. If focusing on her got him through the panic attack faster, maybe focusing on something other than his shitty predicament would do the same thing. Maybe working on the auction would be a good thing.

Chapter Twelve

Before she left work on Thursday afternoon, Dani called Mrs. Becker to tell her to pick up the puppies in the morning. The woman was overjoyed. Then it was home to have a late lunch, walk Otis, and get what she needed for her meeting. As they walked, she fumed about having to work with Nick. It wasn't fair. Here she had a chance to get to know people outside of the clinic but to do it he had to be her partner. It was a bad joke. She'd seen him three times in two days, and each time she went back and forth between wanting to kiss him or kill him.

She needed to keep from doing either.

It wasn't until Otis barked that she noticed they were standing on the porch. "Sorry, boy. I'm a little distracted." He bumped up against her leg as if to tell her he understood. She appreciated the dog's support and decided to bring Otis with her. It made sense for Presley, too. She'd take the hound when she left—Nick was going to be relieved—and having the dogs meet where Presley was comfortable would help the transition. The dog had been through enough.

So had Dani.

She put her laptop and the project notebooks in her Fable Notch Veterinary Clinic messenger bag, a welcome home gift from Aunt Rosie and Auntie Helen, designed by Helen, and got into the car. That's when she realized she didn't know where Nick's street was. For the first time since moving back, she opened her phone's GPS and put in the address. As she drove, she wondered where she was headed. Several of the condo developments had separate houses for those who wanted more space while having extra benefits like plowing and a pool. But as soon as she turned on to his street, she knew she was wrong.

There was no sign to announce the development, and the narrow road wound through a heavily wooded area. She passed one other house and if its size was any indication of what Nick's would be like, it was going to be huge. A minute later, her suspicion was confirmed. A mailbox set in a stone pillar with a number two on it told her she arrived as her phone gave a confirming ding. As she turned into the circular driveway, pulling her Honda Element behind his Lexus, she couldn't stop herself from whispering, "Oh my God, Nick. You really did it."

He'd built the home he'd drawn when they were kids. As she stared through the windshield, she remembered when they'd spent hours talking about what they wanted to do and have once they were on their own. She'd look up pictures of dogs she wanted to adopt—Cynthia never allowed pets of any kind—and places she wanted to visit. He'd flip through library books and websites on architecture, stopping at homes in the Prairie style and sketching versions of his own.

Nick spent so much time drawing houses inside and out she once thought he'd become an architect. "Not lucrative enough," he'd said. "You're at the mercy of every bad economy. It's almost as tough as construction. I like working for Mr. Franks, but the only way I'm going into real estate is if I can own it."

He was always driven to be as financially successful as possible as quickly as possible. And here were the results. It was impressive, but also a good reminder that plans and success came first for Nick. Everything else was a distant second.

It didn't matter how well he kissed.

She was still staring when he opened the door and stepped out, Presley close on his heels. She got out of her car, and Otis followed. As they walked toward the house, both dogs barked at one another, communicating awareness and, in Presley's case, territory. As Otis went over to meet his new friend, Presley took a step back, almost hiding behind Nick.

"Your dog is a beast," Nick said as he put a protective hand on Presley's head.

Dani laughed. Most people were startled when they saw Otis for the first time. His back came to her waist and at 5'7", she wasn't short. "Not exactly," she said. "He'd be much bigger if he were a purebred."

"What breed is that? Polar bear?"

"Great Pyrenees."

"You always wanted a big dog." As she knew his dreams, he knew hers. "Your dog makes mine look small."

"Otis makes every dog look small." Otis gave a quieter bark and waited for Presley to respond. Because he was used to seeing and calming pets at the clinic as well as when Dani fostered puppies, Otis was good around nervous animals. It didn't take long before Presley took a cautious step forward, then another to come meet the other dog.

"I'm glad you could adopt one." She heard genuine pleasure in his voice and couldn't stop the blush. Most people thought she was crazy to have such a large animal.

"And I get to bring him to work." She gestured to the house. "In the some-things-never-change-file, I see you kept your love of Frank Lloyd Wright architecture. I thought this place wasn't in the plans until your forties."

"You remember?"

Damn, she shouldn't have said anything. He didn't need to know how little she'd forgotten. "Your plans were always very important to you." *More important than me.* No, she wasn't going to go there. Well... she wasn't going to stay there.

"This did happen sooner than I expected. When this parcel of land became available and I had the money, I decided not to wait. Come on in."

She followed him, and the dogs scampered off to explore. She was aware of being alone with him in a way she hadn't been the other times they were together. Tonight, there was no committee nearby, no Beth to interrupt them. She stood there feeling strangely vulnerable and wishing Otis had stayed nearby.

Walking from the foyer into the large living room, she was struck by the different colors of wood that made up the decor. It was luxurious and obviously expensive. Uncluttered and chic, but also warm and inviting. In addition to a fireplace, there was a long, deep brown leather couch taking up most of the space, so different from the threadbare one that had been in the last home of his she'd been in.

She had an image of Nick sipping brandy with some skinny super model-type who would join him for a ski weekend. The blond—Dani always pictured them blond—wouldn't know the first thing about skiing, but she'd look great in and out of everything. Dani picked at her thumb's cuticle. She never resembled those women, the ones who looked like the country club wives and daughters her mother wanted Dani to emulate. Nick may have said her kisses drove him crazy, but that was a long time ago.

Why did her thoughts keep going back to kissing him?

"I can give you the five-cent tour, if you'd like."

"It may have been a while since we've seen each other, but I know you. Nothing around here is five cents."

"You have a point," he acknowledged. "Still, you're one of the few people who saw the plans for this place when they were a bunch of drawings in a sketchbook made by a boy with a lot of dreams."

There was a time when seeing those drawings was the best part of her year. She'd arrive for the summer, and he'd show her the new ideas he'd drawn. He didn't share them with many people, and she'd treasured the knowledge he'd let her see and comment on them. When friendship turned to love and I turned to we, he'd put her dreams in his plans, and she'd seen him in hers.

Until New York.

She wouldn't think about that. The auction was the reason she was here. She took her bag off her shoulder. "Show me where I can put this first." He led her to the dining room off the kitchen, where there was a table big enough to seat twelve people. Dropping her stuff, she said with more bravado than she felt, "Lead on."

They went upstairs where there were two bedrooms around a cozy open area. For a second she pictured children playing video games together as they had done once, but she moved off that image as quickly as it came.

Back downstairs, he took her down one hall which held a home office and another bedroom, then the opposite hall which had the master bedroom suite. His bedroom. As soon as she walked across the threshold and saw the hastily made bed, she took a step back and banged into him. Turning around to face him made it worse. He was close enough to kiss, close enough to smell the soap he used, something spicy. They stared at each other until she stepped around him and into the safety of the hall.

Auction. Dog. Auction. Dog. She had to stay focused on *her* plans. She had to do this right. She walked quickly back to the dining room. "It's an amazing house. Big. Planning to do a lot of entertaining?"

"Not really. I mean, when I built this place, I assumed I would use it as another rental property, so I made decisions based on that. After it was done last month, the realtor called me asking when I'd be ready to list it. I couldn't do it. I didn't want anyone else living here, even short term. Guess that turned out to be a good thing."

She remembered what he'd said last night. "Are you going to tell me why you're here for so long?"

He didn't answer immediately, and she watched his face change as thoughts went through his head. Anger, grief, worry. She was about to prod him when he said, "I've been put on a work suspension until the beginning of September."

"Holy shit." Dani slapped a hand over her mouth after the words slipped out. Nick was out of work? His goals had goals. She'd never seen him have a setback. She couldn't imagine what this was doing to him. "I kind of want to give you a flip response about not remembering that being a part of your plans, but as someone who knows how important those plans are, I'm going to stick with saying I'm sorry."

"You'd be justified in saying the first, but I appreciate the second."

She couldn't help but ask, "What happened?"

He rubbed a hand along the back of his neck. "I screwed up a major deal. Lost some big clients some big money."

"You can't be the first person to do that. You always said there was a volatility and risk to your work. Bigger risk, bigger payoff."

"I missed some red flags which could have prevented the problem. Truthfully, if my track record hadn't been so good, they probably would have fired me. I suppose that's still a possibility." He opened one of the notebooks. The subject was closed. "How about you fill me in on this project?"

Dani considered pushing him about what happened, then decided this was a good reminder. His life was separate from hers, and when his plans got back on track, he'd be gone. She gave her hair a pull, tightening her a ponytail, and opened her computer. "Everything we've done so far is in these books and the spreadsheets Nancy created. I'll give you the link to the shared drive."

"You said at the meeting you're still looking for donations, so I assume there aren't enough items to hit the goal."

She shifted in her chair. "Not yet. Nancy has some good ideas for people to ask for larger ticket items, but we're getting down to the wire."

"Then let's get to work."

For the next two hours they went through everything Dani had on the auction. She appreciated his taking it seriously. Maybe working with him wouldn't be a complete nightmare, although she had to admit there were more than a few times when she got distracted by his nearness and had to mentally brush the memories and attraction away. When she felt she'd told him as much as necessary she said, "Given what happened the last time, I'm not sure about asking, but do you have any questions?"

"Yes, but it's not about the auction."

"Does it involve kissing me again?"

He gave a half smile that—damn it—melted her and said, "Not at the moment, but I'm not ready to take it off the table. I want to know why you left me that summer."

Chapter Thirteen

♥

H e hadn't expected to blurt it out. He'd been sitting for the last few hours, trying to concentrate on the auction but every time she tightened her ponytail, he was distracted by the bare slope of her neck and found himself thinking about kissing her under her ear; a spot he knew was sensitive. Only their history kept him from reaching out. Before she left today, he needed to know why she left then. "After all those years of friendship and more, all I got was a one-line note."

She shifted in her seat then started to pack her things. Not looking at him she said, "I didn't think you'd have time to read more than that."

"You knew before you joined me I was working long hours." While she was finishing her senior year, he'd graduated early and started work. Most of their conversations that year had been brief calls and lots of texts.

"I did, but I didn't know how that was going to feel, how left out and separate I was going to be." She stopped putting things away and looked at him. "From the first week I arrived, I could feel how much you'd changed. Even on the few occasions we did things for fun, if there was more than the two of us, things always turned to business."

He crossed his arms. That wasn't fair. "The only people I knew in New York other than Henry were people I worked with. Who else were we supposed to see?"

"I know. I can't explain it exactly." She went searching in her bag for her keys. He knew it was a ruse. She always put them in the same spot—big pocket on the side. "I understood—understand—why you were so driven. But that summer, there was no room for me."

"Of course there was," he said, but before he could say more he stopped, not certain that was the truth even though he wanted to be. Had he cut her out? "I thought there was."

"You once got out of bed moments after we'd finished having sex to check the Japanese markets." Her voice cracked, and the sound made him wince more than her words. "Yes, you came back, but you got up again to work when you thought I'd fallen asleep."

He wanted to tell her she was wrong, but the last few months had shown him how unbalanced his life had become. The seeds for living this way had been planted in that first year, and there had been no reason to do things differently. After she left, someone at work thought he was slacking when he had trouble concentrating. He locked down what he was feeling and didn't allow any more distractions. Had he stayed locked down? "You're right. I didn't notice that I pulled away."

Her look told him he'd missed the mark. "You did more than pull away. You were gone. Nothing but work and the occasional blonde got your attention."

"What blonde?" He had no idea who she was referring to.

"Twice I came to meet you at bars near your office. Both times when I arrived there were these skinny women fawning all over you."

"The women on the hunt for rich husbands with fat portfolios? Please, I never noticed any of them or took their attention seriously." Sure, after she was gone, he took advantage of their interest, but it never mattered to him. He was about to say as much to Dani, then saw the sadness in her eyes as she blinked away tears. Apparently, she took it seriously. "I'm sorry. I didn't know you felt that way."

"It was more. About a week before I left, Auntie Helen's dog died. I'd been crying all evening, and I needed comfort. You came home railing about something that had happened at the office. 'Listen to this' you said and didn't stop. After you finished the story, you opened your laptop to work."

He remembered the project. He'd gotten his first big bonus from it. He'd used the money to get her something special. "Why'd you leave the necklace? I'd been so glad to finally give you something expensive."

She crossed her arms in front of her. "As if that mattered to me. Do you remember what the card said?"

He remembered how happy he'd been to buy it, but didn't have a clue what he wrote. "I'm guessing it wasn't 'I love you and you mean more to me than any necklace could,'"

She gave a sour laugh. "Not even close. 'Sorry I haven't been around. I'll make it up to you soon.' I had a jewelry box filled with apologies. I wasn't about to accept them from you, too."

Nick's stomach dropped. Gifts rather than attention or physical availability had been her father's style after the divorce. 'I can't be there for your birthday... holiday... graduation. Here's a check, here's a computer, here's a car.' If Nick hadn't noticed that's what he wrote, then he hadn't been thinking, and if he hadn't been thinking, then she was probably right about how he treated her. "I... holy shit, Dani." There were no good words.

"That card told me was no place for me. I didn't know if there ever would be again, so I left." And he'd driven her to it. She hadn't been selfish. She'd been alone.

Apparently he'd been missing warning signs for years. Maybe it was amazing his life hadn't blown up sooner.

Staring at her, he said, "To quote *When Harry Met Sally*, what's the statute of limitations on apologies?"

Dani gave a faint smile. She remembered. She'd gotten bronchitis just before winter break of their freshman year at college. He'd stayed with her and watched a marathon of rom-coms. The Meg Ryan ones were her favorite. "Her answer is ten years. You're definitely under that."

"But will you accept it?" As he watched her consider her answer, he came over and pulled her into a gentle hug. Friendly, not asking for more, but his lips were by her ear when he said, "I'm sorry."

They stood there in silence. He wished he had the right to ask what she was thinking. Not yet. Maybe before he left.

A bark at the back door alerted them there were things more urgent than talking about their past. "Someone wants to go out," Dani said, ending the hug.

One bark became two. Nick rolled his eyes. "And what one wants, the other wants."

"That's usually the way. They're like children. Have you used the word 'out' around Presley? Does it immediately get a response?"

"Every time." As he grabbed Presley's leash, she came walking over as quickly as her brace would allow. "And, as you can see, so does the sound of her leash. Do you have time to take them for a walk?"

Dani glanced at her watch and took out Otis's leash. "We can make time."

Nick remembered the man from the night before and stopped what he was doing. "Other plans? That guy from the meeting?"

Dani shook her head. "I owe Chris a beer." Nick didn't understand. "He said you might think there was something between us."

"There isn't?" Good.

"No, he and David have been going out for a few months. It could be getting serious."

It took Nick a second to understand what she was saying. He chuckled and finished getting Presley ready. "I'm an idiot."

"Sometimes," she agreed, and they headed to the door.

As they walked down the hill from his house, Presley tugged at her leash, hoping to go faster, but Otis kept a steady pace which made her settle. "Otis is good with her."

"He's been trained to be careful with other animals. He's a big help at the clinic. People sometimes warm up faster to him than to me." He was about to comment on her self-deprecation, but she continued. "We probably shouldn't go too far. Uphill could be difficult for Presley."

They turned and headed back. Otis changed directions so quickly he wrapped the leash around Dani and then banged against her as he went by. As she lost her balance, Nick reached to catch her. Because he was not prepared to have his arms suddenly filled with a woman, they both ended up falling into the grass next to the drive. Fortunately, it hadn't rained in the last few days, and they didn't land in mud. The dogs thought their owners had decided to play and immediately there was a pile of people and pets on the ground.

Before Nick could ask if Dani was all right, she let out a laugh he hadn't heard in years. He didn't know how much he'd missed it until the sound rang out and loosened something inside him. He rolled over to look at her, flat on her back, the light of the afternoon sun making the red in her hair glow. She was so incredibly beautiful. No one had ever captured his thoughts or his heart the way she had.

"Guess I should have seen that coming," she said, pushing herself onto her elbow and giving Otis a belly rub.

"Does he do that a lot?"

"Shuffle me aside, yes. It's not intentional. He gets enthusiastic and forgets how big he is."

Nick looked down into her shining eyes. She was, as always, irresistible. "This is a very Hallmark movie moment," he said, and brushed her hair out of her face to prove it. He hoped she could see what he was thinking. "And I know what's supposed to happen next."

He watched as she swallowed, liking that she was a little nervous. He was. "That depends on where the couple are in the story."

"Nope," he said. "There's only one thing to do at this point," and he closed the short distance between them and kissed her. He waited a breath to see if she'd push him away and when she didn't, he opened her mouth with his tongue, wanting more, hoping she'd give.

When her hands moved up his chest and over his shoulders, a voice inside him cheered, "Yes!" He wasn't imagining the attraction between them. If they had been inside, he'd be looking for a way under her clothes, to touch more of her, to be closer. Her t-shirt wasn't much of a barrier, and the area was secluded, but it wasn't the time for that. Instead, he allowed himself to enjoy the feel of her against him and the heat of her kisses. He could have continued for hours, but Presley tugged on her leash and howled. Otis joined in with barks.

"Squirrel," Dani said when they stopped. "It's a constant challenge around here." Nick tried to think of a way to recapture the moment, but before he could, she untangled them, stood, and continued walking to the house. "It's time for us to go. I'll check Presley's splint to make sure this little romp didn't aggravate her leg before the three of us head out."

"What do you mean, three of you?"

"I didn't tell you? Sorry, I guess the Festival took precedence. The quarantined puppies are going home in the morning. You're off the hook. Presley can come with me tonight, and tomorrow I'll start the process of having her transferred to a shelter."

His heart rate jumped, and he tugged on the leash, bringing Presley closer. "No."

"What do you mean, no?"

"You can't take her." The words were out of Nick's mouth before he could stop them. He hadn't consciously thought about keeping Presley, but the moment he said it, he knew it was the truth. "She's happy here, and I'm happy to have her stay with me."

He picked up his pace, glad Presley could keep up, then stood at the door, keeping the dog close. Dani and Otis were close behind. "She's not a cool new watch or a sleek feature on your car, Nick. She's an animal who needs care, comfort, and consistency."

He didn't like her tone. "I'm aware of that."

"Are you? I understand with your plans up in the air, you're not sure what to do, but that's not a good reason to get a pet. That's like having a baby to save a relationship."

How could she go from kissing to criticizing him in such a short so quickly? "Yes, I'm at loose ends right now, but having Presley here and taking care of her has been great. She's given me something other than my shitty situation to think about. We're having a good time together, right girl?" Nick put his hand out, and she nuzzled him.

"Two days ago you wanted to pay for her care and go. Now you're offering to keep her as long as necessary? What are you going to do when it's time to go back to New York?"

"I don't know. I suppose you may be taking her then, but people own dogs in New York, so maybe she'll still be with me." He was sure he could hire someone to walk her during the day while he was at work. Assuming he had a job to go to. Maybe he'd start a dog walking business.

Dani looked as though she might continue to argue, then changed her mind. "If I let Presley stay with you, promise me you're not going to flake out in a few days because she's not new or fun anymore."

"I won't. Does it look like she's been neglected? That I'm screwing up?" It came out harsher than he intended, but he wanted—needed—her to believe him, to believe *in* him. "Look, I get it. My track record sucks, but you can trust me. With the auction and with Presley."

He waited for her to say something. It was clear she was having some sort of argument in her head. "Don't let me down, Nick."

There was a world of meaning in her words, and Nick knew that if he wanted to heal what had happened between them, he had to do this right. "I won't."

She nodded but didn't look convinced. He watched as Dani and Otis got in her car and drove off. Presley barked, then howled. Nick assumed she wasn't ready to say goodbye to her friend. Nick was a little more conflicted. The auction. The dog. Even telling Ed he'd be back in the morning. Nick had made more promises and commitments in the last two days than he had in the last several years. How had that happened?

Chapter Fourteen

♥

The parking lot of the Seven Brothers Brewery was more than half full when Dani arrived after dropping Otis at home. Laurel greeted her as she came in, putting her arm around Dani and giving her a squeeze as they went over to the owner's table in the back corner of the restaurant, similar to how Aunt Rosie had her space. "Whatever it is, we'll figure it out."

Tears stung Dani's eyes. She loved that she didn't have to say anything. No one understood her like Laurel did. It had been that way since Dani's first summer with her aunts. Rosie took Dani and her brother, Xander, to the Stewart Lodge and Cabins for dinner, where Dani had been overwhelmed by the family of ten, seven of them boys. But before dinner was over, she and Laurel had started a friendship that lasted through the years, no matter the distance. When Dani left Nick in New York, she'd called Aunt Rosie and Laurel. Laurel met her at the bus and brought her to her aunt's and came over every day to hold her as she cried.

As Dani sat, Laurel said, "I'm going to have Jennifer bring you a Blueberry Summer Ale, and I'll join you in a few minutes."

"Are you sure you're not too busy tonight? We could get together tomorrow for lunch if that would be better." Nights were busy, and Dani didn't want to distract Laurel. Nick wasn't going anywhere, so neither were Dani's problems.

"I wouldn't have asked you to come if I didn't think I'd have the time. Sit, relax, drink. I'll bring food when I come back."

That was something else Laurel had in common with Aunt Rosie—they were good at taking care of people, especially with food. Soon Dani had her beer, and as she drank, she looked around at the business her friend had created.

It had been open for three years, and the brewery, housed in one of the area's refurbished paper mills, was getting a reputation for its excellent beers and as a place to go after a day of skiing. It had high ceilings, wood floors and walls, and ample space for diners, including a huge wrap around bar which would be filled before the night was out. It didn't surprise Dani that her friend ended up in a male-dominated part of the hospitality industry. Seven older brothers could do that.

It wasn't long before Laurel came back with an appetizer sampler plate and a beer for herself. "Start talking."

"Nick is my new partner for the silent auction, he's keeping the dog, and I have to stop kissing him," Dani said. She hadn't intended to blurt out that last part. She popped a fried pickle in her mouth, then quickly took a sip of beer to cool the burn of the hot food.

Laurel waited for her to swallow before asking, "Want to repeat that last one?"

"I need to stop kissing Nick."

Laurel tilted her head from side to side. "Probably. Possibly, but why don't you back up a few steps first and tell me how it got to that."

Dani told Laurel about the kiss in her office, Nick being assigned to help her on the auction, the fact that he was going to be around for longer than a few days, and their most recent kiss. "Somehow when we're alone together, I end up kissing him."

"Just kissing?"

"So far, but when I see him, I think about more." Memories swirling with new desires. It was a terrible combination.

"Guess that means he's still a good kisser." Dani's cheeks flushed. She was grateful the light in the brewery wasn't bright, but her friend's laughter told her it was no help. "So you two still have as much chemistry as ever."

"But I can't let it distract me. Nick will be gone as soon as he can." She had to remember that. Just because he was willing to take care of a dog didn't mean he'd changed.

"Why is he here for so long in the first place?" Dani shared what Nick told her. "Holy shit, Nick Hanson without a plan. Time to make that Hell Froze Over Lager."

She was grateful Laurel understood. "I'm sure it would be a big seller. Which reminds me, this is very good." Dani took another sip of her beer, then saw a familiar face. "Isn't that Casey Shaw?"

Laurel looked toward the bar where Dani gestured with her chin. "Looks like."

"She's on my list of people to talk to about a donation." Casey worked at the senior center where Dani sometimes brought Otis to visit with the residents. She also ran a side business dressing in costume and leading princess parties. Dani was hoping she would donate a party appearance. "Think she'd be okay with a quick chat?"

"Don't bother my customers." Dani was about to apologize when Laurel waved a hand. "I'm kidding. I love when people connect while they're here."

Dani had made enough mistakes with friends. She didn't want to make a misstep with Laurel. "Are you sure?"

"It's a bar. Not church." Laurel stood, grabbed Dani's hand, pulled her out of the booth, and gave her a shove. "Go. Talk to her."

Dani went to the bar, hoping the woman wouldn't mind being interrupted. As soon as she mentioned why she'd stopped by, Casey pointed to the open stool next to her and said, "Sit and tell me what you need."

In less than fifteen minutes, Dani had two donations, one for a princess party and another for a makeup lesson. Several hundred dollars added to the total. Time well spent.

When she got back to the table, Janelle was sitting in Dani's seat eating nachos. She liked the other woman, but Janelle was one of those women who made looking good seem effortless, and that intimidated Dani. Janelle's blonde hair was loose around her face in messy waves and her outfit, a bold orange and pink wrap dress, looked as though it were made for her. It probably was. Janelle ran a thrift store, Tailor Thrift, and she repurposed vintage clothes. Dani felt plain by comparison. "Hello, Doctor Dani," Janelle said, giving her a bright smile. "Working the room?"

"Hoping to get this auction filled," Dani said.

Before she could sit down, Janelle said, "What on earth are you wearing?"

Given the combination of surprise and horror in Janelle's voice, Dani was certain she had a stain on her top, but when she checked, she saw nothing out of the ordinary. Between being on her feet all day and not knowing if an animal was going to get something on her, she dressed casually for the clinic, usually an oversized top worn with leggings and comfortable shoes. "My work clothes."

"It's not doing you any favors."

Everything inside of Dani curled inward, and every time she'd said or done the wrong thing vied for attention in her thoughts. Loudest was mother's critical voice. *You cannot go to the club wearing that. Put on a dress.* Janelle was right. She looked awful. "I know, I need to lose some weight," she said, sitting on the opposite side and hoping she didn't sound as defeated as she felt. She took a nacho, but all she tasted was disappointment.

"You do?" Janelle tipped her head to the side. "Not that I can see. I meant that shade of lilac isn't good on you. Gray undertones. Very few people can wear it well. It's washing you out. You're like Eden—you don't wear make-up at work, so you should choose colors that make your skin glow. More rosy hues. Bring out the red in your hair. The v-neck is nice, though. Keep that. I'm going to look through my inventory and see what I have. I'll put some things aside, and you can choose."

Dani could almost hear her negative thoughts screech to a halt. Janelle wasn't criticizing. "I'd appreciate your help. You've got a great eye." That gave her an idea. "I know you donated a gift certificate to your store for the auction, but what would you think of donating an hour of personal shopping time? You could give someone one-on-one advice to help them pick out pieces that make them look fabulous. Some people don't know how to shop in a thrift store."

"Are you kidding? That's a fabulous idea. I wonder if it's a service I should think of offering?" Janelle grabbed a notebook out of her oversized bag and made some notes. "I could gauge interest level by the number of people who bid on it. This is brilliant. You're brilliant. Where should we set the value?"

Dani and Janelle discussed the new donation until Laurel came back with a plate of her baked mac and cheese and a to-go bag, which she handed Janelle saying, "Dinner's ready."

"Wonderful. Sorry I can't stick around, but I've got inventory to process and a video to edit." Janelle had a YouTube channel where she showed how she repurposed some of her more hideous thrift finds.

"Did you ask Dani your question?"

Janelle snapped her fingers. "Nope. Forgot. Laurel says you can settle an argument for me. I said Ryan

Reynolds had never been married before Blake Lively. Laurel insists he was, but can't remember who."

Without hesitation, Dani answered, "Scarlett Johansen. Lasted two years."

"Told you," Laurel said.

Janelle stuck out her tongue. "Thanks again for the idea, Dani. See you two soon."

Laurel took Janelle's seat. "What idea?" Dani explained about Janelle's new service and the donations. "Sounds like you had a very productive few minutes."

"I did. You don't think Janelle thought it was odd that I knew about Ryan Reynolds, do you?" She still worried about over sharing, giving people a reason to tease or turn on her.

"Just because those assholes in Texas made fun of you, doesn't mean other people will. We could have checked our phones, but I told her to ask you."

Deciding this was a worry for another day, Dani dug into the cheesy goodness of her meal. She couldn't stop the sigh. "Carbs make everything better."

Laurel swiped a bite from Dani's plate and said, "No argument."

"Now if I can keep being creative about ideas, there will be enough donations to make the goal."

"We," Laurel said.

Dani stopped the fork midway to her mouth. "What do you mean?"

"You said 'if *I* can keep being creative.' You have a partner for this, and as much as it may be uncomfortable to work with Nick, don't start doing everything yourself. You need to trust him." Trust Nick. Again. Give him the opportunity to disappoint her. Again. "You know, this could be an opportunity to close the book on your past with Nick."

"It was closed," Dani said. Wasn't it?

Laurel gave her a pointed look. "How many serious relationships have you had since him?" Dani ate another bite of the mac and cheese so she didn't have to say anything. Didn't matter. Laurel knew the answer. Dani dated a few guys after getting her degree, but there'd been nothing lasting. "You left Nick because you saw how money was taking over his life. This could be a chance to see what a jerk he's become."

"It would be nice not to have to avoid him every time he comes to visit."

"Exactly. Some relationships aren't meant to be." Dani heard the frustration in her friend's voice and knew she was thinking of Hunter Davis. Hunter was best friends with Laurel's oldest brother. She'd been in love with him for years, but he'd made it clear he saw her as a little sister and off limits. "Maybe this is a chance to be free of him."

Dani doubted her heart would ever be completely free of Nick, but Laurel was right. Her past with Nick had been a shadow over most of her romantic relationships. She'd never been able to find the combination of friendship and love she'd shared with him, and without it, something had been missing. Even if she and Nick acted on their attraction, eventually she'd see how attached he was to work and that no amount of chemistry could make her a priority in his life or turn him into the type of man who would stay in Fable Notch. She lifted her glass in a toast. "Here's to getting Nick Hanson out of my system once and for all."

Chapter Fifteen

♥

On Friday morning, Nick got to the Kinsman Diner with time to spare. He'd left Presley at home since he couldn't bring her into the diner, and it was too warm for her to sit in the car while he had breakfast with Theo. He sat in the parking lot, stalling. No more avoiding Rosie or any accusations she might lob at him. He deserved them, but he wasn't looking forward to them. His choices were to text Theo and suggest some place else and never come here again—which was a depressing thought since he'd been missing the food here for nearly a decade—or face Rosie.

Deciding he'd put off the inevitable long enough, he got out of his car and went in. The smells of home fries and coffee hit him and made his mouth water. For all the things that changed—and all the things he wanted to change—the Kinsman wasn't one of them.

He was two steps in and looking for Theo when Rosie greeted him. "Good morning, sunshine. Took you long enough to come by. Grab any seat you want." He tried to detect if there was anything in her tone, but all he heard was welcome. "Coffee?"

"Please," he said, sliding into a booth and facing the door so Theo would see him when he arrived.

She put an empty mug on the table along with a silver creamer, then poured. "Is it just you this morning? Did you finally decide you couldn't live without my pancakes and bacon?" It didn't surprise Nick that Rosie remembered his favorite.

"Never found a place that made them better." And that was true. He'd had breakfast in some of the fanciest places in New York, but nothing was like the food here. "Theo is joining me, so don't put the order in until he gets here."

"Can do." She sat opposite him, and he looked at the woman who was practically an aunt to everyone who came in. Short, energetic, and round in a way that made you want to hug her, Rosie was as an important a part of Fable Notch as the diner her grandfather started. She and Millie had been best friends since childhood. Nick had met her at a Sunday night dinner at the Sinclairs'. Like everyone else, he'd loved her immediately. Would she forgive him for hurting her niece? "But I'm not going to put off asking you why you haven't been here in years. You've come up on a few weekends and never stopped by."

Rosie was always direct. It was one of her good qualities. Usually. Today it made Nick feel as though he were the bacon on the griddle, jumpy and sputtering. "I didn't know if I'd be welcome after what I did to Dani."

"Sweetheart, you're always welcome." Hearing her say that was a balm, but he was still concerned.

"I screwed up. Big time. I didn't want you to yell at me for what I'd done. Didn't need you to tell me what a shit I'd been. Especially since you'd be right."

"Nick, if everyone who ever made a mistake in a relationship wasn't allowed in, the diner would be empty. Heck, if I banned everyone who'd hurt me a time or two, I'd lose the company of some great people. Including my wife and Millie."

Nick gave her a weak grin. He knew people made mistakes, but not everyone would forgive you for what you did. "I appreciate that, Rosie."

"So after all this time, you've decided to come in. What's changed?"

There was a loaded question. What hadn't changed? "I'm going to be in town for the next few weeks, and I can't go that long without having your breakfasts. Or your open-faced turkey sandwiches. It was tough enough to stay away on those short trips."

"I'm glad you came to your senses," she said, giving his wrist a pat. "What about you and Dani partnering for the auction?"

Nick wasn't surprised she'd heard. "She wasn't thrilled, that's for sure, but we worked on it yesterday, and we talked about that summer."

"How did that go?"

He took a sip of his coffee before answering. "It wasn't the highlight of my week, but I think it helped. I missed a lot of signals back then. Hopefully, I'm smarter now."

She sat back, taking in the information. "Does this mean the two of you may be friends again?"

Nick flashed on their kisses, the feel of her lips against his. That wasn't exactly friendship, but he didn't know what it was. Better not to say anything. "It's too soon to tell. It's possible, and I'll take that. I've missed her. And you."

"I've missed you, too." As she slid out of the booth, Theo came up, and she gave him a bump with her hip. "This one I get to see all the time. Still can't quite believe it."

Theo gave Rosie a quick squeeze. "Me either. Has he ordered his pancakes?"

"Waiting for you."

"Then I'll have coffee and the breakfast special." Eggs scrambled with cheese and chunks of ham. Nick and his brothers loved it. When they were kids, they'd ordered it whenever they could because it was filling and one of the lowest priced items on the menu.

Rosie didn't bother to write it down. She never did. "You got it. Anything for Harlow?"

"No, she's at the house this morning, sleeping in with Eden, but thanks for asking." Rosie went to the kitchen to put the orders in, and Nick stood to hug his brother. What he thought would be a quick squeeze lasted longer, and Nick got an unexpected lump in throat. It had been over three years since he'd seen Theo. Cole's band, Emporium, had been playing at Madison Square Garden, and Cole had gotten them tickets. Theo had driven up from Maryland, and they'd spent a few hours together before everyone needed to leave again. As they pulled apart, Theo's coffee arrived. "I was surprised to get your text. I've heard you don't come up often."

Nick shrugged. "My plans changed."

"I'm thinking that's an understatement because, first, I've rarely known you to change plans. And second, Eden told me you're working with Dani to run the silent auction, which means you're in town for more than a few days. Spill."

Somehow he hadn't considered the need to repeat this humiliating story when he thought of coming here. His mistake. Maybe he should print cards so he could hand them out and make things quicker. *Yes, I'll be here through the end of August. Because I was suspended from work. No, that wasn't part of my plan.*

Nick was still trying to figure out where to start when Theo said, "I don't have anywhere to be this morning. I can wait as long as it takes, so talk. What's going on?"

He looked at his brother. Theo hadn't changed much since the last time Nick had seen him beyond growing a narrow beard and mustache. It suited him. And he looked happy, which also suited him. Nick considered giving his brother the same version of the story he told Martin and Millie, then changed his mind. "Do you remember Henry?"

"Your friend from college, right?" Nick nodded. "Millie mentioned him. He came to the house a bunch if I remember correctly."

"That's because his parents sucked, too. He was a planner like me. We finished school in three years and moved to New York together after graduating." Nick could feel the emotions coming to the surface. The therapist would tell him to let them come, but the middle of a diner didn't seem like a good place for another breakdown. "He died in April."

Theo let out a sigh and ran a hand through his hair. "Damn, I'm sorry. What happened?"

"Undiagnosed heart condition. Nothing to be done. All of a sudden, he was gone." The hole he left in Nick's life remained as big as always.

"I've lost people suddenly." Theo had lost friends while deployed in the army. "I know how tough it can be."

"It was awful. I took the day off for his funeral, drank myself sick that night, and went into the office the next day as if nothing happened. Thought I could get through it by working. I was wrong. I ended up making mistakes, personally and professionally, and they suspended me. Gave me three months to regroup, then they'll decide if I'm worth having back."

"The only one of us who didn't get suspended in high school and you get suspended now?"

Nick couldn't quite appreciate the irony. "Maybe I should have gotten it out of my system earlier."

Theo leaned forward. "I don't see you often, so I could be reading you wrong, but it seems like there's more."

He both hated and loved that Theo could tell. "Besides losing Henry, I've made some poor investments and lost almost everything. The day the deal went south was the end for me. I lost it. I couldn't breathe. The edges of my vision darkened. It was awful. I nearly passed out. They took me to the hospital on a stretcher. I thought it might be the same thing as Henry. Turned out to be a panic attack."

"Holy hell. When was this?"

He had a feeling Theo was not going to like the answer. "Almost two months ago."

"And you didn't tell anyone?"

Nick put up a hand. "Can you keep it down? People in this town talk enough without us giving them a new topic."

"I don't care. Wouldn't be the first time they talked about our family," Theo said, but he did lower his voice. "It's one thing to lose a job. It's another to wind up in the hospital and not tell anyone."

He hadn't exactly lost his job, but it wasn't the time to correct Theo. "This is the first I'm telling anyone. Why do you look like you're going to hit me?"

"Because I'm strongly considering it."

"What was I supposed to say? I had a bad day at work and overreacted? Nothing to see, folks. Go back to what you were doing."

Theo's features softened. "Nick, it could have been serious."

"And then I would have called you." If he'd had a chance. He remembered a few scary minutes where he wondered if he would never get to speak with his brothers or the Sinclairs again. "It's not like you reach out often."

Theo tipped his head in acknowledgement. "True. And it's not like I ever shared about my panic attacks."

It took Nick a moment to absorb what Theo was saying. "You?"

"Made it back from Afghanistan in one piece, but when you've seen people killed and their lives destroyed by fire and war, it has a lasting effect. I still get nightmares. Shocked the hell out of Eden the first time I woke her with my screaming." Theo told Nick about how he nearly left because he believed he was too broken to have a good relationship. "Medication helps but doesn't cure. So, how long did you see a shrink? A few weeks? A month?"

"Little over a month." He'd stopped the week before coming here.

"That's about how long I lasted. Was sure I could do better on my own."

"Did you?"

"What do you think?" Theo gave him a look that allowed Nick to see some of the shadows that lingered. "After a few months on the road with Cole, I was a mess. He forced me to go. That time it helped. Finding work I liked did too, although it can be triggering. So, let me see if I've got this straight: Henry died, you messed up at work, had a panic attack, and got suspended. Am I missing anything?"

"The part about me losing nearly all of my net worth." Nick practically mumbled it. Of all the pieces, that was the most upsetting because that he could have – should have - controlled. Instead, he had almost no financial buffer. It was as though he'd picked a game card that said, 'Start over.' "Want to hear about the dangers of cryptocurrency?"

"Not really. I'll take your word for it. What have you been doing?"

Moping. "Beyond therapy? Not a lot. When I got tired of the nothing, I drove up."

Theo smiled. "Because it's so exciting here?"

"I needed to get out of the city. I needed to not see everyone else going about their lives. I needed—"

"Family," Theo finished. It would have been easier if Theo had hit him. He must have looked stunned, because Theo went on, "Yeah, that was a shock for me, too."

Before Nick could manage a response that didn't come out as an emotional croak, Rosie came over with their breakfasts and conversation stopped as they ate. After they made a sizable dent in their food, Theo said, "Time for a subject change. Eden told me you have a dog and are volunteering for the auction for the Festival. Both involve Dani Vaughn. How has that been?"

"Wonderful and terrible. Was that what it was like when you saw Eden again?"

"Pretty much. Are you having a hard time keeping your hands off of her?" Nick choked on his coffee. That was a little too close to home. "I'll take that as a yes. Something else we have in common. Be careful."

"What do you mean?" Theo raised one eyebrow. Okay, he knew what Theo meant. "I'm not you. My plans aren't here."

"Plans change. Mine did. Yours could." Everyone had been shocked when Theo decided to stay in Fable Notch. Looking at his brother, Nick could see how happy the decision made him.

Nick shook his head. "I'm done with change. I have to get back to New York. Set things right and get back what I lost. I... had to tell Martin I couldn't put money in the joint account we set up for them." God, he hated saying that.

"But Nick—," Theo started.

"I know, I know. We promised to help them. I'll get back to it as soon as I can." Before Theo could say something more, Nick put a hand up. He didn't want to hear it. He felt like enough of a failure. Letting down the Sinclairs was hard. As his heart rate increased, he changed the subject. "Let's see if we can reach Cole."

They weren't sure where their brother was on his current band tour. Nick worried for a second that they might be calling him too early if he was on the West Coast, but after one ring, Cole answered, a bright smile on his face. "Hey baby bro. Long time — hey, is that the Kinsman?" Nick turned the phone. "And Theo. Holy shit, you're at home."

Propping up the phone on the napkin dispenser so he and Theo could both see Cole and he could, mostly, see them, Nick asked the obvious question. "Where are you?

"No idea," Cole said then thought for a second. "Atlanta for one more night. We're working our way up the

East Coast. Will you be in New York when I get there in three weeks?"

Nick's stomach fell. Time to tell one more person. "No, I got jammed up at work, and I've been put on temporary leave. It's a longer story, as you can imagine, but the result is I'll be here for the next few weeks."

"Damn, Nick, I'm sorry. Do you need anything?"

That was his big brother. Always looking to take care of everyone around him. He'd been doing it Nick's whole life. Part of him actually wished there were something Cole could do, but no one could help. He made the mess. He'd fix it. "Nah, I'm good."

"Is he," Cole asked looking toward Theo.

Theo gave Nick an appraising look. "He seems tired, and a bit burned out, but nothing fresh mountain air, Rosie's cooking, and Mom's hovering can't fix. Of course, he does have to see Dani so that might be a challenge."

"Dani Vaughn is in town?"

"More than in town," Nick said. "She's moved here permanently and is in the process of taking over Doc Wheeler at the veterinary clinic."

"Good for her. That's what she always wanted, isn't it?" Cole asked."

"Since we were kids," Nick said. It was nice one of them got what they dreamed of. "We ran into each other when I found an injured dog and we're partnered for the Dog Days Festival in a few weeks."

"This I've got to hear." Nick gave him the full run down of how Presley and Dani came into his life. When he was done, Cole said, "Nothing like one unexpected turn of events becoming several more."

"Tell me about it," said Nick trying not to roll his eyes. He was used to business drama, not personal.

"You, um..." There was a pause before Cole continued. "Neither of you have seen Mia, have you?"

Interesting, Nick thought. Mia had held Cole's heart the way Eden held Theo's and Dani once held his. "Sorry, man. I only needed a vet, not an ER nurse," Nick said.

"Me either," Theo said. "Although I think Eden sees her from time to time when she gets together with friends."

Cole looked as though he were about to say something, but then he turned away from the phone when something distracted him. "Sorry, guys, someone's at my door and since no one is usually up this early, I'm going to check on that. I'm glad you called. I'll check in with you both soon."

Nick had no doubt he'd be hearing from Cole. Once Cole started worrying about his family, it was hard for him to stop. As they signed off, Nick wished he could reassure his brother, but he didn't have the words, and Cole wouldn't have believed him anyway.

As they returned to their breakfasts, Nick asked, "Think he's still hung up on Mia?"

"Wouldn't surprise me. Like you and me, he didn't want to end their relationship, but life had other plans." Nick didn't want other plans. He wanted the once he'd made. They were the ones that would get him what he wanted. "And speaking of plans, what are yours for the rest of the day?"

He almost didn't want to say it. "I'm working with Ed Franks while I'm here so I'm heading to the site where they're renovating a garage into a playroom." Nick told Theo about how this came about.

"You really are falling into old patterns," Theo said with a laugh.

Nick wasn't sure he found it funny. Yes, he was glad to have put things behind him with Rosie and grateful he and Dani had discussed their past, but the reminder that he was practically where he'd been when he left this town sat like a weight in his stomach. His father had called him worthless as a child. Nick couldn't—wouldn't—let that be true. Theo may be hap-

py here, but Nick's success and happiness was elsewhere.

Chapter Sixteen

♥

Over the next several days, it was clear to Dani that everyone in Fable Notch had not only heard that Nick was in town but that she was working with him on the auction. No matter where she went, whether or not she was working on the Festival, she'd gotten into conversations like, "Heard Nick's helping you with the auction. Is the old spark still there?" "So, do you think the two of you will get together?" "Theo and Eden found each other and look how that turned out. Maybe you two will, too." She wasn't comfortable with so much attention on her or that talking about Nick reminded her of how she was struggling with their partnership.

They were adding to the donation list and getting closer to the goal. That wasn't the problem. The problem was, ever since their last kiss, she couldn't stop wanting more. Whatever else had changed between them, her desire for him hadn't.

Every day when he'd text, she'd smile. If he sent pictures of him and Presley, her heart jumped, and if they got together, she practically had to sit on her hands to keep from grabbing him. He'd been back a little over a week, and it was getting harder to resist him. But she'd also had important reminders that he wasn't going to be staying.

Last night, he'd come to her house for the first time. Initially, she'd worried about what he'd say about her small two-bedroom home, so different from his sprawling place, but instead he'd noticed all the things she'd loved about it. The open floor plan, the big picture window in the front, the cheerful, cozy kitchen. When he'd banged on a wall and commented on how sturdy it was, she teased him that a week in construction was turning him into a builder.

He'd rubbed his hands together and given her a curt, "Yeah, like that's ever going to happen."

She tried to make a joke of it, but it fell flat, and Nick changed the subject. While they were together, the knowledge that he was leaving was almost constantly at war with her desire to be kissed, and last night she could hardly focus with him so near. At her place, they were seated closer, hands brushing against each other if they reached for the same thing. The zing that traveled through her body at his touch was nearly too much. She was grateful she hadn't given herself away by gasping. Nick's ego was strong enough without her adding to it.

Having him there for a few hours had made for a long night. In addition to having to fight her attraction, she'd been frustrated at the bottom line not growing fast enough. Nick had brushed her worries aside. She wished she had his confidence.

Worry and want had made it hard for her to sleep, and today she was tired and having trouble focusing. As she attempted to fill out forms for insurance companies and tried not to think about Nick and the auction, Dani's phone buzzed with a message from her Aunt Helen. *Piece is ready. Come see when you can.*

Helen was a fine arts painter and had promised an original piece for the auction. It was in her database at seven hundred dollars. Given the current totals, she hoped it would go for more. Needing the distraction, Dani texted she'd be over shortly. She confirmed with

Beth there were no patients for a few hours, grabbed her bag, and drove over to her aunt's workplace.

Aunt Helen ran the local Artist Cooperative. She taught classes, nurtured young talent, and repainted the brightly colored converted church regularly. Besides flying the pride flag, the building resembled one. Helen met Dani outside her studio. She was dressed for the day in baggy paint colored cargo pants and a purple tank top. A tall woman with her long gray hair pulled back in a braid, Helen had this wonderful air of strength and love that Dani found irresistible. She greeted Dani with a hug, then covered Dani's eyes before walking her into a room that smelled of oils and turpentine. "Ta-da," she said when she let Dani see.

Dani gasped and brought her hands to her mouth. There was Otis, running through the woods, heading for a patch of wild blueberries. "It's gorgeous, Auntie Helen."

Helen clapped her hands like a child. "I wanted to combine the two Festival aspects." Besides the "dog days" theme, each August there was a blueberry competition. Foods from breakfast to desserts were entered. "I'm glad you like it."

"Like it? I love it. More than love it. I want it." Dani stared at the painting, at the clear joy in Otis's body language, and did some math, then decided she didn't care. She was dipping into savings if necessary. No matter what anyone else bid, this picture was going on her wall. "It's wonderful. You do the best work."

"Thank you, my sweet. You do pretty great work yourself."

Dani gave a shrug. Her aunts gave compliments freely, but Dani had never been good at accepting them. Each time she heard one, she finished the sentence with 'if only you.' Years of her mother couching criticism in kindness made her leery. Today she heard, 'if only you had everything together for the auction.' "Unfortunately, we have less than two weeks and not enough donations yet." As she said the words, Dani found herself unexpectedly emotional. She turned to hide her reaction from Helen, but her aunt had noticed and shuffled Dani into her office.

Helen sat Dani down on an oversized sofa, took her hands in hers, and asked, "What's wrong?"

Dani wanted to say she was fine, but the words wouldn't come. Instead she said, "Everything. It's been months, and still there are people coming to the clinic who are disappointed to see me and not Doc Wheeler. And the auction is coming up fast, and all we've been getting recently are donations of smaller items. It's not enough." *I'm not enough.* The words were loud in her head, but she didn't say them. Too many times she'd thought she was fitting in, only to discover she was wrong. First with the girls from the country club who were friends with her so their mothers could get in good with Dani's mother. Then the people at her last job, where she learned, through a series of unintentional group texts, they made fun of her behind her back and thought she was too competitive. That had been the last straw.

"It's more than enough. Why wouldn't it be?" Auntie Helen looked genuinely confused.

This was Dani's fresh start, and she was determined to do it right, and she couldn't stand the thought of disappointing the people. "I want people to like me for me, not for who my aunts are."

Helen looked as though she were going to say something else, then changed her mind. "Is that all that's worrying you?"

Dani dropped her head and groaned. "Why did he have to come back now?"

Helen didn't ask who 'he' was. "When would have been a good time?"

"When I could have prepared in advance? When I was sure about things with Doc Wheeler. When I'd lost some of the weight I've gained since I've been here."

Helen put her hands on Dani's shoulders. "Stop. That's your mother talking." Dani looked at her aunt and couldn't stop the tears from welling. "Oh, sweetie, come here." Helen sat them down on the sofa and put her hand behind Dani's head so she could rest it on her aunt's chest. It was the position she always curled up in whenever she'd brought a problem to Helen. Where Rosie jumped in to solve a problem—usually with an offer of food—Helen was great at listening. She'd let Dani talk forever until Dani came to a conclusion on her own or could ask for something specific.

Dani let every worry tumble out—Nick, the auction, Nick, work, whether the other women she'd met through Laurel actually liked her or only tolerated her. Nick. As she talked, she noticed he was an even bigger part of her thoughts than she realized. After a while, she sat up and gave a sigh. "What am I going to do?"

"Trust yourself."

Aunt Helen's answer was quick and simple, but Dani didn't know what to do with it. "I'm not sure I can."

"I'm not sure you have a choice." Helen brushed a stray hair out of Dani's face before continuing. "It's clear that your work and the auction matter to you, but there's only so much you can do for either of them. You have to trust that you're doing enough, that you're giving your best, and people will see that."

"But—"

Helen put a finger to Dani's lips to silence her. "I know. The critical noise in your head has always been loud, and those people in Texas didn't help. But you're not there. You're here. Where you belong. Believe that. Trust that."

"What about Nick?" Bet her aunt didn't have an easy answer for that.

"Trust will help you there, too. You left him years ago even though you loved him because you trusted he couldn't be what you needed or wanted." It was true. She refused to have a marriage like her parents did. Even her mother's second marriage had placed a priority on money. "I know your emotions are bubbling over when it comes to him, and it's hard to control. But I believe you know what's right for you."

Dani wasn't ready to agree, but before she could say anything, a call from Beth interrupted them. Dani gave her aunt a final hug and headed back to the clinic. As she drove, she thought about Aunt Helen's words. She agreed she was where she wanted to be. Everything and everyone in her life mattered more than anything had in a long time. That was scary. But she was also grateful to be here and to have opportunities to be a part of this town, both in and out of work. Could Aunt Helen be right? What would it take for her to trust herself?

Chapter Seventeen

The next several days fell into a predictable pattern Nick enjoyed more than he could have imagined when he arrived. He and Presley would wake around eight—two hours later than his New York mornings—and he'd put coffee in a travel mug to drink as they took a walk. When they came back, Presley had her breakfast and either he'd eat, or they'd drive to the diner to get something to go before heading to the job site. He'd slip on the coveralls and start on the playroom renovations. At lunch, he'd sit with the guys or he'd find a corner to eat and spend time with Presley. More and more often he'd bring his notebook and instead of brainstorming ideas to present to the team at Jeffries and Waters, he'd draw house plans. He'd forgotten how much he enjoyed it.

It was the Festival that was driving him crazy. Every time Nick spent time with Dani, it became harder to concentrate. Time had not changed how attracted he was to her. He hadn't kissed her since the day they'd fallen over with the dogs, but he wanted to. He wanted to hear her sigh, feel her nipples harden under his touch, lose himself in her body. They'd been working together less than a week with nearly two weeks to go.

He wasn't going to make it.

Working at her house had been an exercise in madness. From where they sat at a table in the kitchen, he could see into her bedroom, which had his thoughts racing and his pants getting uncomfortable. He didn't know how much longer he could trust himself to be alone with her.

Tonight, as he sat at home idly sketching while she had dinner with her aunts, he found himself thinking about what would happen if he and Dani ended up in bed. Would that be so terrible? He was pretty certain she was having the same feelings. They both knew his living here was temporary. They'd have no expectations of it becoming more.

And after?

He'd go back to New York, and she'd go on with her life here. She'd become more and more successful at the clinic, have fun with Laurel and other friends at future Festivals, and meet someone new. Someone who would hold her, touch her, make her laugh. The thought punched him in the gut. He shouldn't—couldn't—let it bother him, but it did.

He looked down at the sketchbook and groaned. He'd been drawing the exterior of her house. There was a full page as it was currently, then another with an expansion and possibilities for a second floor. Even when she wasn't there, she was. He shut the book with a slam, went to his office to get his laptop, and brought it to the couch so he could review the ideas he'd had for possible financial projects. This was where his focus needed to be. Not on how Dani made every pair of leggings—no matter the crazy animal print on them—look sexy. He needed to concentrate on what he could do to get back to his plans.

The next morning, Nick woke to see he had a text from Terri Allen, a work colleague. It had arrived at 7:30. Nick imagined the other man had been in the office for an hour before sending it. *Give me a buzz when you have a chance.*

Nick was suspicious. Despite being in the same department, he and Terry worked better separately. They'd been on the same project once early in their careers, and their competitive personalities didn't mix well. Wondering why Terry had reached out, he replied, *What's up?*

Three dots immediately appeared. *Working on a proposal. If you have time, I'd like to run something by you.*

The 'if you have time' was a dig at his employment status, but if Terry was reaching out, it had to be a last resort. Nick considered waiting to respond, but he was too curious. *I need coffee first. Call or Zoom?*

Zoom. I'll send you a link. See you in a few.

As Nick dressed, he thought about what could have made Terry call. Had he heard something and wanted to gloat? No, he mentioned a proposal. There was something specific. He suspected something had gone wrong, and working with Nick meant no one in the office would find out. He made coffee and hoped Presley could wait for her walk. When she followed him into the office, he took it as a good sign.

By the time he clicked into the Zoom conference room, Terry was waiting. Nick couldn't stop the pang of longing when he saw Terry's office in the background. The bookcase on the right with manuals, awards, and plaques. The window to his left looking out onto the city. It felt like a lifetime and a thousand miles away.

As if to underscore the difference in their locations, Terry leaned forward and squinted. "Are those mountains out there?" Nick had a window behind him as well, but with a very different view.

"There's grass, too." And if Terry could see the dog sitting across from Nick, he'd be even more amazed. "So, what's the problem?"

Leaning back in his chair, Terry said, "Same old Nick. Always wanting to get to the heart of the issue."

Same old Terry. "As if you called to shoot the shit. What's going on?"

Nick watched as Terry debated between making light of the situation and owning up to the problem. The problem won out. "I'm working on the deal for McCutcheon Enterprises, and we're stuck." Terry explained the goal, what he'd been thinking, and why it wasn't working. Nick could hear the other man's growing concern. "I know I'm missing something, but I can't see what it is."

Nick understood the challenge. Not specifically what Terry needed, but how you could work your way into a box and not see a way out. When he'd been in similar situations, he'd talk to Henry, who often asked the right questions. Nick wondered if one reason his last deal had blown up was because in addition to the grief, he'd lost a key part of his own process by not having Henry to bounce things off of. Where would he find it once he returned?

A beautiful face with auburn hair in a high ponytail floated into his thoughts. Lips unendingly kissable and a laugh he could listen to forever. No. Go away, Dani. This was not a place for her.

"Think you can help?" Terry's question brought Nick back to the present.

Nick couldn't deny that even with the momentary distraction, Terry's request was tempting. "Send me the proposal files. Nothing confidential, just the overview and whatever notes you can. I'll review it, see what jumps out at me."

"Great. How long do you need? Are you available tomorrow?"

He'd forgotten the speed things worked in New York. "Not that soon. Maybe by the end of the week."

Terry wasn't happy about Nick's lack of urgency. "But it's Tuesday."

Nick understood the other man's concerns. In their business, every day—every hour—could mean lost money, someone else getting ahead. "If I come up with something before then, or if it turns out you don't need me anymore, we'll talk sooner."

Nick saw Terry straighten at the crack about needing. "This could help you, too. I know the Nash project got you got suspended." Ouch. Nothing like a dose of reality first thing in the morning. *Should have known better. Should have done better.* "Work with me on this, and if it goes well, I'll let Jeffries know you contributed. You'll be back in your office in no time. You've been missed."

Nick doubted that. It was a big firm. People were focused on their work and didn't notice the comings and goings around them. He'd been in his share of meetings where he learned someone left weeks after it had happened. He hadn't noticed. Very different from life here where Rosie remarked if he skipped a day coming into the diner. While he didn't trust Terry or his motivations, it was the first break Nick had, and he wasn't going to toss the opportunity aside. "As soon as I have the details from you, I'll go through it. Something's bound to stand out."

"Sounds good. Hope to hear from you soon."

Terry ended the meeting, and Nick turned in his chair to look out the window at the mountains Terry found so unusual. He wondered what the other man would think of the star-filled night sky. Presley took the silence as a cue to come over and put her head on his leg. As he rubbed her between the ears, he thought about Terry's request. It would put him back in the game, at least tangentially, and Terry was right. It could be what he'd been looking for since he'd been suspended—a way back. The fact that Terry had come to him made it a bit sweeter.

A month ago, he would have turned all his focus on the deal, frantically doing research and making calls. Instead, he made a few notes, then went to his bedroom, took off the polo he'd put on for the meeting, and changed into a t-shirt. He gave Presley her pill as his to-go mug filled with coffee, took her for a walk, then headed to work with Ed.

There would be time to think about New York later.

Chapter Eighteen

♥

D ani's voice was frantic when she called him at lunch time the next day. "Nick, there isn't enough."

"What are you talking about?" Yes, she was talking about the auction, but he wasn't sure what she meant specifically. The last time he'd checked, the numbers looked good. Not goal, but close.

"We're under by almost $3,000. Nancy had the old goal listed for the total, and we were comparing against that. That number changed a few months ago when the library had to increase their cost estimations."

It couldn't be that bad. "People will bid more than items are worth. Won't that make it up?"

"Not by enough. And as many people bid under as over. They like a bargain. Nick, this is awful."

She sounded near tears, and the urge to hold her—even though she was on the phone—was strong. Since he couldn't do that, he did the next best thing. "You can handle this. We can. I know we've only got a little over two weeks, but we'll figure it out." He listened as she took a shuddering breath, then went on. "What's your schedule today?"

"I've got patients into late afternoon, and I need to make a dent in my paperwork. I've fallen behind."

"That's why you've got a partner, remember?"

"What are we going to do?"

He was glad she said we. "We are going to have dinner together then spend the night brainstorming ideas. Can you be at my place by 6:30 or would you rather me come to you?"

"Are you going to cook?"

He grinned at the concern in her voice. "No, I'll grab takeout. You should be safe. And bring Otis. Presley loves to see him."

He heard her sigh and knew she was probably playing with the cuticle on her thumb. "We'll be there." He heard a phone ring behind her. "I have to go. And Nick?"

"Yes?"

"Thanks." He could hear her gratitude. She sounded calmer than when she'd started the call, and he was glad he could do that for her.

As he helped the crew pack things up for the day, he did a mental inventory of what he had in the house for dinner. Negating each idea he came up with, he made two calls. One to Cobblestones to place two orders of their steak dinner complete with salads and double stuffed baked potatoes, and one to Demarco's to see if they had some of their amazing cannoli available. He was in luck. He hoped they were still Dani's favorite.

When Dani and Otis arrived, the dogs ran off to play, and the two of them went into the kitchen. As he took the food out of the oven where he'd been keeping it warm, he turned and stared at the peach-colored blouse she was wearing. It looked soft and inviting and had him thinking about the lyrics to the song *Centerfold*. Too magical to touch. She hadn't worn it to tease him. That wasn't her style, but his fingers itched to undo every button and enjoy everything beneath it.

It was going to be a long night.

As he plated the food, she asked, "Is that from Cob-blestones?"

"It is, and you'll be happy to know that I got also got a $100 gift certificate donation from them while I waited."

"That's another step forward. I'll add it to the spread-sheet after we eat."

He put dinner on the table, then went back for a bottle of wine he'd bought. Her laptop was open, and he thought they'd end up working and eating, but the meal required both hands, so she put things away and they enjoyed the food, talking about their day. Her patients. His building work.

Everything was fine until dessert. She squealed when he brought out the treat from DeMarco's and dove for the plate. As she bit into the cannoli, the shell broke and pieces fell on her shirt. "There's no way to eat these neatly, is there?" she said as she licked her fingers of the sweet ricotta filling and powdered sugar. It was all Nick could do not to leap across the table and ravish her. As soon as she was done, he suggested they move to the living room to work, hoping a change of location would cool him down.

They sat on opposite sides of the couch, computers on the coffee table, folders and notebooks between them. At one point, he thought about telling her about Terry's call, but didn't want to bring it up, didn't want to change the tone of their time together. She'd never respond well to hearing about NY.

As they worked, he couldn't get over how comfortable he was. "If someone told me a month ago that I'd be sitting here after working for Ed Franks for the day, vol-unteering on a Festival project with two sleeping dogs and you, and wondering if I could rip your clothes off, I would have said they were crazy."

She looked at him, smiled, and took a lazy sip of her wine. "Isn't it great having a dog around? I'd wanted one for so long, but I never imagined how much I'd love it. Ever since Otis...."

Nick slid across the leather couch, letting everything fall to the floor, and pulled her into his arms. She had her chance to say he was being ridiculous about pulling off her clothes. She chose to tease him and talk about dogs, and now she would pay. She responded immediately to his kiss, opening her mouth, letting him taste the wine along with the sweetness of her.

When she shifted underneath him, he was sure she was about to push him away and tell him this was a bad idea. Instead, she put her wineglass on the coffee table then both arms around him.

"Yes," screamed the voice in his head as her hands held his waist. This is what he wanted, what he needed. Dani, as hungry for him as he was for her. Finally, he could undo the top two buttons of her shirt and enjoy the warmth of her skin. Hearing her sigh, he kissed his way down her jaw and to her neck, his hand sliding beneath the shirt, teasing a nipple through her bra, feeling it harden with his attention.

He was wondering how many more buttons she'd let him undo when the sound of breaking glass followed by running feet had them jumping apart. Nick looked to the kitchen. "Do I want to know what that was?"

"My guess is there was food left on a plate and one or both of the dogs decided to help themselves. We should clean up before they do any more damage or get glass in a paw."

He hated watching her close her shirt, but she took his hand as they went to the kitchen to see what the damage was. "Cock blocked by my own dog. That's rough."

"They can be worse than having parents in the next room."

Sure enough, they knocked over a water glass over and there was glass and stray food on the floor. She went to pick up the pieces as he got a broom and trash bin.

It didn't take long to clean things up. When he came back from putting the broom away, she had the dishwasher open and was about to put the remaining plate in the rack. Before he could think, Nick grabbed her wrist. "What are you doing?"

She gave him a strange look as she took her arm out of his grip. "Loading the dishwasher."

"That's not necessary. Put everything in the sink. I'll take care of them later."

"It's no big deal. You probably won't have enough to do a load tonight, but it will be ready to go for another time."

She reached for another dish, but he put his hand on hers and stopped her. "I don't run the dishwasher. Ever."

It came out harsher than he intended. She waited for him to explain, then asked, "What's going on?"

Shit. Why couldn't he have let her put the dishes in and kept quiet? He could have taken them out later. "It's nothing."

"Try that on someone else."

They stared at each other. He wanted to change the subject. It wasn't as though he'd kept this from her. It never came up, but this was Dani, and if there was anyone he could trust with this story, it was her. "The night my dad left, the fight that set everything off, was because I broke the dishwasher." When she remained silent, he continued. "Cole, Theo, and I were cleaning the house to surprise my mom. My dad was on the road and not expected back until the next day. The sink was filled with dishes. To get things done faster, I overloaded the dishwasher, cramming things everywhere I could and using extra soap."

"Uh oh," she said softly.

"Yeah, it didn't work. The dishwasher flooded the kitchen. When my mom arrived, I was sure she was going to freak, but instead she laughed and helped us clean. She turned it into a game. We were having a great time and still mopping up when my dad came home. He took one look at the mess and lost it. Screamed at us, wanted to know what the hell happened. I owned up to it, but that made things worse."

You stupid, irresponsible little shit. How could you not know how to load a damn dishwasher? Nick could hear his father's voice as clearly as if the man were standing next to him. "He raged about what it would cost to fix and said he wasn't made of money. Told me I was a waste of space. He came at me with his hand up, ready to smack me. He'd done it once or twice before, to all of us, but he was furious. I was scared. I braced myself for the impact. It never came. Cole stepped in front of me. Dad cracked him hard across the face. The sound... I'll never forget it. I swear it echoed. From the way Cole's head flew back and the blood that came out of his nose, I knew it was broken. My mom screamed and told us to go upstairs. Once we were out of the room, they tore into each other."

Nick could remember every detail of that night. His father saying "I told you three kids was a bad idea. A family of five is too damn much money. Well, I am not paying for a new dishwasher. Put that little worthless shit to work." Holding an old shirt up to his bleeding nose, Cole tried to give Nick a hug, but he drew away, pulling his knees to his chest.

"Don't listen to him, Nick," Cole said. "He's just mad."

But Nick heard the truth in his father's words. "He didn't want me."

Theo came and sat on his other side and said, "I don't think he wanted any of us, dude."

"Yeah," Cole added. "Have you noticed it's not nine months from their anniversary to my birthday? They got married 'cause Mom was pregnant. All of us are probably a mistake to him."

Nick understood what Cole was saying, but all he heard was that he wasn't worth it.

Dani took his hand in hers and brought him back to the present. "I can't imagine how awful that must have been."

"That night, I learned what my dad really thought of me. In my memory, the yelling goes on forever, but it was probably only a few minutes. We heard the front door slam, then another when Mom shut the door to their bedroom. We didn't come down until we smelled something burning. I thought maybe the dishwasher had caught on fire or the water caused a short circuit, but my mom had left dinner cooking on the stove. We didn't know what to do since we couldn't put anything in the sink—it was filled with wet dishes. Cole tossed everything, pot included, into the trash outside. I didn't sleep that night, waiting for Dad to come to my room and yell at me some more, maybe even beat me after all. But he didn't come home. And I was relieved. I was so damn relieved. I didn't want to face him knowing what he thought of me. And then he didn't come back, not that night or the next. I never saw him again." Dani said nothing, and Nick was grateful for the silence. "I only had a dishwasher installed because it's expected, and I thought there would be renters here, but I don't use it."

She brought his hand to her heart and cupped his cheek. "I'm so sorry. I didn't know."

"Guess we've never been around a dishwasher together." He tried to make light of it. It felt weird to be talking about this. The only person he'd ever told was Henry, and they'd both been drunk. "Not like it's something that comes up in conversation. 'Hey, wanna talk about my unresolved childhood trauma?' It's a lousy icebreaker."

"Nick, stop. You don't have to joke with me or brush it aside. I know you had it rough before and after your dad left, even if I hadn't heard the details. You were a kid. You did nothing wrong."

No, it was worse. He *was* something wrong. That's what he'd learned that night and could never forget.

As he struggled to release the memory and the feelings it brought up, Dani lifted herself up on her toes and gave him a kiss. He expected it to be quick, something to offer comfort, but she put her arms around him. The warmth of her body eased a coldness he didn't know had crept in as he unburied the memories of that horrible night. When her fingers threaded through his hair, sending tingles down his spine—and lower—he released the emotions churning inside.

He reached for the band holding her hair back and yanked it out, letting her hair fall around her face, giving him the chance to run his fingers through it. With a growl, he put his hands on the small of her back and pressed her against him, letting her feel his arousal and need. Part of him expected her to stop him, tell him it was too much. Instead she matched him, kiss for kiss, opening her mouth to him, her tongue dancing, igniting other memories.

When her hands moved to his neck and down his back, he reopened the first buttons of her shirt, this time to the bottom and pushed it off her shoulders. His touch moved to trace the edge of her bra, and it hit him.

This was Dani. The only woman he'd ever loved, but also the only woman he'd ever hurt. He didn't want to be a hero, not in this moment, but he wouldn't put her through that again. Not unless she was sure. He took her hands off of him and pulled back. She moved forward. Not fair. She was not making it easy for him to be reasonable. "Dani, I don't know if we should do this. I've wanted to since the first day I saw you again, and definitely since you arrived tonight, but if we go any further, I will not be able to stop."

"I'm hoping you won't stop for quite a while."

That didn't help. "You know what I mean. Please, I don't want to do something you might regret."

She looked at him. "Are you going back to New York when your suspension is over?"

He wasn't going to lie to her. "Yes."

"And I'm staying here. We're clear. We can enjoy the time we have, and neither one of us is going to get hurt."

Nick let her words sink in and watched a slow grin play at her lips. Nothing coy or fake. So different from the women he'd met who preferred to learn his bank balance before his name.

Over the last few months, he'd wanted so many things he couldn't have. He wanted his job back. He wanted Henry back. He wanted to not need the Xanax or even know what a panic attack felt like. Tonight, all he wanted was Dani.

He captured her lips in a soul searing kiss then lifted her by the hips. She wrapped her legs around him, and he walked them to the bedroom.

Chapter Nineteen

♥

As he picked her up, Dani thought to complain she was too heavy for him to carry, but before she could break the kiss and say anything, they were in the bedroom. He put her in the middle of the bed and turned on the nightstand lamp. She almost asked for it to be dark, but this was Nick, and there was no one she'd ever been able to be herself with more than him. If he could tell her the story of what happened the night his father left, she could have sex with the light on. She could be herself with Nick.

Which reminded her of a minor aspect of reality she thought to mention. As he got onto the bed with her, she said, "There's something I should tell you."

He looked at her, concerned. "Second thoughts?"

"No, not at all, but I haven't... It's been a few days... And I don't wear shorts so... I mean it's nothing really..." She sounded like an idiot. Maybe she shouldn't tell him.

"What is it?" He looked completely confused.

She picked at her thumb nail. "I didn't know this would happen tonight."

"Neither did I," he said and moved to kiss her jaw, then neck. Okay, she needed to get this out fast before she lost the ability to form words.

"I know, but that means..." Helen had told her to trust. This was as good a time as any. She blurted it out quickly. "I haven't shaved my legs in a few days."

He looked at her and for a second she panicked. He was used to New York women, polished and perfect, not an ounce of fat and nothing out of place. The rejection was going to sting, but it was better to get it out of the way than have him make a remark when she was naked. She wasn't expecting him to burst out laughing. "Damn, Dani. I adore you. And I couldn't care less. As long as your legs are attached to you and wrapped around me, that's what matters. Now, let me get rid of that maddeningly soft shirt the way I've wanted to all evening."

Kissing and undressing and touching while also pulling down the blankets required a fair amount of acrobatics, but even with the fumbling, it didn't take long before she and Nick were naked. They lay side-by-side, their bodies pressed together, their hands roaming everywhere. As she was about to see if he was as aroused as she was, he snapped his fingers, stopping her.

"One more quick pause, because I will not want to stop later." He jumped out of the bed and walked to the bathroom, giving her a nice view of his ass. Damn, he was gorgeous. When she'd first seen him, she was surprised she hadn't remembered how blue his eyes were. But there was more she'd forgotten. How his muscled chest felt under her hands, the strength in his legs.

Before she could ask what he was doing, he came back, showing her the strip of condoms he'd taken from the other room. "I thought you didn't expect this would happen tonight."

"I didn't, which is why they weren't in the nightstand drawer, but I always have some in my shaving kit."

"Something to be grateful for." She liked that he didn't assume protection was her responsibility.

He got back into bed and asked, "Where was I?"

She took his hand and put it on her breast. "Right about here."

"Are you sure? I thought I might have been here." He put his hand at the top of her ass then slowly caressed his way over her curves.

"That's a good place, too."

"They're all good places," he said.

She had to agree. There wasn't any place she wasn't hungry to touch or taste. She moved her mouth from his lips and worked her way to his jaw, then to the spot beneath his ear that drove him wild. It was interesting to be with someone and have it both new and familiar at the same time.

She ran her hands between them, letting the hair on his chest tickle her skin. His nipples were hard, and she teased him with the tip of her finger, enjoying when he reacted with a sharp intake of breath. And as she rediscovered him, letting memory and desire guide her actions, he did the same, finding all the places that shot tingles through her body, that made her wetter and left her aching.

She'd not only forgotten things about how he looked, she'd forgotten how he made her feel. The tingling sensation of his hands on her hips, his mouth on her breasts. The way he explored and found every sensitive spot. And if she moaned, he'd spend more time there.

He shifted his position, claimed her mouth with his, then rolled her onto her back. She loved the weight of him on her, the feel of him covering her. They kissed for a while longer before he moved from her mouth to her neck. As he worked his way past her collarbone, she had a moment to be sorry she could no longer kiss him, but the regret disappeared as soon as his mouth locked on her nipple and sucked it deeply.

The rush of pleasure focused first where he touched her, then pooled between her legs. His hand covered her other breast, fingers playing with the sensitive peak until he switched his attention and moved his mouth. The air on her damp nipple added to the sensations. As he continued to excite her, he rolled to her side so his hand could travel down to her stomach. He teased the juncture where her thighs met her hips, and she ached for more.

"God, Dani, I love the feel of you. You are so damn sexy." It wasn't a way she ever saw herself, but as he touched her, kissed her, she believed him.

Part of her could hardly believe this was happening. For years, Nick had been part of fevered dreams where she'd wake sweaty and breathing fast or memories used to coax solo orgasms that left her missing him all over again. Nothing was close to how it felt to be with him tonight.

He kissed his way down her body, his hands teasing the curls between her legs. "Spread your legs, Dani. Open for me," he said, his voice low and husky.

She did as he asked, feeling the cool air on her wetness for a moment before his mouth was there, his tongue licking at her. She jumped at the sensation. There were no thoughts anymore. She was at the mercy of whatever her body wanted, and it wanted Nick completely.

His tongue lapped slowly at her entrance, and her body responded with a surge of heat. "Yes, that's it. Let me taste you." His voice was low, hungry.

It wasn't long before he had her moaning again. Whether he used the flat of his tongue or pointed it for a more precise sensation, all of it was driving her insane. Just as she thought it might all be too much, Nick inserted first one, then two fingers into her. As his fingers probed and his tongue raced along her sensitized flesh, she knew there was no holding back her climax.

"Nick, I'm going to... I don't think I can't stop."

"Then don't." His words vibrated against her, and as soon as his mouth touched her again, she came apart, screaming his name. The wave of pleasure engulfed her, her breath caught. Her hands gripped at the sheets as her back arched off the bed. Nick moved with her and didn't stop until she was panting. Even then, he continued to stroke her, sliding his fingers out slowly, bringing her down from her peak.

He kissed his way up her body, licking and nibbling as he went. By the time he reached her lips, she was mad for him.

"I love it when you come like that," he said.

"That makes two of us." She wasn't sure how she put so many words together.

She reached between their bodies and wrapped her hand around his cock, happy to find him hard. She stroked the length of him, reveling in the groan he couldn't hold back. She felt powerful and sexy. She continued to tease him, running her fingers around the sensitive tip of his erection, loving the heat and silky skin. Wanting more, she kissed his chest and worked her way down to his stomach, making her intent clear. Before she could get lower, he stopped her.

"I am not going to tell you I don't want what you're about to do, because heaven knows I do, but Dani, I don't think I can last if you start. I can't wait. I want to be inside of you."

His words thrilled her. Knowing that he wanted her so much was exhilarating. To give them both what they needed, she reached over him to the nightstand and ripped off a condom package. After taking it out, she stroked him several more times before rolling it down as slowly as she could.

"You are driving me mad."

She gave a low chuckle and before she could say anything, he grabbed her hand, finished sheathing himself in the latex and then in one smooth move rolled her onto her back and positioned himself between her legs. A breath later, he was inside in her.

As soon as they were joined, he froze and stared into her eyes. For a moment she worried something might be wrong. Then he brought his hand to the side of her face and kissed her softly. She understood. There was something magical, something inexpressible about being together.

The kiss shifted from sweet to passionate, his tongue diving into her mouth as his body drew back, then thrust into her again.

"God, Nick. Yes," was all she could manage as she stretched to accommodate him. She was swollen from her orgasm and the sensation was exquisite.

It didn't take long to find a rhythm that excited them both. Once they did, he reached his hand between them to find her clitoris and increased her pleasure. She gasped at the assault on her senses, wanting more and not sure if she could take it. She raked her nails down his back. His hissed "Yes" told her it was something he still liked.

As her desire built and their kisses became heated, Nick growled, "Give me what I want. Wrap those legs around me."

She did as he said, making it easier for them to move together. When he pulled out, she used her legs to push him into her again and hold him as she rocked her hips and ground against the base of his shaft.

"You drive me crazy. I need..."

"I know."

It wasn't long before their speed increased and Nick said, "Dani, I'm there. Please. You. I'm going to..."

She loved his incoherence. He surged one more time as her hips lifted to take all of him. As he came, he kissed her, and she encircled him with her arms, wanting to be as close as possible. She loved the heat of his skin against her, the light sheen of sweat covering him. She took a slow, deep breath, savoring the scent of the two of them together.

As she reveled in the gentle shivers of her body, he asked, "Am I crushing you?"

She shook her head, not trusting her voice, and answered him with a kiss. Once again, he rolled to the side, taking her with him, keeping her close. He grabbed a tissue from a box by the bed and took off the condom. He kissed her softly, running his hands through her hair. Her thoughts were reeling from what they'd done, from what she was feeling. How was she going to get out of bed and say goodnight?

Maybe this wasn't such a good idea.

Before she could think of something that wouldn't embarrass them both, the dogs came bounding into the room. Otis jumped on the bed and Presley howled for help to get up. Nick gave her a boost, then covered sensitive areas as she tried to snuggle between them. "Thank goodness they didn't come in a few minutes ago."

She giggled at the thought. "That would have been awkward."

As the dogs tried to find their territory, Nick asked, "Now, what do we do?"

"What do you mean?"

"I don't know if there's room for all four of us," Nick said, and she realized he wanted her to spend the night. She almost hated how much that pleased her.

"We're going to have to think of something. Otis sleeps with me."

"And Presley with me. It's going to be crowded." He looked at her and gave her a wink. "Guess we'll have to be close."

It took a little while, but eventually they got the dogs settled and, yes, they needed to be close. It was wonderful. Nick asked what time she needed to get up and set the alarm on his phone. This was the Nick she remembered—kind, considerate. Aware of her. That was as sexy as anything he did with his hands and mouth.

Well, almost.

He turned off the light, and she curled against him. She couldn't remember the last time she'd been so relaxed after sex, but she was fairly certain Nick had been in bed with her when she had. As she lay next to him, trying to fall asleep, her thoughts raced.

How had she forgotten how being with him made her feel? Not only in bed, but when they spent time together. And how had she managed to not find anyone to feel this with in the years they'd been apart? Had leaving him hurt her so much that she kept herself from caring? It certainly was possible. Maybe that would be the upside to being involved with him for this contained amount of time. She'd remember how to let down her walls. She'd rediscover how to let someone get close, and when he left, she wouldn't shut down. She'd stay open to the possibility of love and a relationship with someone who wanted to be with her, who could make her a priority.

She told him she wouldn't get hurt because they were going into this with their eyes open. She had no expectation that he'd stay. She understood the importance of his plans, even better tonight after what he shared. But she'd lied.

As she lay there listening to his slowing heartbeat beneath her ear, she knew without a doubt she was going to get hurt.

Chapter Twenty

♥

Nick couldn't remember the last time he'd reached for a woman in the middle of the night to make love to her again. Then again, he couldn't remember the last time he'd wanted someone to spend the night. Normally he left or made sure she did, but he wanted Dani with him, and when he woke and saw her sleeping, he couldn't resist. He'd kissed her shoulder, then worked his way to her neck. By the time he got to her jaw, she was almost awake and before he'd gotten to her lips, she'd pulled him on top of her.

Everything about her excited him. The fullness of her breasts, the curve from her waist to her hips, the slightly rounded mound of her stomach. It was all Dani, and he couldn't get enough. The sound of her moans, his name on her lips, the taste of her passion. How quickly she was wet and ready for him. How it felt to sink deep inside of her. How in a few hours he'd want her again.

The second time had been as wonderful—if a little less intense—as the first. Before he fell asleep, he made a mental note to buy more condoms—and to drive out of town to do it. No need to fuel rumors.

In the morning he woke before her and considered another round of sex, but knowing what Dani was like in the morning, he thought better of it. Deciding to bring her coffee in bed, he slipped on a pair of sweatpants and went to the kitchen to start a pot. It wouldn't be as fast as the Keurig, but this way there would be plenty for them both. The dogs, having moved to the floor when he and Dani had sex again, followed him. He took out an extra bowl so he could feed them both.

As he watched the carafe fill, he thought about the night before—from working on the auction, to kissing on the couch, to his spilling the details about the day his father left. It was a memory he avoided as much as dishwashers. He'd had a few evenings with women ruined when they used theirs or tried to use his. Once the memory was back, the evening was over. But he'd never explained why. Instead of ruining things with Dani, it brought her closer.

She wasn't feeling pity, was she?

Last night he'd been too caught up in the pleasure and need to think about why Dani chose that moment to kiss him and let him take her to bed. Did she feel sorry for him? He didn't want to believe it, but without the haze of desire to color his thoughts, he wasn't sure. Doubt was a shitty thing, and he'd been experiencing it more than he wanted.

He was still wondering if he should ask when Dani came into the room wearing nothing but a sleepy look and the button-down shirt, with very few buttons done. He was instantly hard. All concern flew out of his head, replaced by new questions. Did she have anything on under it? How long before he could find out? "Good morning," he said.

"Coffee," she managed, and he smiled. In the some-things-never-change file was Dani's inability to be human before caffeine.

"Your timing is perfect." He filled a mug, leaving room for her to add what she needed. He motioned to the island where he'd put things on the tray he intended to bring to the bedroom. "I don't have cream, but there's milk and sugar."

"That will do." She turned her coffee a light brown then took a sip, letting out a happy sigh and closing her eyes.

"Bet I can make you sigh more than that."

"I don't know. Morning coffee is so good," she said. Eyes still closed, she took another swallow, then held the cup in both hands close to her chest, as if she were cuddling it. "And if you try to come between me and my socially acceptable addiction, I may hurt you."

"I will wait." He tried to sound contrite, but he must not have managed it because she opened one eye to look at him. He held up a hand in surrender. "I'll be good. Honest."

"For how long?"

"Half a mug?" He liked teasing her.

She shook her head back and forth. "I can't guarantee it will be safe at that point."

He laughed, unlocked the iPad that was on the island, and opened up the *New York Times* app to read the headlines. She stepped close and leaned against him as he read. It was the coziest morning he could remember. When she was willing to hold the mug with one hand and moved an arm about his waist, he figured it was safe to give her a good morning kiss. It tasted of coffee and Dani.

A noise at the door followed by barking and scampering startled them both, and she asked, "Do you need to check that?"

"No, I'd rather keep kissing you. It's probably a package from Amazon. A few things I needed. More toys for Presley." He nibbled at her ear and whispered, "Maybe I should get some toys for you. Something that vibrates and makes you scream."

"I didn't scream enough last night?"

"Who's to say what's enough? There's nothing wrong with more." Especially when it came to her pleasure. Watching her shuddering orgasm last night had been one of the sexiest things he'd ever seen. "And I love it when you yell my name."

"I liked when you called out mine, too." He kissed her again, but before he could get lost in the pleasure, an idea hit him. "Oh my God, Dani. Packages! Holy shit, I can't believe I didn't think of that yesterday. That's it."

"Clearly, I haven't had enough coffee. What are you talking about? What is it?" She looked at him as though he'd grown a second head. Or told her she couldn't have more coffee.

"We need packages to auction off, not for a high price, but for a higher amount than the combined value, because there's no way to get it unless someone wants to do all the work for themselves."

"Obviously, your brain is working more than mine is. Run that by me again, this time slower. Pretend I'm not awake yet, because I'm not."

He opened a drawer, took out a notepad, and starting writing. "We need to create something that's greater than the sum of its parts. If we get a hotel to donate a weekend, then it's worth the cost of the room, and not something unique. Anyone can book a stay. And people only bid more than the value if they want to make a donation." He looked to see if she was listening. When she nodded, he continued. "But, if we get the weekend at the hotel, then call the spa and have them include an in-room massage for two, then find out who can donate chocolates, secure an evening on the dinner train up the mountains, and either ski lift tickets or something else for them to do during the day—then we've got a complete romantic getaway that's worth more than the cost of the items because it's all done for them."

As he continued talking, Dani stood straighter as what he was saying sunk in. She joined in the process and said, "And since there are so many people who come here to get away with their kids, we could also create one for families. A stay at in a cabin at the Stewart's hotel along with tickets to the mini golf course, and ice cream at The Bright Spot..."

"And a bottle of wine for mom and dad after the kids are in bed."

"Nick, this is inspired. This has real possibilities for helping us get over the top of our goal." She put her coffee down threw her arms around him. "My head is spinning. Too many ideas."

"Better than coffee?"

"Don't push it," she said, but kissed him to soften her words. Like last night, the kiss quickly went from sweet to hot, and as he wrapped his arms around her, he discovered she wore nothing underneath the shirt. With a groan, he lifted the hem to grab her naked ass. He was about to repeat his actions from the night before and carry her back to his bedroom, but stopped when he recognized a muffled ringing. Carnival of the Animals.

"Sorry, that's me," she said against his lips. She broke their kiss and went to the table to find her phone in her bag. "First client in less than an hour. I need to go." She gave him another kiss and darted out of the room. He watched her sexy legs and wished they had more time.

This morning. He wanted time this morning. Nothing beyond that, he reminded himself.

Refocusing on the auction and finishing his coffee, Nick set about writing ideas for places they could bring together to create the packages. Dani came back, grabbed her mug, and drained it. He noticed her hair was back in its ponytail. He couldn't wait for the chance to get rid of it again.

"Do you need coffee to go? I probably have an extra travel mug somewhere."

He went to look, but she said, "No, I'm going to dart home to change clothes before going to the clinic. I'll get one there."

"I gave Otis food when I fed Presley. I hope that's okay."

At the mention of their names, both dogs came in. "It is if you want a friend for life."

"I'll take another kiss."

She gave him one, then noticed the list he'd made. "Are you around tonight to discuss this? Maybe make some calls or send emails? We need to move on this fast."

The only thing he wanted to move on was her, but he didn't say that. "I'm flexible. What time works for you?"

"I can be available after three. Do you want to come to my place?"

He made a mental note to bring condoms. "I'll be there by 3:30. Let me know if your schedule changes."

"Absolutely. Come on, Otis. We need to go." Otis gave Presley a bump with his nose as if to say "see you" to his friend, then followed Dani to the door. Nick walked behind them. Before she stepped out, she turned back, smiling. "And Nick? Last night was wonderful."

He was glad she didn't have any regrets. He certainly didn't.

* * *

The next several days fell into a new pattern. Work in the mornings, Dani in the evenings. They'd meet at her place or his, although his was easier because the king-size bed meant more room for the dogs who seemed to like the arrangement as much as he did. He looked forward to her texts, their dinners, and the sex, which got better every night. He was happier and more relaxed than he'd been in months, possibly years.

And he didn't want to think about what saying good-bye to her was going to feel like.

Monday morning, they were having breakfast at her place and going over the final details of the package he was pitching to five different businesses at the Castle on the Hill hotel this afternoon. This was the couple's package, and they were excited about the boost it would give to the auction if all the businesses agreed.

Nick was certain it was going to be an easy success. It was a win for everyone, but Dani was on edge. "I'm sorry I can't be there. I feel like I'm throwing you into the deep end of the pool on your own." She wasn't going with him because the time all five owners could make it work coincided with a spaying she had scheduled.

"Do you know the size of the last deal I managed?" Of course, it had gone to hell, but that was a different issue.

"Still, I wish I could be with you," she said, playing with her thumb.

He'd accepted that Dani was going to be worried about this event until it was over. He took her hand, kissed the raw skin of her thumb, and said, "It's going to be great. I'll call you as soon as we're done, and we'll celebrate later tonight."

She took a calming breath, gave him a kiss, and said, "Something to look forward to." He had lots of thoughts of how to celebrate with her and which parts of her he was going to celebrate first.

He worked with Ed until lunch, then went home to shower and change for the meeting. As he took out a pair of chinos and the polo shirt he'd brought with him, he thought of the difference in meeting attire from New York to Fable Notch. At some point, he was going to have to wear a tie again. He was looking over his notes when thoughts about returning to the city collided with how he and Dani came up with the pieces for the package. From one second to the next, he knew exactly how to help Terry with his current problem.

Terry had been prodding him daily, and Nick dreaded every text because it reminded him of how useless and out of the loop he was. Mostly he focused on things here, but those messages sent his blood pressure up and his spirits down. "I've got nothing"—which is what he'd text back—was too close to "I am nothing."

Nick went to his office and booted up the computer. He checked his watch. Plenty of time. He took the next hour to do some research, made a few calls to people from other departments, and did a quick run of the numbers. He couldn't write fast enough as thoughts and possibilities jumped into his head. Then, heart racing with excitement, he texted Terry.

I think I have an idea. But he didn't think. He knew. He recognized the tingles that came when he was on the verge of a new plan. It was like being buzzed on coffee, but better.

Terry texted back almost immediately. *You available now?*

Send me a Zoom link.

The link appeared in his inbox seconds later, and in two clicks, Terry was on his screen. It took a little while to explain the idea in part because Nick was so fired up he was having trouble completing sentences, but soon the other man could see the concept. It was the same, in many ways, as what he and Dani were doing for the auction. Pulling pieces from different places, getting support and buy in from different departments to ultimately create something greater than the sum of its parts. Everyone involved was going to benefit from it.

Once Terry could see the big picture, he jumped in with ideas of his own. As they brainstormed, getting rid of things and adding new ones almost as fast as they could talk, it was clear this had the potential to be even bigger than what Nick initially envisioned.

An hour into the call, he asked about bringing in a few other colleagues, but because of Nick's status with the company, Terry suggested they hold off. Still, it was clear to Nick this was some of the best work he'd ever done. Every idea led to another, which led to more research and more people to contact. More work, but also more excitement.

Nick could see how the possibilities were huge not only for this client, but for bringing new ones to the firm. Once this succeeded—and Nick knew it would—companies were going to be clamoring to work with J&W. This was everything and more than he'd been looking for since his suspension started.

He had his ticket back.

Chapter Twenty-One

D ani went through her day lightheaded and joyous. By the time she went to bed tonight, they'd be one very big step closer to hitting the auction goal, and not a minute too soon. They were a little closer to the deadline than she'd like, but it would be worth it once they could punch through that number.

Nick had turned out to be an amazing partner. In and out of bed. She didn't know which one she marveled at more. He'd been focused and supportive on the project, willing to follow up with donors and find new ones. Instead of the stress she had been experiencing, she was enjoying the process, which was what she'd hoped for when she first volunteered. Sure, she couldn't stop blushing when people asked her about working with Nick, and that probably gave them something new to talk about, but it was worth it to have him there every night.

Oh, and the sex. Better than it had ever been, and if it was because he had more experience than when they saw each other last, she let thoughts of other women go because her own experiences told her that Nick's attentiveness and care were worth it. Every night, they found new ways to please one another. She'd even been willing to be on top, riding them both to intense climaxes. She'd never been comfortable with the position in the past—it made her self-conscious—but he'd insisted that she be in charge. The power and control had been thrilling. She couldn't wait to do it again.

She kept an eye on the clock, thinking about Nick getting ready for the meeting until it was time for her to start a cat's spaying process. Then her focus shifted solely to her patient. It was a smooth procedure, and Dani was confident the cat would heal easily.

She sat at her desk to make notes in the file when she heard her phone buzzing in the drawer. She couldn't wait to see the text telling her the meeting was a success. Instead, caller id told her it was the hotel. Worried something had happened to Nick, she answered.

"Is this Dani Vaughn?"

"Yes?" *Oh God, what had gone wrong?*

"This is Robin Amsden from the catering and sales department at the Castle on the Hill. We were expecting Nick Hanson half an hour ago, but he hasn't arrived. I've tried his phone several times, but it goes to voicemail. Are you still interested in creating the Festival package?"

"Absolutely. I'm so sorry. Something must have come up." She couldn't imagine what. He was supposed to stop work at lunch. "I could call him, although I'll probably have the same result as you. Could we reschedule?"

"We could, but you know it's a challenge to find a time five people can meet, and I know the auction is soon."

That was an understatement. Damn him. What was he doing? She looked at her watch. "If everyone can stay a little longer, I can be there in twenty minutes."

"I'll have the kitchen bring in some more snacks, and we'll be waiting for you when you get here. Have the front desk direct you to the River Room."

"Thank you, Robin, and I'm sorry you had to wait. I'll be there soon." She was grabbing her things before she hung up the phone. Dani found Beth and explained the problem and what needed to be done for the cat in recovery. "Could you please let Doc Wheeler know I had to go out? I think he was about to leave. Bella should be out of the anesthetic any minute. He'll want to call Mrs. Jamison to let her know."

Beth made some notes in the file and said, "I hope Nick's okay."

"If he is, I may have to kill him." As she and Otis drove toward the hotel, her thoughts were a jumble. Nick had the information they were going to present. All she had was her notebook of papers, not quite as professional looking or complete. She'd have to wing it and hope she remembered everything.

She drove as quickly as she could to the Castle on the Hill, but the fates were against her. "Three lights in town, and we have to hit every one," she said to Otis as the light closest to her destination turned red. She drummed her fingers on the steering wheel. How could he screw this up? They'd been talking about this almost nonstop for the last four days. Except for the times they stopped for sex.

She couldn't think about that. She was serious about what she'd said to Beth. If he wasn't in the hospital, she was going to put him there.

She watched the light, her foot itching to move to the gas. As soon as it was green, she accelerated, looking at the dashboard clock, thinking about how much longer before she got to the hotel, too distracted to notice the SUV that ran the light.

Chapter Twenty-Two

♥

Nick's head was spinning when he got off the call. He couldn't remember the last time a deal had gotten him so energized. He sat there looking at his notes, light-headed on the potential of the plan. Terry had a lot to do on his end, while Nick would continue to do research and review the numbers as the project continued. He wanted to do more, but this was the most he could offer, given his situation. A glance at his watch told him had been talking with Terry for over three hours.

Shit.

He was an hour late for the meeting. He found his phone and saw four missed calls from the hotel, two from Dani, and three messages. Not good.

"Presley, I'm late. Gotta go." He grabbed the portfolio and laptop with the presentation, his coat and keys, and ran for the car. As he drove, he called the hotel but couldn't reach his contact. Next, he tried to get ahold of Dani, but it went straight to voicemail. He needed to get in front of this. Let her know he'd screwed up and apologize. Damn it. Before he got in touch with Terry, he should have set an alarm on his phone. He couldn't let this ruin their plans for the auction. He'd promised her he'd be there.

He was less than a mile from the hotel when he saw the emergency vehicles with their lights flashing. A police car, fire engine, ambulance, and tow truck. Great, just what he needed. Another delay. A cop directed him around the accident, and as he drove past, he looked to see the damage.

And saw Dani's car.

It took all his strength not to slam on the brakes. The driver's side door was gone, deployed airbags hung like deflated balloons. The SUV that hit her was still pressed against the engine.

He drove beyond the accident, then pulled onto the shoulder. Getting out of the car, he ran back. The officer monitoring the scene stopped him. He had to find out what had happened. "Dani. Where's Dani Vaughn? That's her car. I need to talk to someone in charge."

He continued yelling, demanding someone answer him until he heard, "Nick, what are you doing here?"

Nick felt a jolt of both panic and relief at the familiar voice. The officer let him pass and he raced to Martin. As the town's fire chief, it made sense for Martin to be at the scene, but it confirmed the accident was serious. "Where's Dani? Is she okay? How badly is she hurt?" He looked over at the ambulance, but only saw a stranger with his head in his hands. His thoughts raced. "She isn't...." He couldn't say it, didn't want to think about it.

Martin grabbed Nick's shoulders and gave a steadying squeeze, then turned him away from the sight. "No, son. They took her to the hospital. She was bruised and had a few cuts, probably from broken glass. I don't know if she lost consciousness, but she was talking to the paramedics when they loaded her into the ambulance. The front of the car took most of the force. It would have been worse if he'd hit her door."

The relief made his legs weak. She was okay. She had to be okay. "I need to get to the hospital and find out what's going on."

He started for his car, but Martin stopped him. "There's nothing you can do for her yet. She's probably still in the ER, and they'll only let family in. I called Rosie. Dani won't be alone."

But she was at the hospital, and that was his fault. The voice of his father calling him a screw up rang in his head. He needed action to drown it out. "I have to do something. I can't go home and wait for someone to call me."

"You could take Otis."

"Otis was with her?" Of course he was. He would have been at the clinic when she learned Nick missed the meeting. Things were getting worse by the minute. "Is he hurt?"

"Not that I could see. My guess is he was on the other side of the car, but he's pretty shook up. He almost didn't let the paramedics take her. I've got him in the fire truck. He knows you and seeing a familiar face might help."

"I'll get him. Bring him back to my place to stay with Presley." He could do at least this for her. "This is my fault."

Martin looked confused. "How could it be?"

He rubbed a hand across the back of his neck. "I was late for a meeting about an auction donation. I was supposed to be there over an hour ago." His voice broke. He'd let her down. Again. "That's why Dani was here. She wasn't supposed to be. Martin, if she's hurt..."

"She's going to be fine. She's getting the care she needs. You need to do the same. Take Otis and either go home or go on to the Castle to see about the meeting."

Martin was right. He needed a plan before he saw her. "I can do that." Otis started barking and jumping when he saw Nick. At least someone was happy to see him. He could imagine the conversation he was going to have with Dani. Otis leaped from the truck as soon as the door opened, and Martin went with them back to Nick's car, where he'd left the engine running.

"Are you sure you're okay to drive?"

Nick wasn't sure of anything at the moment. The day had gone from good, to great, to horribly wrong, but he wasn't going to say that. "Yeah, I'll take a minute before I get going."

"I'll check in with you later," Martin said, giving Nick's shoulder another squeeze before closing the car door.

"Thanks, Dad." Nick watched in his rearview mirror as Martin walked back to the scene. He couldn't take his eyes off the sight of Dani's car. She'd been hurt because he hadn't kept his word. As he watched the tow truck take the SUV away, he noticed the full extent of the damage. He didn't know a lot about car repair, but he had a feeling hers was going to be a total loss.

As he looked away, he caught his own reflection in the mirror and saw the panic in his eyes, his pupils large, sweat running down his face. He couldn't go over to the hotel looking like this. He banged his hand against the steering wheel several times and cursed himself loudly. A whine from Otis told him he was scaring the dog.

You're a waste of space. As he heard his father's voice, his heart rate shot up. It had been fast before, but this was different. The edges of Nick's vision darkened. Recognizing the signs, he tried to calm himself.

In for four counts, hold for four.

He didn't know how long it was before he noticed the weight on his leg. Otis's head. He ran a hand between the dog's ears and the constriction around his heart eased. Another dog helping him through. Time to get moving. He'd get Otis home and call the hotel. Then go to the hospital.

It wasn't much of a plan, but it would do.

He drove the car to the nearest left turn, changed directions, and headed to his house. Once on his way, he used the car's blue tooth system to call the hotel sales manager. He apologized for missing the meeting, then told her about Dani's accident. She told him not to worry—too late for that—and she would do what she could from her end to make things work. He said he'd email the presentation to her and check in again tomorrow to see what they might be able to do.

At home, he fed both dogs and took a Xanax. When he got to the hospital, he needed to be calm. He hoped he'd be allowed to see Dani when he got there. He hoped she'd agree to see him.

Panic and the August weather had him sweating through his clothes, so he ripped them off and jumped in a shower. Once he was under the spray, he raged, letting out a howl that Presley would have envied and beating his fists against the wall until they were sore.

It didn't help.

He slid down until he was sitting on the cool tile floor, pulling at his hair as the water cascaded over him. He was startled by a sound at the glass and saw both dogs on the other side. Presley had a paw on the door. Otis was leaving marks with his nose. Not wanting to worry them, he stood, turned off the water, and got dressed.

But he couldn't think about anything other than how he'd screwed up. Again. And this time it could have been a much bigger loss than money. Dani was priceless.

He held out for another half hour, alternating between pacing and staring, before he jumped back in his car. On the way to the hospital, he tortured himself by listening to the messages on his phone.

"Hi, Nick. Robin Amsden at the Castle on the Hill. According to my schedule, our meeting was for four o'clock. It's fifteen past. Everyone is waiting. Hope you're on your way."

"Nick, Robin again. It's four thirty. Is there a problem? Please call me."

"Nick, I'm sorry, but we can't stay much longer. I'm going to call Dani Vaughn to see if she can help. I hope you'll call soon or that you're on your way."

And the last one from Dani. "Nick, where the hell are you? Robin has been trying to reach you for almost an hour. I can't believe you forgot. You said you weren't working this afternoon. I'm heading over there. If you get this message in time, get in your car and meet me at the hotel."

He wished he'd lost track of time on the construction site. She'd be pissed, but she'd be more likely to forgive him. As much as he wanted to see Dani and know she was okay, he was dreading the moment she heard he was on the phone with New York. When she found out that work was the reason he'd missed the meeting, it was going to make everything so much worse.

Chapter Twenty-Three

♥

Dani lay in the Emergency Room hospital bed, an IV in her arm, an oxygen tube in her nose, and tried to do a self-assessment of her injuries. She kept getting distracted by the noise around her and flashes of how she'd gotten there.

One minute she was driving, the next, pillows of airbags surrounded her, and broken glass was everywhere. Otis was barking, and a car's horn was blaring nonstop. She didn't know how long she sat there before someone in a uniform was by the side of the car, pushing things away and asking if she was hurt. She wasn't sure how to answer. She'd been dazed but nothing unbearable. She tried to get out, but her vision swam, and the door didn't budge. Neither was good. "I need help," she managed.

The next minutes—it could have been hours—were a blur. She remembered someone getting in the backseat and putting a collar around her neck, then the warm rush of air when the door of her car was opened. They put her on a stretcher, asked her if she lost consciousness. She wasn't certain.

They were expecting her at the hospital. As soon as they wheeled her in, there had been a flurry of doctors and nurses asking more questions, taking her vitals, inserting an IV, asking her blood type. She changed out of her clothes and into a hospital gown. They made sure she wasn't pregnant, then after doctors ruled out broken bones, the cuts on her arms and face were cleaned and bandaged. A head CT was ordered to see if the impact or airbags had caused any other damage, and after that, they brought her to a curtained area to wait for the results.

And while she waited, she worried.

The auction didn't need two bed-ridden volunteers, and she didn't want Doc Wheeler to discover things were better without her or for patients to get used to seeing him again. Okay, maybe she was overreacting. A day or two out of the office shouldn't set her back, but what if it did? With nothing to keep her company but her thoughts, her own fears were getting the best of her. When Aunt Rosie stepped through the curtain, Dani sighed happily. Rosie would help.

Unfortunately, her aunt's first reaction was an uncharacteristic gasp. "Yikes, that answers the 'How bad do I look' question."

Rosie sat on the edge of the bed, took her hand, and gave it a gentle kiss. "Honestly, it's not as terrible as I feared. You've got a good size bruise on the side of your face, and they've bandaged a few cuts, but I don't see any stitches."

"Then why did you gasp?"

"Relief. All Martin told me was that you'd been in a car accident and taken to the hospital. Then they wouldn't let me back to see you. I imagined the worst." Dani could admit Rosie wasn't the only one. "How are you?"

"You know that joke about feeling like you've been hit by a truck? Turns out it's no joke." In spite of her words, she gave a small chuckle, then groaned. "I think it's more than a few bruises." Dani told Rosie about what had happened since they brought her in. "I guess we're waiting on the results of the CT scan before they let me go."

Rosie looked concerned. "You're not going to be admitted?"

Dani hadn't considered that. No one had said anything about her staying. "I hope not. I don't think it's anything serious, although I have a feeling the car is a total loss. Oh my God, Otis!" Maybe she did have a head injury. She'd been worried about him as they were taking her to the ambulance, but she hadn't thought about him since she'd gotten here. "Where is he? He was in the car with me. Who has him?"

"I don't know, but as soon as we know more about you, I'll call Martin and find out."

"No, please, Aunt Rosie, call him. I need to know." She sat up straighter, gave her aunt a push, and couldn't stop the wince of pain.

"Okay, I'll call." Rosie took her phone out of the giant bag she carried and made a call. She mouthed the words 'voicemail,' before talking, "Martin, it's Rosie. I'm at the hospital. Dani's concerned about Otis. Could you give me a call as soon as you get this and let me know where he is? Thanks."

"I hope he's not hurt," Dani said as tears formed and fell from her eyes. For the first time since the accident, she allowed the fear of what happened to roll through her. With Aunt Rosie here, it was safe to fall apart. "I was so scared."

"Of course you were, but you're going to be fine." Rosie rubbed her arm. Dani could see how much her aunt wanted to hug her, but between the tubes and the bruises, she held off. "Martin said the other driver ran the red."

"I didn't see him at all. I was too focused on getting to the—oh shit."

"Lived here all my life. I don't know where that is."

Dani couldn't be amused. "I was heading to the Castle for a meeting." Dani explained where she was going and why. "I need someone to call and tell them what happened. And I need to find Nick."

"You need to relax." Rosie sounded stern, and Dani remembered the times Rosie had kept her in bed when she'd gotten sick or hurt in the summer. Dani never wanted to stay in when things were happening elsewhere. "The calls will get made, but you're not going anywhere for the time being."

"I'll have to agree with that," the doctor said, pulling back a curtain and stepping in, saying hello to them both. "You are a very lucky woman. The airbags did their job, and the CT scan was clear. However, even though there are no outward signs of a problem, we're not certain you didn't lose consciousness, so I'm having you admitted overnight for observation."

"I'd rather not," Dani said. The auction, work. She couldn't stay.

"Danielle Vaughn," Rosie said, and Dani had a moment to be grateful her aunt didn't take out her middle name as well. "You know better than to argue with a doctor's recommendation. If he says you need to stay, you need to stay."

The doctor stepped forward and said, "It's a precaution. We'll monitor you, and if everything looks good, you'll be discharged in the morning."

Dani wanted to argue, but the look in her aunt's eye told her that if she tried to leave, she'd be walking home. "I understand. Thank you."

"Do you have any questions for me?"

"No," Dani said, although she had plenty of questions for other people.

"If you need anything, press that buzzer and someone will come. Transportation will be here shortly to bring you to your room."

"Thank you, doctor," Rosie said, echoing Dani, as the doctor left. "If you think you'll be all right on your own,

I'm going to give Helen a call and tell her what's happening."

"And call again about Otis?" She needed to know he was okay.

"And call again about Otis." Rosie gave her a kiss on the forehead, and Dani managed a deep breath. Her aunt's love and comfort always made her feel better. "Be back in a flash."

As Rosie walked out, a new nurse came in. This, at least, was someone she recognized and seeing a familiar face was nice. Dani knew Mia Durant through her dog, Bowie, a beautiful Saint Berhard/Husky mix, a pet almost as big as Otis. They were also connected through the Hansons. Years before, Mia had a serious relationship with Cole, both personally and professionally, until she was forced out of the band, or at least that's what Dani had heard. "Hello, Dr. Dani," Mia said with a smile that had Dani relaxing. "I saw your name on the board, so I thought I'd check in. At the risk of asking a dumb question, how are you?"

"I'm fine, but they're keeping me overnight." She was still trying to think about who had Otis and if they'd know what to do for him, but it was hard to focus.

"From your tone, I'm guessing you're not happy about this."

"Is anyone ever happy to be admitted?"

"Other than those heading to maternity? No, usually not. Let me look at your file and see if I can tell you a little more." Mia left the room and was back a few minutes later with a laptop. After a few clicks, she said, "As the doctor hopefully told you, there are no major concerns, but you have some pretty serious bruises from the impact and airbags, and those are going to feel worse in a couple of hours. Once you're in a room and have some food in your system, you're going to be getting some IV painkillers for the evening. The good stuff. I wouldn't be surprised if you sleep through the nurses taking your vitals during the night. As much as you want to leave, I think you'll be happier not to have to worry for the next several hours. Let someone else take care of you."

Mia's words reminded her again of Nick. She was going to take care of *him*. "You wouldn't know where my bag is? I left it in my car. I need to make a few phone calls to let people know what happened."

"I can check, but for now, at the risk of stating the obvious, try to get some rest."

Dani had a feeling she was going to be hearing that a lot over the next several days. She already hated it. As Mia left, a nurse and someone from the hospital's transportation department came to take her to her room. She was allowed to move from the emergency room gurney to the bed on her own. And she tried not to wince. Mia was right about the bruises. Maybe it wasn't a bad idea to be here for the night.

Once in a room, her new nurse got her hooked back up to the monitors, checked her vitals, made sure the IV was running properly, then asked if Dani wanted to order dinner. Her stomach growled in response. "That's a good sign," the nurse said as she took a menu from the bedside drawer and told Dani to call in her meal when she was ready. "Order whatever sounds good. Even dessert. The medication you'll be getting later works better on a full stomach."

Dani had finished ordering a grilled cheese, tomato soup, and carrot cake when Rosie came in. "Found you."

"Yes, welcome to my suite. It's not the Ritz, but I can't complain." Well, she could, but it wouldn't do any good.

"I know you're not happy about staying, but I'm relieved. This way, I know you'll get what you need and not overdo things."

"I do not—"

"Do you remember the sprained ankle? I had to practically tie you to the bed to get you to stay off of it for a day. Or the stomach bug when you insisted you wanted to go out, even though you couldn't be away from a bathroom for more than an hour? You have many virtues, my sweet, but patience isn't one of them."

Dani couldn't argue. She'd already been calculating when she'd be able to go back to work. "I'll try to be good."

"That's all I ask. There's one other thing," Rosie said. "I made some calls. I reached Xander, and he says he'll check in with you tomorrow." She was glad Rosie had thought to tell Dani's brother. They weren't in regular contact since he lived in Seattle, but he deserved to know. "And I called your mother."

"Why?" The question was out before Dani had a chance to stop herself. She didn't share details of her life with her mother. Dani had her appendix taken out during her junior year of college. When she called from the hospital, Cynthia's response was, "Well, it's not like you were wearing bikinis before, so I don't suppose it's an issue." That was the last time Dani told her about any crisis.

Rosie took Dani's hand. "This could have been serious. She'd want to know."

Dani wasn't convinced. "You and I both know that mothering isn't always in her schedule."

"Well, it's going to be this time because she's catching the first flight she can out of O'Hare."

"She's what? No, don't repeat it. I need to let that sink in." As if Dani didn't have enough going on, she was going to deal with her mother, too. How could she relax with Cynthia around criticizing her every choice, from clothes to food? One of the bonuses of living in Fable Notch was knowing her mother was never going to visit. So much for that.

Her mind raced in a new direction. Could she get them to keep her in the hospital for a few extra days? She could complain of a headache or say the pain had gotten worse. Cynthia would never stay if she had to visit Dani in the hospital. The worry built as Dani's thoughts swirled in her head. She wished Otis were here. She could use his quiet comfort. "Did you find out about Otis? Is he okay? Where is he?"

"He's with me." Dani gave a small start at the voice and looked to the door where Nick was standing with a bouquet of pink roses, her favorite. She gave a quick glance down his body, looking for broken bones or signs that he'd been violently ill or viciously attacked. He looked fine. Good.

She was going to kill him.

Then she really looked at him. The circles under his eyes that weren't there a few hours ago. The concern and guilt on his face telling her there was nothing she could say that would make him feel worse than already he did. And the traitorous walls around her heart, which she thought were so strong when it came to Nick, cracked.

Chapter Twenty-Four

♥

When Nick arrived at the Emergency Room, they told him they had admitted Dani. His stomach fell. How bad was she? He'd raced up to her room, worried about what he'd discover. Seeing her lying in the hospital bed, bruised, pale, and bandaged, had his heart stopping before it raced again. He stepped into the corridor before she noticed him, and stood against the wall, giving a thought to whether he'd need another Xanax. This would be a bad time for a panic attack, although it wouldn't be surprising. He practiced the square breathing techniques, and when he had himself under control, he went into the room, giving her the roses and telling her about Otis.

She barely looked at the flowers. "How did Otis end up with you?"

He listened for the accusation in her tone but didn't hear any. "I was late for the meeting—which you know—and was heading to the hotel to see if I could salvage anything when I passed the accident scene." He explained how Martin had told him what happened and suggested he take Otis. "He's settled in with Presley. A little jumpier than usual."

"That's to be expected," Dani said and visibly relaxed. He was going to have to savor the small smile she gave him because it could be the last one for a while. "Thank you. I know he was scared after the crash, and it got worse when they took me away. Being with Presley will help."

"I'm going to let the two of you talk," Rosie said as she stood and gave Dani a kiss. "I'll be back after the breakfast rush tomorrow. If you need me sooner, call."

"I can't. Still don't have my phone."

"I'll see what I can do about that." As she walked by Nick, she whispered, "Don't screw this up."

It was probably too late for that, but he'd do what he could. He walked over and took the seat Rosie had vacated next to the bed. "How bad is it?"

"Not as terrible as you might think, or apparently looks. They're being cautious in case I lost conscious-ness. I get to be on some fun painkillers for the night. Rosie thinks it's a good idea because, as she was quick to remind me, I tend to rush things."

When she heard why he missed the meeting, she was going to think getting involved with him again was another thing she'd rushed. "Is there anyone you want me to call for you? Or do you want to use my phone?"

"I'd like to call Laurel. She may have already heard what happened through the town grapevine. It will be good to talk to her."

Nick put in his passcode and handed over the phone. "Anything I can get you?" He probably sounded overso-licitous, but he needed to be of some help.

"Maybe a vase for the flowers?" So she had noticed. He was glad he stopped to get them.

He left the room to give her some privacy and, he admitted to himself, so he didn't have to hear her talk about what happened. What happened because of him. She was fine, he reminded himself, but this wasn't like breaking a dishwasher. She could have been seriously hurt, or Otis might have been.

For the rest of the time he was here, he couldn't screw up again. He was going to make sure the auction was the most successful one in the town's history, whatever that took.

When he returned with a vase, Dani was off the phone and her dinner had been delivered. He arranged the flowers and sat down again. He wanted to pace. He wanted to scream. He wanted to beg for her forgiveness but didn't know how.

Instead, they sat in silence as she ate. After taking a few bites, she asked, "Should we talk about the elephant in the room?"

"Probably. Elephants aren't good for hospitals. Or patients." Or him. He needed to face this and take whatever was coming.

"At the risk of stating the obvious, you missed the meeting. Where were you?"

Now that they were talking, he didn't want to answer. He considered lying. He'd thought of several plausible excuses he could give. He'd fallen asleep reading. He'd taken Presley for a walk and didn't notice it had gotten late. But the truth was eating him up, and he needed to be honest. Better to get it out and disappoint her. It's not like it was the first time. "A few days ago, I got a call from a colleague who asked for my help on a project. I'd been thinking about it but didn't have any recommendations for him until today. As I changed for the meeting, I realized our ideas for creating the auction packages could also work for him. I thought I had enough time to do the initial research and give him a quick call. It wasn't a quick call."

She said nothing for a while. Waiting for her to respond was killing him. "You lost track of time. Because you were talking to someone from work."

He nodded. He wanted to throw up. He sat on the edge of the bed and took her hand but couldn't meet her eyes. "I screwed up. I know." She didn't answer, and he looked at her. "I'm so sorry. This is all my fault."

Before she could reply, a nurse came in, introduced herself, and said she'd be in charge of Dani's care overnight, explaining she'd be stopping in every few hours. Nick remembered that from his hospital stay. The interruptions were constant. After a quick check of Dani's vitals and a reminder to Nick that visiting hours ended soon, they were alone again. The silence was agony.

"Please say something," he said. "Yell at me. Tell me what an asshole I am. Throw me out and say you never want to see me again."

When she didn't say anything, he watched her face, hoping she wasn't considering his suggestions. Finally she said, "I don't think you need my help to feel like shit for what happened." He shook his head. "Would you feel better if I told you you're a selfish prick who never thinks about anyone but himself and all my friends will hate you forever?"

Ouch. "Maybe."

She gave his hands a squeeze, and he let himself hope. "I won't tell you I'm not upset. I am, along with being frustrated and worried. I was counting on this package coming together so I—we—could relax about the auction, but this project was my priority, not yours."

He hated her being so agreeable, as if she'd expected this, and he'd lived up—or down—to that expectation. "I should have waited. I should have called Terry after the meeting or tomorrow."

"Agreed. Then again, the guy who hit me should have waited at the red light. By the way, thank you for taking Otis."

No, he would not let himself feel like a hero. Otis deserved to be mad at Nick, too. "Rosie would have done that."

"True, but having another dog around will help him, and he wouldn't have that with my aunts. I will sleep better knowing Otis is with the two of you."

"I still feel like shit." But was grateful to have taken at least one right step since his latest screw up.

"I know. And I'll admit that I'm not entirely sorry that you do."

"Guess we can't go back and fix these things," he said. And there were so many places in his life he wanted to do that.

"Nope." And in the silence that followed, he wondered if she was thinking about their past as much as he was. He'd hoped this time would give him a chance to make up for some of his mistakes. But he'd fallen into an old habit of putting work before her—before anyone—and this was the consequence. No, he couldn't have foreseen the accident, but her needing to go to the hotel was his fault.

The nurse knocked on the door and told Nick it was time to leave. He stood and gave Dani a gentle kiss. "How about I come in the morning to take you home when you get sprung?"

"That's not necessary. Aunt Rosie said she could come by." She yawned. Good. Sleep would help.

"I know, but this way she won't have to worry if you're released during the breakfast rush, and you won't have to wait. I'll tell Ed I won't be in tomorrow."

"He won't mind?"

Nick gave a shrug. As if he was really needed. "I'm an extra hand and probably not as much help as I think. He's being kind, letting me pass the time by working on his crew. They won't notice if I'm not there." It surprised him to realize he didn't like that thought, although it was probably true. "I'll stop by your place to pick up some clothes before I come over."

"That'll be great. The door is unlocked."

He wasn't surprised. "Anything else you need?"

"Not that I can think of, although my ability to think is fading by the second," she said as she snuggled into the pillows.

"Get some rest and when you wake…" Dani was out before he finished the sentence. He stayed with her to be certain she was sleeping. The thought of leaving her made him nervous. He could have lost her today. She accepted why he'd missed the meeting, but he wasn't letting himself off the hook. For the rest of his time in Fable Notch, he was going to make certain he was there for her. He wouldn't let her down again.

He went to bed as early as he could, but couldn't sleep. He didn't realize how much he was tossing and turning until Presley and Otis, who both wanted to be near him, complained and jumped off the bed. Sometime around four, he managed to sleep for longer than an hour, but by seven, he was awake and out of bed. Coffee and a cold shower were the best he could do before dressing, walking the dogs, and heading out.

His first stop was Dani's house, where he grabbed clothes from her room. When he saw the blouse from their first night together hanging in the closet, he was tempted to bring that, but instead he went through her t-shirts until he found one he thought was the softest.

Once he had everything in a bag, he drove to the diner. He'd grab something for himself, and he'd get something for Dani. He'd also let Rosie know he'd be bringing Dani home. He took a stool at the counter and waited to place his order. When Rosie poured him coffee in a thick mug, he said, "No, this is to go. I'm heading straight to the hospital, in case they let her out early. I want to bring Dani her favorite omelet."

"Nick, it's barely eight o'clock. With any luck, she's still sleeping. It's going to be hours before the doctor clears her. And when was the last time you ate anything?"

"Last ni—" he started, then remembered that wasn't true. He'd fed the dogs, not himself.

"That's what I thought. Sit. You'll have a proper breakfast to get you going before I give you food to take to Dani."

He was about to argue, but it was pointless, especially since Rosie was right. It was too early to go to the hospital, and he needed to take care of himself a little if he was going to care for Dani. He sat down and sipped his coffee.

News of Dani's accident had spread through town, so Nick's breakfast was interrupted by people asking him how she was doing. He was surprised to discover he didn't mind answering the questions. A few months ago, he would have preferred anonymity. This morning, the attention and concern was a much-needed balm. So many people cared about Dani, him included.

When he was finished, Rosie handed him a bag with three containers and a large cup of coffee. He wasn't surprised by the amount of food. "She needs rest for the next few days. Do you think coffee is such a good idea?"

"It's decaf, and if you tell her, I will spread embarrassing rumors based on truth about you." She could do it, too. "Go get our girl. Let me know when she's settled, and I'll be over as soon as I can."

"See you then," he said, and gave her a kiss on the cheek.

As he was walking to his car, his phone pinged. *Getting sprung around 11.*

He replied, *On my way. Maybe we can get you out sooner.*

Before he could get on the road, Theo called. He'd barely said hello when his brother said, "Martin told me about Dani. Is she okay? Are you?"

He put his seatbelt on and said, "She's being discharged in a few hours. I'm heading to the hospital and bringing breakfast from the diner."

"That'll help. What about you?"

Guilty. Miserable. Worried Dad might have been right. "Me? I'm fine."

"Try again."

"I'm not the one in the hospital."

"Martin told me everything." Including, Nick assumed, the part about Dani driving because Nick missed a meeting.

"Fine, I'm still blaming myself, but I deserve to."

"No, you don't." Theo went 'big brother' on him. "It's called an accident for a reason. And if she's coming home today, then it wasn't too serious."

Nick appreciated Theo's effort, but he wasn't ready to give up responsibility yet. Before Theo could offer any more ways to make him feel better, Nick said, "I need to go. I'll call you later."

It was almost nine thirty when he got to Dani's room. She was sitting up with a tray in front of her. He barely managed a hello before she said, "Please tell me there's a decent breakfast in that bag. Look at this." He did. It was depressing and colorless. He took the tray and put it on the windowsill, then unpacked what Rosie had given him.

As she sipped her coffee, Dani took a deep breath of the wonderful smells and gave a smile and a sigh. Realizing he could have lost her yesterday and never seen that smile again punched him in the gut. Maybe he shouldn't have eaten at the diner.

When she saw what he brought, she asked, "Do you think I can start with the blueberry muffin?"

"I think you can start wherever you want. Patient prerogative."

"Oh good," she said and snatched off a big piece of the pastry and popped it in her mouth, licking her fingers. Nick's body reacted to her pleasure, and he mentally smacked himself. There was a good chance after what he'd done, she'd never want him in her bed again, and as much as he'd hate it, he'd deserve it.

He let her take another bite before asking, "How are you feeling this morning?"

"Better than I expected, although whether that's because I wasn't badly hurt or all the pain killers, I couldn't say. How's Otis?"

"Fine, but he misses you. I don't think he ate much this morning."

"This is the first time we've been apart for a night since I adopted him when he was three months old."

Another thing he was to blame for. What was a little more guilt on top of what he already had? "We'll go straight to my place and pick him up."

When her face brightened, he was grateful he could do something right. After she was done eating, they sat watching morning talk shows, waiting for the doctor to give her the all-clear to leave. Nick snuck glances at Dani, making sure she was comfortable and worrying she seemed tired. She had a few colorful bruises and more bandages than he liked. Everyone one of them was because of him. Nothing other than time was going to heal her body or the damage he'd done, but during the sleepless hours the night before, he'd come up with a way to help.

No matter what it took, he would make certain the auction was a success. He knew what it meant to her, and now it mattered as much to him. He may not know if New York was going to take him back at the end of his suspension, but he knew that before he left, he was going to do his part to make sure Dani had her dream of a life and community in Fable Notch. His new plan was going to work.

Chapter Twenty-Five

♥

Time had never moved so slowly for Dani than it did as they waited for the doctor to come to the room, give Dani her discharge plans and prescription, and tell her she could go home if she "promised to take it easy". She would have agreed to give up coffee for a week if it meant should go home.

Okay, maybe not a week.

As soon as the wheelchair arrived, Nick left to get his car and meet her at the entrance. He was waiting when they got to the lobby and helped her up and into the SUV. She'd been in his car a few times and didn't remember it being so high. Maybe she needed more help than she thought.

"Let's go get your dog," he said once he was seated beside her. She was grateful the drive to his place didn't take long and annoyed that Nick was right when he suggested she wait while he get Otis. She'd felt fine as they left the hospital, but by the time they arrived at his house, the aches were returning. The thought of getting out and back into his car wasn't appealing. As he went in, she heard a chorus of happy barking, and moments later

Otis bounded out. She'd barely gotten the door opened when he jumped into the vehicle.

"Ouch, Otis. Gentle." She understood his joy—she'd never been happier to see him—but he was a lot of weight on her bruised body. "Gentle, please." Responding to the tone in her voice, the same one she used in the office around sick pets, he gave her a nuzzle, then after a few more hugs moved to the back.

"That looked like a happy reunion," Nick said, getting into the car.

"For us both. You're not bringing Presley?"

"Maybe later. Let's get you settled without having two dogs underfoot. I'll check on her this afternoon and bring her by then."

"Thank you again for watching him, Nick."

"It was the least I could do. He's a very easy house guest." Dani wasn't surprised Nick was still feeling guilty and worried. She could tell from his constant glances and the way he took her hand as he drove, squeezing it occasionally. She was surprised not to be madder at him, but there was no changing what happened. She hoped he was serious about staying focused on the auction going forward. Starting tomorrow, even if she was home, she'd make calls and get things going again.

When they turned on to her street, the sight of an unfamiliar white sedan parked out front deflated her happiness at seeing her house. Oh damn, she was here already.

As Nick parked in the driveway, the car's driver got out. Looking in the rearview mirror, he asked, "Who's that?"

She couldn't keep the dread out of her voice. "That's my mother."

Nick did a nearly comical double take. "One more time?"

"Yeah, I'm shocked, too. Aunt Rosie called her, and she decided to fly out. Truthfully, I'd expected to get a text telling me she had changed her mind. Brace yourself."

Nick came to help Dani out of the car as Cynthia walked up to them, looking fresh and put together. How her mother could look so good after an early morning flight, a drive from the airport, and standing in eighty-degree heat was something Dani would never understand. Then again, looking good no matter what was a priority for Cynthia. Dani bet none of her mother's clothes would dare wrinkle in her luggage.

"Danielle, my darling. Oh dear, you look awful." At least there was a good reason for the remark, and it wasn't because Cynthia didn't approve of what Dani was wearing or her current weight, although she'd get comments about both of those soon enough. Her mother put a hand on her shoulder and gave her a brief kiss. "And who is this?"

"Mom, this is Nick Hanson. Nick, this is my mother, Cynthia Phillips."

"So you're the famous—or should I say infamous—Nick. The reason she came up here for college then ran off to Texas for medical school." Oh, this was starting out *so* well.

Dani managed not to cringe when Nick squinted at her and said, "Texas?"

"She never told you? Whatever happened between you that summer was so bad, she withdrew from the University of Pennsylvania and transferred. Moving here is her first time out of the south since then." Done embarrassing Dani, at least for now, Cynthia gave Nick an appraising glance. Dani bet she found very few things wrong other than the casual clothes. "I thought you lived in New York."

"He does," Dani said, "But he's visiting." Dani had no intention of telling her mother more than that, and she gave Nick a look she hoped let him know to keep his mouth shut.

Nick gave a nod and said, "It's nice to meet you, Mrs. Phillips. Let's get you inside and settled."

"Oh, that's fine," Cynthia said. "I don't need to bring my things in."

And so it began. "He meant me, Mom."

"Of course." Otis jumped out of the car, and Cynthia let out a scream. "What on earth is that?"

Dani smiled. This was one disapproval she could enjoy. "My dog."

"Heaven help me," Cynthia said, her hand on her heart.

For a change, Dani agreed with her mother. She was going to need all the help she could get to make it through this visit. Too bad her prescription meant drinking wasn't allowed.

When they got to the door, Dani saw her bag waiting on the doorknob. Something else to like about small towns, and one less thing to worry about. She'd have to find out who brought it back to her and thank them.

"Oh. Well," Cynthia said, stepping in behind them and standing in the doorway. It was amazing how much her mother could convey with two words. Dani looked around the space and saw it through Cynthia's eyes, noticing the places her mother would find it lacking, from the older appliances to the mismatched furniture. Nick's house—and its size—was more her style, but Dani loved the small ranch from the moment she'd seen it. As scared as she'd been to take on a mortgage, not knowing if she'd be successful, she bought it. For her it was a way of saying, 'I'm here, and I plan to stay.' Cynthia stood in the center of the living area, looked around, and said, "I assume this is everything."

It was perfect for her and Otis, but with her mother there, it seemed to shrink. "There's also a basement."

"You didn't consider renting until you could afford something bigger or until..." She didn't need to finish the sentence. There were only two things Cynthia would say. Either until Dani decided she didn't want to live here or until she met someone to marry, and they could buy a place together.

"It's a terrific place, Mrs. Phillips," Nick said, and she was grateful for the rescue. "It's close to the clinic and town, and it sits on a good size piece of land. Between that and the layout of the rooms, if Dani wants to expand someday, it would be easy."

Cynthia said nothing as she smoothed a nonexistent wrinkle from her outfit. "I'm going to use the powder room." Dani pointed in the only possible direction. Her mother wasn't going to like that room any better.

Nick was getting Dani get settled on the couch with her favorite soft blanket and plenty of pillows when Aunt Rosie arrived. "Welcome home, sweetie." Rosie held up two bags that looked heavy. Whatever was in them smelled great, and Otis was hovering, wondering what he'd get. "I know Nick brought you breakfast, but healing takes energy, so I've got sandwiches and cheese fries, gravy on the side, and a Boston cream pie." Her mother came out as Rosie was unpacking the food on the dining area table. "Cynthia, you're here. I told you to let me know 7when you were landing, and I'd pick you up."

Cynthia brushed her hand through the air. "It wasn't necessary. I rented a car and drove myself so no one needs to ferry me around."

Dani suspected it the real reason was so Cynthia could come and go as she pleased, not get stuck where she didn't want to be. It wasn't a kind thought, but Dani didn't kid herself about the limits of her mother's patience. The fact that she was here was surprising enough.

Rosie gave her sister a hug, which was barely returned. "I'm glad you made it. We have to make sure our girl doesn't overdo it." As if Cynthia was going to do anything to help. Rosie gave Dani a gentle kiss before sitting on the loveseat, set at a right angle to where Dani was lying down. "How are you feeling? You have more color than yesterday, but that probably wouldn't take much."

The question made Dani realize her mother hadn't asked about the accident, only commented on how Dani looked. That was the difference between the sisters. One worried about how people looked, the other about how they felt. "I'm a little better. Sore, which I expected. Tired, which I didn't. It's not as if I've done much other than rest for the past several hours."

"Your body's been through a lot. That's exhausting. Let me fix you a plate of food. Cynthia, there's plenty. Come help yourself."

"Is there any tuna? Or maybe a salad?" Dani managed, barely, not to laugh. If Aunt Rosie brought tuna, it would include mayo, and that's not what Cynthia wanted.

"Not in what I brought, but I'm sure you can find something in the cabinets."

Dani was going to tell her mother where things were, but decided if Cynthia wanted to show up, she could fend for herself. The first negative comment didn't take long. "Oh, Dani, you should have more fruit than one dying banana."

"Cynthia, leave the girl alone. I'm sure she eats plenty of fruits and vegetables." Dani gave a mental shrug. She should probably eat more of both. "Today she needs my meatloaf sandwich and a piece of cake."

Nick brought Dani a plate of food, and at the first bite, she discovered Rosie was right. This was what she needed. Dani was grateful for the food, and for Rosie keeping the conversation going during the meal. It saved her from having to talk to her mother and kept her mother from grilling Nick.

After lunch, Nick left to pick up her prescriptions. Dani moved to bring her plate to the kitchen, but Rosie grabbed it from her, telling her to stay seated. Dani piled more pillows behind her and got back under the blanket, loving and needing the comfort. Otis came and dropped on the floor beside her since he didn't fit on the couch with her stretched out.

As Cynthia sat on the love seat looking uncomfortable, Dani tried to fill the silence. "I know the place is small, but there's a second bedroom, and you're welcome to stay there."

"Nonsense," Rosie said, coming over and placing a cup of tea on the table next to Dani. "You have to focus on healing, not having a guest. She'll stay with me and Helen."

"That's not necessary. I'm staying at the Castle on the Hill." Dani wasn't surprised. It was the fanciest place around. "Check in isn't until three, so I'll head over later this afternoon. Is there anything I can help you with in the meantime?"

The question sounded odd coming from her mother. Cynthia must be bored. Dani wasn't mad at Rosie for calling her mother, but she still couldn't understand what Cynthia was going to do while she was here. Dani hoped she wouldn't stay long. "Thanks, but resting doesn't require much." Dani closed her eyes to stave off any more talk. She must have fallen asleep because it seemed only a minute before Nick was next to her, rubbing her arm and telling her it was time for a pill. "I don't think I need it," she said.

"Which is why you should take it. You don't want pain medication wearing off completely before you add more. It's codeine, nothing too strong."

She took the pill and asked, "Where's Aunt Rosie?"

"She went back to the diner," Cynthia said. "She'll be here again tomorrow. Probably with more fried food and carbs."

Before she could say anything about her diet not being her mother's concern, Nick brought over Dani's Kindle and turned on the television. She was grateful for the distractions. At three, Cynthia left saying she'd be back in the morning, and at five, Laurel showed up also carrying bags of food.

Dani walked into the kitchen and watched as Laurel unpacked a mountain of containers onto the kitchen table and said, "There's enough food to last a week."

"Your weeks are different than mine. This would hardly survive an hour with my brothers." Since Laurel had seven, Dani knew the validity of the statement. "Besides, Sheridan is coming over in a bit, and I invited Eden and Janelle, too."

As her stomach clenched, the word came out before Dani could stop it. "Why?"

Laurel gave her a funny look. "What kind of question is that?"

Dani's throat closed over the answer that boomed in her head. *Because they're not really your friends. They'll turn on you, too.* Laurel must have seen something in Dani's features, because she stopped what she was doing and took Dani back to the couch. Grabbing her hands, Laurel said, "Stop. Stop thinking about those awful people and the things they said. Don't let them have that kind of power over you. You're here, and you're wonderful, and I won't let you forget it."

Just as Laurel had been the one she'd cried to when things ended with Nick, she'd told her friend about what happened with her work "friends." For years, Dani accepted their teasing and put-downs as part of the friendship, until they'd shown their true colors and she couldn't ignore the truth—they weren't her friends. She'd been job hunting when, less than a month later, Aunt Rosie told her about Doc Wheeler retiring. The timing had been perfect, and Dani had been so grateful. It was part of why she was determined to do everything right. "Thank you," she whispered, and gave Laurel a hug.

"Anytime," Laurel said. "Every time."

"Well, if the house is being invaded by women, I'll head out." Nick said. She'd forgotten he was there. She wondered what he'd heard and what he thought. "I'll be back in a few hours with Presley, and I'll stay overnight.

In the second bedroom," he added when Laurel shot him a look.

"You don't have to," Dani said automatically.

"Not negotiable. Rosie offered before she left, but I said I'd do it. You need to get a good night's sleep, and hopefully you will, but in case you need someone, I'll be here." Dani nearly argued, but the idea of Nick being there for her was more wonderful than she wanted to admit. She might as well enjoy having him around while she could.

An hour later, the place was bustling with noise and laughter. As unsure as she might be about the new friendships, Dani admitted she loved having them over, even when Eden, who was a physical therapist, did a cursory check of her bruises and range of motion. Dani teased Eden about being off the clock, but Eden insisted and then promised to teach her some yoga stretches to help the healing process. Dani couldn't deny she appreciated the care.

They talked about everything and nothing. About books they'd read and a movie that was coming in the fall that they were all looking forward to. "I wonder if Meryl Streep will be nominated for another Oscar," Dani said. "I'll watch anything she does."

"How many would that make for her?" Laurel asked.

"Twenty-one times, but only three wins," Dani answered without thinking.

"I cannot get over how much you always know about this," Janelle said. Dani listened for the derision but didn't hear any. "You'd be great to have around for trivia games. Hey, Laurel, why don't you do that at the brewery on a slower night? Trivia Tuesday or something."

Dani's skin grew icy. "No!" She didn't realize she'd shouted until she saw three sets of eyes staring at her.

Chapter Twenty-Six

♥

As the silence drew on, Dani wanted to sink under her covers and disappear. She knew it was a bad idea to have people over. Laurel scooted closer and put her arm around Dani. "Tell them. Trust them." It was one thing for Laurel to know, but Dani was embarrassed to talk about it, embarrassed to share what had her running here. What if they thought she was being silly?

Dani's need to feel safe warred with her need to feel connected. Connection won. "Back in March, I accidentally discovered that the people I thought were my friends didn't want me around."

The women looked confused, probably because nothing like this had ever happened to any of them. Sheridan asked, "How do you find out something like that accidentally?"

"By being unintentionally included in a group text." Dani's eyes watered, and she blinked rapidly. No, no more tears for those women. "My friends were my coworkers. I hung with them and a few of their friends after work. It was fun, or so I thought. We'd get together one or two nights a week, and our usual bar had a trivia night. As Janelle guessed, I'm really good. But I also have a competitive streak. One week I was scheduled to work and couldn't make it. Later that night I got a text that said, *Tonight was more fun losing without Dani than it was winning with her around.* The next several texts agreed. They didn't notice I was in the chat. I didn't say anything, but once I knew, I could see other places where I wasn't included. Weekend trips, movie nights. I don't know how I didn't notice it before. When I said something to a coworker, she shrugged it off with a sorry, but clearly it didn't bother her at all. I couldn't wait to get out of there. It's what got me to move back." Dani finished the story and waited. No one said anything.

Janelle broke the silence. "Those bitches." Her tone was so serious Dani burst out laughing. A moment later, everyone was giggling.

Once they'd gotten themselves under control, Sheridan said, "They were never your friends. You're better off without them."

"That's what I've told her," Laurel said, putting her head on Dani's shoulder.

"Absolutely," Janelle said, getting up to give Dani a quick hug. "We'll tell you to your face if we think you're being ridiculous."

Eden said, "And you know she'll do it." As Janelle sat back in her spot, she poked Eden with an elbow, which got them all laughing again. "I'm sorry for what happened, but glad for the result. As someone who had very few friends as a kid, I can honestly say that I love having you around."

The others added their agreement, and a part of Dani she hadn't realized she'd been protecting felt as though it burst free. They weren't here with her because they knew Laurel. They were here for her. Somehow, when she hadn't been looking, she'd created the circle of friends she'd always wanted.

Two hours later, they'd finished the brownies Eden brought when Nick arrived with Presley. They insisted she stay on the couch while they cleaned up in the kitchen before giving her gentle hugs goodnight. After they were gone, Dani snuggled under the blanket and accepted a cup of chamomile tea from Nick. "How are you doing?"

"Not bad," she said. "Tired, but glad they came by." It had been a more revealing night than she expected.

"You have good friends here."

Dani nodded and drank some tea. The personal side of her life was definitely working. The thought reminded her. "We still need to get that package together. The auction is..."

"Ten days away. I know. I'm working on it, and we're closer than you think. I'd promise everything is going to be fine, but I know my word isn't good yet."

"Nick—"

He held up a hand. "It's okay. I'm going to earn back your trust. Here, sit up and take your medicine." She did, and he sat on the couch next to her so she could rest on him. He made an excellent pillow. Presley and Otis were curled up on the other sofa. It was cozy. Then Nick said, "You went to vet school in Texas?"

Dani cringed. She'd forgotten her mother dropped that information. "Philadelphia was too close to New York. I needed a fresh start."

"You needed to put half a country between us?"

"It seemed logical at the time, and it's an excellent school." She was being vague and hoped he didn't push. She had loved her time in veterinary school. It was staying in Texas after graduation because she didn't know where else to go, that things had gotten difficult. She was grateful when he didn't ask anything else and instead turned on the television.

She knew he was catering to her when he agreed to stream *The Gilmore Girls* without a complaint and then asked, "Do you want to tell me something I don't know about the actors in the show?"

Nick had always known of her trivia fondness. "Kelly Bishop, the one playing Rory's mom? She was in the original cast of *A Chorus Line*, only then she went by Carole Bishop. She was also Baby's mom in *Dirty Dancing*."

She turned her attention to the show and fell asleep with her head on his shoulder before the second episode was over.

The next day, Dani didn't wake until almost nine. "Good morning," she said as she came from the bedroom and saw Nick on the couch, reading something on his tablet.

"Good morning to you, too." He got up and came over to give her a gentle kiss.

They went to the kitchen where coffee was waiting. Good. She didn't know what time her mother would be back, but she needed fortification before then. As she took out the creamer, she asked, "Did you put me to bed last night?"

"No, Otis did. You rolled onto his back, and he carried you in."

That was quite an image. "Very funny. Did you stay on the couch or in the other bedroom?"

"The bedroom."

"I'm sorry. I think I had stuff piled on the bed in there." She wasn't much of a housekeeper since it was only her and Otis.

"I'm perfectly capable of moving things to the dresser. I'm not your mother. You don't have to try to impress or please me." He always understood. Summer after summer, he got an earful on how her mother had driven her crazy the year before. "How are you feeling this morning?"

She rolled her shoulders and did a quick inventory. "Less sore. Still slow."

"Well, there's nothing on your calendar today but rest, relaxation, and more *Gilmore Girls.*"

"While my mother hovers nearby." How many hours could she nap?

He gave her a gentle hug before she sat down, holding her mug close. "Do you want me to stay so you don't have to be alone with her?"

She loved that he offered. "No, I can manage."

"I know you can, but you don't have to." He took eggs and bread out of her refrigerator, which was filling up with leftovers, and started breakfast.

"I appreciate that, but you mentioned getting things together for the package, right?"

"That's my plan."

To ensure the auction succeeded, she'd handle a few hours one-on-one with her mother. "Then that's what you should do. I'll be fine."

"If it gets horrible, call, and Presley and I will come over and rescue you. Or at least act as a go between."

"Thank you." It was good to know she could get help if she needed it. After finishing breakfast she said, "I want to take a shower this morning. Do you think you can stay close by, just in case?"

"Absolutely."

She managed the shower without a problem, although seeing all her bruises in the bathroom mirror had been a bit of a shock. By the time she had finished drying her hair, Cynthia arrived, impeccably dressed once again, and carrying bags from the market. Dani watched as Cynthia unpacked fruit, nonfat yogurt, and lemons. Lemon water—hot or cold—was Cynthia's go to drink to keep her weight in check. Dani could hardly look at them without shuddering. Guess her mother wouldn't be having any of the leftovers from the brewery for lunch. Too bad. More for her.

Soon after, Nick headed out, promising to call during the day and to be back for dinner. Dani went to the couch with her second cup of coffee and opened up an entertainment site on her tablet, hoping that reading about the madness of other people's lives would distract her. Maybe she should skip the coffee so that she could fall back to sleep. Being alone for long stretches with Cynthia was more uncomfortable than the bruises. Finally the silence got to her, and she said, "How was the Castle on the Hill? I've never stayed, but the events I've attended are always lovely."

"It was quite nice, and the breakfast had egg white omelets." Egg whites. The other staple after lemons in Cynthia's diet.

"How's Hugh?" Dani had forgotten to ask about her stepfather the day before.

"He's fine. Busy with work, as always." There was something in her mother's tone that had Dani wanting to ask more questions, but before she could, Cynthia continued. "I picked up an assortment of baked goods at that Just Right place when I drove by this morning, and I assume you have plenty of coffee. How much freezer space do you have?"

That was an odd change of conversation, especially since her mother didn't eat those things and didn't think Dani should either. "Plenty. Why do you ask?"

"For your visitors."

Maybe she was tired. Her mother wasn't making sense. "What visitors?"

"Unless things have changed—and I doubt that's possible—they will inundate you with casseroles before the day is over. It's what people do here when someone needs help. They cook and bring over various forms of pasta covered with cheese and swimming in cream-of-something soup."

"I haven't been here that long, Mom. I doubt that will happen." She remembered seeing casseroles on Nancy's table when she went to talk about the auction. She'd brought coloring books and art supplies for Nancy's kids, not trusting her skills in the kitchen. Maybe that would happen for her someday. If she continued to do a good job, then there would be a time when people would bring over food when she had a problem.

"Trust me. I recommend clearing a space on the kitchen counter and leaving the front door open an inch so guests can walk in, otherwise the doorbell will drive you crazy." Dani didn't argue and wondered what comments she'd hear from her mother when no one showed up. "You can get away without make up since you're just out of the hospital, but give your hair a brush before anyone arrives."

Dani smoothed down her hair in an automatic movement. She had brushed it, but what did it matter when she was going to want to pull it out several times before the day was over. She slid down into the couch and tried to disappear into her book.

Much to Dani's surprise, within two hours, people proved Cynthia right. Millie was the first to drop by, bringing a lasagna that smelled so good Dani was tempted to ask for a fork and eat it straight from the pan. That dish was not going in the freezer. Next came Ruth Wheeler, Doc Wheeler's wife, with "my famous Frito pie." She assured Dani that everything was under control at the clinic and not to rush back. Both women stayed nearly an hour talking with Dani and including Cynthia as much as possible before they insisted they needed to go and let Dani rest. Dani would have preferred they stay.

Nick called at lunch and through mouthfuls of lasagna, Dani assured him she was doing okay. A cookie bouquet was delivered that afternoon with a card telling her it was from Significant Paws, and Laurel's mom, Vivian, stopped by with beef stew and biscuits. Dani was grateful for their kindness and attention. It never ceased to amaze her how much she could feel cared for by almost anyone other than her mom.

It was Bea Turner's arrival that afternoon that most surprised Dani. Friends were one thing, but this was different. Before Bea could do more than step into the house and say hello, Dani's mother came out from the kitchen. Bea let out an unexpected squeak that had Otis picking up his head. "Cindy Kinsman? Is that really you?" This couldn't be good. No one called her mother Cindy.

"Trixie? I can't believe it." Her mother called Bea....? Dani was glad no one expected her to say anything because she was in shock.

"What a wonderful surprise. Let me put down this Shepherd's pie and give you a proper welcome."

Dani considered warning Bea not to hug her mother, but didn't know how to say that without it sounding horrible. Before she could come up with a distraction, Bea had her arms around Cynthia, and it looked to Dani like the hug was being returned. Clearly, she needed more sleep.

"How long has it been?" Bea took Cynthia's hand and walked them to the couch to sit.

"Long enough that we shouldn't say the number out loud," Cynthia said with a laugh Dani would have sworn was genuine.

"Too true. Dani, I met your mother freshman year of high school. We were cheerleaders, if you can believe it." Dani was still trying to wrap her head around the warmth between the two women. Bea turned her attention back to Cynthia. "I was so worried when I heard about Dani's accident. She's a wonderful doctor, you know. She took care of my Chandler not too long ago." Bea took out her phone and showed Cynthia pictures of the dog. From there, conversation moved to children and husbands. Dani tuned out after a while, still marveling at a side of her mother she couldn't remember seeing before, not even with women Cynthia called friends.

Bea stayed until Beth came by. As the vet tech put more food in the kitchen and came to sit by Dani, Cynthia walked Bea to her car. Beth filled Dani in on things at the clinic. Dani didn't like hearing how easy it was for them to get along without her. Dani made a mental note to get back to work as soon as possible. Maybe she'd do a half day on Saturday. Once Beth left and she was alone again with her mother, Dani said, "So, you and Bea were friends... and cheerleaders?"

Cynthia gave a smile. "We were. It was a bit of a shock to see her standing in your living room, but I admit it was nice catching up with her."

Dani liked the unfamiliar warmth in her mother's voice. "Do you think you'll stay in touch?"

"Oh, I don't know." Her mother gave a wave of her hand, which was a sign that Cynthia didn't want to talk about it anymore, but Dani was curious. She knew almost nothing of her mother's time growing up other than the fact that Cynthia couldn't wait to leave this town.

"When was the last time you saw her?"

"Probably when we were both home the summer after my freshman year in college. Although if I remember correctly, she'd met Dennis Turner by then, so she was busy with him. That was the last time I was here for more than a week. It didn't occur to me I might see some familiar faces beyond your aunts while I was here. Foolish of me."

Dani wanted to ask more, but if she was reading her mother's face right, the conversation was over. She'd have to hope they'd get another chance. For now, she wouldn't push. "I know I haven't done anything today but talking with everyone has wiped me out. I'm going to go to my room to rest."

"Do you need help?"

Instead of automatically dismissing the offer, Dani accepted. "I might. I'm stiffer after I've been sitting for a while."

"That's why you should probably go for a walk rather than take a nap." Ah, there was the kind of help Dani expected from her mother. Still, as she got comfortable in bed, Dani couldn't stop thinking about the side of her mother that came out while Bea was here—or the fact that Bea had stopped by at all. Between last night with her friends and the visitors today, Dani couldn't stop herself from hoping that she was finding the connection she dreamed of.

Chapter
Twenty-Seven

♥

That morning, Nick was reluctant to leave Dani alone with her mom. He'd heard stories of Cynthia, none of them good. Lousy mothers were something he and Dani had in common, although his mother was absent and spent most of her time with a bottle of alcohol, and Dani's was strict and spent most of her time criticizing. Every summer, Dani arrived in Fable Notch looking too stressed and too thin. For at least two weeks, she would worry about gaining weight because of her Aunt Rosie's cooking, and she'd be so self-conscious, she'd wear a shirt over her bathing suit when they went swimming.

He sat in the car with Presley and considered staying to be a buffer, but there were things he needed to do which had to be done in person. And he needed to look professional, so he drove home, showered, and changed into something business casual—chinos and a button-down shirt with the one tie he'd brought. He wanted to make a good impression on the people he was seeing in the hopes they would forgive or at least overlook the mistake he'd made two days before. And there was a second package he had to create.

He'd discovered yesterday, through calls and emails, that he couldn't get everyone together again, but people were available at different times individually. That was good enough. He was going to visit with more than half a dozen vendors, see what each was willing to offer and, hopefully, by the time he got back to Dani's later he'd have some good news for her.

Part of him still couldn't believe she'd forgiven him. If it hadn't been so close to the Festival, she probably would have tried to replace him. Dani's acceptance fueled his determination to make this right for her. He'd had one text from Terry yesterday and as much as he was curious about how the deal was going, Nick didn't want to be distracted. His focus for the next several days was helping Dani get well and making this auction a success.

She'd looked exhausted when he'd come to her house last night, although whether that was because of her injuries or her friends, he couldn't say. He'd been glad she'd slept through the night. He hadn't. He'd woken several times and gone to her door, cracking it open to hear her breathing. By the time she'd come to the kitchen, he was most of the way through his third cup of coffee.

His first stop was the Castle on the Hill, where Robin asked after Dani before they got down to business. The hotel agreed to include the room for two nights, dinner the first night, and breakfast delivered to the room the next day. From there, Nick went to the Oasis Spa, which donated two massage therapists to go to the Castle and give in-room side-by-side massages. When he finished with the third vendor, he had a certificate for a Saturday night dinner for two on the Mountain Train, which was a tourist favorite and something even locals indulged in for special occasions. As he looked at the list of what the package would include, he found himself thinking about what it would be like to have a weekend like this with Dani. What would they do with that kind of time together?

But they couldn't have that.

What they were sharing was wonderful and special, but temporary. He could see how happy she was here, how she belonged. And he had plans to get back to.

Is that still what you want?

He didn't like the question or that the answer wasn't as easy as it was a month before. Last night, sitting on the couch with Dani while the dogs slept nearby was the most relaxed Nick could remember being. While she watched her favorite show, which he still thought was awful, he'd taken out his sketch book. He'd drawn the inner floor plan of her house and, remembering what he'd said to her mother about how the place could be expanded in the future, he'd add a few pages of renovation options. He should show them to her. Someday she might want more space, maybe for a family of her own.

His gut cramped at the thought. In the not-too-distant future, he'd be back in his office and Dani would be here. She'd start a life with some other man, have children with him, adopt more dogs. He pushed the thought away as quickly as he could, not wanting to acknowledge the jealousy. He was being ridiculous. What they had was only for now. He would never ask her to leave what she was creating for herself here.

With an hour before his next meeting, he drove over to the diner, knowing Rosie would appreciate an update on Dani. It was one thirty when he arrived, and the place wasn't too busy, so he took a booth and spread out the folders with auction information as he waited for his lunch. He was about to open his sketch book when his food arrived with company.

"Thought you weren't on site because you were busy. But look at you. Taking a leisurely lunch in the middle of the day."

Nick looked up from his notes to see Ed standing next to Rosie. The grin told him Ed was teasing. "Man's got to eat."

"That he does. Can I join you?"

"Absolutely." Nick moved the pages into a folder and placed the sketch book on top.

"Rosie, I'll have the French dip too," Ed said, acknowledging Nick's food with a nod of his head as he sat. Ed sipped the coffee Rosie automatically placed in front of him and asked, "How's Dani?"

"Better. It wasn't as bad as it could have been. Did you hear it was my fault?"

Ed frowned. "No, I heard the other driver was looking at his phone and ran the red light."

"That's not what I meant." Nick told Ed about missing the meeting and how Dani never should have been on the road. "If I'd done what I was supposed to, she wouldn't have been hurt."

"People make mistakes. It's what you do about them that makes the difference."

"I know, but that's why plans are so important. When you stick to the plan, then there are no mistakes. You understand. What would happen if someone didn't stick to the plan when building a house?"

Ed gave a snort, and Nick wished he could raise a single eyebrow like Theo did. "Do you honestly think we never make mistakes, even with a blueprint? Or that the original plan accurately estimates how long something is going to take? How do you think construction ends up behind? Things go wrong all the time, Nick. Especially in relationships. You want to hear how many times I've screwed up over the years? I'm sure Leslie can give you a list. There's a limit to what you can control. It's better to learn how to manage when there's a problem than live life trying to avoid problems in the first place."

Nick took a bite of his sandwich instead of answering. He'd grown up with so little control, and so many problems he wanted to solve, he didn't enjoy hearing about limits. He had to believe there was a way to guarantee the outcome he wanted. He had a plan to make things up to Dani, the beginnings of a plan for getting back to New York, and future plans that would ensure his success and security. Wouldn't they?

"Nick?"

He'd gotten lost in his thoughts and hadn't heard Ed. "Sorry. One more time?"

"Is Dani mad at you over what happened?"

"She was at first, but she forgave me." He was still stunned and grateful. "Don't know why."

"You don't? I can think of several reasons."

Nick was saved from asking what Ed meant when his phone buzzed. He looked at the caller ID and said, "I need to take this. It's about my next meeting. Give me a second." He grabbed a folder and his phone and took the call in the parking lot, not wanting to have the noise of the diner in the background. Ten minutes later, he came back to the table. His food was gone, and Ed was eating. "Did you swipe my lunch?"

Ed laughed. "No, when Rosie brought my sandwich, I told her you were taking a call. She put yours under the heater to keep it warm."

"And now I'm bringing it back," she said as his plate magically reappeared.

"Thanks, Rosie. You always know the right thing to do."

"Ha," she said. "Tell that to my wife."

"More reminders that mistakes are part of relationships?" Nick said.

"They're part of life," Ed chimed in, and Rosie agreed before she left them alone. "I'll tell you what's not a mistake, though. These drawings."

"What are you talking about?" That was when Nick noticed Ed flipping through the pages of his sketch book.

"I hope you don't mind, but after watching you draw while on your breaks, I was curious. These are good, especially this one of the ranch."

Nick looked at the picture. It was the one of Dani's house. "It's nothing. Something to keep my mind busy."

"It's more than that, and you know it. You always did have an eye for building. This design is solid, and if you don't mind, I'd like to take a few pictures and show it to a client."

Nick was confused. "What client?"

"A young couple came by the office yesterday. They bought a small house like Dani's and plan to expand it before they move in. They showed me some of the designs they found on the Internet and wanted to know if it was doable. I have to tell you, your design is better than anything they are considering."

Nick was floored. As a kid, he'd never shown his designs to anyone other than his brothers and Dani. He'd only shown Ed his ideas once it came time to fix his old house. With a shrug he hoped covered a buzz of excitement he didn't expect or know what to do with, Nick said, "It's not really a design. It's barely a sketch."

"It's not much different from the one we used to renovate your old place. Gene and I had no trouble turning your sketches into a solid plan. And I know you hired an architect for the new house, but I'll guess it was the easiest job he ever did after you showed him what you wanted."

Nick couldn't stop the smirk. The architect had said almost exactly that. Years of building the place in his mind and making a thousand sketches meant there was very little for the professional to do. He had a framed picture in his office of the drawing that most looked like the finished house. "Feel free to share the sketches. I'll be curious to hear what they think."

Nick couldn't deny he liked that Ed thought his drawings were interesting enough to show a client. The result wouldn't change his plans, but he was curious what, if anything, might come of it.

Chapter Twenty-Eight

N ick arrived as Dani was putting dinner in the oven to heat. She wasn't sure which casserole it was, but it hardly mattered. In all the years they'd known each other, tonight may have been the happiest she'd been to see him. The day had been punctuated by tiny but consistent pieces of criticism. Otis got twice as many walks as usual, although they weren't long because Dani tired more easily than she expected. Anything to spend a few minutes away from Cynthia. "These walks of yours are too short to do you any good." "Where did you ever find this furniture?" "How do you manage with such a big dog underfoot?"

When Dani offered no other dinner options but the comfort food, her mother decided it was time to leave. Dani was more than ready to see her go. After dinner—and another piece of Aunt Rosie's Boston cream pie, so there, Mom—she and Nick sat on the couch watching television. He'd brought her a copy of *People* magazine, and she forced him to watch *Bridgerton*. He lasted twenty minutes—ten minutes longer than she would have guessed—before he took out his sketchbook and a pencil. She snuggled against him and let herself get lost in the romance and intrigue of the story.

When the episode ended, she turned to face him and asked, "What are you drawing?"

"The usual, a house."

"I like that you still do that."

"Truthfully, I haven't in years. I've been too busy, as you know." He held up a hand before she could say anything. "It's okay. Work has taken up all my time. That's how I wanted it. But these last few weeks have been eye opening, to say the least. It's been good to remember things I've missed. I found out today Ed wants to show one of my drawings to a client." He told her about his conversation at the diner.

That was intriguing. "You may sell one of your home designs?"

"Well, I don't know if I can charge for it. I'm not a professional, but it would be kind of cool to have someone build something I drew."

She heard the pleasure in his voice, and as she turned back to the television to watch one more episode, she remembered how, when they were young, she thought Nick should be an architect. Who better to design homes than a man who ached for one? But once he discovered the lucrative possibilities of finances, that was his focus. Of course, that fit well with the challenges of his childhood as well and was, as he liked to point out, more controllable. Still, she marveled at him enjoying both his time working with Ed, and drawing. Not that it meant anything for them, she reminded herself, but it was good to see this side of him again and know it hadn't been completely crushed by years in the city.

An hour later, as the credits rolled and the streaming service tempted her with another episode, Dani let out a large yawn. Nick laughed. "That was worthy of the pups. Time for bed." He stood and held out his hand.

"I don't know how I'm so tired after not doing anything all day. Guess criticism gets exhausting."

Nick gave her a hug, which she needed. "I'll stay with you tomorrow. That should dilute her attention."

"Stay with me tonight, too." The words were out before she thought about them. Maybe it was the heat of the show influencing her, but she wanted him near, wanted to be held.

"Of course. Wasn't planning to go anywhere."

"In my bed."

He pushed a stray hair out of her face and gave her a soft kiss. "Dani, are you sure that's a good idea?"

In these two weeks she'd seen the Nick she'd known and loved, the man with whom she could be herself and know she was accepted. The man she'd missed that last summer. Yes, his call from New York had led to her current situation, but he hadn't been drawn back into work. In fact, he was more attentive than ever. "Please, I've had a long day of listening to my mother take shots at my house, my job... pretty much all of my choices. I could use the comfort."

Nick looked indecisive, then said, "We're going to sleep. You still need rest."

"No argument." Her bruises needed a little more healing, although wasn't sex supposed to be good for that? Maybe she'd try to find out. But not tonight.

It took a little while for them to get the arrangement right with both dogs on the bed, but before long, Dani had her head on Nick's shoulder as they both read, and shortly after, she dropped into a peaceful sleep.

Friday morning, they were finishing breakfast when Nick's phone rang. "It's Ed. I'll be right back." While he was in the bedroom, Cynthia arrived for the day with more lemons and a bag from A Thousand Lives, the local independent bookstore. Before Dani could ask what books Cynthia bought, her mother took out copies of *Town and Country* and *Vanity Fair*. No surprise.

Dani was sitting in her usual spot on the couch when Nick came in and looked from Cynthia to Dani before saying, "Ed had someone cancel on him at the dance studio site and asked if I could join Gene and his team. Will you be okay if I head over there for a few hours?"

Don't leave me with her. "Not a problem. It's great that you can help. Eden will appreciate it."

"I thought you were in finance, Nick. Why are you doing construction?" said Cynthia, stepping in from the kitchen. Dani could smell the lemon in her drink and hear the disapproval in her voice.

"I am, but I've been working with the Franks on some projects while I'm in town. It's nice not to be behind a desk all the time."

Dani was surprised to hear Nick say that even though he'd clearly been enjoying the work. She still imagined him ticking the days off in his head as though he were in prison. Maybe this time hadn't been all bad for him.

After a few hours of television and reading, and another short walk with Otis, Dani looked at her watch and noticed it was after noon. She gave a stretch and glanced at her mother, who was deep into an article. "Mom, I'm going to make myself some lunch. Can I get you anything?"

Peering over the top of the glossy cover, Cynthia said, "Oh, I don't know. What if we went out for lunch?"

"Really?" Her mother wanted them to go out together? "We could go to the Seven Brothers Brewery which Laurel runs. Or the Just Right Café. They've got more than baked goods."

Her mother's features pinched at the recommendations. "Isn't there anything a little... nicer? Maybe something at one of the ski resorts?"

Dani forgot who she was talking to. Of course her mother wasn't interested in the places Dani enjoyed going to. Any place her mother wanted would likely require Dani to change into something other than leggings and a t-shirt. As she tried to think of a place to go, all she could picture were previous lunches and dinners out where Cynthia criticized what Dani was wearing or what she ordered, then spent the meal looking at the other women around them.

If Cynthia felt she was better dressed, the meal and the rest of the day went well. If Cynthia found herself lacking, it would mean an expensive shopping trip to improve her look. If she saw someone Dani's age who looked better than Dani, the criticism would start, new clothes would appear in Dani's closet—and some of her comfy favorites would disappear—and no sweets would be brought into the house until her stepfather complained there was nothing for dessert.

Dani must have been silent for too long because Cynthia asked, "Where should we go?"

Dani was exhausted just thinking of going out. "Never mind. I appreciate the thought, but I think I'll heat something up. I'm due to take my prescription, and that makes me need rest." So what if she wasn't planning to take a pill. Her mother didn't need to know that.

"Fine. I may go out while you sleep again," Cynthia said. Dani hoped that would be the end of it, but her mother added, "Remember, eating and taking a nap is a recipe for weight gain. Maybe another walk first?"

As if her mother knew the recipe for anything. Dani grabbed her tablet, went to the kitchen, and ate there. One reason she lost weight after the summer wasn't only because Cynthia had such specific food choices in the house, but because eating around her mother made Dani self-conscious. The one time Dani could remember Cynthia approving of how she looked was after a nasty bout of food poisoning Dani had before a spring dance at the club. Dani had to literally make herself sick to please her mother. She hated that she was censoring herself because her mother was here, making choices to make the other woman happy—or at least less annoyed. She'd regressed twenty years in less than seventy-two hours.

After lunch, she called the clinic to tell them she'd be stopping by the next morning, and then took a walk.

Otis needed it, she told herself. When they returned, she discovered her mother had gone out. She'd take the quiet reprieve. She wondered how much longer Cynthia would stay and if there was anything Dani could do to hasten her leaving.

But then something occurred to Dani. In a few days, Cynthia would leave, and Dani would have her life back. Her life—here. Where she wanted to be, in a job she adored, surrounded by people she loved. That was what mattered. She didn't have to do or say anything to please Cynthia. Making her mother happy wasn't important.

She let out a happy sigh as she snuggled under the covers. Too bad she hadn't realized this years ago.

Chapter
Twenty-Nine

♥

Later that afternoon, Nick and Cynthia arrived at the same time. For dinner they heated Bea's Shepherd's pie, and her mother made a salad to go with it. Cynthia's plate was more than half covered with the greens, and she'd barely touched the main course, which was too bad because it was delicious. Cynthia said good night soon after, and Dani and Nick cleaned up in the kitchen.

"Good thing I was an expert at Tetris as a kid," Nick said as he worked to find room for the food in the refrigerator. "I've got to ask, does your mother eat anything other than salad and tuna?"

"Chicken breasts as long as they don't have a lot of sauce or anything."

Nick gave a visible shudder, making Dani laugh. "I think I'd go crazy. Was she always like this?"

"Yes. It all goes back to how things look. Weight, clothes, what car she drove, that's what's important. What people thought of you came in close second." Dani hated that the latter still worried her more than she wanted to admit.

"Now I understand why you were so skinny when you arrived in the summer."

Dani put a hand on her stomach, the reaction automatic. "I've probably gained more weight than I should have since moving back here."

Nick came over and put his arms around her. "In case you haven't noticed, I think you look amazing. Sexy as hell." He kissed her gently, but when he pulled her close, he accidentally pressed a spot that was still tender. When she gave a gasp that had nothing to do with pleasure, he stopped. "I'm sorry. I didn't mean—"

"I know. Guess I'm not fully healed. I'm great at reminding owners not to rush their pets' healing, but not so good with myself."

"I have something that will make you feel better." He took her hand and led her to the couch. "Wait here," he said, and went out of the house. A moment later, she heard his car door opening. She couldn't imagine what he was getting. He came back with two brightly wrapped boxes.

As he presented them with a flourish and a smile, she saw the boy she'd once known. The one who loved when she beat him at video games, who listened to her dreams and worries equally, and who'd stolen her heart.

Her pulse jumped. *Uh oh.*

"Open this one first." He handed her the smaller of the two. It was light and wrapped in paper with shooting stars, and she couldn't tell what was inside. She gave it a shake, but that didn't help. Finally, she opened it. Inside was a box of chocolate truffles from The Chocolate Bar and an envelope from the Oasis Spa with a gift card for an hour massage. "Thank you. These are some of my favorite chocolates. I may not even share them with you. And I could definitely use the massage."

"These are more than gifts." The glee in his voice had her smiling but confused. "Open the second and see if you can guess."

The second package was the size of a shoe box and covered in paper with bright colored balloons and a huge bow stuck in the center. It looked like a child's birthday present. Inside, she found a toy truck with the logo from the Tree-to-Tree Adventure Park and a gift certificate for a hot fudge sundae at the Bright Spot. She was thoroughly confused. Not that she didn't enjoy ice cream, but the toy didn't make sense. And what did it have to do with chocolates and massages?

Then she made the connection. "Are these for the packages?"

"They are." With a flourish, Nick brandished two pieces of paper and held them up. "Everything on our lists has been committed. Two complete packages—one for couples, and one for families. Bidding should start at $750 minimum, and I think we'll easily see that go over $1,000."

"You did it! This is wonderful," she said with a squeal and threw herself into his arms, boxes and papers falling onto the floor, dogs barking in curiosity at the sound. "Thank you, Nick. Thank you."

"It was the least I could do after—"

She pulled out of his embrace to take his face in her hands. "Stop. What happened, happened. No more looking back. I am so excited about this. Wait until everyone hears about it. There's never been anything like this for the auction. Even Nancy is going to be impressed." He'd done this because he knew how important it was to her, and she was touched.

"We've got to get the word out," Nick said, breaking her out of her thoughts. "I've got an appointment with Chris to make a video with images from all the donors for the social media sites."

She scrambled around the living room, looking for her bag of auction things. Pulling out her notebook, she said, "I'll call Mayor Brenda and see if she has any recommendations. Maybe we could set up a special table for these items at the Community Center, and of course, we'll list it on the event's website page."

"What about the site where people can bid in advance?"

Dani was confused. "What bidding in advance? Everything is done that night."

"What about people who want to bid but can't come? You're relying on the people who can attend to raise over $25,000?"

The look of shock on his face had her hesitant to answer. "Yes. What else can we do?"

"Put it online on an auction site. We need to attract money from anyone who's ever visited Fable Notch and might want to come back."

She still didn't know what he was talking about. "You mean like eBay?"

"No, we need to contact one of the sites that specializes in fundraising events." Nick grabbed a notepad and pen and sat next to her as he started making notes. "There are several things we can do. We don't want to put everything online because then people at the event might be outbid before things even start, but for these packages, we need to get everyone who's ever visited Fable Notch to hear about it. Then we need to tell the Planning Committee to spread the word so that everyone involved is sharing this on their social media pages and with friends."

"Nick, I don't understand." His enthusiasm was great, but he wasn't making sense. "What are you talking about?"

He stopped writing and turned to her. "There are online silent auction sites that host events for free. Once the items are listed, word of mouth will do the rest." He returned to writing while researching things on his phone at the same time. "We need some good graphics and a QR code for all the businesses. Something visitors can scan to check out the auction and bid while they're in the mood."

Dani enjoyed his excitement. It was contagious. This was sounding better by the moment. "How do you know about this?"

"Henry ran a fundraiser a little over a year ago for his firm's charitable foundation. It was a rite of passage for new vice presidents at his company. It got competitive to see if the newest team could outdo the year before. His team beat their goal by a crazy amount because they used this site. Leave it to Henry to help me again. I can't believe I didn't think of it sooner."

"How is Henry?" Nick stopped working as though someone had hit a freeze button. "I probably should have asked before, but you didn't mention him. I assume this means the two of you are still close. What's he doing these days other than being a vice president?"

When Nick turned to her, the color was gone from his face, and the look of grief stopped her heart.

Chapter Thirty

♥

Dani's innocent question reminded Nick he hadn't told anyone other than Theo about Henry. The pain in his chest radiated out until his whole body was tense. He wanted to change the subject. Rewind time by thirty seconds to the elation he had a moment before.

When he didn't say anything, Dani scooted closer to him and took his hand. "Nick, what happened?"

One more time. He could say it one more time. "He died. Last February."

Dani gasped. "How's that possible? An accident?"

Of course she'd think that. Young men didn't die any other way. "According to the autopsy, he suffered from hypertrophic cardiomyopathy."

"I studied that. Dogs and cats can get it, too. It's genetic and incurable but treatable. He didn't get help?"

Nick fiddled with the pen still in his hands. "You can get help if there are symptoms. In Henry's case, he was asymptomatic until it was too late. One minute everything was fine, and then he was gone."

Dani's eyes welled with tears. "I don't know how I'd handle it if something happened to Laurel. Especially so suddenly."

"There are times I still don't believe it. I expect to hear from him. See him. It's only been in the last month that I've stopped reaching for my phone to call him." He hadn't done it once since being back in Fable Notch.

"I don't know what to say. I'm sorry isn't enough, but it's all I can think of."

"That's all anyone says along with 'Are you okay?' Over and over. It's probably why I got good at saying 'Thank you, I'm fine.' I hoped it would be true. It wasn't."

She let go of his hand and threw herself into his arms, hugging him tightly and bursting into tears. He wanted to look at her, but her arms felt too good. There had been no one to comfort him after Henry died, no one to talk to about the loss because outside of Henry, there was no one he was close to.

After a few minutes, she loosened her grip and moved her head to his shoulder. "I know what he meant to you, and I know he loved you."

He wiped the tears from her face and gave her a gentle kiss. "Thank you."

"For what?"

"For being someone in my life who knew him and cared about him. Who understands what he meant to me. Even for crying. I haven't cried since it happened. Is it any wonder my body or brain or whatever decided to shut down?"

Dani tilted her head. "What does that mean?"

The job. Henry. Time for the final piece. He had to trust that he could tell Dani. "After Henry died, I dove into work. What else did I have? Unfortunately, even though I was working hard, I was working blindly. I made a serious of foolish investments that Henry warned me against and..." He stopped and took a breath. This was going to be hard to say out loud. "And lost my entire portfolio."

"Holy shit!" Dani put a hand to her mouth, as if surprised by her own words. "I didn't... I can't believe..."

"That about sums it up." He pushed away from her, stood, and paced. "It gets worse. After the meeting, where it became apparent there was no way to fix the problem with the deal I was working on, I started having chest pains. In seconds, my heart was racing out of control. I was sweating so much, my shirt was soaked." Like it had been after she'd been in her accident. "I could hear my blood rushing in my ears. I called out to my assistant who took one look at me and called 911. I remember thinking, 'This is it. Henry and I are going to go out the same way.'"

What he didn't share was how in those moments when he was certain he was going to die, he'd thought of Dani and wished he had a way to reach out to her, to tell her he was sorry he had screwed things up with her and how he never stopped caring. He turned to Dani, and she reached out her hand to pull him back. He sat next to her, looking at their entwined hands then up to her face. The truth of his emotions hit him.

It was more than he'd never stopped caring—he'd never stopped loving her. Unfortunately, he didn't know what he was supposed to do with this knowledge. His breath hitched, his heart rate increased. This was going to be a problem.

"What was wrong?"

I'm in love with you, that's what's wrong. Oh, she was talking about when he collapsed. "Absolutely nothing. It was a panic attack. The social worker who came to see me said it was from unprocessed grief and being too single-minded. Guess you were right about how bad that could be for a person."

She looked sad. For him. His heart squeezed. "I didn't want to be right. I wanted you to be happy. I still do."

He squeezed her hand. "The morning they discharged me from the hospital, my boss came in and told me I was suspended. Three months administrative leave, no salary."

"So that's how you ended up here."

"After spending the first six weeks moping around the city, not doing much of anything or seeing anyone except a therapist." He gave a shrug. "Now you know everything. All the ways I screwed up my life."

He looked at her and waited. The silence was killing him. He felt wrung out, exposed. He needed her to say something, ask more questions, give him something to react to. Even say 'I told you so.' Instead, she put a hand on his cheek and her features softened, her gaze dropping to his lips.

He knew she would kiss him the moment before she did. He ran his hands through her hair, loving the little purr of pleasure she gave in encouragement. Her hand moved from his face to the sensitive skin behind his ear, then stroked down his neck. He couldn't stop the shiver and deepened the kiss in response. He wanted her with a fierceness that took his breath away.

The feel of her body drew him in, away from the pain and loss. The more he kissed her, the less he hurt. If he let things continue, he could bury himself inside of her, lose himself, and forget about everything. It was a tempting thought. He was about to carry her to the bedroom when something in him said, 'No, not tonight.' Ignoring what happened and distracting himself was what he'd been doing for months. It didn't help, and it wasn't good for him. And Dani deserved more than him using her so he could forget what a mess his life was. He pulled back from the kiss and said, "Dani, we need to stop."

"Don't worry, we'll avoid my bruises," she said, kissing his jaw and nearly distracting him. "I'm hardly sore, although there are a few places I wouldn't mind being sore."

"That's not what I meant. I don't think we should do this tonight." He watched the pain of rejection flood her eyes. "Stop. Don't go there. It's not that I don't want you. God, I always want you. I've practically had to sit on my hands for the last few days, having you so close and knowing I shouldn't do anything to slow your healing. Wanting you never stops. Even last night as you slept, it took everything not to ravage you. This is about where I'm bruised. I'm afraid taking you to bed will be about running from my thoughts and feelings by using sex. I know from experience it doesn't work, and I end up feeling worse afterward. I don't want that with you. Please, can we do something else?"

He watched as his words sifted through her brain. He hoped she would understand and not think this was a rejection, but he'd had years of meaningless sex that was nothing but a distraction. Having experienced something different with her, he didn't want to use her by falling into bed for the wrong reason. She gave him a soft, quick kiss. "What do you want?"

"Will you be there for me tonight?" The words hung there. He'd never said them to anyone, never asked for that kind of help or support. If she said no, if she laughed, he didn't know what he'd do.

She didn't take long before saying, "I'm here, and happy to be." Simple words. They meant the world to him. "Tell me everything."

And he did. He talked about Henry, losing the money, and how scared he was about what was coming. How he didn't know if he'd be able to pick up where he'd left off or earn back what he'd lost. He didn't add the additional doubts that had been swirling in his head the last few days.

"No wonder that call from your co-worker distracted you," she said. "I knew getting your job back was important, but not all that was on the line."

"It was the first time I saw a possibility. I wish the timing had been better."

"Me, too," she said, then gestured to the boxes on the table. "But it all worked out."

And much to his surprise, it had. For the first time in months, something he did worked.

When they got into bed, nothing had ever felt more right than having her in his arms. Her warmth, the scent of the shampoo she used, all brought him a sense of calm he could never get from a prescription.

He thought she'd fallen asleep when she asked, "You never stopped wanting me?"

He smiled. What was one more thing to admit to amid all he told her tonight? "Not since the day you left New York."

Chapter Thirty-One

♥

T he bed was crowded when Dani woke, and she loved it. Nick, the dogs. This is what happiness felt like. She wanted to curl closer to him, but if she moved, the dogs would wake and want to go out. It was a dilemma. She decided being closer to him was worth it. She wasn't going to get more sleep anyway. In the temporary quiet, she took in how sexy Nick looked. His hair was sticking out at odd angles, he needed a shave, and there'd never been anyone else she wanted to wake up with.

Oh, it was going to hurt when he left. But at least when it happened, she'd not only have a lot of support around her, but she'd know that the reason they weren't together was because they wanted different things, not because she was inadequate. She could accept that. He had his career, and she had hers.

For now, he was here, and she was going to enjoy what she could. She rolled over and put her head on his chest. His arm came around her automatically, and the canine shifting began.

"Good morning," he said. She liked the sound of his voice husky from sleep, but as soon as he spoke, Presley's head came up and she tried to get between them. "She's better than my alarm clock. Can't stay in bed with her clamoring to get out."

"No sleeping in when you're a dog owner. I've seen more than one couple argue about who's doing the morning routine." Dani considered clamoring for what she wanted.

"Fortunately, I'm a morning person, as much as I'd like to linger here." He kissed her softly, and she agreed. Lingering sounded good. Otis barked. "Relax, puppy. We're not getting distracted. We know what you need."

"I'll start the coffee and take them out. You get a little more rest." She gave a wolf whistle as his boxer brief clad bottoms made their way to the bathroom and was rewarded with a chuckle and a wiggle. The dogs followed him, and she heard a "Oh, for Pete's sake, let me pee," as she rolled into the warm space he left. Yes, this was a lovely way to wake up.

She stretched and noted how much better she was feeling. Less sore, which was good since she was going into work. The clinic was opened until one on Saturdays, so it was the perfect day to return. She didn't think her absence would suddenly make Doc Wheeler change his retirement plans, but she didn't want to lose the progress she'd made. Besides needing the chance to use her brain a bit, she needed a good reason not to see her mother for a few hours. Dani told Cynthia before she left not to come by until later, and her mom didn't seem disappointed. Dani didn't think Cynthia was enjoying this trip any more than she was. Which made her wonder, not for the first time, why her mom had come in the first place.

Fortunately, she was healing well. She'd been telling Nick the truth about that, and this morning, she realized she'd slept easily with no painkillers. When she heard Nick return with the dogs, she got out of bed, put dog print leggings on under her t-shirt, and headed to the kitchen to join him. "You'll drive me to work today, right?"

He nodded as he sipped his coffee. "Are you sure about going in? Don't you think you should take it easy a little longer?"

"Unlike you, I'm not building a house. I won't lift any animals bigger than a guinea pig, and I'll be done by one. Please, you have to take me. I don't get my rental car until Monday, assuming all the paperwork goes through." The only thing more frustrating than her mother had been dealing with the insurance companies. She'd have to go car shopping soon, but that was a worry for another week. "Please?" She fluttered her eyelids, and he laughed.

"Fine, but only because I think you'll walk if I don't agree." Dani said nothing. She had been considering it because staying home another full day was going to drive her insane.

Less than an hour later, Nick waited until she got into the clinic safely, like a parent dropping their child off at school. The bell over the door rang and the familiar sounds and smells warmed her heart. She missed coming in. Beth greeted her with a gentle hug and a lot of enthusiasm. The day went smoothly, and her last patient made coming in worth it.

"We're so glad you're here," said Grace Duncan. Her daughter, Molly, had become the very happy owner of a guinea pig three months earlier, and Dani had been there to assure the shy young girl that she was going to make a wonderful pet mommy. "We heard about your accident, and Molly almost didn't want to come because she wanted to see you." *Me. Not Doc Wheeler.* Dani gave the guinea pig her checkup and assured Molly she was doing a wonderful job. She listened to the girl go on about what treats the animal liked and how they played together. Dani loved seeing how much more confident Molly was and was glad that a pet could do that for her.

By the time the Duncan's left, Dani's energy was flagging. Nick was going to have an "I tried to tell you" moment. She made a mental note to send Doc Wheeler a message to say she'd prefer to be at half her normal schedule for the coming week.

When she went into the backroom, Dani was surprised to see Doc still there. She'd expected him to leave after his last patient an hour before. Immediately she worried she'd rushed her return and had made a mistake somewhere this morning. "Is everything okay?"

He looked side to side, as though wondering who she was talking to. "Absolutely. Why wouldn't it be?"

"I thought you'd gone home. I didn't miss something, did I?"

"Not that I noticed." He gestured to the pile in front of him. "Apparently, I've gotten used to having a second doctor in the last four months and forgotten how much paperwork even a few days of office visits can generate."

She pulled up a chair to get to work. She had time before Nick arrived. "I'm sorry. I know there's a lot to catch up on and—"

"Dani, that wasn't a criticism. You're doing a terrific job."

Dani took a deep breath and let it out with a sigh. "You're sure?"

He looked at her as though she'd asked if dogs had six legs. "Of course I am. Why would you even ask?"

Oh, I don't know. Three days of seeing my mother and being reminded at nearly every turn where I'm doing something wrong. "I guess I still worry about letting you down. I don't want you to regret your decision to retire."

"Sit down," he said as he opened up the bottom drawer of the desk where she normally worked and took out a bag of M&M's. "You look like you could use a few of these."

"Always," she said, and ripped open the bag. As she filled her mouth, a thought occurred to her. "You knew about my stash?"

"Yes, and if you want, I'll show you where I keep my bag of Skittles. That's always been my weakness, but don't tell Ruth." He gave a conspiratorial wink.

"Your secret is safe with me."

"Then I'll tell you another one. You're doing more than enough." Dani's throat closed up and the M&M's turned to paste. She blinked and hoped Doc didn't see the tears. He noticed something because he went to the kitchen and came back with a glass of water. By that time, she'd managed to swallow the candy but couldn't have managed any words without the drink. She sipped and hoped he didn't expect her to say anything. "I've seen how hard you've been working both here and on the auction. Honestly, I've wanted to tell you to slow down and relax, but since I've known you most of your life, I know that's not likely to happen."

Doc Wheeler knew Dani well. He was like a father to her, especially since he understood her better than her own father ever had. She'd been coming in since she was thirteen and found an injured rabbit. With tears of worry running down her face, she'd brought it to Doc, who'd let her stay close as he examined the animal and splinted its leg. She would have taken it home, but he'd explained a wild animal probably wouldn't enjoy being in a house. The clinic kept a hutch outside, and the rabbit healed there with Dani coming every day to offer it food and see how it was doing. It wasn't long before she asked what else she could do. Before the summer was over, her career path was decided.

She let herself stay lost in the memories for a moment before managing to say, "Thank you for that. For everything." She gave him a hug and looked up when there was a rap on the door frame. "I think my ride is here."

Nick stepped into the room with Presley on his heels. "Hello, Doc Wheeler. Good to see you."

He shook Nick's hand. "And you. So this is the dog you're caring for. And are you taking good care of Dani as well?"

"Trying to, sir, but she's always got something to do, so it's tough to get her to rest." He gave her a wink, softening his words, showing her he was teasing.

Noticing his red cheeks, she said, "You look like you got some sunburn this morning."

"Unloading trucks meant more time outside than expected. I'm not used to my work needing sunscreen." No, twelve-hour work days meant he saw very little sun. "Let's get you home."

"Sounds good," she said. She turned back to Doc Wheeler. "Am I on the schedule for next week?"

"Nope. I didn't even expect you today until you called. Are you ready to come back?"

"I can do a few hours each morning." It would be a short week anyway with the Festival starting on Friday.

"I'll let Beth know. Now, you two go and let an old man finish his paperwork in peace." Dani gave Doc Wheeler another hug before leaving with Nick.

After they got into the car with the dogs, he took her hand, gave it a kiss, and asked, "Everything okay? You looked as though you'd been crying when I came in. Tough day?"

"No, a wonderful day. Doc was reminding me why I love it here so much." She thought about telling Nick the details of the conversation, but instead held Doc's words close and let them sink in. "Is my mother at the house?"

"I don't know. We could do a drive by and you could duck down. If she's there, I'll take you somewhere for lunch and hopes she leaves before we return."

Dani was grateful for his support. "No, I can manage. Besides, we have so much food, we've got to make a dent in it. It doesn't matter if my mom is there. I can handle her." And as surprised as she was to hear the words come out so easily, she was more pleased to realize they were true. Despite the days of nagging, Doc Wheeler's encouragement and her time with her patients allowed Dani to recover a thread of confidence. She was good at her work, and she made a difference. She was exactly where she wanted to be.

Chapter Thirty-Two

♥

While she and Nick ate lunch, he got a call from Theo asking him to come to the Stewart's Inn and Cabins and help with something for the Festival. "I've graduated from playing in the kids' area to building it. I'll be back in a few hours. Do you need anything?"

More of you. "Just some rest, I think."

She waited for the 'I told you so', but instead he said, "Can Presley stay with you and Otis? It's hot out, and I don't know that there will be any shade for her to stay in."

Dani loved how easily he thought about Presley and marveled at how much he'd changed since the day she forced him to take the dog home. It was too bad other things couldn't change as easily. "Absolutely. I've been so boring recently. Otis will be happy for the company. I'll take them out later."

"Don't overdo it. Do you need me to bring anything? Dinner? Movie? M&M's?"

He knew her weaknesses. He was one of them. "Not that I can think of, but I'll let you know if I do."

Her phone buzzed shortly after Nick left with a text from Xander. *Have you killed mom yet?*

His understanding made her grin. *No, but I was at work this morning, and she's out for the moment.*

She stared at the three dots until he responded, *Keep me posted. I'll fly out to be a character witness if you need. And I've got bail money. How are you doing?*

They texted for a few minutes, filling each other in. Xander loved the West Coast, and even though she missed him, she was glad he was happy. Dani was folding laundry and watching television when her mother breezed in carrying several bags from shops in the area Dani had seen but never gone into. She wasn't surprised Cynthia spent the morning shopping. It was something between a hobby and a sport for her, not to mention her favorite way to feel better. It was also the way Cynthia liked her apologies. When Dani's stepfather made a mistake or had to miss something for work, he'd say sorry with gifts. The worse the mistake, the more lavish the gift.

Dani continued folding shirts and leggings as her mother looked through purchases. "There are so many cute places in Littleton. Do you go there? I found a lovely little boutique and picked up two dresses. I almost got a third. I saw one I thought would look good on you, but I didn't know your size. What do you wear, a twelve? Fourteen?"

Dani gritted her teeth. Three days of comments about what she was eating and wearing. She was done. "I'm a ten, and it doesn't matter, Mom. I don't wear dresses. The two I have are more than I need to get me through any occasion that requires one." One of which she was going to wear for the dance and auction.

"Nonsense, every woman needs dresses. A ten? I think they had your size. I'll go back and get it for you tomorrow. Maybe I'll pick up that other dress for myself. It would be lovely for dinner at the club." Dani tuned out her mother's rambling about life back in Illinois and lay against the pillows. She was dozing off when her mother said, "You're lying on the couch again?"

"I worked this morning. I'm tired. It was more draining than I anticipated."

"I'm simply pointing out that between the food you've been eating and the lack of exercise, it can't be good for you."

"If I get out and take a walk will that make you leave sooner?" Her mother stiffened. Dani hadn't intended to be harsh, but she was done with her mother's bullying. It was time to take a stand and create a boundary. "I'm sorry. I know you came here to help, and I appreciate that, but all you've done is put more vegetables on my plate, glare at me no matter the portion of food I take, and suggest I wear something different. I get it. You don't like my life or my choices. But no matter what you do or say, I love it here in my too tiny home with my too big dog in this too boring town you couldn't wait to get out of and never wanted to see again. I'm sorry if that seems like I'm betraying you."

Her mother was silent as she sat across from Dani, straight-backed and straight-faced. "What happens when this life, this town, isn't enough? What happens if you wake up and discover this is not where you want to be, and you've missed out?"

"On what? On golf? On shopping and dinners at the club? On wondering if Laurel's ass is smaller than mine and if she's more likely to find the right husband?" It was time to be clear with her mother. "This is where I'm happy and I wish you could be happy for me, but even if you can't, that won't change my mind."

Her mother had the grace to look down at her hands. "I wanted what was best for you."

"No, you wanted what was best for *you* and thought I should want that, too. Have you ever listened to what I want?"

"You don't understand. I never wanted you to struggle like I struggled."

Nope, Dani didn't understand. "What are you talking about?"

Cynthia stood suddenly and stepped away. She looked as though she wanted to escape, but there was nowhere to go. "Forget it. It doesn't matter. You'll always prefer Fable Notch and Rosie to any of the opportunities I offered you."

Dani considered denying it, but since she was finally telling the truth, she decided to ask a question that had been bothering her since first she fell in love with this town. "Did you hate it here so much?"

"Yes. No. It's complicated." Dani said nothing, hoping her mother would continue. Cynthia returned to the couch, smoothed her skirt, and said, "In this town, it's hard for anyone to see you as anything other than the person you were when you were a kid. You are some-one's daughter or sister. You family does one thing, and everyone knows it. And the only other thing you get to be known for is for who you marry or maybe who your children become. As long as I stayed here, no matter what I did, I was always going to be the fat girl who smelled like bacon because her family owned the diner."

Dani had no idea what her mother was talking about. "Fat girl? Were you a size four instead of a size two back then?"

Cynthia gave a humorless laugh. "Hardly. I didn't al-ways look like this, Danielle. This is years of work and rigid discipline. When I was young, I was heavier than Rosie. They oinked at me in middle school when I walked by, but I found a way to change all of that."

Having been through her own share of bullying, Dani tried to imagine her mother in a similar position. "By losing weight."

"And dressing right and hanging with the right peo-ple." Dani heard the steel in her mother's voice. "The summer before high school I worked crazy hours in the diner as well as babysitting to make the money I needed. I lost weight, then bought my first bottle of hair dye and went from mousy brown to blonde. My mother was horrified, but I loved it. It felt so right. I ordered the best wardrobe I could from the catalogues I could find, and when I arrived at the regional high school, I felt and looked like a different person. I met Bea my first week of classes. She was naturally bubbly and popular, everything I never was. She suggested we try out for cheerleading together, and the acceptance I wanted followed. The next summer, I refused to work for my parents. I took a job at a day camp held at one of the ski resorts and never walked into the diner again. Haven't been back since."

Dani stared at Cynthia, trying to see the younger, heavier girl she'd once been, but there was no trace. Her mother had made dismissive comments over the years about how small Fable Notch was and how she couldn't wait to leave, but it had never occurred to Dani that Cynthia had struggled with self-worth or self-image issues. Although thinking about it, she never saw a picture of her mother from then. She assumed it was because Cynthia didn't like her childhood. It never occurred to Dani that her mother didn't like herself. Who could have imagined they had something in common? "I'm sorry. I didn't know."

"Why would I want you to know? That part of my life was over. There was nothing more to say about it. I wanted you to have something better, but that's not what you wanted." Before Dani could come up with a response, Cynthia went to the kitchen and said, "I'm going to have an apple and some cheese. Do you want anything?"

Dani couldn't believe her mother could open up like that one minute, then shut it all down a moment later, but when Dani looked at Cynthia, she saw her mother was done sharing. Knowing that a moment like this might never come again, Dani walked to her mother and gave her a hug as tight as any she'd given her Aunt Rosie. Cynthia had no reaction at first, then put her arms around Dani. It was the most connection Dani could remember, and although Cynthia broke it off sooner than Dani would have liked, she counted it as a win.

She and her mother would never agree on much of anything, but Dani felt she understood her mother a little better, and that, combined with setting boundaries, was an unexpected and wonderful gift.

Three hours later, Nick came back, and Cynthia left, announcing that she'd be flying out Monday morning so hopefully Dani could join her for brunch at the hotel tomorrow.

"I feel like I missed something," Nick said, looking from the door Cynthia closed back to Dani.

"It's been an interesting afternoon," Dani said, and told him of her mother's revelations. "I also told her where she could stick her criticism of my life and everything in it."

"You said what?" She didn't know Nick's eyebrows could go up so high. "I need details."

"Okay, I was a little more diplomatic than that, but I'd reached the end of my ability to pretend or ignore her. Guess I snapped."

"And how are you feeling about that?"

She'd been so nervous when it happened, she hadn't stopped to think about it. But his question was easy to answer. "Truthfully? Kind of wonderful."

"Then I'm happy for you," Nick said, and picked her up in a hug and twirled her around. When she squealed, he put her down and gave her a worried look. "Did I hurt you?"

Did I hurt you? The words echoed in her head. In the past, he had. Quite a bit. He'd done it again when he missed the meeting, but not only had he apologized, he'd taken care of her in every way he could since. Yes, he'd hurt her. But their time together had brought healing as well.

He was worried and waiting for an answer. She put her arms around his neck and kissed him instead. She ran her tongue against his lips, and he opened his mouth to her, threading his hands through her hair.

"I want more," she said when they stopped for a breath. Hoping the dogs would stay asleep long enough for them to enjoy each other without interruption, she took his hand, wrapped it around her waist, and walked them to the bedroom.

Chapter Thirty-Three

♥

He was instantly hard. Sleeping next to her these last two nights had been a small form of torture, one he figured he deserved as part of his penance. Today he'd been exhausted after waking up throughout the night needing her and wondered when she might be ready for him again. He was glad she'd answered the question.

"I've missed touching you," he said, kissing her neck, licking around the collar of her shirt. "Being close to you and being chaste is not something I'm good at." As they got to the bedroom, he remembered how busy he'd been during the day. "I should probably take a shower."

"Why? You're just going to get sweaty again." She took a step away from him and he watched as she removed her shirt, then unhooked her bra and slowly took it off. He couldn't take his eyes off of her as her hands traced the edge of her pants, a finger sliding under the fabric occasionally. He watched until he wanted to growl, until she grabbed the fabric at her hips and pulled her leggings and underwear down together. "See something you want?"

Standing before him naked was the most beautiful woman he'd ever known. There were still some fading bruises, which gave him pause, and he hated being the cause of, but if she could move past that, so could he. "I want it all."

She got on the bed, and he followed, covering her and not bothering to take his clothes off. There was something thrilling about being dressed while she was bare, completely available to him. He kissed her fiercely, and she raked her hands down his back. His mouth devoured hers, and he couldn't wait for more. One hand was on her breast, the other on her hip, then between her thighs. He moved his legs to the side, gave the lips of her pussy a single stroke as if to confirm how wet and ready she was, then he drove a finger into her, making her arch off the bed.

She sighed "yes," then said, "I know it's only been a few days, but it's been too long."

"For me too. Every morning when you step out looking sweet and sleepy, I've wanted to drag you back to bed. Every night when you change into that damn nightshirt, I want to run my hands up your legs and pull it over your head. You drive me crazy in the best possible ways. I've wanted to kiss you here," he said, and moved his mouth to her breasts. His tongue made circles around one nipple as his hand stroked the sensitive underside of the other. He drew the hardened peak into his mouth and sucked deeply, then bit softly, making her sigh. "And I've longed to caress you here." His touched moved to the curve of her hip, then to her inner thigh. As Nick let his fingers play over her flesh, she shivered with delight, getting wetter, clearly wanting more. "You like that?"

"Very much," she said and let her legs fall open, giving him greater access to her body. He took immediate advantage of the position.

"Good," he said. He wanted to touch her everywhere, show how her desirable he found her, but he decided to show a little restraint to make sure she ached as much as he did. "Do you want more?"

"Yes."

Whoever said consent wasn't sexy didn't know how to ask for it. "Tell me."

"I want to feel your mouth on me." Her voice broke mid-sentence.

He knew what she was saying. Not yet. "Here?" He kissed her stomach.

"Yes, and—"

"Maybe here," he said as he moved and kissed the sensitive spot at the back of her knee.

She jumped. He smiled. A ticklish spot. He filed the information away. "Not exactly what I meant."

"Then you must mean here." And then there was nothing more to say as his tongue licked softly at her core, and she called out his name. He teased her with the gentlest of strokes, making her slick and needy. He was aware of how her pleasure was building, changing, and before she could scream for more, he deepened the pressure and took her most sensitive flesh into his mouth. He alternated between sucking and licking as Dani moaned his name, grabbed at the sheets, and surrendered to the waves of pleasure his touch brought her.

"Yes, Nick. God, yes," she said as her fingers dug into his shoulders. Maybe this time he'd have bruises.

"I love how you taste," he whispered, then blew gently at her damp skin. "I love how you respond. I can feel your muscles tensing, hear every moan and sigh. It's intoxicating. I can't get enough of you."

As he spoke, his fingers traced her opening before he pushed one then two inside of her. His mouth covered her again, and she screamed his name, then bit her lip to call back the sound. She whispered, "dogs," and he understood. No, it wouldn't do to be interrupted. He was not letting anything stop him. Fortunately, moments later, he heard, "Nick, I'm so close. Don't...don't stop. Please."

He could have come from her words alone.

He increased the speed of his tongue and fingers, and her body started its final rise. Pleasure which had ebbed and flowed, built, and didn't stop until she reached the peak he knew she needed. Her hips came off the bed and her legs opened wider. Her climax hit her with a force that had her covering her face with a pillow as she screamed. The sensations went on, and Nick didn't slow until he sensed her body relax. Her knees straightened as though her muscles weren't able to hold them up any longer. Even then he continued to give her soft strokes with his tongue coaxing additional shivers of delight.

She lay there with her eyes closed, floating, as he kissed his way up her body. When she heard a zipper, she opened them watch him undress. She rolled to get a condom from the bedside table. He grabbed it from her as soon as she held it out, and she laughed at his enthusiasm. He tossed the wrapper aside and covered himself. Reaching out, she stroked his length, then cupped his balls. He gave a soft moan.

She opened her legs to settle him between them, but he grabbed her hips and said, "I want you on top. I want to see you riding me."

Dani shivered, then gave him a wicked grin. "Then get on your back."

The command in Dani's voice was thrilling, and Nick did as she asked, rolling to his side and taking her with him. In one sexy, fluid movement, she threw her leg over his hips and straddled him. Looking at her, he thought he'd never seen a woman look more beautiful. Her hair was wild, her lips puffy from his kisses. This was the Dani he'd seen in his fantasies, the lover he could never forget. The woman who made him want things he'd stopped believing were possible.

"Now I get to drive you crazy," she said.

As if she didn't already. She wrapped her fingers around the base of his shaft and used it to tease herself. In the light of the setting sun, he watched as she excited them both, occasionally letting the tip of his erection enter her, then pulling back to use it against her clitoris. Every sigh she gave sent more shivers through him.

Maybe this position wasn't such a good idea. Having her so close and seeing the pleasure on her face was maddening. His restraint was falling apart. "Dani, you're killing me."

"Hardly," she said.

"I need..."

"I know," and with those words, she stopped teasing and slid down the length of him, taking him fully inside of her. He lifted his hips to meet her and reveled at the feeling of them joined. She was tight, swollen from her orgasm. Perfect.

She arched her back and put her hands behind her, resting them on his thighs to give her leverage. The position pushed her breasts out and he sat up to be closer to her, wrapping a hand around her back to help her keep her balanced as he sucked and lightly bit one nipple and then the other. Soon they were both slick with sweat, muscles heated from exertion and need. She returned his embrace, kissing him deeply. Then she put her hands on his shoulders and pushed so he was lying flat. Their hips moved together, slower then faster again. He grabbed her ass, and she fell forward to take his mouth.

She kissed her way down his chest then sat straight again. God, she looked gorgeous. He covered her breasts, and she put her hands over his, pressing her chest into him, letting him feel the power behind her passion. She threw her head back as she made circles with her hips, taking him so deeply he thought they might fuse.

As he got closer to his climax, he reached between them and found her clitoris, still sensitive and slick from her earlier orgasm. Her voice low, she said, "Yes, Nick. There."

How could simply hearing her bring him higher? "I can't hold back much longer."

"Then don't. Take me." She tightened her inner muscles around his cock, and he was lost. His orgasm ripped through him, and he grabbed her hips, setting the motion to match his need. He lifted his ass, pushing inside her as deeply as he could. "Dani. God. Yes." It was all he could manage.

When he stilled, she came forward and rested on his chest. His heart was racing, the blood rushing in his ears. It was wonderful. They stayed in that position until he softened, then he gently rolled out from under her. "Be right back. Don't move."

"Don't think I can." Her words were barely coherent. He loved it.

He kissed her, then quickly went to the bathroom to get rid of the condom and clean himself off. When he came back to the room, he left the door open in case the dogs wanted to come in, then slipped back under the covers. He reached for her, and she pressed herself against his side. She threaded her fingers through his and brought his hand up to her lips and gave his knuckles a kiss.

"Your hands have changed in the last few weeks. They're rougher."

She was right. He'd stopped wearing gloves. He was developing the callouses that he once hated and couldn't wait to be rid of. He'd been a little proud when he noticed them this time, but now he was concerned. "I didn't scratch you or anything, did I?"

"The only thing you did was excite the hell out of me, in case you didn't notice."

He kissed her and dropped his head back on the pillow. He lay there holding her, feeling blissfully exhausted and happier than he could remember being in a long time. There had never been anyone in his life like Dani. Henry came close, but he'd known Dani longer—and intimately. He didn't realize how big a hole she'd left in his life until she was there to fill it again.

Was he in love with her again?

The idea stopped the doze his body was falling into. He hoped she didn't notice the change because he'd gone from untroubled to aware in the space between one thought and the next.

He lay there trying to understand what he was feeling, then realized even if he did love her, what would it change?

Although the texts from Terry had stopped, Nick knew the work would likely get him his job back. And Dani would be here. It's not like he could commute to New York. When Theo decided to stay, the company he worked for opened a branch in Concord to serve the New England region. Not exactly an option for him.

It was odd that he'd even wondered if there was another option.

He hugged her close and kissed the top of her head, breathing in her unique scent, taking all of her in. She kissed his chest and asked, "You okay?"

Maybe she had noticed. There wasn't anything specific he could tell her, so he said, "Very. How about you?"

"I am so much more wonderful than okay I don't have a word for it. That was better than any pain medicine they've given me."

He loved knowing he pleased her. "Not sore?"

"Not in any places that have to do with my bruises. I feel rather boneless, even a little floaty," she said as she picked her head up and gave him a kiss. Her kisses brought him back to the present, driving out all thoughts of what might happen in the next few weeks.

He might have gotten them both going again, but he heard a stomach growl and wasn't sure who it belonged to. "Was that me or you? Or the dogs?" At some point, Otis and Presley had joined them for cuddles and quiet. It was crowded in the bed, and he loved it.

"Could be me. Could be a dog. I am hungry."

"I already ate," he said. There was a beat before they both broke into laughter. He was going to miss so much about her.

Eventually they got out of bed, showered together—so much better than alone—and made dinner. She wore only a t-shirt. He didn't put on more than his boxers until he had to take the dogs for a walk, then he changed back to next-to-nothing as soon as he could. They were ten minutes into watching a movie before they started kissing. Less than a scene later, he was shutting off the television and carrying her back to her room. She was as tireless and greedy as he was.

It was heaven.

As he drifted off, he found himself aware of how confusing these last weeks had been. Today had been one of the best days he could remember in years, and it hadn't been spent making money. He'd helped his brother and the Stewarts with their projects and gotten sunburned and sweaty in the process. He'd walked the dogs and made dinner. And made love with Dani.

And what he wanted more than anything was another day like this tomorrow.

When he'd come to Fable Notch, his biggest worry was what he was going to do if New York didn't want him back. Now he had a new one.

What if they did?

Chapter Thirty-Four

♥

On Monday morning, Dani waited to see Cynthia one last time before her mother left. At brunch the day before, they hadn't talked more about what Cynthia revealed, and Dani hadn't wanted to break the fragile peace. Enough had been said. For the rest of the day, she and Nick did auction work. And Cynthia visited with Bea.

Dani was pouring a second mug of coffee when Cynthia breezed in with a shopping bag and handed it to Dani. She assumed it was the dress her mother had mentioned the other day and was surprised when she turned it around and saw the Significant Paws logo. "What's this?"

Cynthia gracefully lifted a shoulder. "I never know what to buy you and when I do, it's usually the wrong thing, so I thought I'd get something for Otis instead. It's just a little toy."

Dani didn't know what surprised her more, the gift or that her mother remembered Otis's name. "He'll love it. What time is your flight?"

"Two."

It was barely nine-thirty. "Aren't you leaving a little early?"

"I have to return the rental car before getting to my gate, and I'm meeting Rosie at the diner for breakfast before I leave." Dani didn't know her expression changed until her mother said, "Don't give me that look. I said I've never gone back to the place, but it's been long enough. And even though my sister made choices that I wouldn't make in a million years, or for a million dollars, it doesn't mean I don't love her."

Dani was shocked. It wasn't like her mother to admit to emotions. She was going to say something but didn't want to spoil the moment. "I recommend the omelets, even if you have it made with egg whites."

Cynthia came over and put her hands on Dani's upper arms. "Dani, I know you and I find different things important. I can't change who I am or what I want, and neither can you. And yes, I wanted you to be more like me and do as I suggested, because I thought that would make your life easier and happier. But since my life hasn't always been either of those, I can't say your choices are wrong. I hope everything works out the way you want. The only thing that matters is, are you happy?"

The answer was easy. "I'm happy, Mom. I've got what I want here."

"With your work and Nick."

"With work, Aunt Rosie, my friends. Nick, however, isn't staying. Whatever we have is for the short term." She hated saying it and hated more that she wished it weren't true.

"I'm sorry to hear that."

"Because he's rich?" She almost cringed. She hadn't meant to say that.

"Because you obviously care a great deal for him and, unless I miss my guess, he feels the same way about you." Dani thought about their time together. Yes, her feelings for Nick were bigger than was wise, but there was nothing to be done. "No matter. I can be happy for you, even if I think you should wear a little more makeup. You do have beautiful eyes."

Somethings would never change. "They're the same as yours."

"My best feature, or so I've been told." Her mom gave her a quick squeeze. While it would never be the deep, almost back adjusting hug Aunt Rosie loved to give, it was enough. "Take care of yourself."

"You, too."

Cynthia brushed back a loose strand of hair that had come out of Dani's ponytail. "I love you."

Dani's heart constricted at the words. She couldn't remember the last time her mother had said them first. For a long time it was, 'love you, too,' and then Dani had stopped saying it all together. "I love you, too, Mom."

Dani walked with her mother to the car and watched as she drove off. She'd expected to breathe a huge sigh of relief after her mother left. Instead, she felt a different type of lightness. Her relationship with her mother would never be close, but it was better than it had been before Cynthia arrived. She'd taken a stand for her life, for what she loved, and she trusted her choices.

    * * *

As the week went on, Nick was almost sorry Dani had her rental car and the freedom to drive herself. He'd enjoyed being able to help her. On Thursday she was up before him, and she and Otis were about to head out the door when he came out of the bedroom. She still wasn't putting in a full day, but by next week she would.

He didn't want to think about what was coming. Next week the Festival would be over, and he'd be that much closer to hearing from New York about whether or not they wanted him back. His feelings were more mixed than he liked.

He kissed her good morning and poured himself coffee. "How about you come to my place for dinner tonight? Spend the night with me there."

They'd been switching back and forth since Cynthia had left. "Do you want me to bring something from the freezer for dinner? There's a beef stew from Valerie Stewart."

"Great, her stew is amazing, and my cooking isn't."

"See you then." She gave him a kiss, and Otis followed her out. He put an English muffin in the toaster, settled himself at the kitchen table, and called up the *New York Times* on his tablet. After he read the same paragraph four times, he put it down. Why couldn't he concentrate?

Because he kept thinking about Dani. How he was looking forward to her coming over. How they would talk about their day as they ate. How wonderful it was to go to bed and wake up with her. This is what Theo had with Eden and why his brother moved back to Fable Notch, something Theo never expected or wanted before seeing Eden again. Nick's days were going to be a lot quieter, a lot lonelier, when he got back to New York. It was good that he'd have Presley. He was definitely keeping the dog.

As he got dressed, he kept thinking about New York and the people there. It was after nine. Some of them would have been at their desks for over two hours, and none of them would be dressed in jeans, t-shirts, and work boots the way he was. It was going to feel weird to put on a tie and jacket and go to the gym to stay healthy. How could he have gotten so used to the flow of his days here in less than three weeks? How long would it take to get back into the New York pace?

He was still thinking about this when he drove up to the Elks Lodge being refurbished to be Eden's new business. It was one thing to work on a random project, but different to know that what he was doing was helping his future sister-in-law. When he was here the other day, Eden had stopped by. She kept flitting from place to place and then walked him through the site telling him how they were using the space. To say she was excited was an understatement.

Today they were preparing to build a wall and turn one room into two. After several hours, the team knocked off for lunch, and he and Presley were eating in the building's kitchen when Ed came in.

"Things look like they're coming along," he said, helping himself to coffee and joining Nick.

"They are. Gene thinks he's ahead of schedule, but he told me not to say that out loud so as not to jinx anything."

"The boy knows construction. No sooner do you think you're ahead then you hit a pipe, discover a load-bearing wall that can't be moved, or have a power outage." Nick smiled. The boy Ed was referring to was in his thirties and about to make Ed and Leslie grandparents for the second time. "Heard you helped out over at the Stewart's the other day to prep for the Festival."

"I did. Drew needed extra hands to create a mini ropes course on the field in front of the cabins and get a few other things ready for the kids' events they're hosting there. Given the generous donation he made to the family weekend package from Tree-to-Tree—and the fact that I've known him practically all of my life—I couldn't say no."

"As if you'd want to. How much longer did it take because you kids were fooling around?"

"Hey, we're adults. We know how to focus on a project when it needs to get done." Ed stared at him and said nothing. "It was only an extra hour." More silence. "Maybe it was closer to two, but it's done, and there won't be much he has to add to it later this week. A lot of kids are going to have a lot of fun."

"I don't doubt it. Sounds like you had fun, too."

"I did." As much as he had rolled his eyes initially, he and Theo had had a great time with Drew and Adam. The Stewarts' oldest brother, Gabriel, had shown up at the end, making the work go faster. And making the horseplay last longer. "And I didn't even need gloves to work with the rope. I've got my builder's hands back."

Nick turned his palm up and Ed squinted. "You sure about that?"

"Very funny. Might take a little longer before I have some real calluses, but I'm getting there."

"That you are. Which reminds me. I met with the Butlers, the couple who want to update their house. I showed them your design, and they loved it. It's exactly what they want."

Nick's heart gave an unexpected jump. He couldn't deny it was a kick for someone other than family to see his drawings and like them. Hearing the outside validation was heady. "I'm glad I could give them some inspiration. I'm sure they'll be able to find someone to help with whatever they want to do next."

"What they want to do next is buy the plans from you. They asked me to find out what you charge."

Nick sat there and for a moment, not fully understanding what Ed was saying. "What I charge?"

"Yes. Is something wrong? You look like someone told you they'd run out of coffee at the diner."

That would have surprised Nick less. "I can't charge anyone. It's a silly sketch. Let them take it to an architect or another professional and have that person draw up what they need."

"Nick, these people want to take your 'silly' sketch and turn it into the home they intend to build for their family. I told you when we remade your old house, you have a gift for this. I've been watching you draw plans since you came to work for me as a teen. You've always had a great eye for layout and space usage. You've done your own places. Why can't you design for someone else?"

"Because..." But the sentence trailed off when Nick didn't have an answer. Then he shook his head. It was crazy to think of selling his design. "Ed, I'm not a professional. I have no credentials. Sure, I created the plans to renovate what was left of the house I grew up in and build the one on Prescott, but that was just for fun."

"Why can't you make money doing something fun? Doesn't Dani have fun with the animals she cares for? Why do you think Adam Stewart went and opened an ice cream parlor? And you can't tell me Drew doesn't love running the Adventure Park. There are people in this town who bake for a living or teach skiing. We're sitting in Eden's future dance studio."

"Yes, but..."

"Do you think I'd have been doing this for so long or encouraged one of my sons to join me if it wasn't something I found fun? Maybe not every minute of every day, but overall." Ed opened his arms, taking in the space around them. "I love what I do."

Nick hadn't considered that. All he saw was a man who worked hard but couldn't always count on the business he'd chosen to do to bring in enough money. There had been some lean times. Yet year after year, this is what Ed did. What he loved. What made him happy. How had Nick never noticed? "I have no idea what home designs are worth."

"Then I suggest you do a little research and give me a number I can tell those folks. They were ready to write me a check then and there. I almost considered asking them for a deposit, so you'd know I was serious."

"They'll still need to hire an architect, so I should probably figure that into what I charge."

"Not necessarily. We didn't need one for your homes. If you put this design into that fancy software you bought when you did those projects and create something I can use, we'll be all set. Besides, I don't think they're worried about money. She's a doctor, and he's some kind of tech whiz. Charge what you think it's worth."

What it was worth? Nick didn't know how to respond. It wasn't worth the paper it was printed on. Or so he thought.

His head was spinning. He was a doodler, not a designer, regardless of the two places that existed because of the ideas he'd put on paper. Years ago, he'd considered becoming an architect until he saw the upper limits of what they earned plus the additional years of school and interning. His income goals were much bigger, and he didn't want to wait.

But this was a thrill unlike any he'd experienced in a long time. Not since the deal that earned him his office had anything been exhilarating. He kept hoping each new project would give him the rush he missed and not leave him so drained. Even before Henry died and work had blown up, he'd worried about burning out. The project plan he'd created with Terry had been the first thing he'd tried that gave him that zing in years.

And now this. There was definitely a zing when he thought of one of his drawings being turned into a home.

"Nick?"

He didn't know how long he'd been quiet, but from the look on Ed's face, it had been a while. "Sorry. My mind went off on a tangent or two. Or six. I'll find out what plans go for and get you a number in the next few days."

"Good. And there better be a comma in that cost or I'm not accepting it."

"Yes, sir," he said with a smile.

"Stop distracting my workers, Dad. I don't want to fall behind then have you asking me why I can't keep to a timeline." Gene came over and gave his father a pat on the back. Other than the full beard, he looked exactly like Ed.

Ed laughed and finished his coffee. "Nick says you're ahead."

Gene turned on him with an expression that was part scowl, part smile. "Damn, Nick, you know better than to say that out loud. Thought we taught you better."

Building superstition. Never curse construction progress by saying it was going well. "Sorry. I'll sacrifice a two by four to the gods and ask for forgiveness."

"You better." Gene turned to Ed and continued, "Are we still meeting with the library tomorrow?"

"That was the other reason I stopped by. Meeting's been moved to later next week, after the Festival when they have a better idea of what the event raised and if they are going to be able to do the complete project or if there need to be changes and cuts."

"The young adult room may not happen?" Nick didn't know the plans weren't solid.

Ed shrugged. "The loans are contingent on having enough of a financial base. Less money raised means a smaller loan, which means they may back scale some pieces."

"Damn, I hope it all goes through," Gene said. "That job could carry us for months."

"We've got plenty of work," Ed said.

Gene stroked his beard. "Never hurts to have more. I like being busy." Whenever Nick heard conversations like this in the past, he heard the worry about money. Today he heard two men who loved their work and wanted more.

"Speaking of busy," Nick said, "I don't want Eden to blame me if she doesn't have her studio in time, so I'm going back to the room I was working on. Ed, I'll have that number to you soon."

Nick threw away the rest of his lunch, grabbed some more coffee, and went to work. What Ed said about work and fun continued to bounce around in his head. Was there a way to bring some of this fun back to New York? Maybe he needed to make sure that was part of any new plan. Along with not waiting too long between visits here. He enjoyed seeing the Sinclairs and Theo.

And Dani? Would he see her when he came up? Maybe at first, but at some point she'd move forward with her life and start seeing someone. His stomach tightened. Yeah, he would never like that, but what could he do about it?

"Nick?" Gene's voice brought him out of his thoughts. "You okay? You looked as though you were about to argue with that wall."

"Fine. Sorry. Let myself get a distracted. I'm good." Gene didn't look convinced, but gave him a nod and left.

Six months ago, everything had been so clear. He couldn't say he was necessarily happy, but he was on track to get what he wanted. And now? Now he was remembering why he preferred plans, because this not knowing what to do was driving him crazy.

Chapter Thirty-Five

♥

As much as Dani was feeling better every day, she was grateful to only be working mornings this week. There were a lot of details to oversee for the auction, and she checked in regularly with Nancy.

Thursday was her last day in the clinic before the Festival. It wasn't particularly busy, but the morning had taken an unexpected turn for the worse when an emergency arrival had to be told his beloved pet had come to the end of his life. The dog's liver was no longer responding to treatment and additional measures would be costly and mostly non-beneficial. It was time to make some very difficult decisions. This was the first time she'd had to do this while in Fable Notch, and she was grateful Beth was there to help. The owner hadn't agreed to euthanasia yet, but Dani had a feeling she'd be seeing him soon. Or the animal would pass at home. It was never easy, but it was part of the job, and she always did what she could to make the process bearable.

After finishing with her last patient, Dani went to speak to Beth, who she found preparing bills to send out. "I want to thank you for your help with Mr. Pearson. I couldn't have gotten through that appointment without you."

"I don't know how you do it sometimes. Veterinarians. It's the only thing about this job I hate. I've watched Doc

Wheeler have these conversations, and it always breaks my heart. Never gets any easier, does it?"

Dani shook her head. "Not that I've seen or experienced. I'm glad you were willing to be with me."

"No problem. I love how you talk to the animals and the patients. I've learned a lot from you. I have to say I was a little nervous when Doc Wheeler announced he was retiring and someone new was coming in, especially since I didn't know you before you started."

Dani never thought about that. She met Beth on her first day of work. "Did you like some of the other candidates he interviewed?"

Beth gave her a quizzical look. "What other candidates?"

"The other doctors who applied for the job."

"I don't think there were any." She gave a shrug and went back to the bills. "I didn't even know Doc was retiring until he told me you'd been hired."

Dani took in the information. Aunt Rosie told her Doc was looking for someone to take over so he could retire. Had Rosie said anything about how long he'd been looking? Or other people who might be Dani's competition for the job? She couldn't remember. She'd been too relieved about the prospect of escaping the social mess of her life to be anything but overjoyed by the possibility of moving back. Thinking about it, she'd only had one conversation with Doc Wheeler. She'd been on pins and needles for two days before he called and offered her the job. She'd assumed she was the best candidate. Turns out she was the only candidate.

She needed to talk to Rosie.

She dropped Otis at home and minutes later, she was walking into the diner, taking a seat at the back table. Rosie was busy working on her blueberry creation for the festival, so Cathy took her order. Dani chose the chef salad. When Rosie joined her, it was the first thing she commented on. "A salad? Who made you angry?"

Dani stabbed at her meal. With her mouth full, she said, "What makes you think I'm mad?"

Rosie tilted her head. "Other than the way you attacked that defenseless piece of lettuce?" Dani put down her fork. "Is it Nick?"

She didn't know how she was going to say this. She didn't want her to hurt her aunt's feelings, but she had to know the truth. It took her two tries to swallow her food. "Did you convince Doc Wheeler to retire so I could move here?"

When Aunt Rosie didn't answer, Dani's heart fell. She'd hoped Rosie would immediately deny the question. Just when she was feeling confident. When Rosie finally responded, Dani was barely listening. "You were so miserable, so heartbroken over what those girls did. All I wanted to do was give you a hug, and I couldn't. And then I wanted to take you away from the pain, and I realized maybe I could. No, I didn't convince Doc to do anything. He'd been talking about it for years, but I many have... encouraged him to move up his timetable."

"So you're the reason I got the job?" She pushed the salad away. She wasn't hungry. "This is like when I was growing up. I got invited to parties because those girls' mothers wanted to be in good with my mother. It wasn't about them liking me or being good enough. I was included as an obligation."

"You think you were hired as an obligation?"

"No. Yes. I don't know." She drank some water before continuing, hoping it would help clear her thoughts. Instead, all the pain rushed out. "I'm so tired of all of this. Isn't there anyplace I can be myself and not feel as though I have to prove myself? I was never good enough for my mother, I was an annoying know-it-all to the people I thought were my friends in Texas, and here I'm... a charity case?"

"You're not a charity case." Rosie reached for Dani's hand. She pulled it away. She hated the pain she saw in her aunt's face, but she didn't care. "Doc Wheeler wouldn't have brought you on if he didn't think you could do the job."

"But I'll never be certain of that, will I?" Rosie had been the one she could trust, someone who loved and accepted her. But she'd manipulated a situation and Dani. Yes, it was great to be here sooner rather than later, but Dani could have waited. "I'll always wonder if he wished he had interviewed other doctors. Was I really the right person or was Doc afraid of angering you? Why weren't you honest with me?"

Her voice cracked. So much for her growing confidence. Her dream life hadn't been earned; it had given to her because of Rosie. Dani got up from the table. Rosie called out to her, but Dani didn't turn around. She'd never walked out on her aunt before. She couldn't even remember being angry with Rosie, but this was too much. How could she expect her patients to accept her if she wasn't certain Doc wanted her?

She needed to talk to Nick or Laurel, but a glance at her clock told her they'd both be busy. Instead, she drove home, went to her bedroom, and had a good cry. She found herself reviewing the last several months, looking for places where she might have made mistakes, not lived up to Doc's expectations. Did she spend enough time with patients? Were her notes complete? He hadn't started training her on all the financial pieces necessary to take over the business. Was that because he wasn't sure about her skills?

Was it too much to ask for a place where who she was could be enough?

After an hour of tears and snuggles from Otis, she got out of bed and went to the bathroom to splash her face with water. Looking in the mirror, she took a steadying breath. The next time she was in the clinic, she'd talk to Doc and make certain he knew she was determined to be the best vet possible for the practice and their patients. He'd know he made the right decision, and so would she. In the meantime, there was the auction. By

Saturday night, she'd have one clear success under her belt. She'd build more from there.

Chapter Thirty-Six

♥

B uilding a wall was grueling work. Nick didn't think he'd ever put in a more physical day on the job. It had taken three tries before they'd gotten the placement right. Since the rooms needed to be soundproof, it was more like putting up two walls and there had been miscommunication on which side needed to go where. The amount of cursing and yelling was off the charts. Once it was clear everything was right, Gene sent them home. There was still more to do, but what was there was in the right location and things should go smoothly moving forward. Before leaving, Nick reminded Gene he wouldn't be in tomorrow since he was helping Dani with whatever they needed for the Festival.

Nick was glad to get home early. All he wanted was a shower, a quiet dinner with Dani, and a few hours to make love to her before they fell asleep. He'd just gotten out of the shower and slipped into sweats and a clean tee when his phone buzzed. The caller ID read *Bronson Jeffries*. Half a dozen thoughts flashed through his brain. There were any number of reasons for a call from his boss, and most of them weren't good. Walking to his office, he answered on the third ring as he sat down at his desk. "Good afternoon, Mr. Jeffries."

"Nick. Have I caught you at a good time?"

An interesting question, and Nick had several of his own. Was it ever a good time to hear from your boss when you're out on suspension? Did Nick want to know what his boss was calling about? Was there a way to delay the news, whatever it might be? Being called two weeks before his suspension was over couldn't be a good thing. Maybe Bronson heard Nick helped Terry and was annoyed that he'd interfered. As his brain continued to spin through the possibilities, Nick noticed something unexpected.

He was calm.

His heart wasn't racing and no matter what thought popped into his head, he wasn't concerned. It didn't matter what Bronson was about to say. The worst had already happened. He'd lost Henry, he'd lost a fortune, and for a while, he lost himself. If he was about to lose his job, he would manage. "It's a fine time, Sir."

"Good. I prefer to see people when I talk to them. Can you take this on Zoom?"

"Of course." In a few clicks, Nick was looking at his boss. The last time they spoke they'd been in a hospital room. Today Nick could see the New York skyline through the windows of Bronson's corner office. He couldn't help but think how much had changed since he'd last been in the city. "What can I do for you, Mr. Jeffries?"

"It's more like what I can do for you. You've been involved on the McCutchen deal. The interdepartmental contributions were your idea." A statement. Not a question.

"They were," Nick confirmed.

"Tell me how this came about."

Nick wished he'd had some idea of what the man knew. He couldn't tell from his boss' tone if he was pleased or annoyed. How much had Terry told Bronson? Had Nick's involvement put the company or the deal at risk since he was on suspension? He supposed it didn't matter. "Terry called me when he was stuck on how to give McCutchen the reach they wanted with their next merger." Nick explained the details and unlike with Terry, he explained how the Festival gave him the idea. "Once we'd gotten the initial buy in from the other departments, Terry was able to run with it. At least, I assume he was. I haven't spoken to him in a while. Is it going well?"

"Very. This explains why I got a call from the head of Asset Management yesterday. He was concerned because someone on his team was trying to reach you, and you weren't responding to emails."

This was not good for his coworker. "Terry didn't tell you he'd involved me."

"Or that this multilevel project was your idea. After hearing from AM, I made some calls. Then I spoke to Terry to ask him for the details. His answer was less than convincing."

Nick did not envy Terry and the shit that was about to come down on him, but he tried to help. "Sir, we all get into situations where we can't see the answer. Terry wanted to do a good job for the client. As you reminded me recently, perception in our business is key to success. Reaching out to me made it more likely no one would know he was struggling, and then the client wouldn't know either."

"Reaching out to you made it more likely no one would find out he needed help at all. That hasn't worked the way he'd planned, but it's not something you need to concern yourself about." Now Nick heard emotion in his boss' voice. The man was pissed. "Nick, this is the best work I've seen from you or anyone in a long time. I'm very impressed."

Nick warmed to the compliment. "Thank you, sir. I'm glad it helped."

"It was more than a help. It's brilliant. I've spoken to the other partners. We want you to come back as soon as possible. What you did for this project has some significant possibilities for our current clients and for acquiring new clients."

They wanted him back. After months of trying to think of ways to impress his bosses, he'd done it. There was a buzz of excitement in his ears, and he had to ask Bronson to repeat what he said because he'd stopped focusing once his boss mentioned coming back. "The presentation to the team from McCutchen is scheduled for Wednesday. I think you should be a part of it."

"In person?" Maybe it was a stupid question, but he was still stunned at how fast things had changed.

"If you prefer, we can connect you via Zoom. There will be others attending virtually, but I assumed you'd want to be here. Which makes me ask, where are you? I see a forest behind you."

"White Mountains, sir. Visiting family."

"Nice. Get to an airport. Join us in person. Consider it your first day back."

Only days away. Could he just leave? Nick thought of the work still needed at Eden's studio. "Can I let you know?"

"By Monday, close of day." Nick had forgotten how Bronson talked in orders. Nick agreed, and they got off the call.

He'd done it.

He'd proven he was a valuable member of the team. He had expertise and skills they needed. Wanted. They wanted him back. He did a fist pump in the air accompanied by a yell that startled Presley. This was amazing. He had his invitation back to New York. They were practically rolling out the red carpet for him. He couldn't wait to tell....

Dani.

There was no one he wanted to tell the good news to more than her, but even if she was happy for him, it meant their time together was ending. His heart rate picked up uncomfortably.

He took a deep breath. Tomorrow was the Festival. Saturday was the auction. This could wait.

Chapter

Thirty-Seven

♥

At five, Dani headed over to Nick's house. She'd stopped crying and hoped her eyes didn't look too puffy. She reasoned there would be no feeling better without talking to Doc, and that wasn't going to happen for a few days. For now, she'd keep her focus where it could do some good, on the auction.

Presley didn't even come to the door when she and Otis let themselves in. Clearly, the dog had gotten comfortable with their being there. Dani put her things on the couch and the beef stew in the oven before going in search of Nick. Talking to him would help. Make it hurt less.

She heard voices coming from the office, but as she was about to push open the door and mime a knock to let him know she was there, she heard a voice she didn't know.

I've spoken to the other partners. We want you to come back as soon as possible.

She froze and her throat tightened for the second time that day. She stood there, unable to walk away, and listened as Nick became more animated. There was no mistaking the pride in his voice. Nick had gotten what he wanted, an invitation to return to his job. At least one of them was wanted at their office.

His cheer and Presley's bark broke her out of her trance, and she went quickly to the kitchen. She would act surprised and pleased when he told her. No matter what was going on for her, she was happy for him. She was getting plates out when he came in.

"Hey there," he said. He sounded distracted and looked serious, not smiling from ear to ear. Wondering why, she crossed to him and gave him a kiss. When he put his hands on the side of her face, she leaned into him.

"Well, hello to you, too," she said when they stopped. She was going to miss his kisses, how they made her feel, the connection she had with him. Something else to think about later. "I noticed you were in your office, so I didn't want to bother you."

"I was on the phone with someone from New York. They had questions about the deal I was helping with."

It wasn't a lie, but he wasn't giving her the full truth. She waited for him to tell her more. "Is something wrong?" He was looking out the kitchen window and didn't answer. "Nick?"

"Sorry. No, nothing's wrong. There were a few things to clear up about how this all came together, and which departments were a part of it. Sounds as though it's going to be a success. How was your day?"

Dani burst into tears. She didn't know that was possible until this moment. So much for being done crying. Nick wrapped his arms around her and walked her to the couch. Curled in his arms, the whole story came tumbling out, along with all her concerns that she'd gotten the job because of Rosie and, as her mother always made certain she knew and the women in Texas reminded her, she was inadequate.

He listened and only made sounds to encourage her to continue. When she was talked out and it was quiet, he said, "I understand how you're feeling. You know I do, but let me ask you a question. Do you think Doc would have brought you on if he thought you weren't right for the job? Does that seem like him?"

With a sniffle, she said, "No." She appreciated his ability to be logical in the face of her emotions. She'd been trying to tell herself the same thing for the last several hours, but she hadn't gotten there yet. The fear was so big it was hard to hear anything else.

"And I know I'm just one opinion, but truthfully, I don't think there's anything inadequate about you." Her heart melted. Great, it wasn't as though she didn't adore him enough. He had to be extra sweet when she knew he was leaving. He kissed the top of her head and continued, "I've never known anyone to work harder than you, and on Saturday, when the auction is a massive success, you'll see that, too."

She snuggled closer, taking in his warmth and strength, hoping she could remember it after he was gone. Which reminded her. He had some things to share, too. "Bet your day didn't make you want to cry."

"No, but I did get some unexpected news."

Here it comes. She commanded her heart to stop racing as she shifted to face him. "Oh?" It was all she was able to manage. *Hold it together, Dani. Be happy for him.*

"Remember when I told you Ed showed my design to a client? Turns out they loved what I did, and they want to buy the plan from me."

Not what she was expecting, but hearing the joy and surprise in Nick's voice made her smile. "That's awesome. Congratulations." She gave him a hug. "I always said your drawings were good. Guess you believe me now."

"Only if you believe me about how incredible you are."

Why did he have to be so wonderful? It wasn't fair. "What did you tell Ed?"

"I was so shocked I stared at him with my mouth hanging open and said I couldn't charge for it because I wasn't a professional. Can you imagine—me? Turning down an opportunity to make money?" There was something much bigger that he wasn't going to turn down, but if he wasn't ready to bring it up, she wouldn't push him. It had been a rough enough day. "I have to do some research and decide on a value I'm comfortable with, although it still feels weird."

"But good?"

"But very good. The list of things I didn't expect to do when I came back here keeps growing. Adopting a dog, volunteering for the Festival, doing construction work." He kissed her. "Spending time with you."

Too bad it was all ending soon. Needing to cling to what she could, Dani said, "Any favorites on that list?"

He pretended to think. "Well, Presley's very special, as you know, but there's nothing like you."

He kissed her, and she let the pleasure push away the other thoughts in her head. Tonight was not the night to talk about how things were going to change. He was here, and she was going to enjoy it. She could pretend for the next few days everything was fine. That he wasn't leaving and that her heart wasn't going to break.

Chapter Thirty-Eight

♥

The next morning, Dani was out of bed before the alarm and looking through her notebooks before Nick got up. After coffee, they brought breakfast over to Nancy's house and talked through the timeline of what needed to be done. Dani was worried about how they were going to get to everything, even with how she'd tried to prepare in advance. But whenever she got nervous, Nick was there, giving her hand a squeeze.

"We've got this. It's going to be great," he said as they walked to the car. "Everything is in place, and we have offers to help from everywhere." It was true. Auntie Helen had texted her to ask what Dani needed, and Theo had called Nick to say he would be around all weekend. She could almost believe everything would be ready to go when the auction happened the next night.

The day had passed in a whirlwind of activity. By the time the Festival's opening ceremony happened at the gazebo in the center of town at five, Dani had enough check marks on her to-do list to breathe easier. They'd left the dogs at his house, and she stood in front of Nick with his arms wrapped around her, listening to the opening speeches. They cheered as this year's queen and her court were crowned and did her best to let go of her worries about the event and beyond. She wanted to enjoy the moment and whatever time she and Nick had together.

He would let her know about the job when he was ready, and when things ended between them, it would be different from that horrible summer. This time she understood priorities and the decisions that went with those. If she wanted to be loved and accepted for who she was, she could do the same for Nick.

Because she did love him.

She turned in his arms and drank in the smile he gave her and the happiness she saw in his eyes. She wanted to tell him how she felt. How glad she was that he was here, how grateful she was for his help and support, but the words wouldn't come. Instead, she kissed him and allowed herself to forget everything else until they heard someone say, "Get a room."

Pulling apart, she saw Theo with his arm around Eden, holding Eden as close as Nick held her. "Get away," Nick said.

Theo came over and banged his shoulder into Nick's. "There are young people about. Not to mention Martin and Millie are here somewhere."

"Yes, we are." Dani turned and a moment later was getting a huge hug from Millie before she moved on to Nick. "You two enjoying things?"

Dani hoped no one saw her blush. She'd been enjoying Nick, that was for certain. Fortunately, Nick answered, "Everything's great, Ma, but Dani and I have a big day tomorrow, so we should probably head home for the night." Nick took a step closer to Theo, and Dani heard him add in a low voice, "Don't need a room. I've got a whole house."

Theo turned his bark of laughter into a cough. Before they could leave, Millie pulled Dani aside and said in a low voice, "Call your aunt. Please."

Dani wasn't surprised Rosie reached out to her closest friend. If Dani had the time, she'd have told Laurel. Thinking about love and acceptance, she said, "I will."

"Soon," Millie said, and Dani could hear concern in the woman's voice.

Dani gave Millie a kiss on the cheek and said, "I promise."

Nick grabbed her hand as they said goodnight to everyone but getting to Nick's car wasn't as quick as she might have hoped. People stopped them to talk, ask about the auction, update Dani on their pets. They ran into Gene Franks and his family, who Dani hadn't met, and spent time chatting with them. It was nearly an hour before they were back at Nick's place.

The dogs demanded their share of attention, and it was another half hour before Nick grabbed her and give her a kiss. "Where were we before Theo so rudely interrupted us?"

Dani was only too happy to show him.

On Saturday, before going to the Community Center to do her shift at the ticket table set up for the dance, Dani made a quick trip to the diner. The moment she walked in, Rosie put down the plates she was carrying, and pulled Dani into a hug so fierce, Dani thought she'd feel it forever. She held her aunt equally tightly.

Rosie whispered, "I'm sorry."

Dani simply responded with, "I know. I understand." There wasn't more to say, no additional explanations necessary. Dani's worries weren't completely gone, but she couldn't fault Rosie for wanting to help. Love made you do crazy things.

As the day went on, she stayed in touch with Nick by text, including who was taking care of the dogs and when, and almost forgot to stop at her house to pick up her outfit for the dance. She drove to Nick's, and together they drove to the Castle on the Hill to get everything ready.

Dani set up her laptop at a table in the corner where she could keep track of winners and results. Bidding on items ended at different times of the night so winners could be announced throughout the evening, and they could share the fundraising progress being made. She was so focused on her work, she jumped when Laurel appeared at the table. "Time for you to take a break. You need to eat and get ready."

Looking back at her spreadsheets, she said, "You're as bad as my Aunt Rosie, always trying to feed me."

"Occupational hazard, and I've brought along help for the getting ready part." Laurel motioned over her shoulder, and Dani saw Sheridan and Casey arriving with clothes bags over their arms.

"That's not necessary. I've got my dress and shoes in the conference room they're letting us use. It'll only take me a few minutes to change and brush out my hair."

"Nope, it's going to take a little longer than that," Casey said, holding up a small piece of luggage.

Dani had no idea what was in the case, but it couldn't be good. "You need all of that?" Was Dani such a lost cause?

Casey laughed. "Don't look so horrified. I brought way more than any of us need, but I like to be prepared. We're going to have fun."

Dani didn't think this looked like fun. Laurel took the pen out of Dani's hand. "Stop whatever you're doing and come with us."

Dani sent Nick a quick text to tell him where she'd gone, and the four of them went to the room where Dani had been keeping her things. In no time, they'd covered the center table with food on one side and dress prep pieces on the other. They ate the sandwiches Laurel and Sheridan brought and chatted about nothing important. It was wonderful. When they were done, Casey announced it was transformation time and took out mirrors, curling irons, and more. The woman brought more makeup than Dani owned in her lifetime.

The first thing Casey did was wet Dani's hair and put it in big rollers, then had her sit and wait. Dani watched with pleasure as Casey turned the other women into princesses. She used makeup to bring out the blue and gold in Laurel's eyes and created a gorgeous up-do from Sheridan's wildly curly hair.

"Your turn to be experimented on," Sheridan said to Dani after Casey finished with her makeup.

"Very funny," Casey said. "As if you don't love what I did. Before I start, let me see what you're wearing."

Dani's first thought was that she was going to look drab by comparison next to her beautiful friends, but it didn't matter. The auction was what was important, not how she was dressed for the night. She took out the cap sleeve green lace cocktail dress she had recently bought. When she'd picked up Janelle's items for the auction earlier in the week, the dress was waiting for her. It had a v-neck collar and nipped in at the waist with a full skirt below. Dani had been thrilled when it fit perfectly. She didn't even mind Janelle's, "Told you so." She'd brought black kitten heeled shoes to wear, knowing she'd be on her feet most of the night. The three women ooh'd and ahh'd over her choice, and Dani couldn't hold back the grin. She'd never had this experience with girlfriends before. Their warmth—and lack of criticism—was wonderful.

"That's gorgeous. I know exactly what I'm going to do," Casey said. "Step into my salon."

As Casey got to work, Dani wished she could see what the woman was doing. Sheridan and Laurel kept making encouraging sounds and giving her a thumbs up, but that didn't help. Casey worked on her longer than Dani had ever taken with her own appearance. Eventually, she spritzed something called setting spray over Dani's makeup, and said Dani was done.

"Put on your dress, then I'll take out the rollers and brush out your hair." Dani did as she was told, and a few minutes later she was being doused with hairspray. Neither her hair nor her makeup was going anywhere tonight.

Dani stood up and gave a spin, making the skirt of the dress flair out. "So, what do you think?"

Laurel spoke first. "You look amazing. Like Emma Stone in *La La Land*."

Not likely, Dani thought. "Sure, if she gained twenty or thirty pounds."

"Stop that. First, most Hollywood actresses could stand to gain at least that much. Second—see for yourself."

Laurel positioned Dani in front of the mirror Casey set up against a wall. Dani's first reaction was to move away, but her friend held her still, so she looked.

And hardly recognized her reflection. Thanks to Casey's talent—and a set of false eyelashes that took way too long to put on—her eyes looked huge. Dani didn't know how Casey had managed it, but her lips were lush, and her hair bounced when she moved her head. She never looked so good. "Holy shit. If you ever wanted to leave the senior center, you could do makeup full time."

Casey looked pleased. "Does this mean you like it?"

"Very much. Thank you." Dani gave Casey a quick hug.

"You are quite welcome. Nick is going to swallow his tongue when he sees you."

Dani wasn't sure about that, but given how often she felt like the caterpillar in a room full of butterflies, she couldn't deny it was fun to feel beautiful.

She picked up her phone to see what she'd missed while getting ready and was surprised to see the time. There were minutes before the doors opened. Her stomach flipped. Time to get out and do a last walk through. She thanked her friends again for their help and headed to the ballroom.

Since she'd been gone, the last of the decorations had been put up and the space was festooned with gold and blue—balloons, streamers, twinkle lights. Dani made certain each of the tables with auction items was properly grouped by what time the bidding would close. She went to her computer—the command center as Nick had called it earlier—and took out the clipboard with the list of things she'd be doing for the night. She'd barely stepped away when she saw Nick staring at her. Really staring. She smiled.

He looked as though he'd swallowed his tongue.

Chapter Thirty-Nine

♥

Nick was speechless. It wasn't as if he'd never seen Dani dressed up, or that he cared if she wore makeup or not, but tonight she looked amazing. Her friends had done something with her face and her hair, and then there was the deep, sexy neckline of her dress, which invited his eyes to feast. And yet it was more. It was a look of sheer joy and excitement that almost brought him to his knees. She glowed, and he hoped that part of her happiness was connected to him.

"You look amazing," he said as he walked up and put his arms around her waist.

"Thank you. Casey worked her magic. She's a fairy godmother in addition to being a princess. I think it's the false eyelashes." She batted them, and he laughed. "They feel a little weird, but I like how they make my eyes look. My mom would approve."

"It's not the lashes. It's you. It's all you." And to prove he meant what he said, he drew her in for a kiss. He intended for it to be quick but gave that up the moment she was in his arms. All he wanted to do was find the zipper on the back of the dress and get her out of it.

Later. He'd do that later. For now, they'd get through the night, and as soon as possible, he'd take her back to the house to celebrate.

Naked.

"So much for wearing lipstick," she said when they broke the kiss.

"Put more on if you want, but I am going to kiss it off again the first chance I get." He couldn't hide his hunger for her.

"Right, forget the lipstick."

"You'll be lucky if I don't also ruin your hair by running my hands through it."

She patted a curl and said, "You'll get stuck. I think there's a can of hairspray on it."

"Another reason to prefer ponytails."

"I have to say you clean up quite nicely yourself, Mr. Hanson." He knew this was a dressy event, so besides a tie, he'd borrowed a jacket from Theo. He was glad he made the effort. "Do the final walk through with me before they let guests in?"

"Absolutely. It's going to be a hell of a party. People started arriving at seven thirty. We directed them to the bar. I think the hotel's going to be thrilled with the dance committee when they see how much people spent."

Nick did his best to focus on the tables and the items up for auction, but all he could do was look at Dani. She looked gorgeous. Animated and smiling, he couldn't get over how happy she was. When she wasn't looking, he took a picture of her, wanting to capture her excitement. He understood part of her energy was nerves and until this ended successfully, she was going to be on edge and checking through the list of things that needed to be done. But, damn, if he didn't have a list of his own—a list of ways to distract her from worrying.

An hour later, the event was in full swing. The room and the dance floor were crowded, the first round of bidding had closed, and Mayor Keller announced the winners. Dani was concerned a few items had gone for under their value, but he reminded her the night was still young and there were plenty of chances to make that up. Bidders proved him right with the next round, which also included the people who'd won the packages. The items had gone for over a thousand dollars each, both comfortably over their baseline as he'd hoped. Dani had squealed and jumped into his arms when she saw the final total. He couldn't remember the last time he'd been so happy to be part of a deal.

We want you to come back as soon as possible.

Bronson's voice popped into his head as it had throughout the day. Two days until Monday. Bronson was sure what Nick's answer would be. A few weeks ago, so was Nick, but every time he thought about the offer, his heart raced and his stomach clenched. And at some point, he was going to have to tell Dani.

But not tonight.

A tap on his shoulder had him turning to see a couple he didn't recognize. The man asked, "Excuse me, are you Nick Hanson?"

His thoughts distracted by the New York offer, he said, "I suppose I should ask 'Who wants to know' before I answer that."

"I'm Chris Butler and this is my wife, Monica. Ed Franks pointed you out. You drew the home we want to buy." Chris put out his hand and Nick took it.

"I did. It's nice of you to introduce yourselves. I'm so glad you like the design."

Monica offered her hand next. "We did. Very much. Ed said you'd be getting back to us soon with a price. We were so relieved to find what we wanted. I can't tell you how many hours I spent online looking at plans and not seeing anything that worked. We were afraid we'd have to tear it down and start from scratch."

"Definitely no need to do that. You should see what I was working with when I redesigned the house I grew up in."

As Nick chatted with the Butlers, he learned about Chris' tech start-up and Monica's dermatology practice. They were also excited to talk to him about the plans he created. He listened to what they liked about the design and asked if there was anything they'd change or add. He promised to do his best to make the living room and kitchen a little bigger. As the conversation ended, Monica asked, "Do you have a business card?"

He almost laughed. For years he handed out business cards like pieces of gum. His social life was mostly networking that involving the mandatory exchange of cards. He hadn't thought about them since leaving New York. He was curious though. "Not on me. Why do you ask?"

"My sister and her husband recently inherited the house where he grew up in Jefferson. It's a great place and a good size but it was built in the 30's or 40's so the layout is terrible and the closet space is nearly non-existent. I'd love to give her your information and see if you could help her give that house a second chance."

Second Chance Houses. The business name popped into Nick's head. He instantly saw a logo of a house drawn inside of another house. There were lots of homes like Dani's and the Butlers' that could be renovated. His head started swirling with thoughts of websites and how to reach clients locally and beyond. He didn't realize he'd been silent for so long until Monica asked, "Are you okay?"

"I am, sorry. You caught me by surprise on an already crazy week." How had his head taken such a leap? "You'll have my contact information when Ed gives you the design." He almost added, "She can reach out to me whenever she's ready."

He said goodbye to the Butlers and went in search of Dani, trying to get thoughts of home design out of his head. He found her staring at her laptop, frowning and talking to herself, her hands threaded through her hair. Apparently, the hairspray wasn't a deterrent after all.

As he came closer, he heard her saying, "No, no, no. This has to be a mistake. Why didn't we catch this sooner?"

He sat down next to her and pulled one hand free of her hair and took it in his. "What's wrong?"

"I was putting in the final bids and I noticed that a number wasn't changing properly. I went through the formulas on the spreadsheets. There's a programing error, and we've double counted some of the entries. The totals are off. Nick, we're over eight hundred dollars away from our goal."

All the joy he'd seen in her face earlier was gone. She took her hand back, stood, and paced as she rambled. "We raised more than ever, and we still didn't make it. No, it's fine. I can fix this. I can make up the difference. I'll add the money to my bid on Aunt Helen's picture. No one will know. We'll be able to announce the good news before the end of the night. I can't let everyone down."

Nick watched as tears filled Dani's eyes. They'd reach the goal, but it wasn't how she wanted it to happen. He imagined her hearing the congratulations on the event's success in the coming weeks and feeling as though she'd faked the results. It would be a blow to her heart every time. He had to do something. "I have an idea."

"Final bidding has closed. There's nothing else to do."

"I need you to trust me." She looked as though she might argue, then she nodded. His heart swelled. The Butlers' praise was good for his ego, but Dani's trust meant more. He gave her a quick kiss, and he ran up to the microphone, motioning for the DJ to stop after the song was over. "Ladies and gentlemen, can I have your attention? I have a special announcement. We are not quite at our goal, and you know how important this library room is. To help us reach our target, I've got a surprise item. I'm not going to tell you how much we need, but as soon as we break the goal, I'll stop the bidding, and we'll have a winner."

Dani came up to the stage and covered the microphone. "Nick, what are you doing?"

"Getting us over the finish line. This is going to work." He kissed her, and there were a few whoops. "Sorry, not that kind of auction. How would up to four of you like an all-expense paid weekend in New York City? That's right, I am offering a two-night stay in my apartment in New York. It will include parking—which on its own is worth a fortune—dinner both nights, and tickets to the Broadway show or sports event of your choice." There were boo's followed by cat calls. "I didn't say you had to root for the home team. Museums, shops, Central Park, and the Empire State Building. However you want to spend your time, I'll make it happen. Name the weekend, and the place is yours. I'll make the value of the weekend at least two thousand dollars, so I'm going to start the bidding at five hundred."

"Five hundred dollars," was called out from somewhere in the room, but he didn't see who had said it.

"Six hundred." That was from Theo, and Nick gave his brother a look. Theo called back, "I figured it'll be fun to see how you've been living. It'll also give me a chance to trash your room the way you once trashed mine."

Nick groaned into the microphone. "I probably deserve that. Come on, folks, don't make me spend the weekend with my brother. Dig deep for this one. Four of you could get together and split the cost. It will be worth every penny."

"Seven hundred," came another voice.

"Eight hundred."

"I heard that. I want to hear nine." Nine was called out from the back of the room and Nick gave a wave to Janelle. "So close to what we're looking for. Tell you what, when we hit this number, I'm going to add ten extra Chrome books to whatever the library purchases for our students." It would be a good use of the money he was getting for the house design.

"Twelve hundred dollars," called out Chris.

"Chris, you're about to be very popular because you're going to New York. And Fable Notch, you are going to have a new young adult room," Nick said, halting the bidding. A cheer went up in the room and his heart soared as he looked over at Dani and saw the delight in her expression. He went over to her, and she jumped into his arms. He picked her up as he hugged her and swung her around. He hadn't felt like this in forever. Part of it was helping Dani, but part of it was helping everyone else. When was the last time his actions had mattered so much?

"I can't believe you did that," she said. Her smile was everything.

"I had to. Besides, I'd been feeling like the only person in town who hadn't donated to the auction. I finally got my chance."

"You certainly did it with flair. Cole may be the one with the singing career, but tonight you are totally my rock star."

"That means the world to me." And it did. Doing this for the library and the town felt good, but being Dani's hero felt amazing. The music started again as the party continued. Nick wanted to celebrate. He held out his hand to Dani. "Dance with me?"

She put her hand in his and said, "I'd love to."

They joined the crowd on the dance floor, and Nick was pleased when the second song was slow. There was nothing like having her in his arms. She felt so right there.

As they danced, she asked, "Where will you stay when Chris and his friends come to New York and invade your apartment?"

Here with you.

The answer came to him so fast he nearly stumbled. Second Chance Houses. Was there a way to have more time with Dani? Did things have to be over when he went back to his job?

And would she want that? More questions. They hadn't talked about how they felt about one another because they'd agreed this was something short term, but things had changed for him. Had they changed for her? He didn't know. First, he had to tell her about the job offer—and decide what he was doing. Deciding not to overwhelm her with everything he was thinking, he said, "There are plenty of hotels. I can find something for a few days. I'm relieved my offer worked. It could have fallen completely flat."

"Guess you and your offer were irresistible."

"As long as you think so." She wiggled her eyebrows, making him laugh. When the music changed to an up-beat song, he asked, "Do we need to stay until the end of the dance?"

"Nope, I've got all the paperwork and information to get in touch with the winners. Monday I'll start contact-ing people and acknowledging the donors. The dance committee will take care of things here."

"I am one of the donors now, and I have some ideas about how you can acknowledge me. What would you say to getting out of here and celebrating a little more privately?"

"I'd say let me collect my things."

It took longer than he would have liked. People stopped them to say thank you and congratulations. It was the longest half hour of his day as they gathered everything she'd brought to the hotel and headed to his house. He'd never been more grateful for so little traffic and everything being close by. They gave the dogs a few minutes of attention until he couldn't wait. He grabbed her and kissed her deeply, loving the feel of the woman he loved.

There it was. He wasn't going to pretend that it wasn't true. He'd done enough pretending, enough ignoring the truth. He was done with that. He was in love with Dani. He didn't know when it started, but he suspected it never stopped.

He reached for the zipper at the back of her dress at the same time as she loosened his tie. When the dress came off her shoulders and dropped to the floor, he saw the lacy black bra and matching panties she wore and wondered if they'd make it to the bedroom or if he'd have to take her against the nearest wall. The idea had appeal. "If I had known that's what you were wearing under that dress, I probably would have hauled you up to a room in the hotel and not wasted time getting here. How is it you keep getting sexier?"

He grabbed her by the waist and picked her up. She wrapped her legs around him and, after giving the wall a glance and changing his mind, he walked quickly to the bedroom, shutting the door once he got there, and hoping the dogs would understand the message. No interruptions allowed.

He turned on the bedside lamp and climbed into bed with her "I've been aching to have you all to myself all evening. No, strike that, for the last two days. We've been too busy."

He kissed her again as she unbuttoned his shirt. "I forgot how sexy it can be to get you out of your serious clothes. You've been so casual since you've been here."

"If wearing a shirt and tie means you undress me more often, I promise to wear them for you."

"I'd like you to be wearing a lot less."

"No argument." His shirt was undone, and he jerked it out of his pants and tossed it to the floor as she got to work on his belt. Deciding it was taking too long, he helped her, and in no time he was naked. He brought her to him, loving the feel of her skin against his. His hands cupped her breasts, and he broke the kiss to work his way down to lick the lacy edge of the bra that still covered her. Her nipples were hard beneath the material. As wonderful as she looked, he needed her naked. He unhooked the front clasp, and as soon as she was bared to him, he took her into his mouth, licking and gently biting her sensitive flesh, loving how she moaned and how her legs worked back and forth.

Her hands were in his hair, on his shoulders, running down his back. She was as needy as he was. He almost reached for a condom to give them both the release they craved but changed his mind when his hand slid into her underwear. She was so wet, so slick. He grabbed the sides of her panties to drag them over her legs. As he worked them off, he noticed she was still wearing her shoes. Blood surged to his erection at the sight of her naked except for the pumps. Those heels were going to be leaving marks on his skin before the night was done.

Before he could continue, she sat up and pulled her legs under her. Had he done something wrong? "You first," she said.

"Me what first?" Instead of answering, she gave his shoulders a push. He lay back on the bed as directed, and she kissed her way down his torso, pinching his nipples, her nails teasing his chest and stomach before her hand wrapped around his cock. He couldn't take his eyes off of her and when she looked at him and took him into his mouth, only years of control kept him from coming instantly.

He sank into the pillows as her hands and tongue created magic. For the first time, he wished she was wearing a ponytail, as he pushed her hair out of her face so he could watch what she was doing to him. Had there ever been a sexier sight? Maybe when she rode him. Or maybe when she was coming as he licked her. God, it didn't matter. Everything she did drove him crazy, and he adored it. She sucked and swirled, stroked and tantalized him. Wanting more connection, he reached out for her and found he could touch her pussy. As he stroked her slit, she moaned, and the vibrations added to his pleasure. Such glorious madness.

There had been other times when he'd come in her mouth, but tonight he wanted to be inside her. "I need you," he said.

"You have me." He liked the desire in her voice.

"I need to be inside you."

She stopped sucking, but kept a hand on his erection. Kissing his inner thighs, she asked, "Now?"

Tease. He would make her pay for that. He grabbed her shoulders, pulled her up. As he kissed her deeply, he reached for a condom, then rolled her on her back. "Now."

Chapter Forty

♥

Dani loved that she could please Nick in so many ways. Sometimes she didn't know which was better, when he licked her or when she licked him. Both had their benefits.

As she spread her legs, he settled between them, but when he didn't slide inside her immediately, she asked, "Is something wrong?" She said it lightly, but when he didn't answer, she put a hand on his cheek. "Nick?"

"You are so beautiful. Being here with you, looking at you. You take my breath away." He brought his mouth to hers and kissed her so tenderly she could have cried. It was so unfair to have this connection again with Nick, knowing it was something she couldn't keep. Some relationships aren't meant to be, Laurel had said. It sucked that she was right.

As they continued to kiss, she slid her hand between their bodies and wrapped her fingers around his erection. He gasped as she expected, and she reached her tongue into his mouth to tease his. Lifting her hips, she let the tip of his shaft tease her entrance. It was as if a dam broke inside of him. One moment his touch was soft and loving, and the next he was demanding and hungry. Her hand was trapped as he slammed into her and stretched her swollen flesh. When he drew back, she removed her hand and grabbed his shoulders as she wrapped her legs around him to draw him back into her.

It wasn't long before they found a rhythm that had them both desperate and crying out. Nick kissed her mouth, her neck, her breasts. Her nails raked down his back to his ass, loving the feel of his muscles as she caressed him. She swore she could sense his desire through his skin. He continued to take her deeper, harder, and she met his every need with hers, letting him know with her body how he excited her.

"Oh, God, Dani. What you do to me."

She'd never tire of hearing that. "Do I please you?"

"Very much."

"Drive you crazy?"

"Yes." It was practically a moan.

"Make you want?"

"Yes."

She loved every clipped answer. "Then take me. As hard as you want, as fast as you want."

It was as if her words stoked a fire in him, gave him permission to unleash all he was feeling, and he drove into her more fiercely than before. Every stroke brought her higher, took her with him.

As he reached his climax and yelled out her name, a voice in her head screamed, "I love you." How she managed to keep from saying out loud she wasn't sure, but she was grateful for the modicum of restraint. This might not be the time to say it, but she could let herself think it, feel it.

Accept it.

When he rolled to get a tissue from the nightstand, she saw red marks on his back. "I scratched you."

He turned to look over his shoulder. "Really? Your nails or your heels?"

She looked closer. Since some marks were near his shoulders and others were lower, she answered, "Both."

"Excellent." He sounded pleased.

That wasn't the answer she expected. "Why is that excellent?"

"It means you got carried away." He ran his hands down her legs and took her shoes off. "Don't think you need these anymore, but in case you were wondering, I find you wearing heels while you're naked very sexy."

"Good to know." Not that there would be many more times for them. No, she wouldn't think about that. Tonight, and for as long as they had together, she'd stay in the moment. She'd enjoy what they had, what she'd learned, and everything she felt for him. If she was going to get hurt, she was going to let herself hurt big. No more holding back. No more living her life while spending most of her energy wondering if she was doing it right.

* * *

After the madness of the past week, it was wonderful to sleep in. They'd made love a second time in the middle of the night, and Dani had fallen into an exhausted sleep, drained by the day's events and the acceptance of her feelings.

She'd slept so deeply, it took her a minute to notice Nick wasn't in bed with her when she woke. She got up to find him and, realizing that her change of clothes was in his car, put on one of his t-shirts. She went to the bathroom to brush her teeth, and he walked in with a tray of coffee and food as she came out.

He gave a whistle. "I didn't think you could look sexier than you did last night, but my shirt is now my favorite thing you've ever worn. Let me put this down so I can kiss you and say good morning properly."

He put the tray on the nightstand, took off his shirt, and pulled her back onto the bed for a kiss that quickly turned improper. "So, coffee and then I can ravish you, or does the ravishing come first?"

"As much as I enjoy a good ravish, the coffee smells awfully good, and those are cinnamon buns are from Just Right. I'd recognize them anywhere. Aunt Rosie carries them at the diner because they're so popular."

He pretended to look hurt. "Blown off for coffee and cinnamon rolls."

She reached over to him, grabbed a roll, and bit into it. With her mouth full said, "They're beyond good. How'd you manage to get them? The place must be packed. I would expect her to run out early."

"Ah, this is the advantage of knowing the owner. I called and asked Sheridan if I could sneak around back and pick up a to go order. She suggested the rolls and let me park behind the cafe because the area is so crowded. So, if I want your attention in the morning, bring coffee, and cover myself in icing."

She stuck a finger in the white sweetness and painted it on his chest. "Let's see how it works."

It worked very well. They needed to reheat both the coffee and the breakfast in the microwave when they were done. Nick also insisted on a shower to make certain all of the icing was gone. It was almost noon before they left the house with the dogs. Dani had no complaints.

Fable Notch was usually busy on weekends with tourists, but Festival weekends brought that to another level. What would normally take them ten minutes to drive took more than twice as long. Fortunately, Auntie Helen had reserved them a parking space in the lot behind the Artist Cooperative. As Nick said, it helped to know the owner. She and Nick went into the cooperative to visit Auntie Helen, but she was so busy all they could do was give her a quick hello and a hug.

They headed outside where Aunt Rosie and two of her servers were serving up blueberry silver dollar pancakes; the Kinsman Diner's entry into the blueberry competition. To keep all the entries within walking distance of one another, businesses that didn't serve food hosted restaurants whose establishments were not on the four streets that made up the downtown. Sheridan would be serving outside Just Right, but Laurel would be at A Thousand Lives. People could sample and turn in their votes until three o'clock. Dani had offered to help her friends, but they'd told her she had enough to do with the auction and by Sunday she'd want the day off. They'd been right. She was glad not to have to think about anything other than walking around the Festival with Nick.

They left the coop and joined the crowds in the center of town. They stopped at different places, looking at what vendors had put out, and sampling foods. She found Laurel with a large crowd in front of her, offering samples of chicken and waffles with blueberry sauce. It was incredible. After her second-place finish last year, Laurel was determined to win. Dani thought she had a good shot.

The dogs dragged them into Significant Paws, where they ended up chatting with the owner as well as with strangers who commented on Otis's beauty and size. She was used to his getting attention. She was a little less comfortable with all the attention that was directed at her.

As they walked, people stopped them to talk about the auction. Every few steps, someone wanted to congratulate them and thank them for doing such a great job. Ruth Toor, the head librarian, called them over when they passed the library's tent and hugged them both so hard it took Dani a breath to get the air back in her lungs.

"We are so grateful for all of your hard work. Nick, I didn't have time to talk to you last night. Thank you for what you did for the library. For all of us."

"It was a team effort, Mrs. Toor," he said, and put an arm around Dani's waist, drawing her against him. "It wouldn't have been enough if it weren't for what Dani and Nancy had done before I even got here."

Dani let her heart swell at his acknowledgment and at the difference in Nick. The man she'd left in New York was driven only by his goals. There was no stopping to notice anyone else. Even when he'd first arrived in her clinic four weeks ago, she couldn't have imagined him being a part of anything but his own plans.

It was a perfect afternoon. Every few minutes, or so it seemed, Nick would find a reason to kiss her. She never thought of herself as someone who enjoyed public displays of affection, but it turned out she was. She could kiss him forever and never tire of it. Even if forever wasn't an option.

She'd never tell Nick, but for a few moments this past week, she thought about what it would mean to leave Fable Notch and join him in New York again. The moment she thought it, she knew it was the wrong decision. Being happy with him was one thing, but happiness with her life was much bigger, and she wouldn't find it in the city. Whatever else she felt after he was gone and however long the pain lasted, she was where she wanted to be, in a place where she could be herself.

As she looked at a beautifully crafted set of wind chimes at one of the vendor tables, the sound of a high-pitched voice yelling, "Princess!" startled Dani. She turned to look for Casey and instead watched as a young girl flung herself at Presley and wrapped her arms around the dog.

Chapter Forty-One

♥

Nick heard the little girl's squeal, but assumed it meant Dani's friend was around somewhere dressed as Cinderella or some other princess. It wasn't until Presley jumped up and down and pulling at her leash that he looked in time to see a little girl in a unicorn shirt and pink leggings hug his dog.

"Princess, I found you. Where have you been? I missed you so much. Why did you run away?"

Nick was about stop the girl and tell her to leave his dog alone when Presley's reaction to the child told him the truth. Cold gripped his heart as he tried to think of a way to avoid what was coming.

"Kimberly Ann March, you can't go racing off like that, especially in a crowd. You scared—oh my god." The maternal voice changed from concern to surprise mid-sentence. "I don't believe it."

Neither did Nick. He didn't trust himself to speak. He hoped if he didn't, time would rewind. Then he and Dani could walk down a different street and none of this would happen. But he wasn't that lucky. Presley was spinning in circles around the girl, licking her face and trying to keep her balance while being hugged.

No, not Presley. Princess.

The woman, who had tears in her eyes, and girl were joined by a man who held out his hand to Nick. Nick took it automatically, still silent. "I'm Doug March. This is my wife, Tracy, and our daughter, Kim. I can't believe you found our dog."

Nick looked away from the man and back to Presley. His chest hurt and his heart was racing. The Xanax was at the house. Square breathing. In for four... He was vaguely aware of Dani giving his hand a squeeze before she said, "Nice to meet you, all. I'm Dani Vaughn, and this is Nick Hanson. I'm also Pres—Princess's doctor."

Tracy gave them both quick hugs. Nick did his best not to squirm. "We didn't think we'd ever see her again. Kimmy's been heartbroken since losing Princess."

"What's this thing on her leg?" asked Kim.

"It's a brace to help her heal." As Dani explained Presley's injury to the March's—he was not going to call her Princess—Nick let what was happening sink in. Another change. Another loss.

Dani continued to make conversation as Nick's anger grew. He wasn't ready to hand over his dog. "If you don't mind my asking, how did you lose her?"

Tracy looked embarrassed. "We'd been visiting friends in the area. We'd stopped for gas on the drive home—I think it was one exit south of here—and I took Kim to the bathroom. When we got out of the car, she didn't close the door behind her. Doug was filling up the tank on the other side. Princess had been asleep in the back, and we didn't notice she was gone until we were home, which is three hours away. We called the gas station, but no one remembered seeing her."

Nick wasn't satisfied. "Why doesn't she have a collar or a tag?"

This time Doug answered. "The collar is also Kim's fault. She takes it off Princess when we get home, but this time she did it in the car. She doesn't think the dog likes it. We knew it was a bad habit, but we never imagined the trouble it could cause. All of this could have been avoided."

Nick wanted to yell that clearly this girl was too irresponsible to have a dog. Taking off the collar. Leaving a car door open. Presley should stay with him, or who knew what would happen the next time Kim forgot something important.

Stupid, irresponsible little shit.

As he heard his father's voice, understanding hit him. Kim was a year or two younger than he had been when he broke the dishwasher. Like him, she hadn't done anything intentionally malicious. It was bad luck. Kids made mistakes. Everyone made mistakes. *It's what you do about them that makes the difference*. Ed's voice. Much better. There was only one thing to do, and it was going to suck. "I guess it's a lucky thing you came for the Festival. I have some toys and things I bought her. I'll give them to you if you want to come over."

Kim looked excited. "You bought her toys? That's so great."

Tracy was more practical. "Are you sure?"

"I'm not going to be needing them," he said. He hoped no one noticed the pain in his voice, but when Dani pressed against him, he knew she had heard. He wanted to be mad for not being able to hide what he was feeling. Instead, he was grateful she understood. "Are you free to come get them?"

Kim let go of the dog to ask, "Daddy, can we get Princess's toys?"

"Yes," Doug said, then looked at Nick. "If it's not too much trouble, not that we haven't completely disrupted your day already."

"It's fine." Nick wanted to get this over with as fast as possible. Rip off the band-aid. Let the pain come. "It's going to take us a bit to get to our car and drive there, but it shouldn't be more than half an hour. Come over any time after that."

"Thank you. I can't tell you how much this means to us, to Kim."

Once he'd given them the address and his phone number in case they were delayed, they stood there not moving. Nick was wondering what everyone was waiting for until Dani took the leash out of his hand and handed it to Doug. "We'll see you in a few minutes," she said.

Nick watched as the family took Presley. Otis gave a whine as he watched his friend walk away. Nick thought it was an understatement. When he found his voice, all he could manage was, "Let's go."

They walked quickly to retrieve his car, avoiding people, then drove in silence. He was glad Dani didn't say anything. He didn't trust his ability to respond calmly. He looked in the rearview mirror and saw Otis. Only Otis.

In for four. Out for four.

Once they got to the house, Nick found an empty box and walked around picking up toys and dropping them in. He emptied and cleaned the food dishes and put those in as well. Dani found a few he'd missed under the couch. She reached to touch him, but he moved away. By the time the Marches arrived, he, Dani, and Otis were waiting outside with the toys, a bag of food, and everything else he'd accumulated for Presley. He'd included the blanket she used whenever she was on the couch. He wouldn't be able to look at it anymore.

As the family got out of the car, Presley ran to him. He put down the box and kneeled to give her hugs and scratches. He drew in the scent of her fur and breath and willed himself not to cry. As he held her one last time, he whispered, "Time for you to go with your family, girl. Thank you for coming into my life. I know they think I rescued you, but you rescued me."

He gave the dog a kiss on the forehead and rubbed her ears. He wasn't certain, but he thought he heard Dani sniffle.

Finally, he stood, gave the box to Doug, and walked Presley to the car. She got in and jumped carefully to the back. When she looked out the window at Nick and bumped her nose against it, the rest of his heart broke.

"You'll want to take her to her regular doctor in the next week so he can examine her," Dani told them. "The brace needs to be on for at least another three to four weeks and has to stay tight and dry, so no taking it off, Kim. And you might want to look into getting her microchipped."

The girl gave Dani a hug. "I promise. I'm going to take the bestest care of her."

"The microchip is a good idea," said Tracy. "I can't tell you how grateful we are that you found her and that we found you."

"Glad I could help." Nick was surprised he'd managed that many words.

"We come up to the area every so often. We'd be happy to let you know when we're around if you want to see Princess again."

Presley, he corrected in his head. "No, that's not necessary. I don't..." *Live here*, he was going to say. His heart rate was increasing. "I don't want to complicate things for you."

"Well, if you change your mind, you have my number. Really. It's no problem. And if for some reason you find yourself near Worcester, Massachusetts, give us a call."

"Thanks," he managed. He wanted them to leave. He didn't have a lot of graciousness left.

Doug got to the car, and after too much waving, the Marches drove away. Nick stood there staring until they were out of sight, then went into the house and slammed the door. It was a good thing Dani and Otis had gone in first or he would have shut it in her face.

Dani stood there, looking as lost as he felt. "Nick?"

He looked at her and said nothing, then stormed into the living room. Staring blankly at the things around him, he gripped the back of the couch so hard he was surprised his fingers didn't rip through the leather, then let out a yell of anguish as all he'd held back burst free in a ball of rage and pain.

"It's not fair. It's not fucking fair." It was all too much. Everything that had happened in the last several months hit him like an avalanche, overpowering and icy cold. How much could one man lose in such a short amount of time? Why did he let himself care in the first place if this was going to be the cost?

He wasn't aware that he'd moved from yelling to crying until his legs gave out from under him, and he sank to the floor. A breath later, Dani was there, her arms around him.

"I'm sorry," she whispered as she held him. "I'm so sorry."

His head fell against her chest as he sobbed. Tears for the loss of Presley quickly became ones for Henry. God, he missed his friend. There had been a hole in his life he refused to let himself notice. He hadn't grieved when it happened—it was too big—but as his emotions cycled and his thoughts raced, he searched for the clarity and understanding he craved.

How different would things have been in the weeks before that first panic attack if Henry hadn't died? Or after? He never would have left New York if Henry had been there. His friend would have understood why the loss of his job was so difficult. Would Nick have even made the mistakes at work if he'd had Henry to talk to? Pain became anger and moved back to grief so quickly, Nick couldn't process the feelings. He only knew how much he hurt.

If Henry hadn't died.

If he hadn't screwed up at work.

If he hadn't come back to Fable Notch.

If Dani hadn't been here.

Dani. One more thing he couldn't have.

He needed to get back to his plans so he could stop hurting so much. He'd been offered what he most wanted since the day he lost it. Tomorrow he'd call Bronson.

He'd do what he knew how to do in the place where he did it best. This time, he'd stay focused.

One more band-aid to rip off. He'd make this quick. She knew he wasn't staying. It wouldn't be a shock. He shifted his weight so he could stand and took Dani's arms off him. "I'm fine. I'd like you to leave."

"Nick, no. You shouldn't be alone. You don't have to be alone."

"Why not? I may as well start now. I got the call on Thursday from New York. I've been offered my job back. They found out I was behind the idea Terry presented, and they loved it. Hell, if this becomes as big as I think, I've probably got a bonus coming. They want an answer tomorrow. It's time for me to get back on track."

"Stop, you're upset. This is a lot to deal with. I've been with owners when they've lost their pet and—"

"I'm not a pet owner. Presley wasn't mine. You said at the beginning she was too well taken care of to be a stray. I shouldn't have forgotten. She's back with her family, and I've got to get back to work. The auction is done and—"

It was her turn to interrupt. "And so are we?"

"What else is there? Remember who you're talking to. The man whose plans mean more than people. Who'd rather get the goal than the girl."

"When I said that..."

"You were right. We knew this was temporary. You should go. Make this easier for both of us."

He waited for her to argue, ask to stay again. And if she had, he might have given in. Everything in him ached. He wanted her in his arms again, but he stood still. He watched as her eyes teared and then cleared. She squared her shoulders. "If you're sure."

"I am." He wasn't, but he would be. He had to be.

"Take care of yourself, Nick."

He nodded. He almost reached for her. Asked her to forget everything he said. Instead, he stayed where he was with his hands in his pockets. He heard her in the bedroom, and she came out with her bag stuffed with things she'd left. For a moment, he thought she was going to say something, but she motioned to Otis and left.

He didn't know how long he stood there after she was gone, staring at nothing, trying to think about anything other than Henry, Presley, and Dani, and what these last few weeks had meant to him.

He paced through the empty rooms. The house was overwhelmingly silent. He'd gotten used to the dog's snoring, howling, and need for attention and play. Since finding her, he hadn't been alone.

Since coming back, he hadn't been alone. And it had been wonderful.

Rage and loss coursed through him again. Not knowing what else to do, he threw open the back door, stepped onto the deck and howled. Long and loud, he let everything he was feeling loose in a sound that had birds flying out of trees.

But it didn't help. Nick ran to the bathroom, sure he was going to throw up. He sat on the cold, tile floor, hoping the nausea would pass. There was a rushing in his ears and breathing was difficult. His vision darkened at the edges. His heart rate was soaring, and no breathing technique was going to help.

The last time he'd felt this, he'd ended up in the hospital. It took a few more minutes, but he finally got off the floor. He looked in three different spots before he found the Xanax in the bedside table drawer. Next to the condoms. Which he'd bought because of Dani.

The Xanax wasn't going to be enough.

Because once his heart rate and breathing were back to normal, once he'd stopped sweating and the room stopped spinning, he needed to face the truth. In the meantime, he couldn't do this alone. He took out his phone and found the number he needed. He didn't say hello. "Are you busy?"

"No, why?"

Nick couldn't hide the relief in his voice when he asked, "Could you come over?"

"On my way."

"Door's unlocked." He sank to the floor and waited.

Chapter Forty-Two

D ani was glad she'd left her car at Nick's, or she would have had to walk from his place. There was nowhere to go but home, and there was no one to call because everyone was still at the Festival. She went to her room and curled up on her bed. When Otis joined her, she buried her face in his fur and, once again, cried out the pain.

After all they'd been through in the last few weeks, she couldn't believe Nick had asked her to leave. As if he could shut it all off. And although she didn't expect him to choose staying here over going back to New York, she never imagined he'd push her out the door the way he did.

She must have dozed off because it was early evening when her phone buzzed. She hated that she wanted it to be Nick with an apology and a request to see her. Instead, it was a text from Laurel. *We won!*

It took her a minute to realize her friend was talking about the blueberry competition. She could picture her friend's delight. A little good news. It helped. *You deserve it. So happy for you.*

We need to celebrate. I'm texting everyone. Come over.

Dani was happy for Laurel, but her own heartache was too new and heavy. *Can't make it. Another time.*

Ooh, you and Nick have hot plans? Laurel tacked on an eggplant emoji. Normally, Dani would have laughed.

She considered lying. It wasn't time to let people know, but if Laurel found out later that Dani had kept this to herself, there'd be hell to pay. She squared her shoulders and typed, *Nick is heading back to New York tomorrow or the day after. We're done.*

Three dots appeared seconds after she hit send. *That ass. I'm on my way.*

No, I knew this was coming. Have fun. I'll call you tomorrow. Dani didn't want to make the evening about her. Laurel deserved to celebrate. There would be time to cry with everyone later. For tonight, she'd curl up with Otis and let her heart ache.

Not open for debate. Be there soon.

Dani's next texts telling Laurel not to come went unanswered. She considered turning off the lights so that when Laurel arrived, she might think Dani had gone to sleep. Of course, it was only a little after six, so that plan wasn't going to work. Dani was still trying to come up with a way to disappear when Laurel knocked and came in. She was carrying two bags and headed straight for the kitchen. As soon as she put the things down, she enveloped Dani in a hug. "The others will be here soon."

It must be because Laurel had grown up with such a big family that she was used to doing things with a crowd, but for Dani, it was overwhelming. "I just need chocolate and some sleep. Could you tell everyone not to come by?"

"If you can tell me a good reason why you don't want them to come over."

"I don't want to be a bother. This is a big night for you. You should be celebrating, not listening to my sob story. It was going to happen at some point. So what if it's a little sooner than I thought?"

"Dani, when will you accept that you're not a bother? You're like a sister to me. If you're hurting, I'm here. You don't need to put on a brave face and pretend you're fine. This sucks. How about you let some of us help it suck a little less?"

"I appreciate that, but—"

"If this were happening to me, what would you do?" Dani didn't need to answer. Laurel had only had one serious relationship, and it had ended badly. As soon as Dani learned of it, she was on the first plane to New Hampshire. "Exactly. If you don't want to talk about Nick, you don't have to, but if you need to scream or cry or list his faults alphabetically, then we can do that, too."

Dani didn't have any words. She wasn't used to support like this and was grateful for the reminder of what she had here. Within the hour, Eden and Sheridan arrived. Janelle had a family crisis but promised to make a voodoo doll of Nick from thrifted men's clothes if necessary. Dani appreciated the offer. After a few beers, thick sandwiches on fresh-made breads, and brownies from Eden, Dani's heart hurt in some ways and filled up in others. Having friends to talk with was truly wonderful.

"I still don't understand how he could do this," Sheridan said after something had made Dani weepy again. "I saw you two today. I would have bet that he was in love with you. And look at the way he'd been taking care of you since the accident."

Laurel wiggled her brows. "All the ways he's been taking care of you."

Dani managed a weak smile. Yeah, she was going to miss that, too. "I know he cares, and it may even be love for him, too, but that's not enough. Eden, if Theo hadn't wanted to stay in Fable Notch, what would you have done?"

"What I thought I'd be doing from the beginning. Let him go." She took a swallow of her beer, then continued. "Even though I knew his leaving was going to hurt as much as it had when we were teens, I couldn't have asked him to stay if this isn't where he wanted to be. I thought about joining him in Baltimore, but that didn't feel right, either. Fortunately, I didn't have to make that choice. But you're right, Dani. It's not only love. It's about having the life you want and caring enough about the other person to want them to have the life that makes them happy."

Dani turned her palms up in a gesture of surrender. "There you have it. The life that makes Nick happy is in New York."

"Are you sure?" Laurel didn't sound convinced.

"I know he's enjoyed these last few weeks, but I also know he is very committed to his plans. The kind of big success he craves is more likely to happen for him in New York. As long as that's a priority for him, that's where he should be."

Laurel tilted her head as she thought. "I guess you're right. I still say he's an ass. He can find financial things to do around here. And Concord is less than an hour away."

"He loves the city. It fills him up." But as she said it, Dani wasn't certain it was entirely true. She'd seen other things bring him joy while he was here. Not only her and Presley, but his work with Ed and how thrilled he'd been when he sold the house design. Would that make things different for him when he went back? Dani knew how much she loved her life in Fable Notch. A bad day here was better than a good day anywhere else. If Nick wanted to wake up in New York, if that gave him happiness, then that's what she wanted for him. "We want what we want. Can't help that."

"Well, I'm bummed for you and have to say I'm on Team Asshole," Sheridan said. "He was so pleased when he came to pick up breakfast for you today. You seemed good together."

"We are. Were. Ugh, this is going to suck for a while, isn't it?" Dani's head fell back against the couch.

"Very definitely," Laurel said, offering her a brownie.

Dani didn't hesitate to take a second. With her mouth full, she said, "Will you go jogging with me to take off the weight I'm going to gain from this?"

"Not likely," Laurel said, and Dani laughed. "Besides, you hate jogging."

Dani had to agree. "Still, I can't brownie my way through this."

Laurel put her head on Dani's shoulder. "You can tonight and for the next few days. After that, we'll make sure you stick to crying and yelling and laying off the sweets. No man is worth an extra ten pounds."

"You can come take a dance class with me, Dani," Eden suggested. "We'll get rid of those brownies in no time." Conversation shifted to Eden's new dance studio and what classes might be fun. Dani took in the friends around her. She would be leaning on them in the weeks to come, and as lousy as she was going to feel, she was glad to know she wouldn't go through this alone.

Chapter Forty-Three

Nick closed his eyes and waited. He heard the car pulling up sooner than he expected given the crowds and traffic. Even knowing how close everything around here was, Theo probably broke a few speeding limits to be at Nick's house as quickly as he was. "Nick? Where are you?"

"Back here. Bedroom." He hadn't moved since he made the call.

Nick didn't realize how terrible he looked until he saw the surprise register on Theo's face. "Holy shit." That sounded about right. His muscles felt rubbery, he was still sweating, and his heart rate, while not soaring, remained elevated. Nick imagined he looked rather gray. His brother joined him on the floor, and they leaned against the bed. After a bit, Theo said, "Panic attack?"

"Yeah."

"Thought I recognized it. Wanna talk?"

"Almost. Need the medication to kick in?"

"Can I get you anything while we wait?"

"Water." He'd dry swallowed the pill. He could still feel where it scratched his throat.

"Will do," Theo said, and gave Nick's shoulder a squeeze before he walked out.

Nick listened for the sound of Theo in the kitchen. Having someone else in the house was helping. Theo came back with two glasses of water, handed him one, and sat down. Nick was glad his brother didn't try to start the conversation again. He was feeling better physically, but his head was still a jumble of thoughts, and his stomach was still in knots. After a few minutes Nick said, "Presley's family found her at the Festival. She left with them about an hour ago."

"I'm sorry. Was wondering where your dog had gotten to. Usually when I'm having a tough time, Harlow won't leave my side. Is that what set this off?"

He drank some water and nodded. "It was the trigger. I've also been offered my job back and told Dani to leave."

Theo was quiet. "When you're ready, you're going to need to fill in a few gaps for me." Slowly, Nick told his brother everything that had happened in the last few days including Ed's selling his house design to the Butlers. "At the risk of stating the obvious, that's a lot in a short amount of time. What are you going to do?"

"Go back to New York, of course." Wasn't that obvious, too?

"Why of course?"

"Because..." Nick stopped. *Because that was my plan* was what he intended to say, but when he heard the words in his head, they sounded stupid. He had to do what was in the plan? Wasn't he the one who created it in the first place? And didn't that mean he could change it?

"Oh, I recognize that moment," Theo said.

"What moment?"

"That moment you realize leaving might not be the answer it was all those years ago. It's like that carnival ride where the floor drops out from under you. It's scary and impossible and fun."

That about summed it up for Nick. "I'm not ready to move to fun yet."

"When you get there, it's all worth it."

Could it be that simple? "When you called to tell me you and Eden were together again and you were moving back to Fable Notch, I was shocked. I was glad for you, but later I was envious. I looked around my expensive apartment, at my beautiful view, and knew I didn't have anything in my life that made me as happy as you sounded. Of course, my response was to throw myself into work and add a few more goals to my plans." They both knew how that worked out.

"And now?"

"Now, I have some decisions and changes to make. But there's one other problem. I hurt Dani. Again. The look on her face when I told her to leave." Nick pressed the heels of his palms into his eyes. "I'm such an ass."

"As your big brother, I'm required to agree with that opinion. I can also promise you that if you stay, it will not be the last time you hurt her."

Nick looked at his brother. "That's not helpful."

"Do you think you're magically going to stop fucking up? Never gonna happen. But that's the thing about being with someone who doesn't only love you, but really knows you. They know you're worth it, even when you make mistakes."

And there it was. The heart of the matter. Could he stop living a life that didn't allow for mistakes or setbacks and have one that offered the love and connection he'd found since coming back? He let his head fall forward with the weight of his thoughts. "What if she doesn't accept my apology?" He may have used up his fuck-up quota.

"Then you'll have to find a way to convince her she can't live without you."

Easier said than done. "Before Jeffries and Waters offered me my job back, I considered looking at what it would take to make a go of it as a home designer.

When I was researching what to charge the Butlers for my drawing, I learned you don't need a degree."

"So you're going to take the risk to be an entrepreneur in a business that needs a good economy?"

Theo was using his words against him. More people who knew him well. He liked it. "I'm seeing where some risks are worth it."

"Good." Theo put his arm around Nick and gave him a hug. "Hey, I know an investor who could help you get started."

Nick appreciated his brother wanted to help him, but he wouldn't take money from Theo. "Thanks for the offer, but I think I can find a way."

"Not me, the Sinclairs." Nick's confusion must have shown because Theo said, "You know that account all three of us have been putting money into for years? Turns out they've never touched it."

Nick remembered telling Martin on his first day that he wouldn't be able to contribute to it, and Martin brushing it off. Was this why? "How do you know?"

"Eden and I were over for dinner a few months back, and she mentioned putting together the financing for her studio. Millie offered to be a partner and explained how she could do it. When I asked him later, Martin told me how much was in the account. It's a little insane. Eden didn't end up needing the help, but I'll bet the Sinclairs would be thrilled to invest in your company. Especially if it meant you stayed here."

After being so proud to give something back to the Sinclairs, Nick didn't like the idea of accepting help from them again. Given the changes of the last few weeks, however, he thought it best not to rule anything out. And for the first time, there was something that needed his focus before work, because if ever there was a plan worth making, this was it.

Chapter Forty-Four

♥

As nice as it had been to have friends over the night before, Dani woke up Monday not wanting to get out of bed. The rollercoaster of the last few days hit her hard. Fortunately, she wasn't expected at work until Wednesday. It was meant to be a chance to recover from the madness of the Festival. Instead, it was the perfect time for a complete collapse, and she did something she hadn't done since buying her house.

She locked the doors. Front and back.

When Aunt Rosie knocked at nine, she was glad for the locks. Mondays at the diner weren't the busiest for breakfast, but the fact that her aunt showed up so early told Dani the Fable Notch grapevine was at work, and Rosie was worried. Helen was next. Laurel checked in by text. Eden called. Her phone buzzed so much she put it on silent. She needed to be alone with her thoughts and decide what to do next.

Not that being with her thoughts felt like being alone. The noise in her head was unending. It mostly sounded like her mom and her so-called friends in Texas. Criticisms and I-told-you-so's. The images she called up weren't much better. Nick's anger as he told her to leave. Aunt Rosie admitting that she'd suggested to Doc Wheeler that he retire.

But by the afternoon, Dani noticed not all the noise was negative.

She thought of Laurel and the times with the women she'd met since moving back. Her successes at work. Dinners with Aunt Rosie and Auntie Helen. Hearing her mother say she loved her. All the casseroles that arrived after her accident.

And even Nick.

All the pain she was feeling was because of the pleasure that had come first. The way he was there for her after the accident, the way he stepped up for the auction. The way he fed her desires in bed. Yes, she had several months of healing ahead of her, but there were things to keep her from spending all that time crying, and that was good to know.

On Tuesday afternoon, she pulled herself together and went to the clinic. It was time to talk to Doc Wheeler. By this point, she didn't entirely believe he hired her because he was bullied by Aunt Rosie, but the part of her that would always be insecure needed the reassurance. She found him at his desk eating a sandwich. There was a small bag of Skittles nearby. "Knock, knock," she said, interrupting his reading.

He gave her a smile and tucked a bookmark into the paperback. "Dani, what brings you here? Thought we gave you two days off?"

She sat in the chair next to the desk and her mouth went dry. How was she supposed to ask this? What if she didn't like what he said? Rubbing her palms against her legs, she said, "I know you weren't planning to retire yet. Aunt Rosie pushed you into it and into hiring me."

Doc stared at her, wiped his mouth and hands on a napkin, and gathered his thoughts. It took forever. Dani wished for a hole to crawl into. Finally he said, "Rosie Kinsman is a bold and formidable woman, and most people wouldn't last one round if she went after them, but you've met my wife. I'm used to women like her. Rosie didn't push me into anything. Yes, she told me you were unhappy in Texas, and that you'd love to move here. Based on that, I made a choice. A damn good one, I believe."

"Beth said your retirement came as a surprise. That you didn't interview any other candidates."

He nodded. "That's true."

Dani's heart broke a little, but she held back the tears. They wouldn't change anything. "So, you handed me this job."

He gave her a confused look. "Of course I did. I've always planned to hand it to you." She didn't understand. He put a hand on her shoulder before continuing. "Dani, your love for this work and this place has been clear to me since the summer of the rabbit. When Ruth first asked me about retiring years ago and moving closer to our grandkids, my first thought was, 'I have to wait until Dani is ready to take over.' When Rosie came to ask if there was room for you, I was happy to choose my retirement date."

This time there was no way to stop the tears. They burst out of her with a force suggesting she'd been holding them back forever. Maybe she had been. Doc Wheeler wrapped his arms around her. When she calmed and ended the hug, he took out a handkerchief and handed it to her so she could dry her face. "It never occurred to me—," she started and stopped, not certain what she wanted to say. "When I heard from Beth... and then Rosie admitted... Thank you for telling me this. It matters more than you know."

Before Doc Wheeler could say anything, they were interrupted by screams for help from the waiting area. Doc rushed out. Dani hung back, not wanting to overwhelm whoever was out there. If Doc needed her, he'd get her.

But a moment later, she heard her name being yelled. "No, I have to see Dr. Dani. Please, where is Dani? She knows what Chandler needs. Please, get her."

Dani knew the voice. She raced out. Bea Turner was clutching a limp Chandler to her chest. "I'm here. What's the problem?"

Bea looked at her with tears running down her face. "I killed him. I killed my poor baby." She was so distraught, Dani was surprised she didn't kill them both on the drive over.

Doc handed Dani his stethoscope, and she got to work listening for a heartbeat. It was there. "Tell me what happened."

The words came out in a broken flow. "I spilled his pills. I gave him his usual this morning, then I knocked over the bottle putting the cap on. I thought I'd found them all before he had time to eat them, but a little while later he started whining, and when he threw up, I saw a pill."

"Do you know how many he ate?"

Bea gasped. "I should have counted. Why didn't I count?"

Dani took the dog from a reluctant Bea. "It's okay. We're going to take care of him. He'll be fine. Come with me to the exam room. How long ago did he ingest the pills?" She kept Bea talking and answering questions, even though the answers didn't change what she needed to do. It wasn't long before she got Chandler to intentionally expel the rest of the contents of his stomach, where there were two more partially digested pills. As she gave the dog fluids, she had Beth get something for Bea to drink. As she encouraged the woman to sip the tea, she reassured her. "I'm sure you had many scares with your kids when they were little. This is no different. You did the right thing then, and the right thing now. Chandler is going to be a little lethargic for a day, then he'll be back to his usual loving self."

Dani stayed with Bea until Chandler was ready to go home. Almost two hours later, they walked back to the waiting area, Chandler once again in his owner's arms, this time more alert, if still clearly tired. Before leaving, Bea asked, "You're sure he doesn't need to stay over?"

"He will recover best in familiar surroundings close to someone who loves him."

"Thank you so much, Dani." Bea pulled Dani into a hug. Dani didn't know someone could hold you so tightly with only one arm. It was Rosie-worthy. "I'm so glad you were here today."

"So am I," Dani said. She held the door open for Bea and watched as the woman drove away. She made a mental note to call her tomorrow and check in.

As she turned back, she saw Doc Wheeler leaning against the front desk, a smile on his face. "Any more questions about where or whether you belong?" Dani shook her head, unable to answer past the lump in her throat. "Told you I made a damn good choice."

    * * *

By Saturday she was still missing Nick, but she noticed that although she was hurt, she wasn't broken. The pain was different from when she'd been younger. That summer she'd ached because she was convinced she wasn't good enough to be a priority in his life. Today she understood her own priorities and accepted his. She'd get over him, and it wouldn't take another ten years.

As she updated patient files, she remembered to put "cook" on her schedule for tomorrow night. Nancy's baby had been born two days before, and Dani wanted to make a casserole to bring over. Thinking about it, she considered making cookies. Having tasted what the folks here were capable of, her cooking didn't measure up. Tonight, she was meeting the girls at the brewery and looking forward to their company.

As she was closing down her computer, Beth came into the office. "I hate to do this to you, especially as we're about to finish for the day, but we've got an unscheduled owner in exam room three."

"I'll be there in a minute," Dani said. She put away the files on her desk and motioned to Otis. "Come on, boy.

One more patient, then we'll take a quick walk before seeing our friends."

There was no paperwork in the holder outside the exam room door, so Dani assumed Beth was in there. She gave a quick knock and headed in.

Only there was no patient.

Instead, Nick was there, looking way too wonderful and making her heart leap. She took in how different he looked from the day he arrived with Presley. Then his clothes were tailored and expensive, his manner serious. Today he wore a t-shirt and jeans and looked as though he could be heading over to help Ed when they were done.

A thousand questions ran through her head, but there was only one to ask. "What are you doing here?"

Chapter Forty-Five

♥

"I made a mistake. Well, a string of them, starting with asking you to leave." God, she looked beautiful. Okay, maybe she looked tired and a little sad. He'd played a part in that, but if she'd let him, he'd make up for it for the rest of his life. "I'm moving back to Fable Notch, and I want to know if you'd forgive me one more time for being an idiot."

She didn't respond at first. It didn't matter. He'd grovel as much as necessary for as long as necessary. "You think this will be the last time you're going to be an idiot?"

Oh good, a question with an easy answer. "Probably not, but I definitely won't be stupid enough to let you go."

He could see she wasn't convinced. She put her hands into her lab coat pocket, and he wondered if she was picking at her thumb. "What's changed?"

"After you left, I had a full-blown panic attack, almost as bad as that first one." He told her about calling Theo and their conversation. "I thought the reason my heart raced when I thought about New York was because I didn't know if I could get back on track. But that wasn't it. My plans haven't been making me happy for a while. That's what I didn't want to face, especially since I didn't know what to do about it. Those plans were supposed to be my guarantee of happiness, financial security, and control. Then Presley showed up, and you were back in my life. There I was, completely out of control, not earning anything, and happier than I'd been in ages. I didn't realize it until I almost blew it."

"What happened with New York?"

"I called, said I'd come in for the Tuesday meeting. It was two days of presentations, discussions, and negotiations, and by the time it was done, the firm signed one of the biggest deals in its history."

"Congratulations." To say she didn't sound excited was an understatement.

"Thanks, but that's not the important part. The success put me in a position to ask for what I wanted."

"Which was?"

Yeah, she was going to make him work for this. He deserved that. "I'll be there to make certain the project goes smoothly, but I'm staying on as a consultant, not coming back full time."

Now she looked curious. "That's an option?"

"I made it one." Half the time as he sat in the meetings, he was barely listening and instead making notes on the proposal to consult. "The firm brings on freelancers for special projects or when departments are stuck. I told them hiring someone who knew the company could lead to better results and fewer costs."

"What does this mean?" Was there hope in her voice?

"As I said, I'm moving back here. I'll travel to New York as necessary, and when I'm not consulting, I'm going to try to make a go of it as a home designer." He was still getting used to the idea, but the more he said it, the more he liked it. It felt right.

"You're choosing a risky, economy dependent field?"

She knew him as well as he knew her, and it was wonderful. "People always need a home. And some risks are worth it."

She took a step toward him, then stopped. "Nick, you need to be very sure. This is a big change."

He closed the distance between them. When she didn't move away, he put his hands on her waist. "How many times have my plans changed in the last few months alone? It turns out the world doesn't end when they do. It does end, however, when you give up what you want most." He pushed away some hair that had worked its way out of her ponytail and went on, "When I was a kid, my dad made it clear I wasn't worth anything. And I believed him. So I spent all my energy chasing success and money to prove him wrong. In the process, I lost sight of everything that's ever made me happy. My brothers, the Sinclairs, building things. You."

"Do you honestly think you can be happy here?"

He hated that she had to ask, but he'd shaken her trust several times in the past few weeks. He was willing to do what it took to strengthen it, to be worthy of her trust and love. "I didn't notice it until it was gone, but I've been happier here for the last four weeks than I've been in the last eight years. All of my plans, all the goals I've hit, haven't made me as happy the nights I've spent sitting on the couch drawing as you read."

"Small towns aren't like the city. You can't get anything you want delivered. There isn't a decent sushi place for miles."

She was throwing unimportant details at him. It was a good sign. "The only thing I want delivered is you to our home every night after work. And maybe another dog."

"Another dog?" The look on her face was comical.

"Losing Presley has been rough. I've been missing her all week, but I'll get over it. I cannot lose you. I won't get over that. I didn't the last time." She looked as though she was going to argue more, so he silenced her with a lingering kiss, then said, "This is where I want to be. For the first time, I can honestly say being happy is worth more than money. Besides, I'm going to be married to a doctor, and I'm sure she's going to be very successful."

"You're going to be... Is that a...?"

"I promise to make it official soon, but that's my new plan. I'm going to spend my time doing what I want to do, and I want to spend that time with you. I love you, Dani."

"I love you, too. I don't think I ever stopped."

He kissed her until she melted against him. He was excited at the prospect of starting a new business and building homes, but more excited for the life he was going to build with her. When they broke the kiss, he saw tears in her eyes, but this time he didn't mind being the cause. "Oh yes, this is definitely where I want to be." He kissed her softly. "So, what do you think of the name Second Chance Houses for the new business?"

"I like it. I'm a big fan of second chances."

He took in her joy and her love and couldn't wait for the plans they were going to make together. "So am I."

Epilogue

♥

*C*ole Hanson

The last thing Cole wanted to do at the crack of dawn was a radio interview. Okay, 8:00 wasn't early for most people—he imagined both his brothers were up and at work by now—but when the band was on tour, nights didn't end until the early morning and even travel days were exhausting. It didn't matter how luxurious the tour bus or hotel was, he rarely slept well. When they'd arrived in New York last night, he'd gone straight to his room and fallen into bed, then tossed and turned for several hours before dropping into an exhausted sleep. It seemed as though no time had passed when his phone rang with a wake-up call.

As he got dressed and looked out his window at the expensive view and the people rushing below, he couldn't help but wonder how many more months of this they had before he'd be home in Colorado. And more importantly, could he use the break in their schedule at the end of the year to visit with Theo, Nick, and the Sinclairs for the holidays?

Now that both of his brothers had moved back to the town where they grew up, Cole couldn't stop thinking about seeing them. He considered the three of them close, even though their lives were in different parts of the country, but that hadn't had more than a few hours together in years. They could ski, open presents on Christmas, maybe even ring in the new year as a family. That couldn't count against his promise to never return, would it?

His thoughts were still on home when, less than a half hour later, he was piling into the black Chevy Suburban with his bandmates. Paxton Jones, Brian Flemming, and Hugh Walker. None of them appeared any more awake than he did, although Paxton managed to look picture perfect. He'd never understand how she could always do that. As their driver wove through traffic as though he were playing a live action version of *Grand Theft Auto*, Cole couldn't help but wonder why the fuck were they doing this interview anyway?

Emporium was playing four sold-out concerts at Madison Square Garden starting tonight. The entire tour was sold out as far as he knew, even the added dates. Cole couldn't understand how extra publicity was necessary when ticket sales were so strong, but he didn't control what the label scheduled for them.

He didn't have control over a lot of things.

When they got out of the car a few minutes later — and Cole had to wonder if it wouldn't have been faster to walk — he took a deep breath that immediately had him coughing. The air was heavy with humidity and smelled like a combination of garbage and exhaust fumes. How the hell had Nick managed to love living here for so long? Cole had barely gotten himself under control when a young, excited assistant came to bring them into the studio. She introduced herself and he promptly forgot her name. When they got in the elevator, she asked if she could get them anything once they were in the studio. "Coffee. Black," he mumbled. The others gave drink orders as well.

"And a pizza," Brian said. "I've missed New York pizza."

"Toppings?" the assistant asked, and Cole knew that by the time the interview was done, Brian would have his pizza. It didn't matter how early it was.

They stepped into the studio, gave a nod to the disc jockey and were given headphones and shown where to sit. Moments later, his coffee appeared. As he took a fortifying sip, he got his bearings and was surprised to see a camera set up in addition to the microphones for each of the band members. "What's that for?" he asked quietly, not wanting to be on air.

"We do a video recording of our special guests so people can watch the interviews later," the assistant explained. "Gives our fans – and yours - something to enjoy and share."

Cole closed his eyes and thought, *Fuck, fuck, fuck.* He had to hope they kept the focus on Paxton who was camera ready, smart woman. The rest of them looked like the rock-and-roll stereotype of hard partiers, even though Cole knew it was exhaustion. Oh well, may as well add to the myth. It's what the fans wanted and that never hurt their bottom line.

When the interview started, the questions were what Cole expected. Questions about venues, any notable locations, unexpected mistakes, and what life was like on the road. Nothing problematic until the disc jockey asked Hugh what it was like to be away from his wife and new daughter. Hugh's eyebrows dropped in a scowl, and Cole winced. Not fair. The tour been an extra piece of hell for Hugh. He'd flown home for baby Andrea's first birthday, but he hated missing milestones and moments. If it weren't for knowing that this work ensured his family's financial future, Hugh might have left.

"It's not easy," Hugh answered, "and I'm grateful for whoever created Zoom technology so I can see my family daily, but I'm also grateful the fans want to see us. We've got a break coming for the end of the year holidays. I'll be with them then."

It was a good answer, but the disc jockey wasn't done. "How do you think you'll handle it for the next tour?"

"We don't even know if they'll be another tour," Cole said, hoping to shut down this line of questions. "No group lasts forever."

Dead air.

Fuck me. He was going to be in trouble for that. He couldn't imagine what the cameras were picking up. Probably a room full of people staring at him. Their manager, Brett Searle, was going to rip him a new asshole for that comment.

Sure enough, as Paxton deflected by saying no one could predict the future and talking more about how great Emporium's fans were, Cole's phone buzzed. He didn't have to look to know who it was.

Soon after, the interview ended, and the disc jockey came to shake hands while commercials played in the background. "Come back anytime. That was great stuff."

Yeah, great that Cole screwed up. And there was video proof. Lucky him.

He avoided Brett's calls for another few hours, then — unironically — faced the music. There would be no stopping the news and video from spreading, but Brett was already planning to counter whatever was said with some new footage of the band, which they filmed later that afternoon.

After creating two hours of staged footage of the band having fun together, Cole went back to the hotel. He grabbed food and a drink in the hotel bar where he thought he wouldn't be noticed, but before he got through his burger and beer, he was recognized. Two women came up to him asking for autographs and pictures. And for some reason, they lingered. He wanted to excuse himself, but given his earlier mistake, he continued the conversation and did his best not to be rude.

Until they both asked if he wanted them to go back to his room with him. It had been a long time since he'd been in a situation where sex had been offered and almost as long since he'd been interested. As politely as he could, he turned them down saying he needed a good night's sleep before tomorrow's concert. They promised him a good night – without the sleep.

He left as quickly as he could. Because not only did he not have an interest in sex with two strangers, but it reminded him of the person he did want, and couldn't have.

Mia Durant

Even though it was her day off, Mia was up early. She rarely added more than an hour of sleep to her schedule otherwise it threw off her workdays. Her schedule was typically three days of 12-hour shifts in the White Mountain Regional Hospital Emergency Room followed by two days off. It meant she worked a lot of weekends, but at least she'd earned enough seniority to be able to be off on the major holidays she wanted.

She started her day having breakfast with her son, Dean. Sort of. He ate and scrolled through his phone while she drank her coffee and thought about what she needed to do. Neither of them were much for talking in the mornings. Before he left, she managed to tell him, "Chicken bake for dinner."

"Sounds good. Tell Grandpap I said hello. I'll visit him soon," he said as she walked him to the door and gave him a quick squeeze before he headed out. The new school year had started recently, and she was still a little nervous about him adjusting to high school. It hadn't been long since he'd had to deal with the death of his mother, learning that Mia was his legal guardian, and moving from Florida to New Hampshire. High school wasn't easy under the best of conditions, but he was doing well so far.

When it was time to go, Mia grabbed her things, motioned for Bowie, her huge St. Bernard/Husky mix to follow her, and they got in her car. Their first stop was a visit with her father, Joe, at the Crawford Senior Center.

He'd been there since early summer and was enjoying living close to his peers. Bowie, who had been used to having Joe around all the time, was having a harder time with the change. She usually brought him with her since he was always welcome at the Center and got lots of attention from all the residents. It made twice as much sense today since, after their visit, they were headed to the vet.

They arrived at the Center and the usual fuss was made over Bowie. The receptionist kept dog treats in her desk, and Bowie walked over to her to get his cookie. Then he and Mia walked to the Great Room where he went to Joe first and then got attention from the others in her father's circle before settling at Joe's feet. Mia sat beside her father, and they discussed the book they were both reading, Dean, and whatever other mundane topic came to mind. She'd had mixed feelings when he said he wanted to make this move, and although she missed him occasionally, she could see it was good for him.

A half hour before they were due at the vet, Mia went to find Casey Shaw, the Director of Activities, and her closest friend. They'd met in nursing school, and when Mia returned to the town where she'd grown up after graduation, Casey found work here as well. When Casey wasn't in her office, Mia checked the kitchen, the next likely place. Sure enough, she found Casey getting coffee in the kitchen and chatting with the Center's chef, Emilio Levin.

"Knock, knock," Mia said to get their attention.

"Hey there," Casey said, coming over to give Mia a hug. "I thought I'd be seeing you today. How's everything?"

"Good," Mia said, turning down a cup of coffee but accepting a bottle of water. Casey refilled her mug, and they walked to her office. "I still can't get over how much dad loves it here."

"He's had one of the easiest transitions I can remember. Speaking of transitions, how's Dean doing? High school getting any better?"

Mia had shared her worries with Casey the week after school started. Dean had been closed lipped about almost everything and getting him to share was almost as tough as it had been when he first moved in with her. Mia had called the therapist they'd seen when he arrived, and she told Mia to trust what they'd built together and give it time. She'd been right. In the last two weeks, he'd been talking more. "A little rocky at first, but he's joined a few clubs, made some new friends, and doesn't hate all his teachers. I'm taking the win."

"From what little I know of parenting, you should take those whenever you can." Casey had never been married and didn't have kids, but she did princess parties on the weekends along with her work at the Center, so Mia knew she'd seen a lot of different family dynamics. When they got to Casey's office, they sat on the couch and Casey said, "I feel like I should warn you about something I heard this morning." Mia braced herself. Her father seemed fine. Was he hiding a problem? "Cole Hanson was in the news."

Mia wished her heart didn't flutter at the mention of her ex's name, but Cole always had a hold on her, even after all this time. "Who is he dating now? Some king's daughter?" It was rare for him to make the news, but when he did, it was almost always because of his social life. The first few years after she left the band, his named with often linked to one famous female after another. It had been hard to hear and from her reaction, it hadn't gotten much easier.

"Apparently, he and the band did a radio interview yesterday, and he said something about the group not lasting forever." Emporium was breaking up? Before she could say anything, Casey continued, "Their lead singer covered and made sure no one dwelled on it, but the interview was videotaped so clips from it are making the social media rounds."

"Guess I'll be staying off of those sites for a few days." Still, it had Mia wondering what Cole might have meant.

She certainly understood things not lasting forever, but Cole had created Emporium when he was in high school and, after over fifteen years, she couldn't imagine him without it.

She visited with Casey a little longer before her friend had to get back to work, then drove to the White Mountain Veterinary Clinic for Bowie's appointment. And tried not to think about Cole. She didn't quite succeed, even though she stayed off her phone and put on a playlist rather than turn on the radio. *No group lasts forever.* What did that mean?

She shook her head to dislodge the thoughts and images swirling in her head. It didn't matter. Cole wasn't part of her world, and that was how she wanted it.

Bowie's visit was quick, and when they were done, Bowie stood by Otis, Dani's dog who frequently came into appointments, and gave a bark. Both women laughed. "I don't have another patient for an hour. Do you have time for them to go out and play together?" Dani asked.

"I planned for it," Mia said. Bowie was good with other dogs whenever they saw them at the local dog park or when out for a walk, but he had a special fondness for Otis, who was one of the few dogs bigger than him.

"Wonderful. Let me get my coat." September had some of the best weather in New Hampshire, but even standing in the sun, it was chilly.

The minute they stepped into the fenced area next to the clinic, both dogs took off. Bowie was going to crash hard later. As they watched the dogs, Mia asked, "How are things with you and Nick? Has he officially moved back?"

"You heard about him, about us?"

"You know this town. Everyone hears everything." Which meant Mia probably needed to avoid locals as much as possible for a few days so she wouldn't get more comments about Cole.

Dani adjusted her ponytail and said, "He's still in the process of finishing things in New York and finalizing a new consulting contract with his firm, but by the end of the month, he should be living here full time. Mia heard the joy in Dani's voice. It amazed Mia that Dani and Nick found their way back to each other. She didn't know a lot of the details of what split them up — Mia was four years older than Dani and they had only known each other tangentially when Dani came to visit her aunts in the summer — but she couldn't imagine it was easy getting through the pain of the past.

They watched the dogs in silence for a while before Mia said, "If you don't mind my asking, what's it been like? Having Nick in your life again." She probably shouldn't have asked, but Cole was on her mind. The fact that both his brothers lived in town again made it likely she was going to have to face him in the not too distant future, if only at the weddings she knew would be coming.

"At first it was horrible, and everything I didn't want. When he came into the clinic after finding an injured dog, we stood there staring at each other like idiots. He didn't know I'd moved back. And then we ended up working together for the festival, which...complicated things."

And by complicated, Mia understood Dani meant old feelings sneaking in. That was something Mia worried about. She didn't know what Dani's life after Nick was life, but Mia's feelings for Cole had never gone away. She didn't want to think about what it would take to protect her heart when she saw him again. "Was it hard to discuss what ended your relationship?"

"It wasn't easy, and it took a while before we were ready to poke that bear." Mia had to smile at Dani's use of an animal in her metaphor. "We both had to admit where we screwed up, where we could have been more honest. But now I can see it was for the best that we split up when we did. We both had some things to learn, growing up to do."

Mia nodded, even though for her it was the opposite. She and Cole split up because of the grown-up things in their lives. He'd made one decision to support his brothers, while she'd made another to support her parents.

Dani broke into her thoughts with a question of her own. "Have you ever wondered what you would do if Cole moved home?"

Mia gave a harsh laugh as a memory played in her head. *I don't want to see you in Fable Notch again. My life is here. Make yours somewhere else.* Her last words to the only man she'd ever loved. "I may not be able to predict how busy we're going to be on a Saturday night in the ER or understand why one patient responds to treatment while another doesn't, but I can say with certainty Cole Hanson is *never* coming back to Fable Notch."

Find out what happens when Cole *does* come back to
Fable Notch!
Order ***This Time for Us*** at https://bit.ly/TTFU-books

Acknowledgments

It's been an incredible process to bring Nick and Dani's the page. Loosely based on Hans Christian Andersen's *The Snow Queen*, it's intended to be a story about seeing the through the things that blind us to our own self-worth and which can keep us from having what we want. It's a challenge I face, too, and I'm grateful to the people who continue to support me through the good and the tough times.

I have to start with a special thank you to my dear friend Margaret LaBarge and her dog, Buddy. Margaret lives in the White Mountains and always welcomes me when I want to be in the surroundings that inspired Fable Notch. In addition, Buddy is the inspiration for Presley, so thank you to him for being such a good boy!

For the writers in my life—Sara, Lisa, Paula, Misty, Win and Delia, along with the BFA morning Office gang. I may be responsible for getting the words on the page, but it would be so much harder without your support and encouragement. The challenges of the writing life are made easier because of all of you.

Every self-published author has a team to get the books ready for release. To my editor, Beth at Magnolia Author Services, thank you for your support and recommendations, which made this a stronger book, and to Jessie Cunniffe, who made my story sound so enticing with her blurb. Thank you, Bailee and Gen, who were my exceptional proofreaders. (seriously, I'm terrible at that and any errors are mine – feel free to email me if you find any). Additional thanks to 100Covers who continue to give this series it's visual look and who created the Fable Notch logo, which I love.

To my WW River Sisters, thank you for being there as much, and sometimes more, as any "real" family. I cannot believe how much we've been through in the last few years. I feel every virtual hug, prayer, and cheer you send, and I deeply appreciate your unending acceptance and understanding. You make the good days brighter and the tough days easier.

I am beyond grateful to my husband and sons who are behind me with love, encouragement, and belief when self-doubt tries to take the wheel as I continue my writing and publishing journey. I know how lucky I am to have all of you in my life. I love you so very much.

And to you, my readers, thank you for choosing and enjoying these stories. Knowing you're out there makes every writing day better. Wishing you hot coffee and warm cookies!

Mugs up (___)o,
Elena

About The Author

Elena Markem writes emotionally rich contemporary romances about dreams, love, and taking a chance on both. Her stories reflect her belief that life is about the passions we pursue, the people who support us along the way, and never giving up on what we want.

She can't start work without coffee, fall asleep without reading, or listen to Broadway musicals without singing along (badly). She loves time spend with her husband and sons as well as weekends with girlfriends, rom-com and old movies, and anything that sparkles.

Feel free to join her on her ongoing quest for the perfect planner, the best diner breakfasts, and the gooiest chocolate chip cookie. In the meantime, she hopes you'll enjoy spending time in her sexy books where you'll find strong heroines, heroes who find them irresistible, and at least one scene involving comfort food. Stay in touch by signing up for her newsletter at www.e lenamarkem.com to get sneak peaks and free stories or follow her on Facebook, Instagram and Tiktok!